CONOR DALY

BURIED
LIES

KENSINGTON BOOKS

KENSINGTON BOOKS *are published by*

Kensington Publishing Corp.
850 Third Avenue
New York, NY 10022

Kensington and the K logo Reg. U.S. Pat. & TM Off.

Library of Congress Card Catalog Number: 96-075282
ISBN 1-57566-033-4

First Printing: May, 1996

Printed in the United States of America

For Mary Lou,
Who makes this possible.

CHAPTER
1

Demo Mike tapped the forefinger of his good hand against the computer screen. Dark lines appeared in the powder blue field, whirling out of an imaginary distance and assembling themselves into a roof, walls, windows, doors, even gutters and a patio awning. Every detail accurately drawn by a globe of lasers atop the cab of the Milton Fire Department's spanking new pumper.

Behind me, another fire engine squealed around the clubhouse circle and killed its siren as it banged down the slope of the parking lot. Demo didn't react. He hiked the heavy black slicker higher on his badly sloping shoulders, pushed the oily black firefighter's helmet to the back of his head, squinted hard at the screen.

"Demo, I don't see any smoke or flames," I said, scanning the real windows and roof. "Maybe it's a false alarm."

"We'll find out, Kieran," he said. "This machine doesn't lie."

The din mounted around us. Firemen shouted as they laced the parking lot with hoses, tied in to hydrants that suddenly sprang from the azalea bush beside the sixteenth tee and the pine shrubs lining the practice range. Another truck angled into position, two powerful flood-lights bathing the building in instant daylight. A cherry-picker lowered its anchoring struts and raised its arm while the fireman in the bucket fiddled with a water cannon.

The building in the fire department's crosshairs actually was a con-glomeration of three separate units. Most obvious, and dearest to my palpitating heart, was the pro shop where for four years I had plied my trade as golf professional at the Milton Country Club. A large garage abutting the shop housed the club's fleet of fifty electric golf carts. The club's Hispanic restaurant workers lived in a warren of rooms above the garage. In the good old days before political correctness, everyone at the club called these rooms the monkey house. Now you heard it only from unreconstructed bigots or from people, like myself, who doubted vapid vocabulary engendered kinder souls.

Demo tapped a little box on the screen labeled INFRARED. The building image immediately darkened to black. Slowly, tiny digitalized boxes of color appeared: blues, greens, purples.

"Bingo," he said as a splotch of purple lightened to a pulsating red blob.

"That's a fire?"

"That's combustion."

"Oh," I said. Having practiced law before becoming a golf pro, I understood fine distinctions. This one escaped me completely.

"It could be a flaming gas, or it could be a glowing solid. Very eso-teric stuff to the layman."

Demo tapped his finger again. The image rotated slowly through 360 degrees. The red blob oscillated like a wobbling toy top. I looked at the building again. Still no visible combustion. Maybe the machine can lie, I hoped.

"Damn. Can't get a good depth fix with this friggin' thing."

This was a hell of an admission from Demo, a kid with a genius IQ who would have made Harvard or Yale if a stroke hadn't felled him during his junior year of high school. He didn't fit the normal volunteer fireman profile, but the chief pressed him to join because no one could work the new pumper's computerized fire detection system. Demo, one of those twenty-somethings born with 46 chromosomes and a computer chip in his genes, jumped at the chance to practice applied wizardry. I'm not anti-tech. I just believed the new pumper needed a track record longer than a month before I yielded my undying faith.

"You have any idea where that might be?" he said.

Demo's combustion glowed somewhere behind my shop. Maybe in the bag room, where the membership stored its golf clubs; maybe in the cart garage.

"The bag room has a closet about there," I said. "The cart garage has one directly on the other side of the inside wall."

"The garage has battery chargers, right?" said Demo. "Hmm. The heat source isn't super hot yet. Could be a short in one of those chargers. Could be a smoldering wire touched something off. Anything flammable in those closets?"

My stomach sank. "Lots of things."

Demo killed the screen and shoved off toward the chief. Limping fast, his entire body rose and fell like a piston.

"What's going on?" I said.

"Everything's fine, Kieran. Whatever's burning in there, we'll take care of it. You just back away for now."

I didn't like being dismissed by a twenty year old, especially one who admitted to looking up to me as a role model. But Demo now numbered firefighting among his many bailiwicks, so I stumbled over some hoses to the edge of the practice range where the restaurant workers huddled at the base of a pine tree. Half still wore their dirty kitchen linens, the rest gripped blankets around their shoulders. They were squat, grim men with flat faces and thick black hair who suddenly materialized at your elbow to clear away dinner plates or refill a salt shaker. They seemed even more grim than usual in the stark wash of the floodlights. Worried, as if they knew something Demo's laser-guided infrared homing system didn't show.

Demo spoke to the chief, who waved a few other firemen into a tight circle. After a minute of nodding and shaking and pointing, they broke away. The restaurant workers sensed something afoot and started jabbering something harsher than the Spanish I usually recognized.

A crowd gathered behind me. Neighbors, college kids cruising a summer's night, people attracted off the Post Road by the bright lights and grinding engines. I remembered a fire at a dry cleaners in Milton village on a winter's night many years ago. Only a boy, I'd stood in a crowd, hooting at firemen, wondering when the flames would flash, waiting for something to happen because this was a show and the dry cleaners didn't belong to me. Then I saw a classmate, a pretty Italian girl with dark curly hair, crying as she picked her way through the crowd. Her father owned the adjoining barber shop, and she feared the fire would spread. Right at that moment, I stopped hooting and laughing, stopped wishing for something spectacular to happen.

I glanced again at the restaurant workers. As badly as the fire would affect me, it would devastate them. My insurance was paid up. My summer inventory was mostly gone; my huge investment in fall merchandise luckily hadn't arrived. The workers lived in the monkey house, probably minus insurance. If the fire spread, they'd have their blankets and linens. Nothing else.

The first plume of smoke curled out from under the eaves of the monkey house roof just as the water started arcing up from the ground hoses and funneling down from the water cannon. The college kids applauded. A fireman opened the door to the monkey house staircase.

Thick black smoke billowed out, and almost immediately a red glow appeared in the windows above. One worker screamed, and suddenly I didn't feel as sanguine as Demo.

Glass shattered somewhere. Several more smoke plumes eddied from under the eaves. A flaming curtain flapped in a window. One of the college kids narrated the action sportscaster style while his buddies howled. The fireman in the cherry-picker worked the levers, steering for a better angle at flames rushing along the gutter line.

That's when the building blew.

A tremendous fireball tore upward through the roof. Flaming timbers shot skyward, spinning wildly. Shingles peeled back, fluttering like bats. The cherry-picker's arm rocked, then suddenly buckled, dumping the fireman to the wet pavement with a sickening thud.

Time stopped for a single elongated second. The flames froze; the hiss of the water, the shouts of the firemen, the last echoes of the blast receded into silence. And then everything returned in a crashing rush. Several smaller explosions shook the building in quick succession. An EMS crew surrounded the injured fireman, frantically clapping an oxygen mask onto his face and lifting him onto a gurney.

The flames raged out of control, licking at the sky. Blasts of heat pushed us back into the practice range. The college kids, suddenly humbled, gaped in silence as whole sections of plywood wall cracked and splintered, layers opening like the pages of a book. Through gaping holes in the cart garage, fiberglass shells bubbled and bulged grotesquely. Batteries popped, shooting their cell caps through the air like sparklers.

Some time later, Demo pulled up wearily beside me, wiping the length of his good arm across his brow.

"I never expected . . . the readouts said . . . Maybe we opened it up wrong, created a draft. We're just gonna let it burn itself out now. Can't spread anywhere, you know?"

"What about the guy in the bucket?" I said.

"Mickey? Pretty bad, I heard," Demo said, and dragged himself back to the pumper.

Another section of wall crumbled with hissing, crackling, snapping sounds. My suddenly visible pro shop looked like hell. Literally. Club displays and clothing racks collapsed in flaming heaps. A huge golf bag dangling from a rafter ignited like a mini-Hindenburg. Yes, I had my insurance paid up. But the thought comforted me as much as being flattened by a drunken driver and knowing I could sue from my hospital bed.

Watching soon turned pointless, so I headed for my car. That's when I remembered three items no amount of insurance money could compensate: a framed photograph and the first two golf trophies I ever won. I'd carted these mementoes around with me for over twenty years. College dorm, law school rooming house, my office at Inglisi & Lenahan, a Florida apartment during my professional golf apprenticeship, and finally a glass shelf above the pro shop's cash register. Almost certainly, the fire had reduced them to curled ashes and dollops of metal.

Now I understood why my pretty Italian classmate had cried that night so many years ago. Fire consumes. It doesn't matter that you have insurance. It doesn't matter if tomorrow you'll report it to your agent and he'll cut you a check for emergency cash. Fire consumes, and more than the walls and the carpets and the furniture. It consumes the spirit, the opera that echoed while the barber cut your hair, the sudden putting contests you enjoyed with members on rainy afternoons. The Lares and Penates of the modern world.

I swallowed hard, and slammed shut the car door.

A thunderous pounding rousted me from a nightmarish sleep. In fifteen seconds of staggering down my hallway, my mind replayed the fire in super-fast motion, then plunged forward into a future haunted by insurance forms and irate members who conveniently forgot they stored their golf clubs at their own risk.

A second temblor shook my seismograph.

"Coming, goddammit!" I opened the door and caught Det. Charles "Chicky" DiRienzo in mid-wallop. He snapped to attention and straightened his tie, which I'd have wagered was a clip-on.

"Your shop burned down last night," he said. One cheek peeled back slightly.

"What did you say?"

"Your shop. A fire. Last night." The other cheek trembled, stifling a grin. The bastard thought he bore me the bad news and relished it.

"That's what I thought you said." I stroked my chin, eyeing him, anger rising in my gut. "Haven't you learned doorstep manner?"

"What?" DiRienzo's big eyes flattened to a matte finish. He passed his wadded sport jacket from one hand to the other.

"You know, like a doctor's bedside manner. You ring the doorbell. You ask to come inside. You suggest I sit down. You tell me you have some bad news. And then . . ."

"You already knew," he blurted.

"Demo Mike phoned me. I saw most of it."

"Yeah, well, that's good because the fire marshall wants to talk to you."

"Does he suspect arson?"

"The fire marshall assumes arson in any structural fire unless and until he proves otherwise," said DiRienzo. He unfurled his jacket and punched his arms into the sleeves, narrowly missing me. "And whoever torched that place is in trouble. Big trouble. Mickey Byrne died an hour ago. So let's cut the wiseass remarks and don't say another word until you're asked a specific question."

Common decency in the face of death cried out for me to apologize for my immature harangue. But DiRienzo didn't deserve common decency, and besides, he wasn't Mickey Byrne's keeper. I dressed quickly and followed DiRienzo down the apartment stairs and into his unmarked Plymouth.

I quit the practice of law when my partner, Big Jim Inglisi, became Judge Inglisi. I could have continued the firm under my own name and waited until the county's voters tossed the Judge off the bench at the end of his term. But I needed a break for many reasons, and one of them was a growing distaste for the job. Even in a small town like Milton, the practice of law deteriorated into idiotic posturing on behalf of unreasonable clients. Simple real estate closings became adversarial pissing contests. Routine business deals detonated into lawsuits.

"You can't be introspective," Big Jim told me. "You must divorce the kernel of your being from what you do during the workday."

I didn't buy it. First of all, "kernel of being" was not in Big Jim's parlance, so he obviously ripped that advice out of a lawyer's self-help manual. Second, with every firm victory, we planted another time bomb in a minefield of enemies.

Case in point: Chicky DiRienzo. When I was a green young attorney and DiRienzo was a rookie patrolman, the cops arrested a teenager for a string of burglaries on Poningo Point. The kid lived on the Point himself—the son of some stock market muckamuck—and Big Jim, who continuously trolled Milton's toniest neighborhood for business, landed the defense. At the trial, Big Jim tossed me the job of cross-examining the prosecution's main witness, Patrolman DiRienzo. Even then, Chicky's childish understanding of the Constitution and the wide gaps in his deductive reasoning presaged the type of detective he'd become. The cross-examination was short, brutal, and effective. The kid got off, and I added my first enemy to the firm's list.

Ironically, none of Big Jim's enemies held grudges. He injected just enough buffoonery into his style that people he outright screwed would laugh as if to say, "There he goes again." I was too sullen and serious in my execution; nobody laughed.

Exiting Milton for my golf apprenticeship and returning as a golf pro defused some of the time bombs. Not Chicky's. And after I solved the Sylvester Miles murder while he sniffed up all the wrong trees, he even added a few sticks of dynamite.

DiRienzo squelched the radio chatter and deadfooted the Plymouth to MCC in silence. Despite myself, I noticed some refinements to his bovine image. He'd shaved his squiggle mustache and let his buzzcut grow out, which brought his head into approximate proportion with his bulk. He also traded his sharkskin suit for a professorial look of corduroy pants and tweed jacket. Not the most practical fibers for early August, but then DiRienzo could crack a sweat in a meat locker. I imagined opera lessons couldn't be far behind.

We rounded the clubhouse circle. Several of the restaurant workers sat Indian-style on the grass, staring down at the charred, dripping shell. The white stucco of the pro shop walls had blackened. Most of the monkey house roof had blown, then burned away. Jagged holes gaped in the plywood walls of the cart garage.

DiRienzo eased in between the last remaining fire truck and a Chevy with a county official sticker on the rear window and a brass badge on the bumper. A group of firemen, bareheaded but still wearing boots and slickers, nodded at DiRienzo but pointedly ignored me.

"Surchuck around?" said DiRienzo.

"Still inside," said one of the firemen.

DiRienzo told me to stay put. He ducked under a line of fluorescent orange tape and disappeared into the rubble.

I leaned against the hood of the Plymouth and stared at the building I'd known so well for so many years. The pro shop had been built back in the early 1960s, a small, square building with a steeply peaked roof like a Swiss chalet. No basement, no fancy accoutrements, just a place where the pro could sell balls and tees and the occasional set of golf clubs. Shortly afterward, the club tacked on the bag room, a storage area twice the size of the shop where members could park their golf clubs in between rounds. Again, nothing fancy. Plywood walls, minimal insulation, bare bulb lighting, and no heat.

In the late 1960s, after electric carts became the rage, the club added a garage along the entire length of the shop. Above the garage, the club built six rooms, each outfitted with a full bath. Originally envisioned as a penthouse, the club hoped to accommodate guests and prospective members of substance in convenient luxury. But the grand idea never materialized, and the rooms lay empty until the late 1970s when the club's restaurant manager, Eduardo Rojas, installed his immigrant workers.

Faces came and went; sometimes as many as thirty workers crowded into those six rooms. Immigration agents raided yearly, hauling away the illegals. In my four years as golf pro, the monkey house population stabilized at twelve. Immigration paid it no mind.

Someone shouted from inside, and the four firemen waded into the building. They emerged a few minutes later, carrying large mayonnaise jars filled with charred rubble to the trunk of the Chevy. On their next trip inside, the firemen lugged out a bunch of metal containers. My varnishes, turpentines, thinners, paints, and a jug of gasoline. All were deformed, blackened, bulged, split along their seams. The firemen lined up the containers on a clear patch of macadam. Each was tagged, but I couldn't read the writing. A skinny kid balancing a minicam on his shoulder climbed out of the pro shop and taped the containers with a slow sweep of the lens.

DiRienzo poked out of the shop next, like a movie dinosaur cracking out of its eggshell. A short, red-faced man followed carrying a small satchel. He barked orders to the skinny kid, then focused on me.

"You Lenahan?" he said. I nodded. "Paul Surchuck, county fire marshall."

He shook my hand firmly. Navy blue epaulets decorated his denim work shirt. A gut the size of a basketball cantilevered over the waist of his hipboots.

"Any idea what started the fire?" I said.

"Some, what about you?"

I shook my head, surprised by the quickness of his response more than anything else.

"Doesn't matter. You're here to help me find out. The detective tells me you witnessed the fire last night." Surchuck's voice disintegrated into a wheeze. He reached through the Chevy's open window and plucked a pack of cigarettes from the dash.

"I saw most of it," I said.

"How'd you get to the scene so fast?" Surchuck whacked the Chevy's lighter with the palm of his hand, waited about two seconds, and yanked it out. The cigarette caught slowly.

"A friend in the fire department phoned me when he recognized the call involved the shop. His name is Demosthenes Michaelides, but he goes by Demo Mike."

Surchuck looked at DiRienzo, who grunted in corroboration.

"Okay, you got here. What did you see?" Surchuck slipped a tiny tape recorder out of his shirt pocket, telling me I didn't mind being taped rather than asking if I did. DiRienzo opened a notebook.

I explained finding Demo at the new pumper's computer monitor and watching him work the infrared sensor, which showed something hot at approximately the center of the first floor.

"Near a closet?" said Surchuck.

"That's what I thought," I said, and went on to say I saw the first plume of smoke under the monkey house eaves a few minutes later.

"What color was the smoke?"

"Dark gray, maybe black. Hard to tell because the floodlights were so bright. Then one of the firemen opened a door."

"Which door?" said Surchuck.

I pointed to a dark cavity in the bag room's outer wall.

"It opens into a stairway leading directly up to the monkey house."

"What the hell's the monkey house?" said Surchuck.

"Sorry. The six rooms above the cart garage. The restaurant workers live there."

"Monkey house, huh? If that don't beat all." He scanned the broken windows and cratered roof. "Smoke came out of the door?"

"Lots of it. Thick and black."

Surchuck ushered me to the containers. He eased into a crouch and lifted a gallon tin by sticking a pencil through its bent handle.

"You recognize this?"

"That's a polyurethane," I said.

"Not just any poly. This is Imron, right?"

I nodded. DiRienzo scribbled diligently.

"What do you use that for?" said Surchuck.

"Refinishing wood clubheads," I said.

Surchuck slid the tin from the pencil, scuttled past a bloated turpentine jug, and tapped the pen on the rim of a lopsided can.

"What about this?"

"Lacquer thinner," I said. "I use it to clean the spray guns and brushes."

"Do you know storing these two flammables in that building violates the local fire code? Were you ever cited for it?"

I said nothing. I knew storing this stuff was a violation, just as Surchuck knew I probably stashed it whenever the town fire inspector made one of his unsurprising calls.

"Did you store anything else in there that might have caused a large explosion?" he said.

"Like what?"

"Like a large quantity of gasoline. Or propane."

"You see the only gas I kept there," I said. "Why would I use propane?"

"Well, for one thing, I didn't see any fixed heating system in the garage, or in that other area—" He turned to DiRienzo and snapped his fingers.

"The golf club storage room," DiRienzo read from his pad.

"Bag room," I said. "That's because there isn't any heating system. I use a kerosene heater near my workbench in the winter."

DiRienzo stopped scribbling. "You said kerosene?"

"Right. It's a small unit, made of white porcelain. I drain it every spring and store it on a shelf under the workbench. It should still be there, if the workbench is."

"I'll make a note to look," said Surchuck.

He asked about the cart garage. I explained the club leased a fleet of fifty electric carts from the Boland Brothers Cart Company. Under the contract, my staff performed the routine daily maintenance, like cleaning the shells, watering the battery cells, and recharging the batteries each night. If anything complicated needed repairs, Boland sent a mechanic.

"Who is on your staff?" said Surchuck.

"My shop assistant, Pete O'Meara, and myself."

DiRienzo sucked air, but I shot him a challenging glance. He hated Pete, and firmly believed the kid's checkered criminal history would be an unbroken black line if interlopers like Judge Inglisi and myself hadn't meddled with decent police work. He could tell Surchuck whatever he wanted in private; he wasn't going to accuse Pete of torching the place in front of me.

"You both have access to the building?" said Surchuck.

"We each have a set of four keys. Pro shop, garage, the door between the garage and the bag room, the door between the bag room and the shop."

"Anyone else have keys?"

"No one."

"What about the restaurant workers?"

"Keys to the stairway door, I suppose. No copies of ours, that's for sure."

"And no internal access between their area and yours?"

"None that I ever saw."

"Who closed up last night?" said Surchuck.

"I did. The last carts came in about eight-fifteen. It's getting dark earlier now."

"And nothing was amiss?"

"Not a thing."

"All right." Surchuck snapped off the tape recorder. "Just one more thing to show you."

He and DiRienzo led me around the front of the shop and through the caddie yard. The pro shop's air conditioner had tumbled out of the wall and crushed one of the wooden caddie benches. A small oak in the corner of the yard stood with its trunk blackened and its leaves shrivelled.

Far out in the ninth fairway, a good hundred fifty yards from the shop, two slickered firemen stood in a sand bunker. A fairway sprinkler chucked, spraying them with water. As we neared the bunker, I saw a large metal cylinder embedded at an angle in the sand like a dud artillery shell. Its visible end, once a flat circle of metal, bulged into a jagged, blackened gash.

"Know what this is?" said Surchuck. The spray swept past, pelting us with cold drops we all ignored.

"Never saw it," I said.

"You've never seen this before?" Surchuck said incredulously.

"No."

"That cylinder," said Surchuck, "killed a damn good fireman."

CHAPTER
2

I ducked into the caddymaster's shack and watched Surchuck and Di-Rienzo climb the hill toward the restaurant workers. Surchuck could tape the interview, but I wondered how DiRienzo's note-taking would wrestle with whatever Spanish dialect those guys spoke. On a day like today, you take your humor where you find it.

Despite the early hour, I reached my insurance agent by phone. After a brief stab at commiseration, he reminded me that the policy he shoved under my puss four years ago paid twenty percent of the estimated loss as emergency cash. He'd scramble a claims rep as soon as the main office opened. Committed to at least a few hours of waiting, I phoned the Village Coffee Shoppe and asked for Jackie Mack.

When I quit law to become a golf pro, I aimed for the PGA Tour. Six years after earning my card as a bona fide member of the Professional Golfers Association, my attempts at playing on the Tour were the stuff of myth: Sisyphus rolling his stone; Tantalus dipping his chin in the lake; Ixion lashed to his wheel.

I blew my best chance right after my apprenticeship ended in Florida. The PGA Tour officials "lost" my application for the Qualifying School, an annual tournament to fill Tour exemption spots vacated by last season's money-list bottom-dwellers. They had their reasons, and the reasons don't much matter now. Sometimes, in my more charitable moments, the reasons even make sense.

So I've spent my professional golf career as the pro at the Milton Country Club, the same club where I caddied as a boy and where I competed as a high school golfer. And I've tried to insinuate myself onto the Tour. I usually grab sponsor's exemptions for a couple of tournaments when the Tour swings through the Northeast every summer. Under a complicated set of rules, anyone who finishes in the top ten of a tournament automatically receives a berth in the next week's event. I still have visions of cracking the top ten and leaving Milton forever, like a comet breaking the gravitational bonds of the sun and spinning off into interstellar space. But that's not happened yet.

Last October, I finished fifth in the national Club Professional Championship. I picked up a nice paycheck and even landed a few advertising endorsements in golf magazines. But the most important prize was an automatic berth in the PGA Championship, one of professional golf's four grand slam events. By happy coincidence, the nearby Winged Foot Golf Club hosted this year's PGA, which meant I could compete with golf's finest players and still crawl home to my own bed each night.

For ten months, the idea of playing in a "major" floated in the warm realm of fantasy. Fuzzy images of myself paired with Greg Norman or Nick Price or Fred Couples filled my idle moments. Come August, icy reality chilled my nerves. I needed to prepare. Not on the Milton Country Club fairways, not on the practice tee, not in the backyard. I needed to see my shots fly down Winged Foot's fairways, across Winged

Foot's skies. I needed to putt Winged Foot's greens. So with the tournament one week away, I finagled a practice round at Winged Foot. I would hit about 200 shots while Jackie Mack, my special tournament caddie, annotated a yardage booklet like a copy of *Ulysses*.

Ian MacEwan, alias Jackie Mack, was the best caddie this side of those Tour regulars who earned single nicknames like Brazilian soccer stars. He thoroughly understood every strategic and mechanical aspect of the game. He read greens with a surveyor's accuracy. Nothing escaped his senses, not the subtlest nuance of a golf course's condition, not the slightest puff of wind, not even the minutest change in barometric pressure. More importantly, he tailored his personality, his demeanor, and his tone of voice to fit his golfer's temperament. Jackie saw himself and his golfer as a team, not two egos crashing into each other.

"The game and I just mesh," he once told me. "It's like I walk on a golf course and my senses expand. I hand my golfer a club, and I can feel from the way he grabs it exactly how his shot will fly."

His skills kept him in constant demand. The top players at Milton Country Club wanted Jackie Mack whispering his sage advice into their ears. Successful businessmen, who appreciated talent in any field, beamed with pride when Jackie toted their bags. A few, who saw a glint of promise through Jackie's unpolished exterior, tried to fix him with gainful employment.

"Everyone's disappointed in my life except me," Jackie said after refusing yet another job offer.

Jackie brought unpredictability to a high art. He might disappear for weeks, sometimes during the heart of the summer. Rumors would fly in the caddie yard, with reports of Jackie Mack sightings in unsavory places. Then he'd turn up without warning, sleeping on the caddie bench, stinking and unshaven, his curls matted. Once he even disappeared to pee while his foursome putted on the ninth green and didn't return until November.

The golfers tossed these antics off to typical caddie quirkiness. The caddies revered Jackie as a mad genius. I suspected a shiftless, opportunistic side, which showed itself after a golf ball conked Jackie on the head as he stood over a hill crest on one of MCC's blind holes. He hired a lawyer to sue the country club, the golf course architect (long dead), and every golfer who happened to be within four fairways of the accident. Members shunned him. For two straight months, the fabled Jackie Mack couldn't buy a loop. Caddie yard scuttlebutt said Jackie planned on winning a million dollar verdict and retiring to Florida or Switzerland. A sober-minded county judge dashed Jackie's dreams. He called the lawsuit "completely frivolous," and threw Jackie and his lawyer out of court.

Curiously, Jackie stabilized after this debacle. Caddie yard wags theorized the golf ball knocked some sense into his head. The members, particularly the defendants in the lawsuit, tsk-tsked about hubris. More likely, Jackie's newly discovered sense of responsibility emanated from Melvin Tucker. Tucker was not the club's best golfer and, if the caddies were to be believed, not the best tipper. But he hired Jackie as his steady caddie, and demanded Jackie's services every day. I practically had to kiss Tucker's ring to pry Jackie away for the PGA.

Apparently, I'd kissed Tucker's ring in vain because Jackie hadn't shown up at the Coffee Shoppe, and our appointed meeting time passed a half hour ago.

"If he does show," I told the owner, "tell him the practice round is cancelled."

News travels fast in a small town like Milton, faster still in the working-class neighborhood of Limerick where Mickey Byrne and I lived a few blocks apart. A huge crowd soon ringed the burned-out building. Caddies, club members, Limerick denizens unaccustomed to the fancy trappings inside country club walls but who felt entitled to see where one of their own had died. A police van descended, and two cops erected a barricade with blue sawhorses and fluorescent orange tape.

At 8:00, Pete O'Meara pushed his mountain bike up the tenth fairway. He dropped the bike in the caddie yard, wiped his brow with the sleeve of his hockey jersey, and screwed his baseball cap tight on his head.

"Holy shit, what happened?"

"Fire marshall's investigating," I said.

Out on the ninth fairway, two firemen dragged the metal cylinder on a hand truck.

"What the hell's that?" said Pete.

"That's what killed Mickey Byrne. No one's told me exactly, but I think it ignited and rocketed through the roof. You mean you've never seen it?"

"No way, man."

Pete's face combined the tall forehead and sweeping chin of clan O'Meara with the deep summer tan and dark eyes from his Bolivian mother. Those eyes narrowed as he caught sight of DiRienzo towering above the restaurant workers at the top of the clubhouse hill.

"Bet that bastard wants to talk to me," he said.

"He will. Answer politely, okay?"

"Hey, I'm always polite. But when he starts acting like I'm lying, I go ballistic."

"Keep cool this time," I said. The two firemen pushed the hand truck past us, huffing with effort. "And don't use the word ballistic. It won't sit well today."

Surchuck and DiRienzo came down to the yard while the firemen lifted the cylinder into the back of the fire truck. Their questions to Pete covered the same ground as mine. Pete answered with none of his teenage surliness, and DiRienzo said nothing to provoke him. Maybe, I thought, these two antagonists had turned a corner toward a more mature adversarial relationship. It never struck me as odd that DiRienzo didn't chum Pete's waters with the usual bait. But then again, I'm an optimist.

People piled in all morning. I holed up in the caddymaster's shack, basically hiding from anyone I recognized from the club or from Limerick, and keeping an eye out for someone resembling an insurance man. Surchuck and DiRienzo both left about noon, the last fire truck shortly afterward. Some golfers arrived to play, at least those few who didn't store their clubs in the bag room.

A splotch of red flashed around the clubhouse circle, and a few seconds later the caddymaster's shack vibrated with the hum of a turbocharged engine. The engine idled down, then cut out. I found Judge Inglisi in the midst of his exiting procedure. The Ferrari's door thrown open, the Judge's stubby legs reaching toward the ground, his girth wedged between the steering wheel and the leather seat.

Judge Inglisi and I had practiced law together for eight years, but our history went back to my days as a caddie and his as one of the sorriest golfers ever to line up a putt. He gave up golf years ago, but still followed the game as a spectator and my career, he said, out of morbid curiosity.

The Judge squirmed, finally getting enough purchase to pop himself out of the car.

"Hell of a goddam thing," he said, shaking loose his linen suit as he waddled around the shack. "Paul Surchuck on this?"

"Left a little while ago with DiRienzo."

The Judge snorted. "At least they have one brain between them. Surchuck's a good man. He's testified before me on numerous occasions. He'll turn this thing upside down and inside out."

He leaned on a sawhorse, testing its strength. Being high summer, the nimbus of white hair mid-latitude on his head was shaved as slick as a green at Augusta. But his eyebrows were as dark as the day I'd met him, and they knit together as he surveyed the damage.

"How'd you fare?"

"Total loss."

"I'm sure you have insurance up the ass."

"Not for everything, and the PGA is next week. This doesn't help the psyche."

"That's why I'm here," said the Judge.

It figured. My shop burns to the ground, and the Judge dusts off his version of a Knute Rockne pep talk. Who can fathom the judicial mind, especially Judge Inglisi's. A group of caddies stood nearby, bantering in pidgin English. The Judge cocked an ear and frowned. I expected one of his usual comments about the imminent downfall of civilization, but he motioned me toward the lilac bush.

"Jackie Mack fell in front of a train this morning," he said.

I groped for a lilac branch. In the sudden silence, the Ferrari's engine clicked and hissed as it cooled.

"When?" I said.

"About 8:45."

Despite the shock, my mind immediately constructed a narrative. 8:45. More than an hour after we should have met at the Coffee Shoppe.

"Don't go blabbing this because no one knows. Naturally I found out because Deirdre called." The Judge paused dramatically, partly because he reveled in his self-importance, mostly because he thought me a lunkhead for not marrying Deirdre the moment I met her. And, being a judge, no amount of subsequent history or appeals to reason would dissuade him. "She was waiting for a train when Jackie went down. The engineer slammed on the brakes, but too late. Deirdre jumped onto the tracks to see if she could help. But there wasn't much left of him in one piece."

"Jesus Christ," I said.

"Took EMS and the police an hour to scrape him up. That's when Deirdre called. She was pretty upset because she was the only person who recognized Jackie, but police told her not to say a goddam word because informing next of kin is their job, and they weren't going to do that until they had positive I.D."

"No one else noticed him?" I said. Jackie stood out in most crowds with his huge mane of curly blond hair, skin burned bright red from hours in the summer sun, and a permanent squint that drew the corners of his mouth into a perpetual smile.

"I didn't say no one noticed him. I said no one recognized him." The Judge opened the Ferrari's door and burrowed in behind the wheel. "You know Milton Station. Once the stockbrokers clear out in the early a.m., you might as well be in South America."

"What the hell do I do now?" I said.

"Get yourself another caddie," said the Judge. "Sure as hell is easier than getting yourself a new pro shop."

Not long after the Judge zoomed away, my insurance agent reached me on the caddyshack phone to tell me the claims rep was delayed.

"Any problem?" I said.

"Not at all. Are your business records intact?"

"Doubt it. The shop's pretty well gutted."

"Try to reconstruct them as best you can. Supplier lists, bank records. The rep will be along. His name is Frank Platt."

I had only half my suppliers listed on the back of a scorecard when a club worker delivered a message. Georgina Newland wanted to discuss plans for a temporary shop ASAP. I handed the scorecard to Pete with instructions to finish the list and to interrupt me the moment Platt arrived.

———

MCC's clubhouse was a neo-gothic stone castle built in the late 1860s by a New York City socialite and Civil War draft dodger named Seldon Whitby. In the 1890s, a man named Tilford bought the castle and routed the original twelve golf holes through the surrounding land. Seventy years later, three wealthy Miltonians bought the estate, expanded the seedy course to a regulation eighteen holes, and created Milton Country Club. The club converted the castle's basement into a locker room, the main floor into a restaurant, bar, and ballroom, and the second floor into administrative offices. The restaurant was leased to an outside concessionaire, who was free to solicit business from the general public in return for a percentage of the profits. Smart business move, since Whitby, as the castle was called, was listed in the National Registry and was a popular site for weddings because of stunning harbor views from the terrace.

Recently, the administrative offices outgrew the cramped second floor and relocated in the north wing of the main level. I rarely visited the offices and had little direct contact with the executive committee except for the yearly formality of re-upping my contract. The past October, the committee took the odd step of inviting me to answer questions at the regular monthly meeting. The topic: renovating the pro shop/cart garage complex. I sat at the end of a long oaken table while the committee, six men and Georgina Newland, peppered me with questions. I felt less like a witness than a mouse in a basket of vipers. The renovation project sounded like a sweetheart deal for a local contractor, and I couldn't gauge which member of the committee played what angle. All I knew was that the plan threatened to disrupt my life for a year. My considered suggestion, a kind of reverse *reductio ad absurdum*, was to raze the entire building and start from scratch. They dismissed me summarily, and that was the last I heard of renovation plans.

The door to the admin suite was ajar. Georgina Newland stood at the window, staring down at the shell of the pro shop. She wore a pink blouse and a white golf skirt that was wrinkled and creased from sitting, but otherwise perfect. Real perfect.

I cleared my throat, and she greeted me.

"I came here at nine to play," she said, as if stealing my thought that her outfit seemed out of context today. "I had no idea what happened. I haven't left this office since."

She sat wearily in a swivel chair and crossed her legs. One thigh curved just right over the edge of the desktop.

Club opinion on Georgina Newland varied widely. The caddies salivated whenever she sallied into the yard, her golf skirt riding midthigh on her ex-Rockette legs. The MCC executive committee, less awash in testosterone, resented the first female member of their previously all-male bastion. To them, her sweeping plans to "reimagine" Milton Country Club smacked of hysteria. In the psychiatric sense.

Like the caddies, I felt a tug from Georgina's classy features, long auburn hair, and figure that walked off the pediment of a Greek temple. And being older than the caddies, I also understood the true magnificence of a beautiful woman who topped forty. Yet, like the executive committee, I resisted her plans for general club improvement as annoyances without any real upside.

Between these extremes, my personal interaction with Georgina had been ambiguous. Her first year as an MCC member coincided with mine as pro. A rank beginner, she signed up for a whole slate of lessons. The first installment went well, I thought. Her grip was a mess, her swing stiff and awkward. But with a few weeks of intense work, I foresaw that long body whipping into the ball with power. I even sensed an attraction the way she lowered her eyes when I addressed her directly, and discreetly scoped me when I demonstrated various aspects of the golf swing.

She cancelled the remaining lessons the next day. She never explained why; I never asked. And our encounters in the meantime were cordial but unenlightening.

"The fire marshall interviewed me this morning," I said. "Has he spoken to anyone else?"

"Not to me," said Georgina. Her eyes swept me, like a laser guidance system that illuminates a jet fighter just before the SAM missiles fly. "I suppose he'll find faulty wiring or an overloaded circuit in the monkey house. I suspected something like this could happen. Those rooms didn't meet the fire code, you know."

I didn't, but nothing surprised me.

She spread a survey map on the desk and pinned down the curling edges with books and an empty ashtray.

"One thing I've kept in mind is that the club is the golf course, and the golf course didn't burn. So I've concentrated on getting us up and running as quickly as possible." Her voice carried an unusually sharp tone. Not quite defiance, not quite challenging. More like she wanted to remind me it was the *female* member of the executive committee carrying the ball for the old boys.

"Without a garage," she said, "electric carts are useless because we can't expose the battery chargers to rain. The only other option is gasoline carts."

"We do have caddies," I said.

Georgina scowled. "The membership wants carts. But Boland doesn't lease gas carts, so I lined up Tartan Golf Cart Company to deliver a fleet of fifty."

She waved a pencil over a section of the map. In real life, that was a grassy area behind the starter shack where members practiced chipping in a minefield laid by the greenskeeper's collie.

"A contractor will build a chain-link pen here," she said. "We'll lock the carts inside at night."

"Better think about barbed wire along the top of the fence."

"I'll note that," she said. "I've ordered a large trailer for your shop. It will have heat, air conditioning, phones, merchandise racks. No storage facility, but I don't think you mind."

"When can I expect it?" I said.

"Tomorrow," Georgina said with a proud smile blooming on her face. "I couldn't have my pro inconvenienced for too long, especially before the PGA."

She lifted the book and ashtray. The map rolled up by itself. I felt her radar again as I left the office. Sometimes I wonder if I emit signals when Deirdre and I are on the outs. Or maybe women just know my history and set their watches.

CHAPTER
3

By five P.M., the gawkers disappeared, the caddies mounted their bikes, the caddymaster threatened me with eviction. I made one more call to my insurance agent, who curtly told me Platt was on his way. Soon, Pete and I stood alone in the depressingly quiet yard. I almost blabbed about Jackie Mack. But word hadn't yet leaked out, and a promise is a promise. Between Jackie Mack and Mickey Byrne, there would be little joy in Limerick tonight.

Bored by the wait and intrigued by what might remain in the shop, I ducked under the barricade. The inside smelled like the world's dirtiest ashtray, with traces of rubber and plastic thrown in for the sake of nausea. Sunlight slanted through holes in the roof, highlighting scenes of chaos. Sweaters and slacks lay in twisted, blackened heaps. A pile of golf shoes cascaded from a shelf, their boxes burned away. Golf clubs stood singed and gripless on their display racks. The wire skeleton of a golf bag dangled from a rafter. A sludge of wet ash and fallen ceiling tiles coated the floor. Somewhere water dripped a rhythmic ping on metal.

As my eyes adjusted to the dimness, I saw just how whimsical a fire could be. Parts of some walls had burned through, others stood untouched. One side of a rafter was charred, the other side pristine. But the area I most wanted to search was pretty well destroyed. A rafter had collapsed, crushing the cash register and shattering the glass of the sales counter. Behind that, three feet of charcoal clogged my tiny office.

I started clawing at a spot in front of the counter. The ceiling tiles hadn't burned. But they were damp and heavy with hose water, and split like soggy crackers as I peeled them up. I dug through strata of tiles, finding lodes of tees, balls, gloves, all the minor odds and ends that exploded out of the counter when the rafter hit. I sorted them in separate piles, for no reason other than I didn't want to dig them up a second time. I'd cleared a three by three patch of remarkably green carpeting when Pete crouched beside me.

"What are you looking for?" he said.

"Remember the things I kept on the shelf behind the counter?"

"That old junk?"

"Those mementoes are older than you, and sometimes more relevant to my existence."

"Take it easy, huh? I'm just busting chops."

"Stop busting and start sifting."

"But, Kieran, you won't—"

A bright light snapped on, freezing us.

"What the hell's going on here?" growled a voice.

I scrambled to my feet. The light bounced closer, blinding me.

"I said, what are you doing here?"

I blocked the light with my hand, but couldn't make him out.

"Looking for some things," I said.

The light descended, slowly circling the piles I'd made.

"This place is off limits."

"I know. Sorry. I just wanted to look for the stuff because anyone else would toss it as junk."

"You must be Lenahan, huh? We need to talk. Make sure you trace the same path you came in on. You too, kid."

"Kid," Pete snorted beside me.

"Shut up and follow me," I said.

The man waiting outside looked like a racetrack tout clinging to the rail near the finish line. Gum rubber shoes, plaid pants, green Banlon shirt, matching nylon snap-brim fedora. Pete, catching up, choked back a laugh. We had stocked that exact hat for months and never sold one.

"Frank Platt, from the claims office," he said.

"Mr. Platt, am I happy to see you," I said.

If Platt shared my sentiments, he contained his enthusiasm. He tucked a thick file folder under one arm and waved the flashlight with his free hand.

"Is there someplace we can talk?"

"My car," I said.

We cut across the yard. Platt spread his file folder on the hood, humming tunelessly as he flipped through forms, sheets of handwritten notes, photos of the shop at the inception of my insurance policy.

"Your agent told you I'd need business records," he said. He had blunt features and pockmarks on his leathery cheeks. "Let's have them."

"Everything in the shop was destroyed," I said, handing over the scorecard.

"What's this?" said Platt.

"A list of my suppliers. My agent told me to put it together because all my inventory records were destroyed. I keep my bank records at home, and I've been here all day. But basically, I deposit my inventory receipts, cart rental receipts, and lesson fees into separate accounts. You should be able to reconstruct my sales from that."

"I won't. One of our accounting jocks will." Platt ran a stubby finger down the list, then slipped the scorecard into its proper spot in the folder. "I've got to tell you, there is a lot that bothers me."

"Like what?" I said.

"Like every year you lower your coverage on August one. This year, you increased it by forty, fifty grand."

"Usually my inventory tails off this time of year, and I don't restock until spring," I said. "That's why my agent offered sliding coverage. But this year I decided to stock up with closeouts."

"What the hell are closeouts?" said Platt.

"New but out-of-date merchandise. I wanted to expand my shop business, so I ordered a few hundred sets of golf clubs, a load of last spring's fashions, and a hundred dozen cashmere sweaters from an inventory liquidator in Illinois. Pete here agreed to work right up through Christmas."

Pete broke out in a dopey grin.

"Selling closeouts?" said Platt.

"Lots of pros do it," chimed Pete.

"The clubs are last year's models by now," I said. "I can buy them cheap, sell them cheap, and still turn a profit. Same with the spring apparel, which goes as cruisewear for people taking warm weather vacations. The cashmere, well, everyone likes cashmere."

"You had all this stuff in your shop?" said Platt.

"No, it never arrived," I said.

"Yeah, and we can't get the liquidator on the phone," said Pete.

Platt flipped to the list of suppliers.

"You have a Peoria Liquidating Company listed here. You just said the closeouts never arrived."

"That's a mistake," I said, glaring at Pete. "I'm not making a claim for that."

"Okay," said Platt. He scratched Peoria Liquidating. "You guys want to tell me what you were doing in the shop just now?"

"Looking for some mementoes," I said. "Nothing I'd include in a claim."

"Kieran," said Pete. "I told you—"

I shot Pete a milk-curdling glance.

"What?" said Platt.

"Nothing, man," said Pete. "Mementoes, like Kieran said. I know what that shit means to him."

"What were these mementoes?" said Platt.

"A couple of tacky trophies and an autographed photo of Arnold Palmer."

Platt grunted and made some illegible notes on the inside flap of his folder.

"Mr. Lenahan, is your shop business incorporated?" he said.

"No. I run it as a sole proprietorship."

Platt thumbed through his file, humming again, but louder than before. I got the feeling he was like a wind-up toy that hits a wall, spins around, and starts rolling again.

"I'll need your credit records," he said. "Personal credit. Card accounts, auto loans, whatever."

"What for?" I said.

"Never mind. Do you own your own home?"

"I rent."

"I'll need the name of your landlord."

"Wait a second. My agent told me I should speak to you about emergency money. What about that?"

"Emergency money?" Platt laughed. "I've already spoken to the fire marshall. His preliminary report finds arson."

"Targeted at my shop?"

"That's all I'm at liberty to say," said Platt. "Once the company hears the word arson, it won't make any payments of emergency funds."

"You think I burned my own goddam shop?"

"Hey look, pal, don't get nasty with me. The fire marshall tells me about flammables you stored in your workshop. You tell me about a liquidating company you can't raise on the phone. Ever take a lie detector test, Mr. Lenahan?" Platt gathered his file, set the hat on his head, and walked away with the jaunty step of someone who just hit a trifecta.

"Man, does he suck or what?" said Pete.

"You know what sucks, Pete, is you trying to help."

"Hey, like I'm supposed to know not to list Peoria Liquidating because we didn't get the stuff yet."

"I'm talking about you piping up when he asked why we were snooping around the shop. Don't you see he's trying to catch us in a lie?"

"Yeah, well, I just wanted you to know you wouldn't find those mementoes because they weren't there the day of the fire."

"They weren't?"

"That's what I was trying to tell you. I saw they were gone over the weekend. I figured you finally got embarrassed and took them home."

"I didn't touch them," I said.

"Must have been a real asshole to swipe them," said Pete.

The clubhouse lounge was bleak as February. Chilly gusts of air poured out of the ceiling vents. Dark panelled walls sucked up light from the Tiffany chandeliers. A Spanish language news broadcast blared from a TV perched above the top shelf liquors. Jose Rojas leaned against the cash register, the phone against one ear, his finger in the other.

I swirled the last cottage fry through a drop of ketchup and shot another glance at the three busboys sitting on a bench near the kitchen door. They held the exact pose as when my dinner arrived, their arms folded across their chests, their heads tilted as if cocking their ears toward a distant sound. Or watching me. I couldn't read their eyes in the shadows.

Jose hung up the phone and came back to my spot, hard against a pillar at a turn in the bar. Unlike the other workers, Jose enjoyed exercising his English with customers. I sensed more in his small talk than the idle chatter calculated to elicit tips. Jose yearned to assimilate, and to find work in the United States on a par with the engineering degree he said he earned at a university in Bolivia.

Jose was normally a jovial sort, something a medieval doctor or a modern psychiatric quack would predict from his endomorphic physique. He wore his jet black hair in one of those trendy cuts, shaved around the ears and long on top, with two pincer shaped locks curving to his cheekbones. His looks and his demeanor set him apart from the other workers, and from his older brother, the dour Eduardo, who managed the restaurant. Melancholy gripped Jose's mood tonight, understandable since he'd just been burned out of his home. But he remembered the strand of conversation the phone call had interrupted, and he picked it up immediately.

"I lock up about twelve, twelve-thirty last night," he said. "Eduardo stayed to do the books. I went down the hill. The monkey house was quiet. We had three weddings in three nights, and everyone was tired. A few guys who worked the last shift sat in one room drinking beer."

I turned quickly toward the three workers. One was gone; the other two hadn't moved.

"I went to bed," said Jose. He lifted my empty platter and wiped the counter with short, jabbing strokes of a towel. "Pepe woke me up a little later, after one. Said he smelled smoke. I jumped out of bed. The guys ran from room to room, but couldn't find nothing burning. You ever been up in the monkey house?"

I shook my head.

"Very drafty. You spray cologne in one room, you smell in all the others. Impossible to tell where the smoke coming from. I told everyone to run outside, then I call the fire department. The trucks come right away. Faster than I thought."

"So you reported the fire," I said. "You smelled smoke. But you didn't see any flames, right?"

"That's right."

I remembered the expressions on their faces in the glow of the fire. Something bothered me, and I wasn't sure what.

"Why the panic?"

Jose rubbed his forehead with the heel of his hand as if considering a careful answer. He started to speak, but the words gurgled in his throat. I knew why. I hadn't seen anyone, heard anyone, felt anyone's presence for that matter. But I knew Jose fell silent because Eduardo stood right behind me.

"Jose," said the voice over my shoulder, drawing out the second syllable as if in warning.

I shifted around on the barstool, gave Eduardo the low-beam grin I reserved for casual acquaintances I'd just as soon ignore.

"I need the book," Eduardo said to Jose, then nodded at me as an afterthought. He was a wisp of a man with a bandito mustache and a face as flat and impassive as a pre-Columbian statue.

How Eduardo Rojas remained as restaurant manager was a mystery that rivalled the death of the dinosaurs. It certainly wasn't his personality, which ranged between the suspicious and the outright paranoid. It certainly wasn't his charm, which surfaced as often as the Loch Ness monster. And it certainly wasn't his warm heart, not with his autocratic and imperious handling of his underlings. It could only be because he turned a profit, which, for the executive committee, forgave a host of sins.

My interaction with Eduardo was tepid at best. I'd say hello, he'd respond in a tone that made me promise myself to buy my next burger at McDonalds. The caddies whispered that Eduardo carried a switchblade under his tuxedo jacket. For once, those knuckleheads could be right.

Jose handed a thick binder across the bar. At the same time, a look passed from Eduardo to Jose. I knew our discussion about the fire had ended.

Eduardo took the book to a grinning pair of prospective newlyweds in a private dining room off the lounge.

"Where are you guys staying now?" I said to Jose.

"My brother set up cots in the locker room for us. He told us we could stay there until someone complained."

"And then?"

"He will turn a deaf ear to the complainers."

I nursed a beer and thought about how my life had changed in the last twenty-four hours. We tend to conceptualize our lives as a series of tiny stretches. Point A to Point B, Point B to Point C. Intervals of time and space too short and too close to admit danger. Last night, I locked up the pro shop door, hopped into my car, drove my accustomed route of Post Road to Beach Avenue to Poningo Point Road to Limerick and home. I fashioned a meal from leftovers, drank a beer, and turned in early. My only concern was waking up to play a practice round at Winged Foot. Point A to Point B. What could possibly happen in the interim?

Tonight I sat in the clubhouse lounge, my pro shop in ruins and my tournament caddie dead. Quite a wide gulf between Point A and Point B.

I squared my tab with Jose and stood beneath the clubhouse's *porte-cochere*. Only a thin band of pink remained where the sun had set. Mist boiled off the club's swimming pool. Crickets chirped. An onshore breeze carried the salty smell of the Sound up from the harbor. The tower floodlights suddenly dimmed, Eduardo Rojas closing up about four seconds after I left the bar.

I didn't mind my car being at home. Contemplative walks soothed me, and contemplative walks across the darkened fairways of Milton Country Club bordered on the mystical. I couldn't explain why my psyche melded so perfectly with this amalgam of rolling woodlands and flat coastline. I felt only the throb of some internal homing device luring me back whenever I felt troubled.

As I started down the slope of the parking lot, a dark limousine circled the drive. I thought for a moment of *The Great Gatsby*, and the final guest Nick Carroway saw drive up to Gatsby's front steps long after the last party ended. But the limo didn't stop at the clubhouse. It passed me on the slope and stopped broadside just outside the police barricades. The rear passenger window slid down, then up. And then the limo glided away.

The town of Milton rides the northern coast of the Long Island Sound close to where the state line juts west to claim Greenwich for Connecticut. People with the usual dim understanding of history trace the town's name either to John Milton, of *Paradise Lost* fame, or to a family of Miltons who, by pure coincidence, dominated the seat of Lord Mayor during the 1700s. In fact, Milton is a corruption of Mill Town, the early name for a settlement that sprung up around a gristmill standing where a wide, grass-choked stream called Blind Brook empties into what is now Milton Harbor.

Milton conjures images of understated wealth, inaccessible waterfront houses, ancient estates tucked in enclaves even the locals forget exist. Merchant Street, tree-lined and quaint, runs barely four blocks from the town square to the train station. The city's original telephone exchange gathered such prestige over the years that the addition of a new exchange brought protests from realtors. Yet there are neighborhoods those same realtors will avoid when showing off Milton's charms to prospective buyers. One of these is Limerick, a decidedly downscale neighborhood about a mile up the creek from that same gristmill (now a restaurant) that gave Milton its name.

I grew up in Limerick and sometimes wondered if I'd ever leave. I lived in the current species of Limerick chic: the garage apartment. Most of the pre-World War II Limerick homes had some sort of outbuilding, a garage, a barn, sometimes a toolshed. My landlord's had been a plumbing shop, which he converted in the late 1970s, when the building codes were lax and you didn't need to bribe half of City Hall for a variance.

I found my landlord fuming in the floodlit driveway.

"Look at this shit." He stabbed a hoe at a flowerbed littered with petals. "Goddam cable company. They come to replace a wire and trample my daughter's garden to hell. You talk to them, and they don't even understand English. What the hell is it with this country anymore? You try to speak your own language, and nobody understands a goddam word. Can I sue them?"

Amazing how people's perceptions of you differ from the self-image you carry around in your head. I could live in Limerick another fifty years, win fifty golf tournaments, and people would still ask me for legal advice.

I broke down a full semester of tort law into twenty-five words, stressing that damage to a flower garden wouldn't win him a major monetary judgment.

"Goddam," he said. "Everybody can sue but me."

Up in my apartment, I listened to my answering machine. I thought Deirdre might have called, if not to offer condolences for the shop at least to tell me about Jackie. But the lone message wasn't from her.

"Can't make it, Kieran," said Jackie with static crackling in the background. "But I guess you won't, either. I'll be there at the PGA for you, one way or another."

I reversed the tape and sat for a long time in silence.

CHAPTER
4

A different Jackie Mack greeted me with my morning coffee. Front page, above the fold of the local daily, with a grainy photo of the train stopped in the station, two columns of text, and an insert box squibbing all New Haven Line fatalities in the last ten years. According to witnesses, a young man, later identified as Ian MacEwan, 29, of Milton, was hit and instantly killed by the 8:45 train to New York. The witnesses said he had been acting erratically on the platform before jumping in front of the train as it arrived in Milton Station. No mention of Deirdre, no quotes attributed to any specific witnesses, no gloss on the erratic behavior. The Jackie Mack I knew was daft and unpredictable. But suicidal? Well, Jackie, obviously we hardly knew ye.

If Georgina Newland's planning impressed me, her execution knocked me out. I drove into MCC to find a huge trailer smack in the middle of the auxiliary parking lot. Workmen scurried like circus roustabouts, punching holes in the macadam with jackhammers, sinking thick iron pilings, lashing guy wires to donut-sized eyescrews sprouting from the corners of the trailer. A Con Ed rig sat on the sidelines, its driver drinking coffee and waiting for the go-ahead to tie in the electrical lines. At this rate, I could move into my new shop by mid-morning.

I swung wide of the hubbub and eased my car behind the lilac bushes. The caddies milled in the yard, their usual antics tempered by the death of Jackie Mack. Pete O'Meara spotted me and broke away from the pack. Pete was Deirdre's nephew, a factor which contributed to my hiring him when only gainful employment separated him from six months at a youth farm. I usually didn't ask Pete about Deirdre, considering myself too classy to inject an impressionable eighteen year old into the soap operatic love affair of two otherwise mature adults. But Deirdre's role in Jackie's demise was a safe topic.

"I heard about Aunt Dee at the station," I said. "What did she say?"

"It sucked."

"That's a general impression, not a direct quote, right?"

Pete laughed uncertainly. I have that effect on Generation X-ers.

Con Ed electrified the trailer by nine, and NYNEX installed phones by ten. Now the real work began. Without emergency insurance cash, stocking my new shop proved no easy trick. I dealt regularly with six suppliers, and always kept matters on a strictly cash basis. But to pull off my closeout merchandise gambit, I needed to pay twenty grand up front, which meant I needed to draw cash earmarked for my other suppliers. The reps, who all knew me personally, cautiously extended credit. But now, after the fire, glomming additional credit was a tough sell.

I spent the rest of the morning on the phone, trading on overextended credit, and making enemies. Of the membership, not the reps. The scenes played out like this:

A member would enter the trailer and fidget beside the empty sales counter while my telephone voice echoed in the barren shop. I'd hang up, and the member would ask if I filed the insurance claim.

"What insurance claim?"

"For the clubs I stored in your bag room."

"I have no insurance covering your clubs."

At that point, the sun would darken and the stars would fall from the sky. I would explain that the only service I provided was club cleaning. Members stored their clubs at their own risk.

"You remember my telling you this at the beginning of every year," I would say.

Silence.

"You remember the signs posted in the shop and on the bag room door."

Silence.

"Your homeowners policy should cover it."

About then the member threatened to sue and slammed the trailer door behind him. Multiply that scene by twenty for a fair approximation of my morning.

I knocked off my reverse public relations campaign about two and left Pete in charge of our hollow domain with instructions to ring Peoria Liquidating every fifteen minutes.

"What do I say if I reach them?"

"You figure it out," I said.

Milton's stratified social structure pursued people even into death. Residents of Poningo Point, Harbor Terrace, and Soundview crossed the River Styx from Gray's Funeral Home, a pre-Civil War mansion opposite the village green. Limerick stiffs used Damiano's, not only for its prices but for its proximity to Toner's Pub.

Two dozen bikes poking into the hedges meant the caddies went *en masse* to the afternoon session of Jackie Mack's wake. Leo Damiano stood in the foyer, wearing a seedy chalk-stripe suit to complement his '70s style sideburns and overtoned hair. Behind him, white plastic letters on a black felt signboard announced Michael Byrne in Parlor A and Ian MacEwan in Parlor B. As I stood puzzling over whether I should first pop in to Byrne's, someone slipped an arm through mine.

"I'm glad you're here," whispered Georgina Newland. "I didn't want to go in alone."

"Why not?"

She didn't answer. With the slightest pressure, she tugged me into Parlor B. We waited for a couple of caddies to clear, then knelt at the closed coffin. I didn't pray vociferously at wakes, just ran a quick Hail Mary through my mind and flicked a Sign of the Cross before heading toward the family. Georgina followed my lead.

Una MacEwan sat heaped in a chair beside a large spray of lilies laced with a blue ribbon reading *Devoted Son*. A black sweater was draped crookedly over a faded floral caftan. Thick feet burrowed into old shoes pressed flat at the heels. I lifted a damp hand from her stomach and held it in mine. She sniffled, eyes clenched tightly and head bobbing as I expressed my condolences and introduced Georgina.

A tousled blonde I recognized as Jackie's sister Kate stood beside her mother with one hand latched onto the back of the chair. I remembered her as a dirty-faced tomboy, playing ball in the street with her older brother and his friends. Like so many of the younger Limerick kids, she'd grown up behind my back while I was preoccupied with college and law school. I'd never met her father, but imagined she inherited her cool sleekness from him. She seemed more put out than sorrowful, though I couldn't tell whether she directed her pique at her mother's disheveled state or her brother's inconvenient exit.

"Max," she whispered sharply.

A young man drifted over from the back corner of the parlor.

"Max," said Kate, "this is Kieran Lenahan. He's a lawyer."

She emphasized the last word as if sending him a signal. We shook hands, Max avoiding eye contact. Jackie hardly mentioned his younger sister, except once to say he wished she'd married someone regular like me instead of a twit. Max Ritchie's beard needed a trim and his tortoise-shell glasses sat askew on his nose. His topsiders were too clean and his buttoned-down Oxford shirt was too crisply pressed for Limerick. But he didn't strike me as a twit.

I introduced Georgina, and we all expressed the usual sentiments. Max returned to the corner of the parlor. Kate knelt beside Una and tried to adjust her sweater. Georgina and I took seats behind the caddies in a gallery of folding chairs for a few minutes of silent respect. The caddies rustled, stealing glances at the small patch of thigh Georgina bared for the occasion.

Someone tapped my shoulder and settled on the chair beside me. Melvin Tucker.

"How do, Kieran," he said, and leaned around me. "How do, Ms. Newland."

Georgina nodded, suddenly tightening her hand on my arm.

"Looks like we both lost a good buddy," said Tucker, a touchy-feely type who dug his fingers into my knee.

"That we did," I said.

Tucker leaned around me again to aim a big grin at Georgina. But she stiffened, eyes averted. A whiff of bourbon eddied past my nose.

Tucker was built like a halfback gone to seed and then into hair-dressing with his big blow-dried gray-blond mane. I easily imagined him in one of those Southern college publicity shots, stiff-arming an invisible enemy with a pigskin tucked to his ribs and a twinkle in his eye because he realized the pose was all show-biz.

"Weren't you and Jackie headed to Winged Foot yesterday?" He talked from the side of his mouth, even when he wasn't trying to keep his voice under a roar.

"I never made it."

"Oh, that's right, the fire. Goddam, Kieran, you've got yourself more problems than Job. What you doing for a caddie now?"

"I haven't thought that far ahead."

"Neither have I." Tucker sank his chin into his pink jowls and patted his belly. "Course I'm not staring down the barrel of the PGA." He deflated and stared at Una MacEwan. "Feel bad for that nice lady. No mother should have to bury her kid. I tried to help, but you can't live someone's life for him."

Tucker was one of several members who tried to find Jackie steady work in a more conventional vocation. Funny thing was that no one at the club knew how Tucker funded his hard-drinking, golf-swinging, good ole boy lifestyle. Rumors portrayed him as everything from the owner of a telemarketing firm to a defense contractor to the absentee owner of Atlanta tenements. The caddies believed he played pro football and got hurt and now collected a million a year on a long-term contract his agent beat out of the team. Of course, none of those idiots bothered to check a football almanac to see if a Mel Tucker had ever graced an NFL roster. They didn't understand those absurd contracts for obscene salaries didn't exist in Tucker's era, assuming he had an era.

I remembered Tucker's attempt at helping Jackie two summers earlier. It stuck in my mind because the interview Tucker set up forced me to find a new caddie for a local tournament.

"Do you think Jackie committed suicide?" I said.

"Why the hell else would he be at the station when he should have been with you at Winged Foot?"

"He left a phone message some time that morning. He said he couldn't make it and didn't think I would, either."

"What did he mean by that?"

"Probably the fire. But he said he would be there for the PGA."

"He was headed somewhere?" said Tucker.

"He didn't say so specifically."

"Well, all I know is Jackie and I should be standing on seventeen tee right now, instead of this goddam funeral parlor. But then Jackie had his problems."

"What kind?"

"The usual sins of the flesh, like all of us," said Tucker. "I can't help thinking that if Jackie took that job he wouldn't be laid out here right now."

"What kind of job was it?"

"Investments. Entry level stuff, but with a good future. An old buddy of mine runs an investment firm. Jackie thought about the offer, then said no."

"Too bad," I said, though the thought of Jackie Mack connected with investments was more farfetched than me winning the PGA.

"*C'est la vie*," said Tucker, pronouncing the "st" like a true Anglo-Saxon. He cast a long look at the closed coffin, moisture welling in his eyes. "Don't know if golf'll be the same for me."

He punched my arm and grunted a farewell to Georgina. She smiled, and I didn't need the insight of a therapist to know she faked it.

"You and old Melvin aren't exactly pals," I said after Tucker departed and Georgina let out such a sigh a wave of excitement coursed through the caddie ranks.

"We once dated," she said.

I knew better than to pry for details.

Across the parlor, Kate and Max lifted Una from her chair and walked her toward the corridor. A few seconds later, I felt another tap on the shoulder. So far I'd been punched on the arm, pinched on the knee, and had an elegant arm slipped through mine. This time the culprit was Kate Ritchie.

"My mother wants to talk to you."

Georgina used the shift to take her leave, first patting Kate on the hand. The caddies stirred, jockeying into lemming formation for a rush off the nearest cliff. I followed Kate to a private sitting room adjacent to Parlor B. She didn't go in, just shrugged to make clear summoning me was not her idea.

The air smelled of stale tobacco. Crushed paper cones filled a wastepaper basket beside a water cooler. Una MacEwan slumped in a chair, turned half-sideways. Her sweater slipped completely off one shoulder, her stark white hair was mussed as if she just woke up.

"Here, come here please," she said, barely above a whisper.

Max Ritchie moved a chair so I could sit close.

"I need your help," she said after Max left the room. "He won't bury my Jackie."

"Who?"

"He doesn't know about Jackie, but he can check the books. Jackie went all through St. Gregory's School. Jackie was an altar boy when no one else wanted to be an altar boy. Jackie—"

"Who won't bury Jackie, Mrs. MacEwan?"

"Monsignor Neumann. Because Jackie killed himself." Una wheezed, then broke into a hacking cough. I hastily drew her a cup of water. She slurped it down, pulled some deep raspy breaths, let the cup drop to the floor. "Mr. Damiano told me. I thought there was some mistake, but there wasn't. Jackie's a suicide, and the Monsignor won't allow any priest in the parish to say a funeral mass for a suicide. If we lived on Poningo Point, he wouldn't dare."

"You want me to talk to him?" I said.

"You have respect in town. Talk to the Monsignor. Tell him about my Jackie."

I told Una I'd try. I didn't tell her that my influence at St. Gregory's Church, and with Msgr. Barry Neumann in particular, couldn't fill a thimble with holy water.

The Monsignor came to Milton during my lawyer's incarnation. Calling himself Father Barry, he told mythic tales of growing up German in a tough Bronx Irish neighborhood and of boxing out the young Lew Alcindor at Power Memorial High. The neighborhood stories may have been true, but the future Kareem Abdul Jabbar graduated the year before Barry Neumann entered Power. I looked it up.

Deirdre and I, then living together, heard of the hardnosed priest who breathed fire and scattered brimstone upon the good people of Limerick. Not being churchgoers, we thought we could safely ignore Father Barry, though we did notice the neighborhood was decidedly empty on Sunday mornings.

One rainy Saturday found Deirdre and I lounging in our apartment, wearing something less than our afternoon togs. A pounding shook the door. Having not met Father Barry, I took the caller for a delivery boy or door-to-door shill. He wore jeans, white socks, and pointy black loafers, a look that passed for cool in the Catholic grammar school classes of my youth. A windbreaker hid the clerical collar.

Deirdre instantly covered up on the couch, but no matter. What Father Barry saw didn't compare with what he'd heard, and paled beside whatever he imagined. For thirty straight minutes, he lectured about the sin of cohabitation and the virtues of holy matrimony. By dumb luck, or maybe by divine intervention, Father Barry had timed his visit to coincide with one of our closest brushes with marriage. Despite our annoyance, we accepted his invitation to pre-marriage counseling sessions in the school cafeteria.

I confess, I viewed the Church as an important institution of my youth, and one that would reassume importance in my old age. In the meantime, I expected the Church would marry me, baptize my kids, and forgive my rare appearances within the four walls of its Milton outpost.

Father Barry expected much more. After three evenings of blatant brainwashing, he administered a written test that Deirdre and I failed miserably.

"Can he get away with this?" Deirdre asked as we filed out of the cafeteria.

"I get away with this?" thundered Father Barry. "I am the one following God's rules, Miss O'Meara."

That ended any immediate wedding plans. But I don't blame Father Barry for scaring us out of marriage. Our problems ran deeper than an uncooperative clergy.

I took the back alleys from Damiano's, popping out at the front entrance to St. Gregory's Elementary School. The entire St. Gregory's complex, that is, church, school, and rectory, sat between the Post Road and Poningo Point Road, the latter being the main drag between the Point and Milton village. The church faced the Post Road, its Romanesque bulk flanked by the lofty Gothic lines of the Presbyterians and the whitewashed New England clapboard of the Methodists. Church Alley, the locals called this sweeping curve of highway.

Skirting the schoolyard, I felt a tug of nostalgia. As an altar boy, I'd duck out of class and cross this same pebbly pavement to serve at the nine o'clock mass for Father Laffin, who spat Latin so fast no one needed to know the responses, or for Father DiFalco, who actually seemed transfigured as the moment of consecration passed. Driving on Poningo Point Road, the red brick school seemed small and tame, an attraction in an amusement park of the past. Today, on foot and with an audience with Monsignor Neumann looming, I felt like that altar boy again.

The rectory stood between the school and the church, facing neither, shaded from summer by a canopy of oaks. I rapped the knocker on the large wooden door and noticed where the slick black paint had dripped onto the stonework before drying. The latch clanked, and the door pulled back. Gerdie Maxwell peeked out through the crack.

"I'm here to see the Monsignor, if he's in."

"He's in," said Gerdie, and opened the door just enough to admit me.

The rectory hallway was dark, medieval with slate floor and rough plaster walls trimmed with timbers. A damp chill seeped beneath the blazer I wore for the wake. The smell of cabbage laced the air.

"Can I tell the Monsignor why you want to see him?" she said.

"A funeral mass," I replied.

Gerdie nodded, and moved noiselessly down the hallway. She'd worked at the rectory for a good thirty years, cooking, cleaning, laying out the vestments in the sacristy before mass, logging the weekly contributions in the heavy gilt ledger in the parish treasury. I remembered her lingering in the shadows of the chapel beside the main altar, attuned to the tiny sounds in the quiet before mass. At communion time, she'd kneel at the altar rail with her eyes hooded and her head tilted back as the priest pressed the wafer of Holy Communion to her thick budded tongue. She hadn't changed much in the intervening years. The plain dress of a nun, the thick matronly calves, the red circles beneath the eyes, the mouse-brown hair bound in a net. She knew everything that happened in the parish, Father Laffin once told me, and kept it tucked beneath her heart.

Gerdie returned and led me to a sitting room hardly larger than a confessional. Two chairs faced each other on a bare slate floor. A wooden rack of religious pamphlets covered one wall. An oil of Jesus baring the Sacred Heart hung opposite.

The Monsignor swept in, the hem of his cassock whisking around his white socks.

"I understand you wish to speak about—" He pulled up short. "Oh, this Mr. Lenahan."

We scraped chairs, making room for a face-to-face, each replaying that last night of pre-marriage counseling. The Monsignor opened a red calendar book on his lap, licked his thumb, and brought us up to date. Other than the cassock and the rubber-soled shoes, he'd hardly changed since his Father Barry days. A thick boyish face. Bristly hair shiny with tonic and raked sideways. I wondered if something in the rectory air retarded the march of time.

"Who is the funeral for?" he said, balancing the calendar on a stretch of cassock while he probed his pocket for a pen.

"Jackie Mack."

"Sorry?"

"I mean Ian MacEwan. The man killed by the train."

"Is this a joke, Mr. Lenahan? Because if it is, it is not very funny."

"His mother is very upset about you refusing him a funeral mass."

"The young man killed himself. It is not the practice of the Church to condone an act of suicide."

"Saying a funeral mass for a departed parishioner doesn't condone anything."

" 'Thou shalt not kill,' " said the Monsignor. "I treat the Commandments rigidly, which cuts against the prevailing attitudes of this society. I explained my position to Mr. Damiano. The funeral home may conduct any service it wishes. I can't bar the man's interment in the family plot in St. Mary's. I wish I could, but that's another example of a human contract prevailing over God's law. But I control this church and this parish. I will not use the sacred rites of the Church as a rubber stamp. I'm sure you believe me." The Monsignor stood and shook out his cassock. "Many in the parish will remember Jackie in their prayers. Leave it at that."

CHAPTER
5

I waited until dusk to risk a visit to the O'Meara house. Deirdre and I hadn't spoken in three months, ever since the morning she announced she was moving out of our apartment to seek a new life. I pointed out to her she'd moved back in with me to build a life together. Was that now an old life? Deirdre didn't answer, just kept dumping whole drawers of clothes into gaping mouths of suitcases. Once Deirdre plotted a course, nothing stopped her. Small wonder she and Judge Inglisi were *simpatico*.

She moved in with her sister-in-law Gina and nephew Pete in the O'Meara house in Limerick. Pete kept me posted on her search. Unsolicited, of course.

"She's working only part-time at the med center," he told me one day.

"What?" I said, literally hearing the *boing* sound-effect of surprise reverberating in my ears. For the entire decade of our alternating current love affair, Deirdre worked as a cardiac ICU nurse. She usually added shifts to her work week, not sloughed them off.

"Yeah, she's looking for a new type of job. Wants to be a bank president or something."

I must have passed the O'Mearas' crazy pastiche of a house a hundred times in the last three months, trying to fabricate an excuse to ring the doorbell. Tough to be prideful and principled. Tougher still to be at loggerheads with someone just as prideful and principled. But now I had my excuse. Of course, you can't afford a tragedy every time you need a conversation piece.

I rang the doorbell and stepped back to the edge of the crooked porch. Deirdre's hatchback sat in the driveway. A TV played deep inside the house. I held my breath until Gina cupped her hand to the door screen.

Limerick neighbors remembered Gina O'Meara as a mousy Bolivian woman completely enthralled by her good-for-nothing husband. She kept largely to herself, dutifully dragging groceries home from the A&P because Tom refused to drive her, hanging tons of wash on lines strung in a back alley because Tom didn't want the neighborhood to know he couldn't afford a dryer, and wearing long dresses and sweaters in the summer to hide the bruises Tom inflicted when the mood struck.

Fortune smiled on Gina when Tom pulled twenty-five to life after pleading guilty to murder. For almost a year, Gina refused to speak ill of her husband. She even blamed herself, as if her inadequacies set Tom on his murderous course. But then a change swept over her. She landed a job in the high school cafeteria, which served double duty by keeping her in contact with Pete. She rode taxis to the A&P, and used a pre-approved bank credit card to buy a clothes dryer. The neighbors believed Gina finally realized Tom never was coming home again. I wondered if Deirdre influenced her sister-in-law's new life. Or maybe vice-versa.

"Pete's out," Gina said.

"I'm here to see Deirdre."

That thrilled her almost as much as Tom returning for a conjugal speed-bag workout. She opened the door and pointed me into the den. I couldn't help noticing she'd put on weight. Not much, just enough to pad out the bones of her face and shoulders. She looked pretty in a girl-ish way, not the scrawny, hollow-eyed woman Tom O'Meara left behind.

I waited for maybe two minutes, barely long enough to note Tom's wooden cane lying across the arms of the recliner and to reacquaint myself with framed photos of distant holiday gatherings. A young, reed-thin Corny O'Meara and a dazzling Dolores dancing at some railroad company party. Corny in Santa Claus garb, propping young Tommy and Deirdre on his knees. The extended family, including myself as Deirdre's guest, in front of the fireplace with Corny and Dolores as sullen bookends. The photos had to be Gina's idea. I couldn't imagine Deirdre trying to revise family history.

Deirdre came in wearing a terrycloth bathrobe bundled tightly and double knotted at the waist. Her face was flushed. Tendrils of red hair splayed on the towel around her neck. She unstacked two plastic chairs and slid me one. No one dared use Tom's recliner.

"Jackie Mack, right?" She sat, tugging at the hem of the bathrobe to cover her knees. A slight, innocent gesture, but a bothersome one. Deirdre skillfully employed prudishness as a weapon.

"Monsignor Neumann won't allow a funeral mass because Jackie committed suicide," I said. "Una MacEwan asked me to speak to him."

"I'll bet you got far."

"Exactly nowhere. And he remembered us."

Deirdre scowled. At the memory of our stab at pre-marriage counseling, or at the reference to us as a couple, I wasn't sure.

"Mind telling me what you saw?"

"Kieran, I don't have time right now. I have an appointment tonight."

"A date?"

"An appointment. Business, not pleasure." Deirdre sighed. "But if I don't tell you now, you'll hound me until I do. Might as well get it over with."

She hung her head between her knees, flipped her hair forward, and expertly wrapped the towel into a turban. The sudden lack of hair accentuated her high cheekbones and turquoise eyes. People talked about certain faces being the map of Ireland. Deirdre's was an ordinance survey.

"I had an interview in the City yesterday morning," she said. "The eight forty-five runs local to Larchmont, then skips to Mount Vernon to discharge people who want to make connections for Bronx stops. My father was a conductor, remember?"

I remembered, but my memory did not draw upon the raw material of experience. Rather, I remembered an image of a Corny O'Meara I'd never actually seen, swaggering with perfect balance down the bucking aisles of the old New Haven diesels, plinking coins from the change holder on his belt, and chatting up every lady passenger. Deirdre discovered her father's affairs at the age of sixteen. But finding letters and photos in the drawer of an old desk didn't hurt half as much as her mother's reaction. Dolores already knew. Worse, Dolores planned nothing in response. No retaliation, no confrontation. Just say the Rosary and hold the family together and, when loneliness awoke her, nip at the Jamesons. Deirdre hated her father and feared becoming her mother. Sounds glib, but we had a decade of history to prove it.

"I stood at the back end of the platform," said Deirdre. "It's crowded with Hispanics at that hour because they need to be in the last two cars to change at Mount Vernon. The platform was packed solid. I don't know why people stand right on the edge and lean out to see if the train is coming around the bend. I spotted Jackie shouldering through, sidestepping people, squeezing really close to the edge wherever someone blocked him. I was about a car length away from him. The only reason I noticed him is because I recognized him as your caddie. And he stood out with that curly blond hair and red face."

"Did he seem agitated or disturbed?"

"Not at that distance. I didn't pay him much mind. Just sort of noticed him, like any familiar face in a crowd."

"Which direction was he walking?"

"From the end of the platform toward the ticket office."

"So the train came from behind him."

"That's right." Deirdre's eyes seemed to shrink and focus on infinity as she watched the scene play out in her head. "The whistle blew. Everybody turned to watch the train roll in. That's when Jackie—"

Deirdre unwrapped the turban and furiously towelled her hair.

"I didn't see Jackie fall. Too many people blocked my view. What I noticed were two guys running through the crowd. Just as I was thinking how odd that was, the brakes squealed. People screamed. The engineer and the conductor jumped to the tracks. A Metro North crew working across the way ran over. I stripped off my jacket and jumped down myself. I thought that if he needed CPR or a tourniquet I'd be the only one who knew what to do. But the train basically blew him in half. Part of him lay under the second car. The rest was under the platform, across the tracks, dripping off the front of the first car."

"Jesus Christ," I said.

"I climbed back onto the platform," said Deirdre. "Lots of people were staring down. One woman kept making the Sign of the Cross. The police came, Milton cops and Metro North. They moved the crowd back and started talking to witnesses. I heard the engineer saying, 'He was there. All of a sudden, he was there.' "

"Did they talk to you?"

"For whatever it was worth. One cop asked where I was standing and how far away Jackie was, and whether I saw any contact between anyone else and Jackie. I told him no, not exactly, just about Jackie walking close to the edge, and the two guys running through the crowd. He asked if the two guys could have pushed the victim. I said I knew the victim was Jackie Mack, and he said they didn't know that yet and I should be careful about using names right now. I said I didn't actually see them that close to Jackie. Just that they started running at about the time Jackie fell."

"What did they look like?"

"Hispanic-looking. Thin. Twenties, maybe. I told the cop I would recognize them if I saw them again. He didn't seem too impressed. He said he'd call me if it came to that. He also reminded me not to start talking about anybody specific until they identified the victim and notified next of kin."

"That's about when you called the Judge," I said.

"I gave his clerk an earful until he pulled the Judge out of a trial. I had to talk to somebody, and Big Jim can keep a secret."

"Did you hear the police question anyone else?"

"Some of the Hispanic people. I couldn't understand the answers, but I could tell from the gestures they said Jackie jumped. I wasn't surprised to read the paper this morning."

Chicky DiRienzo webbed his finger together and inspected his nails.

"Goddammit, Lenahan, fifty people saw him jump," he said. Behind him, a window framed the Milton train station, the quaint gaslight lamps along the platform just beginning to glow as the summer dusk shaded toward night. DiRienzo's old office had been on the ground floor of the police station, a small rectangle of anal-retentive neatness tucked behind the holding cells. This one was larger, airier, and, though still a psychiatrist's field trip, different in a way I couldn't quite articulate.

"What about what Deirdre saw?" I said.

"No one else mentioned those two guys."

"Maybe everyone's attention was on Jackie. Maybe those people are protecting someone."

"Last I heard, running from a train platform isn't a crime."

"Maybe they bumped into Jackie and think they committed one."

"You've said three maybes in ten seconds flat."

"She says she can I.D. them."

"I know that. She told the officers who responded to the scene. They assessed it wasn't important enough to pursue. You want the truth, they thought she was another hysterical broad. Everybody else was sure and sober about what they saw."

"Deirdre doesn't see things," I said. "And she's one of the coolest people I know."

"Protecting your girlfriend," said DiRienzo.

"We haven't seen each other in three months."

"I guess that adds to the credibility of your character reference. Which reminds me, when is Judge Inglisi going to weigh in?"

"Aren't you even interested in finding out if two guys dashed when Jackie fell?"

Scowling, DiRienzo yanked open the bottom drawer of a filing cabinet. A bronze Remington cowboy crashed to the floor.

"Damn it, Lenahan!" he said, cradling the piece in his hands.

Now I realized what felt different about DiRienzo's new office. *American Gothic* hung beside the hunting calendar with the carefully ruled X marks. Names like Rockwell and Wyeth graced book spines in DiRienzo's size-regimented crimefighter's library. Another Remington cowboy drew a bead on me from behind the water cooler.

"Did you become an art *aficionado*, Chicky?"

"I'm taking a course in art appreciation, okay?" He steadied the bronze back atop the file cabinet and plopped a thick binder of mug shots onto his desk. "She wants to come in and waste her time paging through this, she's welcome."

"I don't think she'll go that far," I said.

"Then I guess we reached the end of the line. Ha ha." DiRienzo slipped the binder back into the drawer, carefully this time. "Why the hell are you so concerned about MacEwan? Don't you have enough on your hands with the fire?"

"Getting Jackie buried is my problem. The fire is yours. Are you any nearer to finding out who torched my place?"

"We're making progress on several fronts."

"Good," I said. "Be sure to tell my insurance company."

"Oh, I will," said DiRienzo. He threw back his head and guffawed. If only Rockwell could paint his newest devotee in brown tones and exaggerated features. *Small Town Comedian.*

I returned to the evening session mainly to talk to Damiano. He bent behind a small desk and rummaged through the drawers. Outside his office door, the line for Mickey Byrne snaked around the lobby and spilled onto the front steps.

"Why not keep the burial as scheduled?" the undertaker said. "I can have a short service here. Then after you convince the Monsignor that Jackie didn't kill himself, he can always say the funeral mass later. It's not a wedding. The body isn't necessary. God still hears the prayers."

I wondered for a moment if he were poking fun, then decided he wasn't.

"I'll need to speak to my . . ." I caught myself before I said *client*. "No, I don't need to speak to her. Una wants a proper funeral. In the church, with two acolytes holding candles and the Gregorian chant and a priest circling the casket with a thurible of burning incense."

Damiano snatched a set of Rosary beads from the back of the bottom drawer. The loop was broken, two lengths of beads falling away from the crucifix like lentils on a string. He counted the beads to make sure all five decades remained.

"Monsignor won't even send a priest tonight," Damiano said, referring to the local custom that a priest say the Rosary the night before the burial. "He's coming himself to Byrne's tonight. When I heard that, I told Una I'd lead the Rosary for Jackie."

At that precise moment, Una limped through the lobby on Kate's arm. As Damiano watched them pass, his waxy features softened. Kate and Una disappeared into Parlor B. Damiano ejected a staple from a stapler and used it to link the two strands of beads.

"Good as new, eh?" he said. "Look, I can keep him an extra couple of days, all right?"

"You're a good man, Leo."

"Don't stroke me, Kieran. Three days, four at most. Don't even think of asking for more, like I know you will. I have a license to think about."

"If I can't convince the Monsignor in that amount of time, I'll convince Una to bury Jackie."

"Deal," said Damiano. He suspended the rosary beads from his forefinger. "Do you know the Five Sorrowful Mysteries of the Rosary offhand?"

The Mysteries were events from the life of Christ, which the leader introduced at the start of each of the five decades of Hail Marys that formed the heart of the Rosary. The idea, I suppose, was to focus the congregation's collective mind while its collective voice descended into hums, drones, and other glottal aspirations.

"Uh, the Crucifixion," I said.

"That's all I remember, too," said Damiano. "Fine couple of Catholics we are. We'd both better hope the Monsignor gets a transfer."

While Damiano led the Rosary for Jackie, I loitered on the lawn and waited until Mickey Byrne's line dwindled. A color guard flanked the fireman's casket. His ex-wife and two kids stood off to the side, the son's attempts at military stiffness reminding me of John-John at JFK's funeral. I said my quick prayer, shook hands, and lingered only a minute or so. The eyes of the volunteer firemen burned me from all angles.

I spent the last minutes in Parlor B. Kate Ritchie stood beside her mother, her blonde curls pulled back off her face. Max hovered ineffectually near his wife when he wasn't moping in the corner. I wanted to avoid direct contact with Una. Just the sight of me might give her false hope, and I preferred telling her of my failure in private. The caddies once again filled the gallery, so I ducked in behind them. Without Georgina by my side, they paid me little mind.

After Damiano's closed, I followed loose ranks of caddies down a side street that described the curvy route of an ancient footpath. Swamp maples grew thick, their leaves blotting out the sky above the large duplex the MacEwans shared with another old Limerick family. As I crossed the lawn, someone called my name. Kate materialized out of the darkness of the driveway.

"I wanted to personally thank you for coming today," she said. "That meant a lot to my mother."

She'd changed into shorts and a tee shirt. Her hair, unbound, tumbled around her shoulders. The word exquisite came to mind, but didn't stick long.

"What did my mother tell you this afternoon?" She took a slug from a tumbler. Scotch, from the scent.

"She wanted to personally thank me for coming this afternoon."

"Whatever." Kate turned and walked back down the darkened driveway, casting a glance over her shoulder. I'm a sucker for that particular toss of the head, so I followed her to the big old barn of a garage. She gulped Scotch, wiped a dribble from her chin, and giggled mirthlessly.

"Ever hear about Jackie and his Saab?" she said. "When he turned sixteen, he wanted to buy a car. Not just any car. He wanted something like all the rich kids drove to school. He worked hard to save money; he read the used car classifieds everyday. It took him over a year, but he finally found a mechanic at Brennan's gas station selling one secondhand.

"Jackie parked the car right here in the driveway. Months passed. He'd wash it, sit in it with his girlfriend. But he never bought insurance or plates. Then the people next door bought a new car, which meant Jackie's was in the way. Instead of putting his car in the garage, he pushed it in front of the house. The cops warned him about parking an unregistered car on a public street. Then they started giving him tickets. When he didn't pay, they towed the car. Jackie never bailed it out. Even if he did, the car wouldn't have worked because the towing tore up the transmission.

"Now Jackie's done it again. Gone. Checked out. Not following through."

"With what?"

"Taking care of Mom."

Kate drifted into the backyard, this time without the fetching glance. I didn't detect much *veritas* in her *vino*, so I headed around front, where Una MacEwan sat on a rocker in a corner of the darkened porch. Through a window I saw a few neighborhood ladies gathered around the dining room table. Max Ritchie slumped in an armchair, looking beat. Caddies buzzed around a platter of cold cuts.

"Lots of food inside," said Una.

"I'll pass." I settled onto the porch rail.

"He's still here, you know," she said. "Last night, I lay in bed and thought I heard him down in the basement the way I always did. 'Jackie,' I called. But the house became quiet, and when I listened again all I heard were the night sounds. I'll listen again tonight. I'll hear him, I know. But tomorrow he'll be gone, and those night sounds will be just sounds."

"Do you have anyone who'll look in on you?"

"Kate has her own life. It was always Jackie did the looking after."

"If you need errands run, I can send over the caddies."

"I'll be fine," said Una, and tilted her head as if falling asleep.

"Mrs. MacEwan, I talked to the Monsignor, and he adamantly refuses to allow any funeral mass for Jackie. I think I can convince him Jackie didn't jump. But it might take days. The funeral could go tomorrow. Damiano offered to conduct a short service."

"A service is no mass."

"The mass could be said after I convince the Monsignor."

"No. I want a mass for Jackie," she said.

"I thought so. I've arranged with Damiano to hold Jackie a few extra days."

Una grasped my wrist. "Oh, Mr. Lenahan, how can I thank you?"

"Don't thank me yet," I said. "Damiano can't wait forever. He said five days at the most. Maybe I can squeeze out a week. If I can't convince the Monsignor, you may need to bury Jackie and have the mass later."

"But that won't happen," she said. "Five days is enough time."

Maybe *client* was the word for Una MacEwan. One with unreal expectations.

"I need to ask you some questions," I said. "And I need you to tell me anything that comes to mind, no matter how trivial it seems. Did you see Jackie that morning?"

"Jackie kept late hours the last few days," said Una. "Early ones, too. I told him he needed his rest, but he said he was busy. He'd catch up later. He ran some errands for me the day before, things he usually does later in the week, like food shopping. That was the last I saw him though he called up to me when he came in that night. Late, after midnight it was. And I heard him banging around early the next morning."

"What time?"

"Six, I think."

"Did he mention to you he was caddying for me that morning?"

"Yes."

"When did his plans change?"

"I didn't know they did."

"He called me that morning. I don't know the time because I was out early and back late. He said he couldn't make our round."

"That's not like Jackie. He loved to caddy for you, Mr. Lenahan. He said he'd even do it for nothing, he loved it so much."

"Do you know any reason for Jackie to kill himself?"

"Why does someone kill himself, Mr. Lenahan?"

"Debts," I said. "Depression. Terminal illness."

"Jackie was always very good with money. Never wasted what he earned. Always gave me something to help out with the groceries and the bills. He wasn't depressed. And he had no terminal illness."

"How did he get along with Kate?"

She cocked her head as if the question surprised her. "Fine, like any brother and sister."

Interesting, I thought. I'd talk to Kate tomorrow, if she sobered up.

CHAPTER
6

Milton train station, 8:30 on a weekday morning. Latin music blared while cab drivers played cards in the shade of the taxi stand. Hispanic boys and young men dribbled soccer balls in a corner of the parking lot, stopping to line up when a contractor or landscaper tooled past. Women and older men clustered on the platforms, waiting for trains to take them to jobs in Mount Vernon or Norwalk.

This dollop of salsa did not sit well in the stomachs of old-line Milton, prompting a group of "concerned citizens" to write an open letter to the town council, asking them to "clean up the daily third world bazaar at the train station." As if these words weren't inflammatory enough, the letter went on to cite police blotter statistics showing an above average number of quality of life violations committed by people with Hispanic surnames. Drunken driving, vandalism, public intoxication.

The issue hit the council's agenda on a winter Wednesday. The town hall bulged with special interest groups and swirled with rumors of Justice Department observers. The debate, naturally, strayed far afield. But then again, that's life in the United States of the 1990s. Everyone has become obsessed with cute legalistic arguments while completely losing interest in action.

This wasn't Milton's first brush with xenophobia. You need only look at Limerick to understand the simple march of time and the ethnic archaeology left in its wake. In the late 1800s, Milton enjoyed a brief vogue as a vacation spot for New York City dwellers. Developers bought up acres of oak forest near the town's two crescent-shaped beaches, carved out lots, and built cottages connected by buggy paths. By the early 1900s, the vacationers moved elsewhere, and the cottages fell into ruins. Then the Irish came with their Mac's and O's and Fitz's; their rolling Rs; their drinking and vandalism and pugilism; their intoxicated Saturdays and pious, if pie-eyed, Sundays. Landlords unfettered by laws or government programs or delicate sensibilities dumped these newcomers into those wretched cottages. No one complained. Hell, Milton's worst was better than the windswept coast of Donegal or a tumbled-down farmhouse on a rocky patch of Clare.

The men stoked coal on the railroad; the women served tea in the parlors of Poningo Point mansions. Soon lace hung in one cottage window. Then another, and another. More Irish came, and Limerick spread, surrounding a colonial inn named the Carriage House where, local legend insisted, George Washington had slept. Eventually, a band of Irish cops bought the Carriage House and renamed it Toner's, after a Dublin pub.

Now, almost four generations later, Limerick was Irish in name only. Yuppies who stood on the shoulders of working-class parents sold the family homesteads to Salvadorans or Bolivians, and traded up to Poningo Point mansions as the old-line WASPs died off. In another twenty-five years, Toner's Pub would be a bodega.

But like that Wednesday night in the town hall, people argue and politicize and demonize. They quote the words of the Statue of Liberty and handwring about barring the door and pulling up the ladder. For me, the issue isn't an ethnic thing or a racial thing. It's a travel thing. Two weeks steerage on a coffin ship refines the caliber of immigrant a bit sharper than six hours on your basic jetliner.

I pulled into a parking space beside a cable TV van. The crew, a couple of lean, bowlegged toughs, stood at the open rear gate. One slurped coffee from a plastic pint container. The other switched a length of coaxial wire against the rear bumper. Both spoke excitedly in Spanish, but quieted when I cut my engine. I wondered idly if these two guys trashed my landlord's garden.

I crossed to the westbound side through a damp, graffiti-stained pedestrian tunnel, and popped up at the Victorian ticket office. The New Haven line ran four tracks through Milton. The platforms were made of forty foot slabs of prefabricated concrete, maybe twelve feet wide and eight inches thick, and hung from metal frames about five feet above the track bed. The entire length of the platform equalled ten car lengths. Hundreds of people could line the platform before it became too crowded to walk. Unless, as Deirdre explained, people congregated at one end to board a particular car.

I climbed a short set of stairs and walked slowly toward the spot where Jackie died. The sun burned white through the August haze. The woody smell of the railroad ties hung in the thick air. The only remaining signs of Jackie's fall were a few snippets of fluorescent purple tape stuck in the gravel between the rails.

Across the tracks, the soccer play ceased. Two cabbies tossed in their cards and leaned against the side of a taxi with their arms folded. The cable crew slammed shut the rear gate of their van. I had a sense of them all watching me, but passed it off to imagination. A pick-up truck stopped, and a half dozen teenagers vaulted into the back. The two cabbies opened the hood of the taxi. The cable company van slid into reverse.

People slowly gathered along the platform, first in small groups, then in thin lines linking the groups like pearls on a string. I knew commuters were creatures of habit. The people who stood closest to Jackie when he fell would likely stand in the same spot today and tomorrow and the day after tomorrow. But several minutes passed without anyone filling the empty space. Everyone eyed me suspiciously.

Just as I began to doubt my logic, a couple moved into position. He was skinny, nervous, constantly shifting his weight. Half moons of sweat darkened the pits of his satin shirt. She was thick-waisted, stolid even at a distance. A long skirt spread across her wide hips. A derby sat on black hair twisted into ropy braids.

I shouldered toward them, noting how willingly the people moved out of my way. Maybe Jackie had struggled through a tougher crowd. Or maybe these people expected someone like me. The tall, skinny Anglo coming to learn of the other Anglo's death.

"Were you here two mornings ago?" I said as I reached them.

The man passed a crumpled paper bag from one hand to the other. "Yes," he said.

"Did you see the man fall?"

He nodded warily, pressing a finger to his pencil-thin mustache.

"Did you see two young men run away?"

The woman planted herself between us, the derby's brim exactly parallel with the thin lines of her squinting eyes.

"No hablo Ingles," she said, anchoring her arms solidly akimbo. *"No hablo Ingles."*

"You spoke English well enough to tell the cops he jumped," I said.

"No hablo Ingles," she repeated.

The skinny man pushed past her, yelling, thumping the paper bag against his slight chest. The crowd pressed close around me, and suddenly a short flight onto the tracks seemed a much easier trick than it had seemed a minute ago.

A whistle cut through the air. Everyone froze as the 8:45 banged into the station. The doors slid open, and the crowd filed on. No one said a word, but everyone stared at me through the dirty windows as the train pulled away.

Back at the shop, Pete O'Meara proudly displayed the morning's handiwork.

"That's all you did?" I said, pointing at the sparsely stocked shelves.

"That's all they sent."

He spun a crinkled yellow invoice on the counter. Four dozen boxes of golf balls, assorted brands. A gross of small bags of tees, all white. Four dozen golf gloves, all men's mediums.

"Any explanation?"

"I called the rep. He said, 'Sell this and we'll send more.' "

I phoned the rep directly. He said, "Sell this and we'll send more." When I pressed for details, he cited the small matter of my credit balance.

"I squeezed out what I could, Kieran," he said. "When your insurance settles up, and you pay us, we'll be back on the beam."

I rang off and stared out the window as a minivan crested the clubhouse hill and parked at the edge of the barricades. Set way back in the auxiliary parking lot and sealed in the trailer, I felt curiously removed from the club and the golf course, like a detective on a stakeout.

"Any word about the closeouts?" I asked Pete.

"I called twice already," he said. "Still no answer."

"Damn, that stuff is five days late now."

"Maybe they heard about the fire."

"Pete, I paid a twenty grand deposit. They've got to deliver it."

A foursome popped out of the minivan. Toting thin canvas bags, once known as Sunday bags when caddies observed the Sabbath, they saluted the caddymaster as they tramped through the yard toward the first tee. That's when I remembered the caddies. Since these kids looked up to Jackie Mack as a font of wisdom, they'd have scrutinized his every move, hung on his every word. They might have noticed the odd behavioral tics we preoccupied adults blow off as trivial nonsense. I should have known to guard against optimism whenever the caddies are involved.

"He showed me the best place to stand every hole," said one.

"He made me rake all the traps while he tended the pin," said another.

"He tried to make me bet Mr. Tucker couldn't outdrive my guy," said a third.

"He slept in the cart garage a lot."

"What?" I said, zeroing in on a bookish kid on the back bench. "Oh, you mean between loops."

"No. At night. He even kept a blanket and pillow stashed above the rafters."

How the hell could I miss something like Jackie Mack bedding down in the garage, especially since I locked up half the nights? I stormed back into the trailer to ask my other half.

"Oh, yeah, I knew," said Pete. He twisted his baseball cap sideways on his head and folded his arms across his Rangers jersey. Why kids went to such trouble and expense to look dumb was beyond me. At least the long hair and bellbottoms of my era showed some wit, however scruffy. No way could a kid look intelligent with the crotch of his pants dangling between his knees.

"You knew he slept in the cart garage," I said slowly.

"Yeah, well, Jackie didn't drive," Pete said as if revealing a startling news flash. "Sometimes Tucker played early, and Jackie figured instead of going home he'd like just spend the night here."

"Going home from where?"

"Hey, how the hell do I know?"

"So you'd leave the garage door unlocked?"

"No way, man. I made him a copy of the garage door key."

"You what?"

"Hey, Kieran, I figured you wouldn't mind. Jackie was like a main man around here."

A pie-eyed Mel Tucker rolled in at noon. I was listening to the fortieth ring of Peoria Liquidating's phone when he tiptoed toward the counter.

"Shhh," said Tucker. "If we're real quiet, my hangover won't find me."

He stopped mugging when I slammed down the phone.

"Are you here to play?" I said.

"Well, hell yes, Kieran, if it's all the same to you. I need to audition me a new caddie. Any suggestions?"

"Ask the caddymaster."

"I'll do that." He spun around slowly, taking in the shop. "I'll also buy me two dozen golf balls. You feel like joining me for a round?"

"Thanks for asking," I said, feeling a sudden pang of guilt for being so short with one of my better shop patrons. "I need to stick here."

Tucker slid me a charge plate, but my credit card terminal wasn't on-line yet. After hitting up Pete for $1.75, I put together exact change for Tucker's fifty spot.

"I expected I'd be attending a funeral today," he said. "Can you explain to me what's going on?"

"Are you a Catholic, Mel?"

"Presbyterian by birth."

"A funeral mass is a big deal," I said. "And an especially big deal for Jackie's mother. But the Monsignor won't allow a funeral mass for a suicide."

"He hate Jackie, or something?"

"He's a hardass. Nothing personal."

"But Jackie's got to get into the ground, right?"

"He will. The funeral parlor agreed to delay the burial for a few days. Meanwhile, I'll try to persuade Monsignor Neumann Jackie didn't commit suicide."

"What about all those people who said Jackie jumped?"

"I talked to them today. It so happens that everyone standing on the platform at the time is Hispanic."

"What'd they tell you?"

"Not a whole lot. They closed ranks. Made me feel like I could end up on the tracks."

"You think someone pushed Jackie?"

"Not intentionally," I said. "My ex was on the platform, too. She didn't exactly see Jackie fall, but she saw two guys running away about the same time Jackie fell. I'm thinking these guys jostled each other, knocked Jackie by accident, and ran."

"Did your ex get a good look at them?" said Tucker.

"She told the police she could I.D. them, but the police didn't seem interested. I'll poke around, see what I can find."

"Like those two guys."

"That may be expecting too much," I said.

"If you need help, Kieran."

"Actually, I wondered what you meant yesterday about Jackie having his problems?"

"I didn't mean much by it. Just talk, and I don't like speaking ill of the dead."

"You said it within earshot of his coffin. You said something about the usual sins of the flesh. Mel, am I wasting my time with this?"

Tucker glanced back over his shoulder, where Pete slumped in a folding chair and paged through a magazine. Then he leaned close across the counter so Pete couldn't hear.

"Jackie liked to gamble," he said. "Horses, football, jai alai, you name it."

"Lots of people gamble," I said. "You play for some pretty high stakes on occasion."

"There's a difference. I play for goodly sums of money, but never anything I can't afford to lose. Jackie always bet over his head. And once he started losing, anything with the smallest element of chance became fair game. Do you remember the first time he caddied for me?"

"Not exactly."

"I brought three guests here," said Tucker. "And we played for some big stakes. That's why I latched onto Jackie to begin with. Well, along about the ninth hole, one of my opponents tells me my own caddie is betting against me. You believe that? He made separate bets with my opponents. I put a stop to that pretty damn quick."

"But you kept him as your caddie."

"Sometimes you see something in somebody. I liked the kid, not that he was a kid like Pete there is a kid. You know, you get familiar with somebody. You get into their skin. It didn't surprise me to learn Jackie had no daddy. I could tell straight off he needed direction. I gave him what I could. I bailed him out of a couple of jams."

"Gambling debts?"

"Uh-huh. Do you think all his disappearances were sudden desires to travel the world? He usually was runnin' to save his neck. Yeah, I bailed him out. Brought him back home a few times. But when he refused that job offer my friend gave him, all that changed. I told him he needed help, and that if he didn't get help I wasn't about to bail him out again."

"Was he in trouble when he died?" I said.

"I don't know, Kieran. He kept pretty private by then. But I can say this, he damn sure didn't get any help."

That afternoon, the arrival of Randall Fisk coincided with fifty gasoline carts on five flatbeds. The truck drivers were pressed for time, so I enlisted the caddies into offloading the carts. No arguments there, since the caddies rated cart driving a close second to scoping Georgina Newland's gams. Within minutes, engines growled and a haze of blue smoke and brown dust rose over the parking lot. I cringed, expecting to hear the crunching of metal and the ripping of fiberglass any second.

Randall Fisk, suddenly at my elbow, lifted his sunglasses and rubbed the sockets of his deep set eyes.

"I feel an image coming over me. A distant stampede. Buffalo on the Great Plains, perhaps impala on the Serengeti. Any thoughts, Kieran?"

"Why not just call them gas-powered carts?" I said.

Fisk clicked his teeth, clucked his tongue, and popped his lips as if computing the suggestion.

"Too dry," he said.

Fisk, a libidinous Rumpelstiltskin with a bad hair transplant, covered professional golf and high school sports for a local newspaper chain. An odd beat, but, as he blustered during one of our less adversarial chats, "No one else at our sports desk recognized the literary possibilities in golf." Hence the local readership shared poetic visions of golf carts as stampeding fauna.

Fisk fancied himself a wit, but wrote so verbosely his ideas rarely sharpened into quotable barbs. A master at innuendo, he thrived on the underside of the sport he professed to love. "The public sees the green manicured fairways," he pontificated in that same chat. "I want to unearth the worms." I doubted the public cared much about fairways or worms, as my Limerick neighbors demonstrated daily. Despite a profusion of public golf courses, despite golf clubs sold in K-Mart and Wal-Mart, golf was still perceived as the domain of the wealthy. Just check out who sponsors the weekend golf telecasts. It isn't Chevrolet.

"Who do you think set the fire?" he asked after a caddie fishtailed a cart into the pen.

"I didn't know anyone did."

"Trust me, Kieran, the fire marshall will prove arson. And that presents a very interesting situation. A building at once a pro shop, a cart garage, and a dwelling. Who is the target? Why?"

"Don't look at me."

"Wouldn't dare," said Fisk. "Of course, it is odd that you spoke out against a renovation plan that would have included sprinklers in your shop."

"How did you know?"

Fisk tugged at one ear.

"Then you also know why I said what I said and the little stock the executive committee puts in anything I say."

"Calm yourself, Kieran. You are the one person I wouldn't suspect. Remember, I know what playing in the PGA means to you."

And I knew Fisk's empathy was no judgment on my honesty but a subtle reminder of my problems with the PGA Tour. Exile, he called it in his more explicit moments.

"Boland Brothers is in bad financial straits. And I notice these are not Boland Brothers carts," said Fisk. "Maybe a fire was in order."

"And the monkey house?" I said.

"Just bad luck. Unless—"

"Unless what?"

"Let's just say it wouldn't surprise me to see a few people walking around here with smiles on their faces."

Speaking with Randall Fisk rarely intrigued me. But before I could press him for details on this obvious tease, two caddies crashed in a race for the gate. Fiberglass tore. One cart hung up on the other's bumper. I told the caddies to scram and jumped onto the two carts, straddling them Ben-Hur style and rocking until the bumpers disengaged. When I turned back, Fisk had vanished.

We usually close the shop at seven during the summer. Pete and I alternate locking up the garage after the last cart returns. With no garage and no carts roaming the fairways, I sent Pete home at closing. MCC is a schizophrenic layout. The original twelve holes are classic parkland. Lush rolling fairways curve through stands of old growth forest, mostly oak and ash. Ponds nestle in the crooks of doglegs. A stream drains a valley creasing the fairways of 4, 5, and 6. Deep sand traps surround the greens. The six newer holes—8, 11, 12, 13, 16, and 17 on the card—are pure linksland routed across salt marshes lining Milton Harbor. Here dun-colored grass clings to salty hardpan, seamlessly shading from roughs to fairways to greens. Canada geese brood in the weedy banks of brackish tidal pools. Winds whip the sand from shallow bunkers and permanently bend the scrubby trees.

Members talk about their "parkland games" and their "linksland games," and the not so subtle differences between the two styles of golf. The caddies, greenskeepers, and other staff use a different means of demarcating the course. Many years ago, a boatyard operated in a small cove behind our present 8th tee. The boatyard owned an easement across the course, and built an access road between its docks and the Boston Post Road. The club still maintains that old access road, which basically bisects the course. We refer to the two halves as "this side" and "the other side".

I strapped my bag to a cart and chugged down the path. The first tee always excites me. Morning, noon, or evening, I could climb the four steps set into its steep bank and feel a sense of endless possibility. The turf is soft beneath my feet like the welcome mat at an old friend's door. A breeze shakes the petals of the impatiens growing thick between railroad ties. Dark green grass flows down a gentle slope, then rises in a river of lime green fairway. This is the moment when the painter stares at the clean canvas, the writer at the empty page, the composer at the fresh sheet. This is the moment when the round is perfect, when your game is equal to any challenge.

I didn't expect much from the evening's practice, just a brush-up of muscle memory while thunderclouds socked in my conscious mind. My first drive hugged the ground well out into the fairway, then climbed steeply and melted into the fuzzy evening sky. I dropped my eyes to the landing area. The ball slammed back to the turf, bounced once high, once low, and curled to a stop where the fairway bent around a pond. My second shot, a smooth wedge, started left and slowly drifted back to the pin. Even at 130 yards, I heard the dull thud of the ball hitting the green, sticking right where it landed. I dropped my putt for birdie and stood for several moments facing back toward the tee. From here, trees obscured the shop, the trailer, the cart pen. Everything looked as it did before the fire.

A macadam cart path essed through a thick stand of trees separating the first green from the second tee. Coming out of the first turn, I saw a black stretch limousine blocking the cart path where it crossed the access road. I eased off the gas, then slammed on the brakes as the incongruity registered. Something crackled. Two burly guys in black leather broke out of the bushes on either side of me.

I punched the cart into reverse, floored the accelerator. The wheels spun, then bit. The cart raced backward but not fast enough. One guy dove into the empty seat and yanked the shift into neutral. The other guy stripped my hands from the steering wheel and wrestled me into a bearhug. My feet lifted. I flew horizontally toward the limo's back door, which opened just in time.

CHAPTER
7

They flung me onto a cold leather seat. I spun around, dove for the door. But it slammed shut, locks firing into place. The engine ignited. The limo wheeled into a tight turn, and accelerated up the access road. I peered past quickly moving trees to slower shifting vistas of distant fairways. Not a damn golfer on the course, not even the greenskeeper on his evening rounds. No one to stumble across my clubs and sound the alarm. Our pro is missing.

The limo paused at the top of the access road while three caddies flew past on bikes. I pounded the window glass with my fist.

"We are soundproof here, Mr. Lenahan."

He sat in the opposite corner of the limo's huge interior, concentrating his eyes not on me but on the tobacco he tamped into the bowl of a pipe.

"What the hell's going on?" I said.

"I need to speak to you," he said, grinding tobacco flecks to dust between a thick thumb and forefinger. "It has been my experience that personal meetings are the most fruitful."

He raised his head into the path of a reading lamp. Forget the *Masterpiece Theater* diction, the turtleneck and blazer, the elegantly styled hair. He had the battered face and the hard eyes of a welterweight.

"Luis Augusto," he said, extending a hand Thomas Hart Benton might have painted. "Relax. I promise to keep you not one minute longer than necessary."

I settled back, though not comfortably. My sternum ached from the bearhug. The skin of my arms burned from my crash-landing onto the leather. The driver, invisible beyond the smoked glass partition, took the Post Road toward Milton village, veered onto the Merchant Street cut-off, crossed the interstate, and headed into the fast food joints and strip malls the town fathers banned from our streets. Augusto puffed serenely on his pipe, the tobacco aroma mingling with the smell of the rawhide seats. He had an odd build, skinny legs beneath the gray slacks but thick arms and a barrel torso stuffed into his blazer.

The road curved into Port Byram, a working-class town wedged between the Byram River and the Long Island Sound. The tires rippled on the uneven pavement. Sidewalk slabs jutted at crazy angles. Tacky signs painted in primary colors marked Mexican-American restaurants, travel agencies, check cashing joints, and driving schools. Augusto leaned forward, the pipe on his knee, and waved languidly at people who watched us pass.

The limo stopped at Liberty Square, the town's main intersection. A banner stretching from corner to corner announced an Hispanic Fiesta the same week as the PGA. A policeman stood in a glass booth on a concrete island edged with shrubbery. He waved to Augusto as the limo zipped across the square.

The character of Main Street changed. Orange brickwork trimmed smooth concrete sidewalks. Planters hung from wrought-iron streetlights shaped like old-fashioned gas lamps. But the storefronts here were dark or soaped-over, with the names and phone numbers of managing agents prominently displayed.

"Do you like these, Mr. Lenahan?"

Augusto tossed a pack of Lifesavers. I grasped the reference as easily as I snatched the candy out of the air. The Lifesavers company once owned a plant at the north end of town, a brick building decorated with giant Lifesavers candies.

"Downtown Port Byram died when the Lifesavers plant shut down," said Augusto. "People moved out. Shops closed. Then about ten years ago, a coalition of builders and politicos schemed to have federal money pumped into a downtown rehabilitation project. In reality, the plan was to rid Port Byram of its poor, which translated to its Hispanic population.

"The plan failed while Port Byram's Latino population endured and thrived. Port Byram is now an Hispanic town. Granted, some of the Jewish merchants remain. Granted, the Italian kids and the black kids still play football and baseball for the high school. Granted, a WASP banker bought the Lifesavers plant and turned it into condos. But the vibrant end of town is our South Main."

"Great," I said. "Is this why you wanted to talk to me?"

Augusto's face tightened for a second, then eased into his charming smile as he emptied his pipe into an ashtray.

"Mr. Lenahan," he said, refilling his pipe. "People have roamed this planet for millennia. Nations and borders are meaningless inventions. Laws and armies may hold migrations in check temporarily. But in the end, stopping the flow of humankind will be as impossible as holding back the oceans. You have heard of the Latin Cooperative?"

"I've seen mention in the newspapers," I said. "It's a businessman's organization, like a Chamber of Commerce?"

"Businessmen are involved, but our business is not business. You see, the Hispanic people were once welcome in this country. As recently as the war in El Salvador, town governments created havens for refugees by passing resolutions forbidding town officials and residents from cooperating with INS deportation efforts. But these feelings could not last forever. The bad times came, and the American people look to blame others for their ills. They see their jobs going overseas, and they see immigrants bleeding them dry at home. Latinos are not the largest group of immigrants, but we are the most visible.

"The Cooperative fights the type of resentment that led to Proposition 187 in California. We work discreetly. We provide our own social services to all people of Latin descent so that they do not swell the county welfare rolls. We counsel them about the mores of this country. We tell them not to drink and drive, to keep adequate insurance on their cars. We guard against exploitation by unscrupulous employers and landlords. Do you remember the problems at the Milton train station? I brokered the deal to reserve a small corner of the parking lot between seven and ten each morning for the men to congregate."

"You don't come across as the stereotypical Hispanic," I said.

"I've assimilated," he said. "And the Cooperative counsels its members to assimilate. You remember the signs at the south end of Main? English. We don't believe in institutionalized bilingualism, or institutionalized multi-culturalism. Cultures mix, people change, languages evolve naturally. We don't need official proclamations."

The limo swung off Main and whipped around into a parking lot behind the storefronts. Augusto's two henchmen got out and leaned against the doors with their arms folded. They looked like a pair of linebackers.

"I understand you harassed people on the Milton train platform this morning," said Augusto, his charm peeling away like a lemon rind.

"I asked questions. That isn't harassment."

"What is the death of the young man to you?"

"Jackie Mack was my caddie. Monsignor Neumann refused him a funeral mass because he supposedly committed suicide. Jackie's mother is very upset. She asked me to look into it. I went to the station to find witnesses who could tell the Monsignor Jackie didn't jump."

"These people are members of the Cooperative," he said. "They are good people. They work hard to eke a living out of a hostile environment. The Cooperative is their only protection."

"Why wouldn't they talk?" I said.

"They are free to talk if they wish. Their silence was their decision. They reported you to the Cooperative. I must respect their concerns."

"What concerns? Are they illegal?"

"That is immaterial to me," said Augusto. "Their concerns are my concerns. They are not to be harassed about the Anglo caddie."

"It isn't harassment, goddammit. All I need is for these people to tell the Monsignor that Jackie didn't jump."

"Maybe he committed suicide after all. How well did you know your caddie?"

"Well enough. And I know two men ran from the platform right after Jackie fell."

"Who told you that?"

"Never mind. Some witnesses cooperate."

Augusto held his pipe before his eye, watching the smoke curl toward the ceiling. His chest trembled slightly, as if he wrestled to contain an eruption of anger.

"So you think he was pushed," he said, almost too quietly.

"I don't give a damn if he was pushed. I don't give a damn about the two men. Dead is dead. All I want is the Monsignor to allow a funeral mass."

"Nothing else?"

"I'm a golf pro, Mr. Augusto, not a private detective. I'm doing a favor for a neighborhood woman and for a guy who served me well over the years."

Augusto puffed thoughtfully on his pipe. Whatever anger he felt before had subsided.

"I see how my people misinterpreted your questions," he said.

"Understandable," I said, laying it on thick. "I could have been anybody."

Augusto smiled wanly. He knew crap when he heard it.

"I will try to intervene," he said. "But I can't promise I will correct the situation. These people will not tell lies. Especially to a priest."

He opened the door and stepped outside.

"Mr. Augusto," I said.

He stopped smoothing his blazer and leaned in, smiling expectantly.

"While you're at it, maybe you can find out who torched my shop."

"Why do you ask me such a silly question?"

"I saw this limo the other night. You eyeballed the building."

"Twelve Latino men were burned out of their home."

"Are they members of the Cooperative? I hear they are sleeping on cots in a locker room."

"They will be cared for. Their interests are mine."

He slammed the door and waved for the limo to be gone.

We drove back to Milton in the fading light of dusk. I didn't trust Augusto enough to bank on his offer to help. At the same time, I probably didn't need to bother his people. Hell, I had enough of a lead to run down with Tucker's story about Jackie's gambling habit. But something nagged me about Augusto. Was he warning me to stop talking to the members of the Latino Cooperative? Or was he warning me not to look into Jackie Mack's death at all? For someone who spoke such formal English, the confusion made little sense.

The limo descended the access road in almost full dark. My cart and clubs appeared in the headlights, exactly where I left them. We idled for a few seconds, long enough for me to think Augusto's men planned something funny. But then the locks released, and I pushed open the door. I drove back to the yard, stashed my clubs, and locked the cart in the pen.

Jose Rojas poured a shot of Scotch.

"Ice on the side," I said.

Despite my relatively benign encounter with Luis Augusto, the reality of being dragged off the golf course against my will hit me the moment I'd walked into the clubhouse. I knew of a golf pro in Ireland who was kidnapped off a golf course near the border with the North. He was engaged to marry the daughter of a wealthy computer company executive, and his kidnappers, a radical cell spun off from the IRA, sought a huge ransom. To prove their point, they delivered the pro's left thumb to his prospective father-in-law. The police quickly flushed them from their hideout. But the pro never again gripped a club.

What if Luis Augusto hadn't been the leader of a Latino social services organization? What if pure circumstance made me a pawn in a game? The imaginative possibility, coupled with the banality of the clubhouse bar on a weekday night, unsettled the hell out of me.

Jose reached for a tumbler, scooped several cubes out of a basin, set the tumbler on the bar. I must have worn my imagination on my face because his eyes never left me.

I knocked back the Scotch in one huge gulp. I rarely drank hard liquor. Anything more than a healthy sip of distilled spirits hit me like a sock to the jaw. This belt ran down my throat like cheap cough syrup. I slammed down the shot glass and tapped the rim with a finger. Jose refilled, an incredulous look on his face. He'd seen three beers reduce me to gibbering, rubber-legged idiocy. But tonight I stood solidly at the bar, knocking back Scotches like a sailor.

"What happened?" Jose said as he poured a third.

The lounge was empty. No members, no private party. Through the ballroom doorway, a busboy swirled a mop across a corner of the dance floor. I stared at him until he moved out of sight.

"Someone played a joke on me," I said to Jose.

I reached for the shot glass, but left it on the bar. My eyes suddenly burned. My stomach tightened. I rubbed an ice cube on my eyelids, and breathed deeply until the sick feeling passed.

"What do you know about the Latin Cooperative?" I said.

"The Latin Cooperative should be no concern of yours." Jose stuffed a bar rag into the mouth of a shot glass he'd already wiped dry.

"Are you a member?"

"Why? Because I am Hispanic?"

I told him about the limo and the tour of Port Chester. All the while, he fussed with ashtrays and glasses, pretending not to listen but making a poor show of it. At the first mention of Luis Augusto, Jose threw his apron to the floor, ducked under the bar, and ran off shouting for his brother. I followed only as far as the ballroom doorway. Eduardo's private office was behind the bandstand off the far corner. Inside, Jose shouted that same staccato Spanish I'd first heard among the workers the night of the fire. The busboy leaned on his mop. Two dishwashers ran out from the kitchen to join him in the center of the dance floor. After a moment, one ran back to the kitchen, and several more workers returned. They crouched outside the office door, listening to Jose and Eduardo shout at each other.

Glass tinkled behind me. Georgina Newland poured herself a drink at the bar.

"Refill?" she said. "On my tab. Jose and I have an understanding. I'm deputy bartender when he's indisposed."

She wore a denim work shirt and jeans, with her hair pinned up as if she'd been painting. The caddies may have been disappointed. I wasn't. She wielded the Scotch bottle like a pro, pouring two precise measures and turning her wrist at the end so no drops dribbled out of the spout. The shouting from Eduardo's office subsided, but mounted again as Georgina beckoned me to the administrative office.

"How do you find your new accommodations?" she said.

We stood at the window. Down below, security lights aimed beams at the trailer and the cart pen. The old building was lost in the shadows.

"Fine. I should have told you I was impressed."

"Don't be. Half the membership isn't. They want club storage."

"That's one headache I don't miss. I must have had twenty members ask me if I filed claims for their lost clubs. They aren't pleased to learn my insurance doesn't cover them. If they only knew it doesn't cover me, either."

"Pardon?" said Georgina.

"Nothing." I cupped my hand to the window, shading the reflection of the desk lamp. "The way the light hits the shop, it looks almost intact from here."

Georgina cupped her hand as well, so close her cheek almost grazed mine. She breathed softly, her breath fogging the glass.

"You know, the front section of the garage was part of the caddie yard until the club roofed it over," I said. "I spent a lot of summer days there, waiting for loops. One of the other caddies drew pictures on the walls. Scenes of the golf course, caricatures of members. Great stuff. Ever notice them?"

Georgina, her reflection wide-eyed in the glass, shook her head.

"He went on to become one of Disney's top illustrators. When I became pro here, I thought about prying off those plywood sheets and framing them. Too late now."

"You've been a part of this club for a long time," she said.

"Twenty years, one way or another. Caddie, pro, member for a spell while I practiced law. The longest connection still is as a caddie. Nine years."

"It must be nice to have a romantic connection to a place. People move so much now. Everyone is always from somewhere else."

I grunted, remembering how attempts to sever my connection never succeeded. A poignant silence descended. Georgina gently placed her glass on the windowsill. I drained melted ice out of mine.

"The fire hurt you, didn't it?" she said.

"Oh yeah, it hurt." I knew what my tone of voice meant, and recognized the same in hers. We weren't talking now so much as making noises. Circling each other, testing how far we could go.

She made the first move, trailing her fingernails up my forearm. I'm slim, but my arm muscles are blacksmith strong from swinging weighted golf clubs, twisting off grips, and wrenching hosels. Women dig my arms. At least, that's what they tell me. Her fingernails were short, but smooth. Not the chewed stubs I remembered from Deirdre.

Soon we hit the lights, and cleared space on the desk. I thought of lots of wonderful modern inventions, like radar and jets and SAM missiles. And I thought how lucky I was not to be a dopey young caddie.

I cruised home at midnight, expecting to spend long hours indulging the persistence of interesting memories. But the red light on my answering machine blinked, and Kate Ritchie's voice told me she was staying at her mother's house. She'd wait up for me.

I walked the two blocks to the MacEwan house. Kate met me before I hit the doorbell.

"I'm just going out for a minute, Ma," she called back inside, and put her finger to her lips.

"Is anyone there?" came Una's raspy voice.

"No one. I'll be right back."

Kate pulled me down the porch stairs and into the driveway, out of view from the windows on the MacEwan side of the duplex. Facial cream gobbed on her cheeks and forehead looked a ghostly pallor under the streetlight. Sweat pants and a tee shirt bagged around her tiny frame.

"What's going on?" she said. "I wake up this morning, and my mother tells me the funeral is being postponed. When I ask why, she says you would be talking to the Monsignor. Then I call Damiano, and he says you asked him to hold Jackie for three or four days. All day she waits to hear from you. Everytime the phone rings, she says, 'That's Kieran Lenahan. He's going to see my Jackie's buried right.' "

"True enough," I said.

"Jackie should be in the ground. This just prolongs my mother's agony with false hope."

"Your mother asked for my help. I explained there would be a delay, maybe five days. She agreed."

"You should have stayed out of our business. My mother will get over the idea that the only route to heaven is through the front door of St. Gregory's Church."

"I'm not sure Jackie committed suicide," I said.

"Lots of people saw him jump. You didn't."

I didn't know Kate well enough to trust her, but I resented her smirky attitude toward her mother, her brother, and most of all me.

"My ex-girlfriend was on the platform. She didn't see Jackie fall, but she saw two guys run away. So I went to the station to question people who were on the platform that morning. No one would talk to me. Tonight, a fella named Luis Augusto took me off the golf course. He's the head of the Latin Cooperative. The people I questioned complained to him that I harassed them. I think they just plain lied to me."

Kate's smirk faded for a heartbeat. "Why?"

"Protecting someone. Protecting themselves."

"From what?" said Kate. "I never heard of the Latin Cooperative."

"It's a social services organization. I'd bet the people who saw Jackie fall are illegal. They don't want to be bothered by the police, so they say Jackie jumped. Who cares about a suicide? I also heard about Jackie's gambling problem. Mel Tucker told me it was pretty bad."

A breeze lifted the leaves of the swamp maple that spread over the house. August nights could turn chilly in Limerick when the wind swept onshore from the Sound. Kate hugged herself.

"It's too cold to talk out here," she said. "Go around back and I'll meet you."

I waited at the back stoop for several minutes. Through an open window, I heard Kate telling Una she needed her rest and Una telling Kate she wasn't tired. Plates clattered in the kitchen sink. Water hissed, then stopped. A moment later, the back door eased open.

"Quiet now," Kate whispered.

I padded behind her through the kitchen and down a hallway to the staircase. We each took tight turns around the bannister and headed up. In the living room, Una's feet stretched across a hassock, one big slipper rhythmically slapping her heel.

Kate's tiny bedroom was wedged under a sloping section of roof. The twin bed, the nightstand, a small desk and chair were all stained an antique gray. Several coverless paperbacks lay on a shelf, the glue of their bindings yellowed and dry. A Barbie, circa 1975, stood on a dresser, wearing a gown made from paper towels.

Kate closed a suitcase lying open on the bed, but not before I noticed more clothes than she'd need for an overnight. She sat on the desk chair, and I took the mattress.

"You know about our father, right?" said Kate.

I shrugged. I knew nothing specific, other than Mr. MacEwan was conspicuous by his absence from Limerick.

"I don't remember much about him because I was too young," she said. "But he was a great joker. My girl friends would meet him and fall down laughing at the things he said. They would tell me what a fun daddy I had. But I guess he had only his jokes, and when his jokes ran out so did he.

"Mom always doted on Jackie. And after my father split, she started calling him the man of the house. Jackie took it seriously. He signed up for all kinds of odd jobs, like delivering newspapers, flowers, groceries. But Mom always stopped him. She said he didn't need to work to put food on the table.

"Anyway, I think these conflicting signals gave Jackie a weird sense of responsibility. He became obsessed with providing for Mom, but at the same time he couldn't bring himself to find a real job. Just like that car. He loved the idea of owning it, but the registration and insurance were beyond his comprehension. Max says it illustrates Jackie's fatal flaw, which is that his reach exceeds his grasp on reality."

"He planned to support your mother on his gambling winnings?" I said.

"Ridiculous, but that was Jackie," said Kate. "No sense of stability, no desire to work at a steady job. No respect for education. Three or four years ago he was terribly hooked just like Mel Tucker said. It was beyond absurd. And Max was just as bad. Worse, if you ask me. He would come home from work and tell me he'd invited Jackie to dinner. I would cook, and sometimes they would just eat and rush off to New Milford for jai alai, or they would take their dinner into the den and click through all those sports cable channels to keep track of their bets. They would scream, throw food. It was totally insane."

"Your husband and Jackie were close friends?"

"I met Max through Jackie," said Kate. "New Year's Eve at Toner's. Max knew Jackie from one summer when Jackie caddied at Burning Tree. He liked slumming, and who better to slum with than my brother. When the gambling got real bad with Max, we put a stop to it.

Jackie was banned from our house, banned from contacting Max in any way."

"Who were 'we'?"

"Max's parents and I," said Kate. "Mom lives in a dream world. She cooks, she keeps the house clean, she pays the bills. But when the subject turned to Jackie, it was like her eyes glazed over. She'd get calls at all hours from people Jackie owed money. Poor lady, she thought these were Jackie's friends. That's why I'm pissed at you for doing this. That's why you'd better go to Leo Damiano tomorrow first thing and get Jackie buried."

"It's not what your mother wants."

"You leave my mother to me. You're not the big man in this town you once were."

I needed this. An hour ago I lay with Aphrodite. Now I bit my tongue to keep from trading schoolyard insults with Jackie Mack's wiseass sister.

"I wouldn't play with your mother's feelings," I said carefully. "I wouldn't drag her through something I didn't think she could take. Now you can help me or you can leave me alone. But I'm going to get Jackie buried right or explain to your mother why I couldn't."

I think the steel in my tone brought her up short. Sometimes, the more evenly you speak the more crazily determined you sound.

"Just don't bother her, okay?" she said. "And if you want my opinion, Jackie got into debt real bad and decided to check out."

CHAPTER
8

I found Sound Shore Marine Brokerage Inc. at the north end of Greenwich Avenue. Far from the marinas and shipyards, it was a fitting location for a business that played with money instead of labored with hulls and rigging. The receptionist said the young Mr. Ritchie was on a phone call, with two others holding. I told her I was an old friend, and he'd have a gas seeing me pop in unannounced. She shared my sense of fun and waved me past.

Max Ritchie sure had a gas. He dropped the phone, leaped out of his chair, and practically climbed a credenza.

"I'm not accepting anything," he said. "You have something for me, drop it on the desk. Then get out."

"Calm down, Maxie. All I want is to talk."

"That's it? No papers?"

I plucked the sleeves of my golf shirt.

"Wait a sec." He retrieved the phone, apologized profusely, and buzzed the receptionist to tell the others he'd call them back. "Kate didn't send you? Then how did you know where to find me?"

I tapped my temple with a finger.

"She moved out, you know," he said. "That's obvious from my reaction. I thought the way she made a point of introducing you as a lawyer the other night meant something. You're not here to serve divorce papers?"

"I'm not licensed in Connecticut."

"I should have thought. I'm frazzled by all this. How did you get past the reception desk?"

"I told the lady I was an old friend with a surprise."

"Some surprise. Seeing you scared the crapola out of me." He sat, relieved, but not exactly at ease. "So what is it, you looking to buy or sell?"

"I'm here to talk about Jackie."

"Oh." Max's expression darkened. He peeled the wrapper off a fresh pack of cigarettes, but paused before lighting up. "Pretty weird. I never heard of a funeral called off because someone killed himself."

"Monsignor Neumann's pretty strict about Catholics committing suicide."

"It's what happened, isn't it? I mean, the newspapers said he jumped."

"The newspapers only print what they're told. What do you think?"

"I don't think anything. I hadn't seen Jackie or talked to him in months. Years."

"You mean since you two stopped gambling together."

Max's neck snapped as if I'd slapped him. "Kate told you that, huh? Damn her."

"Look, Max, if it makes you feel any better, Kate didn't badmouth you. She told me about Jackie, and the story spilled over."

Max lit the cigarette, took a long drag, and slapped the lighter onto the desk. Beneath the beard, his neck showed a two-day stubble.

"What the hell do you care about this anyway?" he said. "All he ever did for you was lug your golf bag at tournaments."

"Una asked me, and the only way I can get Jackie buried right is to convince the Monsignor he didn't kill himself."

"Good luck."

"Kate thinks Jackie killed himself because he was too deep in debt."

"She would," said Max. "People think because she's a hot-looking little chick anything goes with her. No siree. She's puritanical as all hell."

"Because she joined forces with your parents to stop your habit."

"They cut me off from Jackie, but that's not what stopped me in the end." Max stubbed out his cigarette. "Let's go outside."

We went through the back door to a small parking lot that could have doubled as a fancy auto showroom.

"Hanging out with Jackie was fun," he said, lighting up again. "After getting married, it was a way to hold onto those crazy times. But we were nuts. Jackie gambled way over his head, I almost went in over mine. At least I had resources. The business, my expense account. I tapped into them. I don't know how Jackie survived without getting bones broken.

"Kate and my parents checked me into a boot camp with a twelve step program like Gamblers Anonymous. When I came out, my parents moved Kate and me into a separate apartment in their house. Watched me like a hawk. Monitored phone calls, bills, expenses, income.

"My problem wasn't as bad, but I still wasn't cured by a long shot. And I was smooth enough to get around all the barriers and gamble with Jackie. Plus, I hit an early stretch of luck so I was playing with house money instead of my own. Jackie was still in deep, though. This was Christmas time, two years ago. One night, coming back from jai alai, Jackie noticed a car tailing us. I tried to ditch it on the New England Thruway, but it kept pace all the way into Milton and cut me off right near Toner's.

"I looked over at Jackie, and he had this expression on his face I can't describe except to say it was pure fear. The doors opened, and two guys got out. One had a chain, the other had a tire iron. Jackie said, 'Oh shit.' I'll never forget the sound of his voice, like he was already in pain. Then he jumped out and ran down an alley with those two guys chasing him. I never saw anyone run like Jackie did that night, literally running scared."

"They catch him?"

"I don't know," said Max. "A third guy got out of the car and came back to me. He told me to get the hell out, and I didn't see anything because there wasn't anything to see."

"Do you remember what he looked like?"

"Nope. I was too scared to look him in the eye. I just did what he said. Made a U-turn and got the hell out."

"How did he sound? Any Hispanic accent?"

Max flicked away his cigarette and lit another. "I still hear that voice, too. It was like he had no doubt I'd do what he said. No, he had no accent. He just sounded tough. And he was right. I did just what he said. Made a U-turn and got the hell out.

"All the money my parents spent on that boot camp was a big goddam waste. But I never placed another bet on anything after that night. You know why? I found a big wet spot on the car seat the next morning. Jackie had pissed in his pants."

Back at the trailer, Pete smiled triumphantly.

"I got a busy signal at Peoria Liquidating," he said.

"When?"

"Five minutes ago."

I punched in the number. The phone rang three times, then connected me with dead air. I yelled hello.

"You sure you dialed the right goddam number?" I said to Pete.

But Pete didn't answer. He stared at two uniformed Milton cops who'd slipped into the trailer and now flanked the door. I recognized one from the neighborhood, a tall, loose-jointed kid with a ruddy face he needed to shave only once or twice a week. The other, shorter and bulkier with a trim mustache, was a stranger. Before I could ask what they wanted, DiRienzo bulled through the middle like a fullback.

"Please hang up the phone, Mr. Lenahan."

I didn't like the sound of DiRienzo's politeness.

"Hang up the phone, Mr. Lenahan. Please."

DiRienzo leaned toward me, fists the size of elephants' feet pressed on the countertop. Out of one poked a rolled-up sheet of paper. I knew exactly what it was.

Time stretched again, as it had when the propane cylinder blew through the roof. The two cops stepped forward, thumbing the safety straps off their holsters. DiRienzo unrolled the paper, cleared his throat like an after-dinner speaker. Pete bolted toward the door, but the shorter cop swung out an arm to clothesline him.

I dropped the phone onto its cradle.

"Kieran Lenahan," said DiRienzo. "You are under arrest for arson and murder."

I blanked on the rest of it, all those Constitutional rights people know mostly through cop shows on TV. Pete started yelling, and then I was walking out from behind the counter, allowing DiRienzo to turn me around and cuff my hands behind my back. Odd details seized my senses. The vendor label stuck to the cash register. The stale coffee on DiRienzo's breath. A lawnmower firing up somewhere. Then the taller cop spun me and marched me toward the door while the shorter one body-checked Pete.

"Call the Judge," I said.

"What do I say?" said Pete.

"Just tell him what happened," I said. "He'll know what to do."

My arrest attracted lots of attention on an otherwise routine morning. Caddies poured out of the yard. A foursome stared down from the sixteenth tee. Teenaged lifeguards ran out from the pool. Two older lady golfers, crossing the parking lot in a cart, plowed into an azalea bush. As the cop bent me into the back of DiRienzo's Plymouth, I thought I saw Georgina watching from beneath the clubhouse *porte-cochere*. But by the time DiRienzo chugged toward the exit, whoever I'd seen was gone.

They took me into the Milton Police Department through a side door and directly into DiRienzo's old office, now a windowless gray cubicle cramped with file cabinets. DiRienzo faced me across a small wooden table gouged with initials and obscenities. Paul Surchuck leaned against a cabinet, his thick arms folded atop his gut, a broken, unlit cigarette sticking from the corner of his mouth. The crack investigative team. Mutt and Jeff. I remembered Judge Inglisi's comment about the two of them equalling one brain. At the moment, I didn't find it amusing.

DiRienzo started with all the usual cajolery about making it go easier for me if I talked. Surchuck paced behind him, rolling the cigarette side to side in his mouth and looking annoyed. At DiRienzo's ham-handed technique, or at my adamant refusal to speak without a lawyer, who knew?

"So call one, goddammit," DiRienzo finally said, practically ripping the phone off its wall socket.

"I don't need to," I said.

"Don't press your luck with me and your wiseass remarks, Lenahan. You expect a lawyer to appear out of nowhere?"

"I told Pete to call Judge Inglisi, remember?"

"Not this time," said DiRienzo. "Inglisi's not going to blow in here and order people around. This isn't one of the O'Meara kid's piddling raps. This is murder."

I didn't expect the Judge to jump off the bench and rush down to the M.P.D. Being a judge, he couldn't represent me as a lawyer. But he probably had more markers floating around the county than anyone. Once he heard from Pete, he'd call one in.

Meanwhile, DiRienzo tossed me into a holding cell. A tiny figure lay in fetal position on one cot, completely covered by a sheet. The bars clanked shut, and the figure stirred.

"Hey, K'ran." Lester Bill, Limerick's resident wino, poked out his head. "What're ye in fer?"

"Murder and arson, Les. How about you?"

Lester righted himself, overjoyed at his captive comradeship.

"Got me fer sleepin' on Miz Manning's front porch agin." His mouth pinched like the opening of a gunny sack, his four blackened teeth mashed together jigsaw style. "God durn lady shows some grat'-tude fer me seein' her garbage drugged out twice a week."

I took a deep breath, savoring the last few cubic inches of fresh air before the stench rolled across the cell. Lester always stank as though his entire epidermal layer had died. He lived at large in Limerick, earning the indulgence of the citizenry with favors like dragging Mrs. Manning's garbage can to the curb on pick-up mornings. But the police could run him in any night of the year. And I wondered whether Mrs. Manning filed a complaint or whether DiRienzo rousted him to add ambience to my anticipated stay in the holding cell.

I hung tough, pretending to sleep with my face buried in the moldy mattress while Lester gibbered in singsong cadence before drifting off into either sleep or a coma. One long hour later, the bars rattled. I raised one eye above the sheet, saw who the officer let in, and dove back into the mattress. A hand shook my shoulder.

"Next cot," I said.

"Judge Inglisi sent me," said William St. Clare, Jr.

"Oh my God," I muttered.

William St. Clare, Jr., was the son of a one-term mayor of Milton. He started his legal career as I bailed out of mine, taking referrals from Inglisi & Lenahan as we wound down operations after Big Jim's election to the bench. I never thought much of Willie Junior as a lawyer. The image of his father, swaggering with ridiculous brio up Merchant Street long after his two year debacle at the helm of Milton politics, cast too long a shadow. The Judge disagreed, one of those rare instances where he held someone in higher regard than I did. He believed Willie Junior would make a great lawyer, adding, in one of his typical backhanded slaps, that Willie's extra thick hide was impervious to embarrassment. Unfortunately, I was susceptible to irony.

"What's that odor?" said Willie Junior.

I nodded toward the lump of Lester. Willie Junior leaned over the cot, a scientist studying a specimen. He had thick lips, meaty features, and red welts on his neck and chin as if he chafed himself every morning with a week-old razor blade. A true St. Clare, quarter-sized earlobes hung from otherwise tiny ears, and an equatorial bulge stretched the waistband of his blue seersucker pants.

"Is he dead?" said Willie Junior.

Lester bolted upright, his tiny eyes blinking against the light. An intense wave of his smell staggered Willie and sent me diving into the pillow. Something landed beside my head. A tube of sunscreen.

"Try it," said Willie, rubbing a dab beneath his nose.

I did. The combination of smells had some bouquet. *Eau du coconut avec Lester Bill.* At least Willie Junior won points for being prepared.

Resigned to the fate Judge Inglisi dealt me, I made room for Willie Junior on the cot.

"It's safe to assume you made no statement, right?" he said.

"Not one word."

"Good. Some clients sink themselves before I become involved. Then they expect miracles. Why am I telling you? You've been here, but not exactly here. These few inches are a wide abyss. We're in the same place, but in different dimensions. I think about things like that. I know your opinion of me, Kieran. I earned the Judge's respect long ago. I hope to earn yours now."

Willie Junior pulled his briefcase onto his short lap. The leather edges were frayed. The snap locks needed prying with his thumbnail. He readied a legal pad, tried writing on the severe downslope, then crossed his legs to level his lap. It struck me that Judge Inglisi's tolerance for Willie stemmed from Willie being shorter.

I recounted everything I saw the night of the fire, everything Surchuck and DiRienzo asked me the next morning, and everything Frank Platt asked the next evening. I sketched the building on a legal pad, estimating as best I could where the fire started. Across the cell, Lester interrupted with salient comments about the splinters in his ass from Mrs. Manning's porch. Willie Junior told him to shut up, and surprisingly he did. More points for commanding respect.

Willie ripped off my sketch, reduced our half hour conversation to a few scribbled lines, and started to pack up.

"The way I see it, the idea that you did this for insurance money doesn't withstand scrutiny. Increasing coverage doesn't gain anything if the merchandise isn't there to be burned."

"The prosecution doesn't have to prove motive," I said.

"No, but it helps," said Willie Junior, "and the weak motive is what's going to sink their case. We'll fight 'em at every turn. We won't give up anything."

With that, John Paul Jones St. Clare signaled the guard to let him out.

Another slow hour passed with my face in the pillow before the cell bars rattled. I expected another trip to the interrogation room, this time with Willie Junior and an assistant district attorney. Instead, the same two cops cuffed me and led me out the back door to a squad car, which sped to the White Plains courthouse. Somewhere below street level, Milton P.D. turned me over to the courthouse guards. I got a new set of cuffs and a slow elevator ride to holding pens that made me yearn for my old buddy Lester. I tried to act tough, hard, unconcerned about my future. Too bad I still looked like a golf pro.

Before long, the guards produced me for the arraignment. This courtroom usually was busy as hell, with prosecutors, defense lawyers, defendants, and families shuttling in and out. But with the workday almost over, the courtroom was quiet as a church. A pair of elderly men, the type who hop from courtroom to courtroom in search of free entertainment, whispered in the front row of the gallery. The court stenographer leafed through a fashion magazine. The court clerk dropped a stack of file folders into a shopping cart. Willie Junior waited at the defense table, still wearing that dab of sunscreen under his nose.

"Who is the judge?" I said as the guards uncuffed me.

"Ben Petty," said Willie Junior. "I fish with him."

"Is that supposed to help me?"

"Can't hurt."

A woman slammed a briefcase onto the prosecution table. She was tall and angular, with a round face and light brown hair chopped at the shoulders. Her gray suit was cut along the lines of a Girl Scout jumper.

"That's the assistant D.A., Jayne Sokol," said Willie Junior.

"Do you fish with her, too?" I said.

"Hello, William," Jayne Sokol called over.

"No," he told me through his grin before returning the hello.

Judge Benjamin Petty swept onto the bench. A stranger seeing the waxed mustache and hearing the slight British affect might expect pomposity and theatrics. But Petty judged without fanfare. He called Willie Junior and Jayne Sokol to the bench. There were grins and handshakes all around, and some polite chuckles at comments Petty made but I couldn't hear. Clients often are surprised at the cordiality between opposing counsel, as if they expect brain-bashing and strangulation at every turn. But lawyers slip in and out of character while the client remains simply the client. I would be a criminal defendant today and tomorrow. Willie Junior would defend me today, defend another defendant against another assistant D.A. tomorrow, close a house sale on Thursday, and in between, do whatever sons of ex-mayors do in their spare time. Still, I felt a twinge of paranoia at the grins and chuckles amid a discussion of my fate.

Willie Junior returned to the table.

"I've got a good feeling about this," he said. "We'll fight 'em at every turn."

The court clerk called the case, and *People v. Kieran Lenahan* formally began.

"Ms. Sokol," said Judge Petty, "do you have an indictment or a criminal complaint?"

"A complaint, your honor."

"Mr. St. Clare, do you waive a formal reading?"

"I do, your honor."

Jayne Sokol handed Willie Junior a copy of the complaint, a preprinted carbonized form filled with citations to the state penal code. Willie and I huddled at the table, Willie parsing each count, which charged arson, arson murder, attempted arson murder, several species of manslaughter, and a few degrees of property damage.

"Who did I attempt to kill?" I said.

"The restaurant workers who were in the building when the fire started."

"Ms. Sokol," said Petty, "you know you have seventy-two hours to convene a grand jury and obtain an indictment."

The A.D.A started to speak, then hesitated. She cast an odd glance at Willie Junior, who didn't catch it and asked to approach the bench. Straining my ears, I couldn't pick up more than a few words of the sidebar discussion. But I didn't like what I saw. Jayne Sokol wore an expression that seemed smug, almost taunting. Willie Junior's earlobes deepened from pink through red to scarlet. Judge Petty shook his head as if watching an increasingly absurd tennis rally.

"I don't believe it," he finally said. "Let's go on the record."

Willie Junior returned to our table, and Jayne Sokol to hers.

"What's going on?" I said.

But Willie didn't answer right away, and then Jayne Sokol was speaking.

"Your Honor, the People do not intend to seek an indictment at any time during the statutory period. We stand on the complaint."

"And Mr. St. Clare?" said Judge Petty.

"The defense demands a felony hearing at the earliest possible date."

I couldn't believe my ears. If another second passed, Jayne Sokol would have had to amend her complaint to add another charge of murder—the death by strangulation of William St. Clare, Junior. But Petty immediately asked if there were a bail application, Willie Junior answered yes, the court clerk handed each lawyer a copy of the probation department's bail report, and Willie Junior and I once again huddled at the "defense" table.

"Empty rap sheet," he said. "Very good."

"Willie, what the hell did you just do?"

"I'm fighting 'em at every turn, just like Judge Inglisi taught me."

"Willie, you don't demand a felony hearing when the D.A. waives a grand jury."

"I do," he said.

No sense arguing philosophy and strategy at this point. The felony hearing was a done deal, and I didn't want to upset Willie lest he screw up the world's easiest bail application. Mine.

The door at the rear of the courtroom opened with a squeak, and in waddled Judge Inglisi. I shot him the darkest look I could muster, and refocused my attention on Willie.

"Empty rap sheet. Right. I've never been arrested before."

"Hmmm," he said, staring at a yellow carbonized biographical sheet. "You don't own your home. And we know you're not married. Engaged?"

"No."

"What about that good-looking redhead you dated back when?"

Another Deirdre fan, I thought. "Long gone."

"Could pose a problem," said Willie Junior. "Your roots in the community don't go very deep."

"That's crazy. I've lived in Limerick all my life, except for school and my PGA apprenticeship in Florida. That ended over four years ago."

"This is a capital case, Kieran. Petty's no pushover," said Willie, tugging at an earlobe.

I stole a glance at Jayne Sokol. Her probation file lay closed while she rifled a thick file folder inside her briefcase.

"Wait a second," said Willie. "Judge Inglisi said you're supposed to play in a big tournament next week."

"The PGA Championship at Winged Foot."

"Are you ready, counsellors?" Petty said from the bench.

Jayne Sokol answered ready. Willie Junior signalled he needed another minute.

"You're not likely to run out on the chance to play in it, right?" said Willie.

"You just finished scheduling a goddam felony hearing for the same day as the second round of the tournament," I said.

"They don't know the second round's that day. I sure didn't."

"Willie," I said, reaching a state of exasperation I never thought possible this side of raising kids, "say whatever the hell you damn well please."

He did. Locking his thumbs behind his suspenders, Willie Junior delivered an oration to make Cicero proud. He erected and then dismantled every perceived weakness of my bail application. With Petty leaning intently forward and Jayne Sokol jotting notes, Willie moved on to his strongest argument. His client was a simple golf pro, a man from a working-class background, a man who stood on the verge of realizing a great professional dream. Certainly this client, a man never once accused of even a misdemeanor, would not flee the jurisdiction at this time and in the face of these obviously erroneous charges. Willie ended with a flourish and settled beside me.

"Well, Ms. Sokol," said Judge Petty, "what do you say to that?"

"Quite a bit," she said. "First, you mustn't let Mr. St. Clare's oratory obfuscate the clear facts of the probation report. The defendant has only the weakest link to his community. Second, defense counsel is trying to make you believe that this defendant is no risk to flee because of, listen carefully, a golf game. This, your Honor, is patently frivolous. Third, this may be the defendant's first arrest, but not his first brush with the law."

"Ms. Sokol," said Judge Petty, "his rap sheet is clean."

The A.D.A. strode to the bench, waving a newspaper article I recognized only too well.

During my professional apprenticeship, the Florida State Attorney's Office investigated a complaint of organized gambling infiltrating some mini tour events. PGA Tour hopefuls, like myself, honed their competitive skills by playing in these minor tournaments. Prize purses were small, which opened the theoretical possibility of bribes. The investigation fizzled, partly because I advised the prime targets not to cooperate and mostly because the complaint was bogus. But the PGA Tour never forgot, which was one reason I was never allowed to win a playing card.

The story would have stayed buried in the South, a weird chapter in both golf history and Florida jurisprudence. But shortly after I returned home, Randall Fisk exhumed it for one of his midwinter columns. Four years later, Fisk's embellishments stank enough of moral turpitude to deep-six my bail application.

Petty read the article, his face grim. I glanced over my shoulder and mouthed the word *help*. Judge Inglisi spread his hands in a rare show of helplessness. Winged Foot, the PGA, even my humble apartment with its tenuous roots in the Limerick soil seemed very far away.

Two hours later, we sat in a window booth at the Skytop Restaurant at the new county airport terminal. A private jet taxied noiselessly down the runway and climbed gracefully into the purple sky. Things weren't so serene on my side of the glass.

"I still think Willie Junior is a good lawyer," said Judge Inglisi, who decided he could afford a third dessert after shelling out the premium on my hundred grand bail bond.

"He let himself get baited," I said. "The D.A's office won't present this case to the grand jury because their case is too weak. So rather than lay back, he demands—*demands*—a felony hearing. That's just what they want, evidence from us to help them make their case. And when I point this out to him, all he says is, 'We'll fight 'em at every turn.' "

"He got that from me," said the Judge.

"I know where he got it. You taught me the same thing. But you also taught me there are some straightaways where you just keep your mouth shut and act patient."

"I guess Willie missed that lesson." The Judge flagged down a waitress for another squirt of whipped cream on his chocolate mousse. "But give Willie his due. He got you out on bail."

We sat in silence for a few minutes and watched another plane take off. The bitching session may have helped my psyche but did nothing for my legal jeopardy. I was still charged with half the state penal code, and was still represented by a dolt.

"What do you think is going on?" I said.

"Well, you have an arson and a death," said the Judge. "And the death being a fireman turns up the pressure a notch. Arson is a quick read but a slow case to solve. So closing it quickly makes everyone look good."

"Why me?"

"You have a felony complaint instead of a grand jury indictment," said the Judge. "That means you have the police and the A.D.A. collaborating. We already know DiRienzo doesn't like Milton Country Club and hates you. You throw in Jayne Sokol and you, meaning Kieran Lenahan, have a real problem."

"What's special about Jayne Sokol?"

"Ever hear of *Sokol v. Willow Run Country Club?*"

"No."

"Must have been while you were putting down roots in Florida," said the Judge. "Jayne Sokol's old man joined Willow Run when Jayne was five years old. She played as a junior member until she turned twenty-one, then played as an intermediate member until she turned twenty-five. She got married, and her husband joined the club. Five years later, she was divorced and her old man was dead. The next spring, she went to re-up her membership, and the committee rejected her. Why? Because she was an unmarried woman with no connection to the club. She'd been a member for twenty-five years, but never in her own right.

"She sued, but it was a private club with a clear set of rules. No woman could join unless she was the wife or the daughter of a full-fledged male member. She's had a hard-on for golf and golfers ever since."

"Is that why she was so adamant about scheduling the felony hearing for next Friday?" I said.

"Damn right," said the Judge. "Especially after Willie Junior made that bail pitch. No way will she adjourn it now."

"Does Willie know that about her?"

"No, and we don't tell him. We let Jayney work along and prepare her case. Just before the trial, we tell Willie to make a motion to disqualify her for prosecutorial bias against golf pros in general and you in particular. The D.A.'s office has to scramble a new trial attorney on the eve of the trial. Gives you an edge."

"I won't let it go that far," I said.

It was midnight before the Judge dropped me at MCC and I drove my own car back to Limerick. The neighborhood seemed different in subtle ways. Shacks and fences I never noticed, a stump where a swamp maple once tangled its branches among power lines, a bright new beer sign hanging in a window of Toner's. I wondered if Jayne Sokol had been right, that for all the time I spent living here I hadn't put down real roots in the community. I was an oddity. A lawyer among firemen, cops, and railroad workers. A golf pro among guys who slugged softballs in vacant lots or swigged beer in front of the afternoon's NFL fare. People respected me, yes. Una MacEwan told me so. But did this respect bury a rich vein of resentment? Would these charges rub away a silver-plated civility to expose baser metals beneath?

Before I could decide on an answer, Randall Fisk jumped out of the bushes lining my driveway. I opened my door into his knees, but he recovered quickly enough to chase me to the foot of my apartment stairs.

"Aw, come on, Kieran, say something. I'm the only reporter in the county who doesn't have you hanged."

"Pretty funny, coming from the one reporter who almost prevented me from making bail."

"I did?"

"Your column on the Florida mini tour gambling probe found its way into the D.A.'s file and translated into moral turpitude."

"Oh," he said. "I guess you don't want to talk to me."

"Not now. Maybe not ever."

Fisk retreated with atypical meekness. I expected the usual counterattack, but his car started at the curbside, and he drove off into the quiet Limerick night. Maybe there was hope he'd join that fraction of the human race who understand actions have consequences.

I trudged wearily up the stairs. My screen door was ajar from a large envelope wedged against the doorjamb. I opened up, switched on the light, and emptied the envelope's contents onto the table. Two trophies and a framed photograph of Arnold Palmer. My golf mementoes.

CHAPTER
9

I stood the trophies on the table. The smaller one was a plastic silver cup on a black plastic cube. An old golf ball sat glued in the mouth of the cup, two crescent smiles gouged in its dirty balata. Yellowed tape held a square of paper to the cube. On the paper, the caddymaster had lettered "Keerin Lenahand - High Gross." It was the booby prize for shooting 144 in my first ever round of golf in the annual Caddies Day Tournament. The larger trophy was almost a foot high. Real metal, real wood, an engraved plaque stating simply "Caddie Champ - Low Gross." I'd improved a lot in two years.

The photograph was a shot of a youthful Arnold Palmer, powerfully coiled at the top of his backswing, his club a wispy blur. He'd autographed it for me during the 1971 Westchester Classic, one of his last victories on the regular PGA Tour.

No doubting Pete now; someone had stolen these mementoes from the shop prior to the blaze. I lifted the manila envelope again, and felt some extra weight. A yardage booklet for Winged Foot's west course tumbled out, profusely annotated in Jackie Mack's unmistakable hand.

The yardage booklet was such an obvious idea no one thought of it for 500 years. Invented by a Tour caddie, it spread through the Tour and into the general golfing population as quickly as the personal computer spread across the U.S. But just as owning a computer didn't make you a genius, carrying a yardage booklet in your hip pocket didn't make you a champion golfer.

Basically, a yardage booklet is a hole-by-hole schematic drawing of an entire golf course. Distances are measured from the front edge of the green back toward the tee, and noted in relation to obvious landmarks. For example, the schematic of a 450 yard par four might show a 180 yard reading from a tree or a sprinkler head, tacitly assuming a 270 yard drive. Some schematics also list an oddball yardage labeled JICYFU for "just in case you fuck up." In that 450 yard example, a JICYFU distance might be 270 yards, just in case you duck-hooked your tee shot into the trees.

The yardage booklet Jackie Mack left for me was the standard issue Winged Foot version available in the pro shop any day of the year. When the tournament began, each pro would receive a booklet customized for the day's exact tee and pin placements.

But Jackie could mold a standard yardage booklet into an invaluable tool, a fifteenth club in the bag, a guardian angel sitting on your shoulder. He paced off all kinds of alternate distances from places his golfer—i.e., me—was most likely to fuck up. He noted prevailing wind direction, drainage conditions, tidbits of local knowledge, hidden dangers that appeared harmless until they sucked your ball into their throats. He suggested tactics, and reduced the character of each hole to a five or ten word phrase.

I flipped open to hole number one, a quarter-mile long par four with a dogleg left. "Death down the left side," Jackie had written. My heart pounded out of control. Was this a message? Did Jackie know he was about to die? I read on and found many references to death. But this was just caddie jargon, death not being the absence of life but the absence of any workable shot from the position of your ball. Even a desperate, hyperactive imagination like mine couldn't warp Jackie's notes into a hidden message.

Exhausted, overpowered by confusion, I switched off the light and crawled into bed. At dawn, I peeked back into the kitchen. No, I hadn't dreamt this. I filled the envelope and buried it deep in the Inglisi & Lenahan archives, the extra bedroom where I stored my half of the firm's files.

Una MacEwan sat on her porch, scraps of breakfast tumbling from a small table between her knees. Scouts from an army of ants probed the floorboards for crumbs.

"I found the envelope while I was cleaning Jackie's room," she said. "Ever since he was a boy, he always hid things in secret places. I looked inside and saw your name. So I sent Kate over with it."

"Can you show me where you found it?"

Una dragged the table out of her way and pulled herself upright. She wobbled terribly, moving forward in less of a walk than a controlled fall. Somehow, her feet reached far enough forward to save her.

"We need to be quiet," she said, easing open the front door. "Kate's still asleep."

With excruciating effort, she climbed the stairs. Twice she stopped, caught her breath, and pulled mightily on the bannister to start again.

"She was on the phone with Max all night." Una huffed as we passed Kate's closed door. "I told her she has a husband and a home. She doesn't need to keep me company. I'll be all right."

Poor Una, I thought. She doesn't have a clue.

Jackie's room was as cramped as Kate's, but without any of the childhood trappings. A twin bed, a dresser, a metal wardrobe faced with wood-grained contact paper. Dark panelled walls. Dingy drapes gathered against the morning sun. The air smelled like a mix of cheap aftershave and dirty socks.

"He never let me in here, even to clean," said Una, switching on an old brass fixture shaped like a candle. "I respected his privacy, but now . . . Help me with this."

Together we lifted the mattress off the box spring. The underside had urine stains shaped vaguely like the continents.

"I was changing the sheets," said Una. "The envelope was under the mattress, close to the wall so you couldn't see any lump."

We dropped the mattress, and Una smoothed the covers.

"I thought you could show the Monsignor," she said. "They say people who commit suicide give things away before . . ."

Her voice trailed off, as if she realized the fuzziness of her logic. She reached behind her, groping for the arm of a chair I shoved into place. Her white hair pressed hard to one side of her head and puffed out on the other. Rolls of flesh bulged beneath her mis-buttoned house dress. I wondered how much sleep she'd lost last night, weaving this thin straw into a basket of false hope. Maybe Kate was right. Maybe I should have set Una straight right off and kept my nose out of their business.

The floorboards creaked, and Kate came in looking ragamuffin cute in a man-tailored shirt.

"What are you doing here?" she said.

"I showed Mr. Lenahan where I found his things," said Una, oblivious to her daughter's tone of voice.

"Excuse us a minute, Mom."

Una nodded, her eyes fixed on the floor between us. Kate and I went down the stairs and out to the front gate.

"You promised you'd leave her alone," she said. "If I'd known that junk would bring you over here bothering her, I would have dumped it."

Another one calling my mementoes junk. Between Pete and Kate, Limerick was losing its grip on sentimentality.

"You know what happened to me yesterday?" I said.

"The whole town does. I was hoping they'd keep you in. I would have buried Jackie this morning."

"This isn't just about getting Jackie buried," I said. "The stuff in that package was stolen from my shop before the fire."

"So what?"

"Jackie knew what that stuff meant to me. Maybe he knew there would be a fire."

"Are you trying to pin that on Jackie now?" said Kate, less in anger than in wonder as the idea of her brother as an arsonist took hold in her mind.

I still didn't know how to read Kate. I didn't know how she connected with the web of old Limerick families, or whether, after her flight to Greenwich, she connected at all. But she could give me another line on Jackie, and the first step in winning her help was to pique her interest. I had that, and changed the subject.

"I'm sorry I had to bother Max. Your mother told me you were on the phone all night."

Kate leaned on the gatepost. "He was pretty upset about you showing up because he still thinks I want a divorce. That's the problem with Max. One of many, actually. He wants to know. He wants certainty. Silly for a guy with a gambling problem, huh? I don't know what I want, except something new."

I had no time for this to turn into a soul-baring session. Luckily, it didn't. Kate yawned like a lioness, and clamped her mouth shut.

"Have the police released his personal effects yet?" I said.

"No."

"When they do, I want to see them. Especially his wallet."

Kate yawned again. Tired and bored, and maybe a bit exasperated. Then she broke away quickly, skipping up the steps with her shirttails floating around her thighs. She could be a heartbreaker in her discontent. I didn't envy Max a bit.

Gene "Bear" Burkowski opened for business the minute the morning papers hit the street. Customers reached him at any of a number of telephones, from a lonely roadside booth near the county airport to a black rotary in the back room of Tony La Salle's clam bar on the town boardwalk. Burkowski crossed Milton's borders only in dire emergencies. Still, I needed to cover lots of territory before opening time at the club.

Burkowski was an old client, and amazingly not as a criminal defendant. I formally met the Bear when his daughter broke off her engagement literally on the eve of the wedding, after discovering her fiance's continuing affair with an old flame. The town held its collective breath, expecting Bear Burkowski to exact physical revenge. Instead, Burkowski ambled into the offices of Inglisi & Lenahan. The future Judge ducked out the back door while I prodded Bear toward the conference room.

"I should break every bone in that bastard's body," said Burkowski. "But I got a better idea. I'm gonna sue."

I was hard pressed to draft a complaint. Law and public opinion hadn't yet devolved to the point where we contrived idiot theories to blame other people for every vicissitude of life. I let him ventilate for an hour, explained that a lawsuit would open him up to a potentially expensive countersuit, and sent him home. He'd adored me ever since.

I spotted Bear Burkowski's rusted old Chevy in that most obvious of places, the handicapped parking space outside Philly Casino's lunch counter off Merchant Street. Steamy, greasy air hit me the moment I opened the door. So did the silence. Philly's customers were ninety percent blue-collar Limerick boys, and those who didn't think me con-

victed as soon as my arrest leaked out yesterday were at least stunned to
see me on the loose. The counter tilted one way, the row of tables another. Faces loomed out of shadows, familiar yet strange as if suddenly
stripped of the names I'd known all my life.

"What's the matter?" snarled a voice from the back. "Aintcha all
seen Lenahan before?"

The room shrank back into perspective. Heads lowered. Voices
rose. A hunk of bacon landed on the grill with a sharp sizzle. I made my
way down the aisle.

"Grab that for me, willya?" Bear Burkowski said by way of greeting
as a phone jangled in the metal booth immediately behind his table. I
reached in and pulled out the receiver. Bear flipped a pair of drugstore
reading glasses down from his brow. He grunted a few times, made some
runic markings on a pad, and tore off the top sheet.

"Thanks." He handed back the phone and arched his spine, dragging his belly above the table. His golf shirt had peeled up from the
T-shirt underneath. Both were dark with sweat. "Don't let those mutts
get you, okay? You're innocent until proven guilty, and maybe not even
then."

Not a very encouraging sentiment, since lay people used that
phrase when everyone from the nightly news anchor to the washer-
woman believed someone overwhelmingly guilty. "Oh well, so and so's
innocent until proven guilty," they'll say, as if it's written in the Constitution or the Bill of Rights, which it isn't.

"Ah, Kieran, does anything beat the smell of bacon?" Bear leaned
sideways and squeezed a wallet out of his pocket. Buried among the chit
sheets was the picture of a newborn. "Joshua. Ain't he something?"

"Cute," I said, though all these hospital shots looked the same to
me except for the pink or blue backgrounds. Might as well show me the
picture of a cat.

"You're gonna be godfather," he said.

"I don't even know your daughter or your son-in-law."

"Don't matter. You didn't talk sense, I'da sued him, they never woulda kissed and made up, and there'd be no Joshua in my wallet."

I let that pass, and cleared a pile of morning dailies off the nearest chair so I could sit. Three cups of the syrup Philly Casino called coffee steamed at Bear's elbow. He gulped one down, and shovelled mounds of sugar into the next victim.

"Damn that bacon smells good," he said. "Can't eat it, though. Doctor's orders. Hey, where do parents come up with kids' names these days? Joshua's Jewish, right?"

"Biblical," I said. "Battle of Jericho."

"But the kid's a damn Polack. Three-quarters, anyway. What's the matter with Michael or Eugene? You think a priest'll actually baptize him Joshua? I hear that MacEwan kid's still on ice over at Damiano's because the Monsignor won't give him a funeral mass. I also hear you tried to talk to the Monsignor."

"You're good, Bear."

"Ain't nothin'. You talk to all the people I do in one day, you don't need newspapers. At least not for news."

"This is a personal matter for me."

"I know. The kid was your caddie. You don't think he jumped. That's your business."

The phone rang. Bear swiped at it but missed, so I dragged out the receiver and waited for him to finish his hieroglyphics and hand it back. He didn't.

"Hit the hookswitch and come sit down," he said. "Jackie did lots of business, since that's what you're asking. But I wasn't into him for anything, since that's what you're getting at."

"I'm not."

"Good. Jackie had some rough stretches. Couldn't smell a winner if a horse sat its ass right on his nose. There were times guys chased after him. Guys from out of town because nobody in town would let him go too far without collecting."

"Do these guys have names?"

"Yeah, but they won't do you any good." Bear drained the second cup in two gigantic swallows.

"Why not?"

A recorded voice said to hang up or make a call.

"Shut the fuck up," Bear told the voice. He stifled the earpiece with a meaty palm. "About a year and a half, two years ago, Jackie settled up what he owed. Boom. One shot, all square. Said he was starting a new life. Got himself a sponsor and joined a Gamblers Anonymous chapter up in White Plains or somewhere."

"Do you know the sponsor's name?"

"Nah," said Bear. "Jackie told me, but it never clicked. Just knew he wasn't one of my old regulars. See, a kid like Jackie, who never had his head screwed on right, he needs something like G.A. But if every gambler in the world joined up, I'd need to find a new line of work. Not to mention listening to a bunch of boring people saying they're in recovery."

Just as well Bear couldn't remember the name of Jackie's sponsor. Twelve step groups weren't noted for a willingness to share information about their members.

"So he stopped gambling," I said.

"I didn't say that," said Bear. "Jackie came back maybe half a dozen times. Couple of Super Bowls, the Triple Crown, the Breeder's Cup. Small bets, like he wanted a piece of the same action everyone else in the world had."

"He could have booked other bets with someone else," I said. "Hispanic bookies, maybe."

"Stop jumping to goddam conclusions and listen," said Bear.

The third coffee went down the hatch. A tiny stream dribbled down Bear's chin. He groped for a napkin before seizing a wad of news-paper.

"Week before the last Super Bowl, Jackie comes in to see me. We do our business. Nothing much, the favorite ten times. He walks out and there's this guy waiting for him, right about where the front fender of my car is. It's cold out, real cold, but this guy's wearing only a flannel shirt and jeans. He and Jackie start shouting at each other, and then they're throwing punches. The guy goes down. Jackie takes off. The guy comes in here bleeding real bad from his hand. I figure when he went down he cut it on a piece of metal sticking out of my car. Philly throws him a rag, and the guy wraps it around the cut to stop the blood. The place isn't crowded, but nobody's saying a word. Everybody's watching him. He looks my way. He's pretty big with an even bigger face, huge and round with broad features and thick reddish hair pulled back in a ponytail.

"I'm thinking he knows that's my car he cut himself on. But in-stead he says, 'I don't want you taking any more action from that kid. You hear me?' He's looking down at me, and he's holding his hand out, and the blood's starting to seep through the rag and plop onto the table. I don't usually listen to threats. But this guy looks nuts as hell. So I say, 'Okay, pal,' and he walks to the door, drops the bloody rag on the floor, and heads out with his hand raised over his head so it won't bleed so bad."

"Jackie's G.A. sponsor?"

"Guess so," said Bear.

"Jackie ever come back?"

"Not to bet. And he didn't even come to collect his Super Bowl cash for a good six months. And when I did see him he didn't even want it. Actually, what he said was he didn't need it."

"When?"

"Couple of months back. He seemed happier than a pig in shit, all smiles and gladhanding everyone in the joint. Even left Philly a good tip. He plopped himself right down where you are now and started asking a bunch of questions about when the baby was due. Never figured Jackie to be the type interested in babies." Bear tossed me the receiver. "Hang this yapping thing up."

I did. It rang immediately.

"Fuck it," said Bear. "Point is, Jackie wasn't betting with me, or with anyone else in any type of persuasion. Guys wanting action, needing action, they have this restless look in their eyes. They have this sound in their voice. Not Jackie."

"He wasn't gambling," I said.

"Swear on Joshua," said Bear. "And Kieran, think about being godfather, okay?"

Halfway down Poningo Point the mansions ended and the clubs began. Beach clubs lined the Sound side, their patches of sand demarcated by chain link fences clogged with seaweed and rusted by the briny air. Yacht clubs lined the harbor side, taking full advantage of the protection the Point offered against nor'easters. A few clubs combined both, straddling the curvy road that ran down the Point to a small public quay. The Land's End of Milton.

Demo Mike worked at one of the beach clubs. For many summers, he hustled food, drinks, and towels between the clubhouse and the flimsy cabanas on the sand. Lousy wages, great tips, and rich chicks in bikinis. A high school kid's dream. After the stroke felled Demo's hustle, the club manager created a new job for him. As cabana captain, Demo sat in a tin shack, listened to the radio, and oversaw the cabana boys. Better wages, greater tips, and the same rich chicks in bikinis. A college kid's wet dream.

When Demo entered law school, I thought he'd find a summer job with a firm or work as an intern for Judge Inglisi.

"Are you insane, Kieran?" he'd told me. "How many real summer vacations do I have left?"

I liked that. I always thought the perfect summer job involved a summer activity. A beach, an amusement park, a golf course. There was time enough to devote July and August to your future profession. Maybe it was a sign of our economic times, but too few of Demo's contemporaries agreed.

I found Demo in his tin shack, sipping an iced tea with his good hand while curling a five-pound dumbbell with his weak one. Heavy metal music crashed from an FM station and static hissed on a police scanner. The coconut scent of sunscreen hung heavy. Demo immediately cut the music and dropped the dumbbell.

"I heard you were sprung," he said. "Word got to the fire house last night. The guys were pretty damn pissed, especially at Judge Inglisi."

"He put up the bond."

"Not the way we heard it. Everyone thought he arraigned you himself and released you on your own recognizance."

"You told them that was impossible."

"I'm the kid who works the computer," said Demo. "They don't listen to me about anything else. You got William St. Clare, Junior, as your lawyer?"

"The Judge did. I'd have hired you first."

"I didn't even graduate yet."

"I don't care. You'd do just as good a job as Willie Junior."

"Thanks, but I'm already booked for your hearing. The D.A.'s office sent an investigator to interview me. I may be a witness."

A couple of women strolled by, wearing high-heeled sandals and skimpy bathrobes. Demo grinned, running his hand along his expanded bicep.

"Someone from your insurance company was here with the D.A.'s man," he said after the two women sank into lounge chairs at the edge of the sand.

"Frank Platt."

"That's the name. Is he weird or what? He dresses like he's going to Atlantic City to play the slots."

"He has a distinctive style," I said. "What did they ask?"

"The D.A.'s investigator asked most of the questions," said Demo. "He wanted to know why I called you the night of the fire. I told him I was at the fire house when the alarm sounded, I recognized the building was your pro shop, and I phoned you at home from the chief's cellular while we were en route. Then he asked whether I spoke to you at the scene. I told him about showing you the computer and asking for the location of the heat source."

"Did you tell him that I doubted you?" I said.

"You just told me you would have hired me as your lawyer," said Demo. "No way I told him you doubted me or the machine. I know how that sounds. I told him you were extremely cooperative. Then he asked if I saw you at any other time during the fire. He wanted to know your mannerisms, disposition, and demeanor. Exactly those words. I told him you were visibly upset. Then he said I could be subpoenaed to testify at the felony hearing next Friday."

"Did Platt ask you anything?"

"Personal stuff, like how long and how well I know you, your lifestyle, the kind of car you drive, whether you spend money flamboyantly. I told him you're careful with a buck."

"Thanks. Why didn't you just say I'm a cheap bastard."

"Actually, that's what I did say," said Demo. "He also asked something about mementoes you kept in your shop, and whether I knew anything about them. I told him I didn't visit your shop that often. Hey, did you really snoop around the building?"

"Yeah, I did. Anything else?"

"That was it," said Demo. He hoisted the dumbbell, this time doing one-armed presses.

I mulled the questions the D.A.'s investigator and Platt had asked Demo, squeezing them for any farfetched inference that might drop out. If my alleged insurance scam made little sense to someone like Willie Junior, these questions made even less.

"Demo," I said, "I need Surchuck's report."

Demo let go of the dumbbell in mid-press. It flew out of the shack and thudded into a flowerbed.

"Geez, Kieran, I'm only a volunteer."

"But you're the chief's main man. Without you, that new pumper's in mothballs."

"Which would suit a lot of the crew just fine," said Demo.

"I need that report. I can't rely on Willie Junior."

"Do you have any idea who did it?"

"Some."

Demo sipped thoughtfully on his iced tea. His bad hand trembled.

"Forget about me getting a copy," said Demo. "Maybe I can finesse some information out of the chief. And that's a big maybe."

"Give it your best shot, okay," I said, knowing that Demo's best shot was better than most other's.

Boland Brothers Cart Company was located on the Hudson River within sight of the Tappan Zee Bridge. Sam and Chris Boland were ex-caddies who boasted of seeing the economic possibilities of powered golf carts through a marijuana haze. Back in the early '60s, most golfers walked their rounds, and country clubs housed a handful of powered carts as a courtesy to older members. The costs of buying large fleets directly from the manufacturers was prohibitive, and the maintenance of the flimsy fiberglass buggies a pain in the ass. The Bolands envisioned huge numbers of carts bought from the manufacturers at cut-rate prices, then leased to country clubs along with a maintenance package.

With or without the dope, the vision proved prophetic. For years, Boland Brothers monopolized cart distribution in the tri-state area. For many more, its competitors hardly competed. But in recent months, Randall Fisk spread a rumor that the company had fallen on hard times. The Bolands hadn't kept abreast of new technologies, didn't reinvest, and paid exorbitant salaries to an increasingly inept maintenance crew. "A microcosm of our nation's decadence," Fisk concluded.

Naturally, I passed off Fisk's remarks to the usual news media hyperbole. After all, I saw no obvious decline in Boland's service contract with MCC. A fresh fleet of carts arrived every two years, Pete and I performed daily maintenance, and a mechanic called three times weekly to repair any damage we couldn't handle.

But the sight of the Bolands' warehouse confirmed the rumors. Airlines need their planes in the air; cart distributors need their carts on fairways, not parked nose to ass in a riverfront lot. I'd never seen the club's contract with Boland, but guessed Boland offered favorable terms to one of its oldest customers. I also guessed the contract had an impossibility clause, which extinguished the contract when conditions made performance impossible by one side or the other. Like a forest in a drought, the situation seemed right for a fire.

A familiar mechanic sat beside an overhead door and cleaned his fingernails with a paring knife.

"In there and up those stairs," he said, divining the obvious.

The inside was packed with rows upon rows of carts. White fiberglass shells, vinyl seats and backrests covered with the manufacturer's plastic, shiny black tires. The cool air jumped with a rubbery new cart smell. Not as rich as a new car smell, but distinctive just the same. I plodded up a set of metal stairs, then inched along a catwalk suspended by girders to an office that looked like a box on stilts. The shades on the windows were drawn tight. I knocked. The door opened by itself.

Chris Boland, the paunchy one with curly gray hair circling a pink tonsure, sat behind a terribly messy desk. Sam Boland, the tall one with the salt-and-pepper ponytail reaching halfway down his back, stood in a corner and fiddled with the pull cord of a set of blinds. Sam spotted me first. He dropped the cord, which was tied like a noose.

"Look, Chris, another goddam jackal."

"Easy, Sam," said his brother.

"They sent you, huh?" Sam said. "Figures. Well, I'll save you the time. We owe Milton a rebate. We admit it. Here, you find any money, you write yourself a check."

He shoved a large check ledger from the desk to the floor.

"Cool it, Sam." Chris stared his brother back into the corner, then swivelled his chair to face me. "My brother's pissed off. And I'm not feeling so great myself."

"I'm not here on behalf of the club," I said.

"So what the hell are you here for?" said Sam.

"Quiet," said Chris. "Kieran, have yourself a sit."

I dragged a chair close to the desk, angling it in case Sam went into attack mode.

"The fire—" I said, and kept my eyes on Sam. With good reason because he yanked the cord and pulled the whole set of blinds to the floor.

"The Bulge, Gettysburg, Thermopylae, Agincourt!" Spit flew from Sam's mouth.

Chris leaped from his chair, grabbed his brother's shoulders, and shook him into silence. Sam tried to slap him, but Chris caught his wrist and wrenched his arm to his side. Chris spoke in sharp whispers, making no discernible impact until he squeezed his brother's jaw.

Sam's attitude relaxed, though his eyes still bugged out in fury.

Chris released him, and Sam glared at me before loping toward the door.

"The river," said Chris.

"Yeah, man, I read you," said Sam.

Chris returned to his chair and tucked two tufts of wiry hair behind his ears.

"He's seeing a new therapist," he said as Sam's boots rang on the metal steps outside. "When he becomes agitated, he must find something to count. He likes the ducks that swim up to the quay. Lucky for me there are loads of them."

"What was the yelling about?" I said.

"Artful allusions. Battles, but more than battles. Turning points in great struggles. He believes we are at war, and that the Milton Country Club fire is our turning point. Temper aside, he may not be completely wrong.

"We are in decline, Kieran. Customer after customer decides gas carts are superior to our electrics. Batteries run low during the second round of the day. Batteries take hours to recharge. By August, they become so weak from a whole summer of nightly cooking they can't hold a full charge. Sure, electric carts are quiet. But the muffling system on the new gas models are almost as quiet, hardly more than a decibel or two off. And all you need to do is gas them up."

"What's stopping you from distributing gas carts?" I said.

"Ourselves," said Chris. He rolled his chair to the one section of window with a view of the river. After a few seconds of checking for Sam, he rolled back. "Sam and I got into this when electric carts were state of the art. We knew gas carts eventually would cut out a niche in the market. But we didn't believe they had any place on a golf course, not with all the tractors and mowers and other greenskeeping equipment laying clouds of blue smoke on green grass. So we pledged never to purchase or distribute any cart with an internal combustion engine. It's written right into our corporate charter."

I wondered if Chris Boland understood that the clean electricity powering his carts probably had been generated from an oil or coal-fired turbine. A philosophical discussion, however, did not seem in order.

"Changing the corporate charter is simple enough," I said.

"It requires both our votes," said Chris. "As you can imagine, Sam and I don't agree on much now. So we careen downhill, helpless to help ourselves, losing club after club to a competitor that was once an industry joke. We'll be in court fighting for dissolution before long, unless one of our creditors forces us into bankruptcy first."

"How has your insurance company treated your fire loss claim?" I said.

A guttural titter rumbled in Chris Boland's throat, then exploded into a belly laugh.

"Insurance?" he said, waving for breath. "We had no insurance."

"You didn't insure your carts?"

"We did," he said soberly. "We paid premiums through our broker. The policy lapsed. No one informed us about overdue premiums. I don't know who dropped the ball, but someone did."

"Fight it in court."

"Just what we need, a lawsuit. Truth is, Kieran, we didn't have the money to pay all our operating expenses and cover our premiums. It's gotten that bad. And the fire may not have been just another piece of bad luck."

Chris sifted through scattered sheets of paper and found a letter from the attorney for Tartan Golf Cart Corp. The veiled threats interested me, but not half as much as the name printed at the top in fancily scripted raised black letters.

———

I could have picked A. Theodore Lauretti, Esq., out of a crowd. "Looks like your typical asshole lawyer," his secretary had told me over the phone, after giving directions to the joint where he ate lunch "every freaking day." I soon enough gathered the secretary's loyalty was directly proportional to A. Teddy's work habits. I'd found the joint, a bar in the Fleetwood section of Mount Vernon, around one, and at two-thirty I was still sitting in a booth listening to Lauretti pontificate about "the law" to a mixed group of people who obviously had nothing better to do.

Lauretti was a compact, butterball of a man. His tie was loosened, allowing his starchy white collar to stick up around his ears like the wings of an osprey. His white shirt rode up and escaped between his dark pants and matching vest. Vests went out of fashion ten years ago, but not in Lauretti's world of "the law." He spoke rapid fire, like a machine gun with a lisp, and slipped in a Latin phrase every three or four sentences. I doubted Virgil or Augustus ever heard such creative pronunciation, unless the Roman Empire once extended to the North Bronx.

After four seltzers with the same lime twist I was belching like a frog and tired of listening to Lauretti criticize every legal benchmark back to *Marbury vs. Madison*. His audience laughed and egged him on to further anecdotes. Not surprising, since most people traced their understanding of the legal system to *The People's Court* reruns and *Geraldo*. Sensing a need to act, I dropped a note on the bar and asked the barmaid to deliver it. Guys like A. Teddy Lauretti are intrigued by moves like that. They think they are about to meet someone as smart as they are. They usually don't.

Silence descended as Lauretti read the note. He craned his neck to look at me, stage whispered the rueful statement that "business calls," and tightened his tie with a flourish of elbow and wrist.

"Kieran Lenahan," I said as he slid into the opposite bench. A buzz returned to the bar. None of Lauretti's audience gave much of a damn what type of business called.

"Have we met?" said Lauretti. Delicate features connected an expansive chin to a wide forehead. His short blond hair was tightly curled, almost nappy. Thick cottony eyebrows shaded his eyes.

"I'm a friend of the MacEwan family, from Milton," I said.

"Sorry, I can't place them. Sometimes I'm not so smart," he said.

His voice carried a smug tone no one on earth would mistake for humility. I formed the immediate impression that A. Teddy Lauretti couldn't catch a client with an elephant trap, which made his position as house counsel to Tartan Cart Corporation both extremely fortunate (for him) and extremely incredible (to me).

"Jackie Mack," I said. "Your first lawsuit after passing the bar."

Lauretti reddened instantly. "That idiot suit was Mack's idea, not mine."

"The judge dismissed it as frivolous."

"Hey, I'm the lawyer, not the judge. People deserve access to the courts," he said.

"Jackie fell in front of a train."

"I heard." Lauretti went very still, like an animal waiting for a predator to pass or a lawyer calculating exactly how much to say.

"People say he jumped, which is holding up a full Catholic funeral mass. I don't think he did."

"So what are you getting at?" said Lauretti. "I haven't seen Mack in years, ever since he stiffed me on expenses for that trial. Almost nine hundred bills. That was a big nut for someone just starting out."

"But you're not starting out now. Nine hundred bills is peanuts. I'll bet you pay your secretary that much in a week."

Lauretti puffed despite himself. "Don't I know it. My brother's sister-in-law. Only reason I keep her is her idiot husband's out of work. And he has the balls to complain I don't pay her enough."

"But you could if she deserved it, right?"

"Right."

"With a solid client like Tartan Carts."

"Hey, who the hell are you anyway?" said Lauretti.

"Just someone burned out by the Milton Country Club fire."

"I heard they got the guy who did it. The pro."

"Nothing's certain yet," I said, probing his face to see if he connected my name. He didn't. "Some evidence points to Jackie Mack doing it."

"I thought you said you were a friend of his family?"

"I am. I want to find out who paid Mack, because whoever paid him probably pushed him in front of the train. The way I figure it, Tartan and Boland Brothers have been battling over territory. There's been an exchange of letters, accusations of contractual interference, threats of lawsuits and worse forms of retaliation. Now all of a sudden there's a fire, and a club that's used Boland's electric carts for so long now needs to rely on Tartan's gas carts."

"If you were a lawyer, you'd know the letters I sent to Boland Brothers are in no way improper. And the fire is one of those things that's *res ipsa loquitur.*"

"I am a lawyer," I said. "And I don't care how carefully you word your letters. The fire was arson. In that context, your letters take on a much different meaning."

"You're looking at a libel suit, pal," said Lauretti. He wriggled out of the booth, wrapped himself in suitable indignance, and strode toward his groupies.

Somehow, Lauretti's threats didn't scare me.

CHAPTER
10

Mel Tucker clomped down the trailer steps as I pulled into MCC. "Damn, Kieran, I didn't expect you'd take my Job comment so serious and bring more trouble down on your head."

"Getting arrested wasn't my idea."

"Guess not," said Tucker. "Well, I'm sure you'll get justice from a jury of your peers."

Get justice. Those two words reminded me of my law practice days, and the criminal defendants who demanded that they get justice, get justice. In their mouths, it meant getting off for crimes they obviously committed. The words probably carried a different connotation wherever Tucker came from.

"Thanks, Mel," I said.

Way out on the first tee, three golfers waved their arms and shouted. Their voices carried staccato over the distance.

"The rest of my foursome," said Tucker. "Caddymaster hooked me up with a new caddie."

He told me the kid's name, and I said the caddymaster didn't steer him wrong.

Tucker started down the cart path to the tee. A sudden thought hit me, and I trotted to fall into step beside him.

"Hey, Mel," I said, "did you know Jackie Mack enrolled in Gamblers Anonymous?"

"Is that right, Kieran? Now who told you a story like that?"

"A bookie."

"Well, now there's a reliable fellow, I'm sure."

"More than most. This guy says Jackie settled accounts about a year and a half ago, gambled sporadically awhile, then stopped altogether after having a fistfight with his G.A. sponsor."

"If he says so, who am I to say otherwise? All I did was bail Jackie out of that jam, remember?"

"Isn't it odd that Jackie didn't tell you about joining G.A.?"

"Assuming he did," said Tucker.

"So let's assume it. Odd, right?"

"Okay, I'll grant you that."

"I wonder if Jackie was into anything shady."

"Like what?"

"Anything," I said. "People sometimes die in funny ways when they're involved in funny things."

"Does this get us back to the pastor?" said Tucker.

"Monsignor. It does."

"How the hell do you have time for Jackie Mack when you got the cops barking up your tree like a pack of hounds?"

"Una MacEwan doesn't understand that," I said. "And at this point, there's nothing I can do about my problem except sit back and keep my nose clean while my lawyer does his job."

We reached the first tee. I lagged back while Tucker climbed the steps and began bantering with his three guests. The tee grass and the impatiens sparkled, still wet from a morning spritz from the sprinklers. The fairway curved into a fine August haze. Behind the distant green, fluffy willows stood as motionless as an oil painting.

I doubted Tucker shared my deep, almost religious sense of promise. Golf was serious business for a hustler, and nowhere was this more evident than on the first tee. There is an old saying that golf matches are won or lost on the first tee, where teams are chosen, shots are handicapped, and bets are sealed. Tucker sounded like an old master, bargaining, bartering, holding out here, giving in there. Eventually, the match was set and Tucker won the honor with an expert flip of a tee. He addressed the ball awkwardly, his fingers fumbling with arthritic pain before he drew back a truncated swing and hit a pop fly safely into the center of the fairway.

"Nice acting," I said, after he descended from the tee to continue our talk.

"Well hell, Kieran, I have to give these boys something in return for all those shots I wrung out of them." He raised a hand to quiet me until his first opponent hit. "About Jackie. Maybe he did go to G.A. and get himself straightened out. Maybe I'm too harsh on him and his problems. Sometimes we miss the most obvious things about the people we know best. But about him being involved in any funny business, like you say, I never saw any sign of that."

The rest of the foursome hit their tee shots, and Tucker shagged off in search of another day's pay.

I stuck in the trailer for the rest of the afternoon. A few dozen members passed through. Most paid for gas carts, a few bought balls and tees. All of them did their business quickly and escaped without so much as a *Have a nice day*.

In between these pleasant transactions, I tried calling Peoria Liquidating. Mentally, I'd already written off my twenty grand bath. But the calls gave me the illusion of action, though I didn't know what the hell I'd say if anyone answered.

I avoided the local paper's news section, and paged in vain through sports for the Fiskian account of my arrest. For once, I was actually disappointed. I called his office and raised an editorial assistant, who informed me Fisk was "in the field."

Willie Junior phoned to schedule a meeting. By dumb luck, Pete answered while I hunkered down for some creative thought in the men's room. I didn't return the call, and Willie phoned ten more times before closing. As the Judge said, extra thick hide impervious to embarrassment.

Since I hadn't touched a club in several days, I decided on an evening practice run. I'd certainly play the first round of the PGA as the only contestant charged with murder. I didn't want to hack up the course to boot.

Georgina Newland rounded the trailer as I saddled up a cart.

"Want some company?" she said.

"Spectator or competitor?"

"How about buddy-pal?"

"You're not afraid to be alone with a suspected arsonist and murderer?"

She shook her head. She wore slacks and a golf shirt, and it occurred to me I may have seen the last of the skirts for awhile. The caddies notwithstanding, I liked her better in slacks. I'd dated lots of women during the many lacunas in my time with Deirdre. Flash and glitz may have excited me, but understatement lived on in my memory.

"I drive," I said, patting the passenger seat with my hand.

I parked the cart alongside the first tee and limbered up my golf muscles with a few gentle practice swings. The fairway looked especially

wide in the waning light, much more inviting and far tamer than anything Winged Foot would offer next Thursday. I pressed a tee into the
soft turf, my knuckles grazing the clipped tops of the grass. I adjusted the
ball so the label faced away, leaving only white dimples visible to my
eye as I stood at address. In my mind, I shrank the fairway to half its size
and visualized a towering draw landing in the exact center of that half.
But as I settled over the shot, my concentration frayed. Across the tee,
Georgina sat languidly in the cart, her sandaled feet on the dash and
one long arm extended across the back of my vacated seat cushion. Her
eyes locked on mine, and she raised her chin slightly as if to say, *Go
ahead.*

I heeled the drive into the left rough.

"Not your best," she said, barely shifting as I climbed into the cart
and kicked off the foot brake.

"No, it wasn't," I said.

I'd played in enough tournaments to develop a technique for dealing with galleries. Strolling down the fairway in between shots, I might
check out the people on the other side of the ropes and acknowledge a
familiar face with a wave or a nod. But standing around on tees and
greens, I never engaged anyone's eye. And during the act of making a
shot, which lasted from conceiving the intended path of the ball until
my follow-through, I sealed myself in an envelope of concentration
even the sound of gunfire could not penetrate.

None of these techniques worked with Georgina. Whenever I
stood over a shot, I felt her eyes on me. Not like the radar sweep I'd felt
in the clubhouse the day after the fire, more like two straws drinking me
in. And there was no respite between shots because sharing a golf cart
with a woman can be a sexy experience. The seats are narrow, and the
suspension jounces like a western buckboard, so you spend lots of time
slapping hips and thighs. When those hips and thighs belong to Georgina Newland, concentration becomes damn near impossible.

After three holes of less than a professional performance, I hit a groove. I don't know whether my concentration somehow returned, or if I passed into a state of mental numbness. I stiffed a wedge on the fourth hole, and tapped in for a birdie. I drilled a 200 yard five iron shot to the apron of the seventh green, and rolled in the putt for another birdie. I rocked the pin on my approach shot on the eighth, setting up another birdie. And I drove the front trap on the ninth and lipped out a sand shot that would have made eagle.

"Is that how you always play?" said Georgina as we tooled back toward the yard.

"Sure," I said bravely.

We decided on the clubhouse restaurant for dinner. Eduardo Rojas, doubling as the weeknight *maitre d'*, sat us at a small table in a corner of the lounge. Mel Tucker and his foursome gathered at the bar, tabulating the results of their matches and shuffling stacks of money like the Federal Reserve Board. A complete stranger mixed drinks.

"Jose off tonight?" I asked Eduardo, recalling the shouting match I'd overheard.

"He quit," Eduardo said as he seated Georgina.

"Why?"

Eduardo moved around the table, his back to Georgina. At the same time, I sensed him measuring me, wondering what I knew and what else I should be told.

"I do not know," he said, and waved for a waiter.

"What was that all about?" Georgina said after the waiter lit the table candle and took our drink orders. The glow from the flame caught her face perfectly. She had great features, just enough age to have character without looking tired.

"The bartender quit," I said. "Not important. I'm just surprised."

"Maybe he didn't like sleeping on a cot in the locker room."

"Maybe," I said. "Can I ask you about the carts?"

"Don't you like them?"

"They're fine. Smooth, quiet ride. Hard to believe they're gas, except for the fumes."

A laugh went up from the bar. Tucker and his boys had finished divvying the money, and now turned to liar's poker. I continued: "It surprises me we didn't go to gas earlier."

"Actually, Tartan's been pressuring us for awhile," said Georgina. "Each winter we receive a full-color brochure trumpeting the advantages of gas carts, and promising how the mufflers and catalytic converters on Tartan carts protect the environment. We also get a follow-up phone call, with a point by point sales pitch on how Tartan outperforms Boland Brothers and any other electric cart distributor."

"Is that why the executive committee hired Tartan after the fire?"

"We knew Tartan from their sales pitches. Some of the committee members liked what they heard."

"Why not hire Tartan before we needed to?"

"The general feeling was a moral obligation to Boland Brothers."

"What about you?"

"I felt no moral obligation," said Georgina. "I just didn't think Boland's track record was poor enough to justify a change. Tartan is much more expensive, you know."

The waiter served dinner and another round of drinks. Two of Tucker's playing partners folded their bills.

"I wasn't going to bring this up," Georgina said halfway through dinner, "but you will hear about it anyway and better from me. The committee held an emergency meeting this afternoon."

"I'm fired," I said.

"The actual resolution on the table was to suspend you without pay. The committee voted against it. But don't draw any conclusions of solid support. We need a pro, and if anyone of decent stature were available we would hire one. No one is looking for work this time of year, and we don't have a suitable pro shop to offer. So you're safe."

"Till next week, anyway," I said. "How did you vote?"

Under the table, a knee rubbed mine.

"How do you think?" said Georgina.

Eduardo Rojas interrupted before I could probe this Delphic answer.

"Phone call," he said, looming heavily above me.

I closed myself into the old wooden booth in the lobby and leaned an elbow on the tiny, kidney-shaped counter beneath the phone.

"Listen quick," said Demo Mike. "I cut out of the meeting and need to go back. The big explosion that knocked Mickey off the cherry picker? You know that was a propane tank. Surchuck found loose copper tubing leading from the cart garage closet to the monkey house. He thinks those guys were rigging some kind of heating system."

"Is that where the fire started?"

"No, and now we get to the bad news," said Demo. "Surchuck's vapor detector found traces of kerosene in the closet that abuts the garage closet. He's pretty sure the fire started there, then ignited the propane when it spread. That's consistent with my computer readings and the black smoke we saw before the explosion. Did you mention anything to him about a kerosene heater?"

"The day after the fire. He lined up a bunch of solvent containers I used for club repairs. I told him about the kerosene heater, and that I drained it every spring."

"Did you drain it this year?"

"Sure."

"Kieran, did you drain it?"

"I don't specifically remember. I just know I usually—"

"Kerosene burns with black smoke, Kieran. Where did you store the heater?"

"Under the workbench. Why?"

Demo's end went silent for a long moment.

"I didn't think a vapor detector was sensitive enough to pick up something like this," Demo finally said.

"Something like what?"

"Surchuck says he found a trail of kerosene from your workbench to the closet, like someone dribbled it."

If Demo said anything else, I didn't hear it. I hung up and slumped against the wall of the booth, my mind plunging into a nightmarish scenario. A jury convicts me of murder for starting the fire that led to Mickey Byrne's death. A judge sentences me to fifteen-to-life. The gavel bangs.

I jumped. Mel Tucker peered into the booth.

"You all right, Kieran?" he said.

I opened the booth. "Sure, Mel."

"That didn't have anything to do with our boy Jackie, did it?"

"I wish."

"Well, I'll keep an ear close for anything might help you. And if you get that clergyman to bury Jackie right, you tell me."

"I will, Mel."

"The caddymaster fixed me up real swell. That new kid isn't Jackie Mack, but we put together a nice little charge on the back nine." Tucker thumped the wallet in his hip pocket. "Now you run along before your dessert gets cold."

Back at the table, I found a fresh round of drinks.

"Compliments of Mel Tucker," said Georgina, with all the gusto of a Temperance Society member.

I laughed, wondering how to take Mel's dessert comment. But the levity lasted only until my fears from the phone booth rushed in to catch me.

"Something wrong?" said Georgina.

"What about these?" I said, ducking the question. I didn't crave a third belt but sure felt I could use it.

"You can have yours," she said. "I won't accept anything from that man."

We shared a glider on a redwood deck. Down below, ceramic elves lit by spotlights danced and cavorted in a garden. Beyond a screen of evergreens the weekly fireworks display boomed over the town beach. Behind me, a bug light zapped another winged marauder.

This was Soundview, a neighborhood more akin to Poningo Point than to Limerick. I estimated the ranch with a split rail fence went for half a mil. Georgina hadn't given me the grand tour, but on the way through the dining room I saw the sewing machine, the patterns, the charcoal design sketches on an easel, the blue chiffon and yellow gauze pinned to a headless mannequin.

"I wanted to stay in the business." She gathered her long hair off her neck and twisted it with her hand. "I wasn't bent for teaching or choreography. But I always had an eye for design. When I was a little girl, we lived on a farm. My father had a job in town, so it wasn't a working farm. But it had a barn, and my friends and I would put on stage shows in the hayloft. I designed all the costumes, and sewed them from scraps on my toy Singer.

"I work my own hours, in my own house. I've developed good contacts and some lucrative accounts. I've designed for the Rockettes. I've designed for grammar school dance recitals."

She went inside to fix refills. I rocked idly on the glider and concentrated on the moment. The ceramic elves. The sounds of fireworks. The smell of honeysuckle. The rough texture of the redwood lumber. I wondered if next year would find me in a jail cell, pining for the simple pleasures of a summer night.

Georgina rapped on the sliding glass door and waved for me to come inside.

"I thought we'd be more comfortable here," she said, leading me into a den.

Two candles guttered on a coffee table. Jazz played on the radio. She curled up on the love seat, drawing her tumbler onto her lap. I lifted the window shade and checked the street for demons before joining her.

"What is it between you and Mel?" I said.

"I've told you, we dated."

I snuggled close, giving her one of my cutely skeptical looks guaranteed to melt her like candlewax.

"Oh, all right," she said. "A couple of years ago, Mel and I were teamed in a mixed Pinehurst. We started dating every Saturday night and one weekday night, usually a Tuesday or Wednesday. He was great fun, but the rigid schedule bothered me. Is there still such a thing as female intuition?"

"We'll need to check with the language police," I said.

"Well, if there is, that's what told me something was amiss. Not that I wanted any more from Melvin than two dates a week. I felt he was hiding something from me, probably a wife. So I did something I'm not proud of. I snooped through his membership file."

"You what?" I said. Under the club's by-laws, membership application files were confidential.

"I was just elected to the executive committee," she said. "I was in the office alone, it was late at night, the files were locked in a cabinet, I had the key."

"Is he married?"

"No. But his first club application was rejected by a man named Walter Walcott."

"The General himself," I laughed.

"Isn't he that nice old man whose picture hangs in the clubhouse lobby?" said Georgina.

"That nice old man was a Poningo Point eccentric who ran the executive committee like a private fiefdom back when the club was owned by a three man partnership. He had full discretion in deciding who joined and who didn't, and he played it for all it was worth. You could be the son of a President, but if General Walcott didn't like your politics, your membership application came back with REJECTED stamped in large red letters."

I never had to pass muster with the General. By the time the owners hired me as pro, he was well in decline. My chief memory of the General was seeing him march up the eighteenth fairway in the early morning, his khaki pants wet to the knees and his golf shoes green with grass clippings. But I'd heard stories from village sages like the Dutchman, who attested to the General's professed belief in conspiracies ranging from UFOs to JFK.

For my money, General Walcott's rejection of Mel Tucker's initial membership application was a big mark on the plus side of the ledger. But I've experienced some of my shallower moments when sex was in the offing, and this was one of them. Georgina opened my shirt button and skimmed her fingers through my chest hair. Thoughts of defending old Melvin drowned in a hormonal flood.

Later, much later, Georgina propped herself on an elbow.

"I have a confession," she said. "I never danced for the Rockettes."

"Where are my clothes. I want out of here."

She rolled onto her back and lifted one leg well over her head.

"I know what people at the club say. I didn't start the stories."

"The caddies believe it. They believe anything."

"Hey, wise guy. I was good enough. Things were just crazy, that's all."

"How crazy?"

"I was young. Actually, I lied about my age. There were guys. You can imagine." She exchanged legs. "So I missed the big time. But if there's anything you want to know about the Catskills or the Poconos, I'm your woman."

I grabbed her leg and pulled her over the top of me. She certainly was.

I woke before dawn and left my spare apartment key wrapped in a corn-ball note on the nightstand. It was the kind of thing I could do only in the dark.

I had no logical reason for slipping out while Georgina slept. But something drew me to the wheel of my car and guided me along the quiet streets of a sleeping Milton. I drove for half an hour before pulling abreast of Toner's and rolling down the window. Air conditioners kicked on and off, and semi-trailers whined on the interstate. A family of raccoons dove into a storm drain. The traffic light winked at an empty intersection. Orion, harbinger of the winter sky, dragged his sword across the eastern horizon.

We cherish the moment, and the romantics among us cherish the memory of the moment. Tonight, I wanted both. I wanted Georgina, and I wanted the memory of Georgina tucked under my shirt while I meandered home like a teenager who still believed magic infested a summer night. It could be my last chance.

CHAPTER
11

Kate Ritchie knocked on my door during morning coffee.

"I tried calling you all night. I thought the cops might have thrown you back in jail."

"Don't sound so disappointed."

Kate brushed past me, then stopped as if suddenly intimidated by the messy living room. She wore fluorescent pink jogging sweats and incandescent white sneakers. The neon sunglasses evidently were left at home.

"The cops returned Jackie's effects yesterday." She scooped a worn leather wallet out of her jacket pocket. "I told them to dump what was left of his clothes. This was the only other thing."

The wallet spoke of a life even more hollow than I'd imagined for Jackie. No pictures, no club cards, no pocket calendar. No credit cards, which was nothing short of amazing in this society. Just a drivers license with Jackie staring red-eyed at the DMV camera, a scrap of yellow paper with a phone number scribbled in faded ink, and lots of twenties and fifties.

"Nine hundred eighty dollars," Kate said as I riffled the stack with my thumb.

"Any idea where Jackie got this kind of money?" I said.

"Gambling."

"I'm pretty sure Jackie's gambling days were long over," I said.

"Okay, then he stole it," said Kate. "You don't think he made it lugging golf bags?"

I punched up the phone number. A recorded voice told me no such phone number existed in this area code. I copied the number onto a sheet of paper and slipped the scrap into the wallet.

"Whose is it?" said Kate.

"No one's."

"I mean the money. I haven't shown it to Mom."

"Did Jackie leave a will?"

"Yeah, right," said Kate.

"If not, it belongs to your mother."

"I was going to give it to her anyway. I just wanted to know."

"Did the cops ask you about the money?"

"They just made some comments about Jackie's luck running out. They knew him." She folded the wallet into her pocket. "This is four days now. Are you getting anywhere?"

"Somewhere."

"Does this help?"

"Maybe," I said. "How's your mother holding up?"

"Better than I am."

Kate trolled the silence for a moment, but discussing her problems with Max didn't interest me. She wasn't gone two minutes before Damiano called.

"This is the fourth day, Kieran. Are you getting anywhere with the Monsignor?"

"Sure, Leo, I'm getting somewhere."

Actually, I was getting nowhere fast.

I found MCC in the full swing of a summer morning. Shafts flashed on the practice range. Caddies swarmed in the yard. A parade of surreyed golf carts lined the path curving around the first tee. Everyone ignored me, until Georgina kissed me hello in the shop. Forget my prediction about seeing the last of the short skirts. Georgina wore a pleated white job that almost sucked the eyes out of my head. Across the room, Pete fared little better. He exaggerated a double-take and slipped out the door. The kid obviously was torn between gawking at us and blabbing what he'd already seen to the caddies.

Georgina walked me to the counter, where breakfast was neatly spread out on a red checked tablecloth. Grapefruit, oranges, bagels and cream cheese, fancy coffee ground in one of those Merchant Street specialty shops Limerick people like myself hardly could fathom.

"I found your present," she said.

"I'm not very good at that sort of thing."

"I think you're very good. When can I test it?"

"Tonight, unless I get hung up with something, which I'll make sure I won't."

Mornings after are never easy, even for someone of my age and experience. You guess and probe, reading the way she works the cream cheese with the knife, interpreting the swirls of cream in the coffee, trying to gauge the other's expectations while shielding your own. You hope for one of those movie scenes, where you both blurt out similar sentiments at the same time, then collapse into laughter over this silly posturing. Not so with Georgina. We ate in such relaxed silence I almost forgot my legal entanglements.

Pete returned but stayed at the far end of the shop, stacking sleeves of golf balls like building blocks and stealing glances beneath the bill of his baseball cap. By the time we finished breakfast, he slouched in a director's chair, thumbing a golf magazine with his ears pricked like a jackrabbit's. Georgina noticed.

"How about seven tonight?" she stage whispered.

"Seven's fine," I said.

She swept up everything into the tablecloth.

"Goodbye, Peter," she trilled.

"Uh, g'bye, Miss Newland," said Pete.

After she left the shop, he swaggered toward me with his thumbs hooked suggestively in the empty belt loops of his huge pants.

"Pete," I said, "don't ask."

He headed back to his chair with considerably less swagger.

"Oh yeah, that St. Clare guy called again," he said. "He sounds like one pissed off nerd."

I picked up the phone but called the local newspaper's sports desk. Randall Fisk was back from the field.

"I have no column planned about you," he said. "The PGA wants no bad press prior to the tournament, and we are honoring that request. You'll be omitted from the blurb bios of local pros in the field, and don't bother complaining. This isn't my doing."

"I don't give a damn about your column, Randall."

"You don't?"

"Well, I did. But now I don't. I have a question. Remember what you said about some people walking around here with smiles on their faces?"

"I said that? Why?"

"Don't play dumb, Randall. It was in connection with the fire, the same fire you said you believed I didn't set."

"Guess I'm in a distinct minority, huh?"

"Randall."

"Okay, Kieran, I remember. You want to know what I meant?"

"Bingo."

"Hold on." Fisk partly covered the phone with his hand while he snapped orders at someone. After some dramatic paper shuffling, he returned in whispers. "You remember E. Gerard Corrigan, right? Contact him. Ask him about the Doomsday Plan."

"You're kidding, right?"

"Like hell I am. Corrigan. The Doomsday Plan. He will want to talk to you. I can guarantee that."

Fisk clicked off, and I checked my morning schedule. The only blot on an otherwise clean slate was an eleven o'clock lesson with Mel Tucker.

"I have to go out for awhile," I told Pete. "Apologize to Tucker for me. Tell him he knows why I can't keep the lesson."

"How long will you be gone?" said Pete.

"No idea."

"So what do I say when St. Clare calls again?"

"Take a message," I said, then thought better. "Tell him I'll drop by his office when I have a free moment."

As I crossed the parking lot to my car, the caddie yard erupted in cheers. One caddie poked through the lilac bush and shoved a scorecard under my nose.

"What's this for?"

"Your autograph."

"You want my autograph. Why?"

" 'Cause, like, you're gonna play in the PGA."

I actually made the opening stroke of a K before I dragged the kid back through the bush.

"All of you, in a circle."

They gathered around, snickering, elbowing each other's ribs. I tried to formulate an extempore speech on how a man and a woman can be friends. Somehow, I decided this wouldn't play in the caddie yard.

"Guys, don't be jerks, okay?" was all I said.

The storybook intrigue of the Doomsday Plan didn't sound so ridiculous when I pulled off the Platinum Mile. E. Gerard Corrigan was an executive vice-president of an oil company. The Platinum Mile was the sobriquet for Westchester Avenue, a widely divided highway boasting more corporate headquarters than any other strip on Planet Earth. In keeping with pre-millennial skittishness, four guards met me at the gate to the visitor's parking lot. One asked me for I.D. and a brief explanation of my visit. Another eyeballed my car's undercarriage with a mirror while the last two planted themselves menacingly at the front bumper.

"Have a nice day," the first guard said when the security check was complete.

"You'll need a new exhaust manifold soon," said the guard with the mirror.

The visitor's parking lot was a good quarter mile from the closest corner of the immense glass-faced building. That was as the crow flies. On foot, I wended through a maze of concrete barriers sculpted to resemble modern art. Or maybe vice-versa.

Inside a three-story atrium thick with greenery, I waited in line to pass through a metal detector. Finally through that, a security guard again asked for an explanation of my visit, then directed me to a receptionist. Several intercom buzzes later, I learned Corrigan would not be free until four p.m.

I almost decided to park myself in the reception area and kill five hours reading splashy trade magazines. But I had another item on my Jackie Mack agenda that was more important than avoiding another run through the security gauntlet.

Fleetwood was a long way from the Platinum Mile, figuratively if not literally. It technically was a neighborhood of Mount Vernon, but evolved its own charming identity to prop up the values of its high-rise condos when urban blight struck at Mount Vernon's core. A. Theodore Lauretti's office was on the ground floor of a Tudor-styled brick behemoth. The extent of his security system was a fish-eye lens in the door and a sign directing you to knock before entering. I did exactly that.

"He's gone to lunch already," said his secretary.

"Good. You're the one I wanted to see."

She dropped her jaw, playfully aghast at the interest of a total stranger. She was pretty in the face and thick in the waist, cutely intellectual in glasses even as she worked a wad of gum around her mouth. I'd felt a spark when I talked with her on the phone yesterday, and felt it again as she closed her paperback romance over a tasseled book mark and dropped it into her desk drawer. Not a physical spark, more like the immediate apprehension that our personalities clicked.

Her name was Angie. She offered me a chair behind her desk rather than the cheap naugahyde bench reserved for waiting clients. A good start, I thought. Maybe she felt the same spark. I fanned it with a humorously accurate account of my meeting with A. Teddy. She laughed right through a lunch delivery I gallantly paid for.

"So what's the big deal with this Jackie Mack?" she said.

"Have you heard about the fire in Milton?"

"Oh yeah. You're the guy they arrested."

"You knew? But Lauretti—"

"He doesn't read the papers like I do. He thinks he just absorbs his smarts from the atmosphere like a sponge. I knew it was you yesterday. How many Kieran Lenahans can there be?"

"Do you think I—"

"Did it?" Angie popped the top of her soda and spit her gum into the wax paper wrapping of her turkey sandwich. "Buster, if I thought you did it, would I let you in here?"

"Thanks, Angie," I said. If my self-help crusade failed, maybe Willie Junior could dig up twelve people like her.

Ripping a healthy bite out of the sandwich, she motioned me into A. Teddy's office.

"Know what I don't like about him?" she said, clearing a spot on his desk and opening his diary. "Lots of things, but mostly his ties. So boring. You can tell a lot about a guy by his ties, especially his sense of humor. Gee, you know what I just realized? My husband doesn't even own a tie. That tells you something, too.

"Jackie came in here within the last two months. Do you have trouble remembering when things happen? You think it's a week ago and it turns out it's a month. That's why I said two. Here goes."

She pointed at Jackie Mack's name, written into the last slot of the day almost two months earlier.

"Do you know what they discussed?"

"Oh sure," said Angie. "Jackie Mack was Teddy's first client. That was a long time before I worked for him, back in my husband's glory days when he had a job. Jackie stuck Teddy for expenses, like he told you. Teddy doesn't forget something like that. If I borrow a quarter for bus fare home, I'd better put a quarter on his desk first thing the next morning, or I'll hear about it."

The spark I felt for Angie quickly dimmed in the chatter. "Did Teddy call for Jackie to come in?"

"Oh no. Jackie called for the appointment. Teddy thought Jackie finally wanted to pay him back. But Jackie wanted Teddy to draw up a will."

"Did Teddy do it?"

"That Teddy's such a hypocrite," said Angie. "He's mad at Jackie for those expenses, but he likes to hear himself talk. He told Jackie so much about probate, Jackie decided he didn't need a will."

Late afternoon found me waiting in the afteroom to E. Gerard Corrigan's major league corner office. Outside the smoky glass, rush hour traffic choked the Platinum Mile in both directions. Beyond the highway, a gap in the trees opened on a public golf course with three foursomes stacked up on each tee. People, people everywhere. Corrigan's secretary had twice assured me himself would spare a few minutes. The only question was when, petroleum being such an unpredictable industry.

Several pro-am pairings had fueled a superficially pleasant friendship between Corrigan and me. He played a passable game, sprinkled with blatant attempts at aping the mannerisms of certain Tour professionals. The caddies called him a fendo, which doesn't appear in the dictionary but fits his oblivious egotism on a non-verbal level. He served on the executive committee for several years before tapping out his MCC bond and joining the Westchester Country Club.

A red sun hung just above the treetops when Corrigan stopped bellowing into the telephone and his secretary invited me inside. Corrigan was a tall man with a bulky torso balanced precariously on legs gimpy from Cornell football and five knee operations in the days before arthroscopic surgery. Sunburn crusted his face and brightened two wings of gray hair sweeping over his ears. He brushed aside the preliminaries with a quick handshake, then half dove onto a sofa.

"When I heard about your arrest, I considered phoning your attorney to volunteer testimony on your behalf. But I was called out of town, and when I returned Randall Fisk told me you were on the way."

"So you know I'm here about the Doomsday Plan."

"Pretty wacky, huh?" Corrigan said with a laugh. "Proves you better watch what you say in jest. Someone might take you seriously."

"It was your idea?"

"It was my joke. Unfortunately, the joke may have been on me. And on you." Corrigan rolled until he sat upright, gingerly lifting each knee with his hands and placing it down again. "Most of the committee's acts are secret, you know that. But it's no secret the committee's basically divided between those with heady ideas for improving the club and those who want to preserve the status quo, especially the membership fees. I thought the place could and should be improved, and with the improvements it might be possible to attract a professional event. Not the main Tour, more like the Ladies or the Seniors. The first step was to renovate the pro shop complex. You're familiar with the resistance to that idea."

"I was part of it," I said.

"I heard about them dragging you up there last fall," said Corrigan. "Never would have happened if I'd still been there. Anyway, at one of our subcommittee meetings—that's what we called our faction—I suggested how convenient an Act of God might be. No one laughed. Before long, we were speaking in hypothetical terms about how, if an Act of God occurred, we could keep the club running while a new building was constructed."

"You planned this?" I said.

"We talked about it. At least, all I ever intended was talk. Winter was the best time to pull it off. Your shop inventory would be low. Fewer carts would be garaged because Boland would have retired some of the fleet and not replaced them yet. The only sticking point was the monkey house. Someone suggested we prevail upon Eduardo Rojas to move his workers to new quarters. But no one volunteered for that assignment. Eduardo can be very scary."

"What were the exact details of the plan?"

Corrigan grinned sheepishly. "House your pro shop in a trailer in the auxiliary parking lot. Switch to gas carts, which would be penned in the grassy area behind the starter shack. Let the restaurant workers fend for themselves. Put up with minor inconveniences like no club storage facilities. Promise a vastly modern replacement complex that would make the disaster seem worthwhile." He paused to re-angle his knees. "I can't tell you who authored these details."

"You don't need to," I said.

I stopped at my driveway without turning in. Georgina's car was parked across the street. The sight should have sent my blood flowing south. Instead, it set off a surge of adrenalin.

I punched my car into gear and headed for Poningo Point, where I weighed my options while clambering over the large stones of the small public quay. Did I trust Georgina, the woman whose bed I shared but who was little more than a familiar stranger as late as one week ago? Did I believe Corrigan, a man with no logical agenda, hidden or otherwise? A man willing to stand up for me in court, but a man who, unfortunately, had been Randall Fisk's contact on the MCC executive committee.

I returned home with a decision. My apartment throbbed with a life I hadn't felt since Deirdre decamped. Music on the stereo, water rushing in the kitchen sink, saucepans gurgling on the stove. Thick spicy air. In the kitchen, Georgina chopped vegetables on a cutting board.

"Hi, doll, you're late," she said cheerily. "I saw you pull up before. Did you forget the wine?"

Seeing her wrapped suggestively in an apron, I almost changed my tack. But she caught the expression on my face, and the knife stopped.

"No I didn't," I said.

She looked me up and down. Not with her usual radar sweep. More like she searched for some clue to my attitude and, finding none, almost lost her nerve.

"I guess not," she said, and wiped her hands on a towel.

"I needed to think," I said.

She sat on the living room sofa, her knees pressed tightly together, her arms grasped across her stomach.

"Getting arrested changes your perspective," I said, pacing with the coffee table between us. "Things I thought were odd but plausible now look suspicious."

"Things about me?" she said.

I swallowed back a sarcastic laugh. "I was impressed with the way you got the club up and running so quickly after the fire."

"That's my job, Kieran. If we had to wait for the men on the committee, you would be selling golf balls out of the trunk of your car, and the membership would be playing out of Sunday bags."

"So you say," I said. "And what about Jackie Mack? You attended his wake because he was a part of our country club community."

"He was. He caddied for you in tournaments. He was to caddy for you in the PGA. I knew what he meant to you."

"What Jackie meant to me is my damn business," I said. "You know, when Jackie got killed I worried about what it meant to me. I thought I was being selfish. After all, Jackie was dead. But now that selfishness may be the one thing to save me."

"What are you getting at, Kieran?"

"Gerry Corrigan told me about the Doomsday Plan."

Georgina took that in for a second, then forced a laugh. "The Doomsday Plan was a joke. He must have told you that."

"He said he was joking when he tossed off the idea of an Act of God, but other people took it seriously."

"I wasn't one of them."

"No? Prove it."

She sputtered. I cut her off.

"My own caddie set that fire. I know that, and I promise you I don't give a damn where the trail leads."

Years with Deirdre conditioned me to fireworks. But as T.S. Eliot wrote, the world ends not with a bang but with a whimper. So do little parts of it.

Georgina slipped off her apron, folded it neatly, and laid it over the back of the sofa. She turned off all the gas jets, slung her duffle bag over her shoulder, and walked to the door. She said only two words, more in sadness than anger or defiance.

"You're nuts."

I sat on the top of my apartment stairs and spooned boned chicken and wine sauce directly out of a pan. Down below, my landlord tended a patch of garden lining the foundation of his house. Working under a floodlight, he loosened dirt, pulled weeds, tied broken plants to tiny stakes. More than once, he leaned on his shovel and cursed the men who wrecked his daughter's flowers. Meanwhile, television light played against the shade of the girl's bedroom window. In a better mood, I'd have laughed at the irony.

Georgina's exit left me more than just lonely. I'd been so certain of my accusation that I failed to run the Doomsday Plan to its logical conclusion. If the committee faction hired Jackie to torch the building, did it pay him the grand he carried in his wallet the day he died? More important, did it pay someone to push him from the platform to cover its tracks? Once again, the Doomsday Plan sounded as ludicrous as when Randall Fisk first uttered its name. And that presented a new possibility. Maybe I was nuts.

Kate showed up a few minutes after my landlord killed the floodlight. She paused at the foot of the driveway, searching the shadows until she caught sight of me and hurried in.

"Great, I need someone to drink with," I said.

She drew up on a middle step, and I went inside. The aroma of Georgina's stillborn meal lingered. I dumped the rest into the garbage, twisted the plastic liner tight, and switched on the exhaust fan before lifting two beers from the refrigerator. Kate now sat on the top step, her legs crossed and her arms gripped across her waist. She moved just enough to allow me to squeeze beside her, took a slug, and held the bottle in front of her face, staring through the shiny silver label.

"When we were young," she said, "we had a secret place in the basement where we stashed our prized possessions. Jackie used a cigar box. I used a box from one of Mom's pillbox hats. We'd wrap our treasures in newspaper, close them in the boxes, and cram the boxes into cubbyholes above the rafters. I don't know what made me look there today."

She handed me a bank book. In the thin light, I could see the account was opened by Ian MacEwan in trust for Una MacEwan with right of survivorship. The balance was twenty-five grand and change. The deposits, of differing amounts but at regular monthly intervals, ran back eighteen months.

"I didn't tell her yet," said Kate.

"Fair enough," I said. "No rush. She's entitled to the money without any hassles."

"What does it mean?"

"I don't know exactly," I said, though I knew enough to wish Kate had shown me the bank book before I opened my big mouth to Georgina.

Kate worked the bank book into her hip pocket. She lifted her beer bottle and traced a finger across the sweaty glass.

"Can you be so wrong about someone for so long?" she said.

"Happens all the time."

"I realized the other day how much I'd grown to hate him," she said. "Not because of the stupid things he did but because he made nothing of himself, and because I was just a simple 'I do' away from a very similar life.

"I'm the daughter. I'm the one who should take care of Mom in her old age. That's the natural order of things. But I went off with Max and hoped Jackie would take over, and when he didn't I resented him. Now I see he was taking care of her all along."

She drifted off into her own thoughts, scraping small bits of the beer label into spitballs and flicking them into the dark. I'd been to bed twice with Georgina, had visions, at least until late, of constructing a relationship with her. Yet right now I felt a deeper understanding of this young woman who had been only a name and a face in the Limerick gallery. I wondered if we sensed a shared Limerick experience, growing up in a working-class neighborhood where perspectives rarely extended into the future. We weren't exactly street urchins as kids. We didn't run around singing songs from *Oliver* or panhandling shoppers on Merchant Street. In fact, we thought everyone lived as we lived until we grew out of St. Gregory's elementary school and mucked in with the rich kids in junior high.

Kate crossed over by marriage. I crossed over by profession. But something clung to us, like the peat stains ground into the pores of our bogmen forebears.

A moment descended when Kate gently placed the bottle on a step and hugged her knees. I knew I could take her into my arms, pull her tiny body close to mine. I knew she would respond, and we'd both believe that tonight we somehow deserved each other. But the moment dissipated, and I knew we both felt relieved.

"I better get back," she said.

I walked her home and watched from the fence post. Inside the blazing living room, she unfolded a thin blanket from the sofa arm and covered her mother sleeping in a chair.

CHAPTER
12

Una MacEwan phoned at seven the following morning.

"Oh, thank you, Mr. Lenahan. Thank you, thank you. I'll never forget what you did."

"What did I do?"

"Stop being so modest. The Monsignor's saying a funeral mass for Jackie at nine."

It took a moment for the news to sink in, like rain on hardpan.

"That's great," I said. "Is Kate there?"

"Yes, she is. I knew you would get my Jackie buried. People doubted you, but I didn't."

Kate took the line.

"What the hell is going on?" I said.

"You didn't do this?" she said.

"Between you and me, I'm surprised as hell."

"The Monsignor didn't explain," she said in a conspiratorial whisper. "Sorry, I have to go. Mom wants to make lots more calls."

I hit the hookswitch and rang Pete first. He answered groggily, geared for the late shift. I told him to get his ass to the club and open up. I'd be in about noon. Maybe.

Leo Damiano picked up halfway through the first ring.

"He got me out of bed at six," he said, meaning the Monsignor. "You cut it pretty close, Kieran. I was going to bury Jackie today no matter what. Now I need this line clear. I'm trying to round up pallbearers."

The inside of St. Gregory's Church was laid out in typical Renaissance cathedral fashion, though downsized to village proportions. At five minutes to nine, the church was quiet enough I could hear the organist rustling papers in the choir loft. A girl wearing a hooded cassock reached a burning wick to the altar candles. I slid into the last pew on the extreme right side, an inconspicuous few steps from the rear door. About a dozen people sat or knelt toward the front. A few caddies. Mel Tucker, sitting stiffly erect. Some older women from the neighborhood, the type who attended the eight o'clock mass daily, then hung out if a funeral followed. Max Ritchie at the extreme left, head whirling toward the rear at the slightest noise. None of them noticed me.

A bell rang. Four altar servers led the Monsignor from the sacristy. They fanned out across the altar, genuflected toward the tabernacle, and walked slowly up the center aisle as the organ droned dolorous chords. The coffin appeared at the rear of the aisle. Damiano's pallbearers lowered it onto a gurney and draped it with the same white satin as the Monsignor's vestments. The organ died away. Two of the servers flanked the coffin, their candles guttering. The Monsignor opened a prayer book, the thick pages whispering as he flicked thumb and forefinger. He said a prayer in sing-song Gregorian chant. Then the organ rose again as the entire procession returned to the altar.

Una, leaning on Kate's arm, followed the coffin at a slow limp. Both women wore black, as did a few ladies trailing behind them. They took seats in the first pew. The Monsignor mounted the altar and spread his arms. The mass began, and I ducked out to the rectory.

Gerdie Maxwell fixed me with a stare that was especially harsh for all her usual meekness. One hand held the door like a shield, the other pinched a black cardigan to her throat. She cocked an ear as if listening to the muffled organ music from inside the church.

"The mass is on," she said, and flung the door against my foot.

"I need to know what happened," I said.

"You've got what you wanted. Isn't that enough?"

"I need to know why."

"Oh, you do? There's precious little sympathy for you in Limerick. I remember Mickey Byrne as an altar boy."

"You remember me, too," I said. She pushed the door again, this time with considerably less force. "Gerdie, you've seen more in this parish than anyone. You've seen sinners go to heaven and the pious go to hell. You know things aren't always what they seem. Was it a man in a limousine? A tough guy with a distinguished accent?"

Gerdie chewed her tongue, then slowly stepped aside. I shouldered through the narrow opening and closed the door behind me before she could change her mind. The thick cabbage air smelled oddly comforting.

"The first of them came during supper yesterday," she said. "A skinny man with a mustache and a big woman with a black hat. They wanted to see the Monsignor, and when I asked why they said they were on the platform when Jackie was killed. I brought them into the sitting room, and the Monsignor spoke with them after supper. They told him they saw the accident. Two boys were jostling each other and brushed up against Jackie as the train pulled in. The boys ran, and everyone on the platform told the police Jackie jumped to protect them. They are illegals."

"The Monsignor believed this?" I said.

"Not at first. He asked why they came forward with this story now. They said they regretted the pain their lie caused, and wanted to tell the truth before it was too late. The Monsignor asked them if anyone pressured them to speak. They said no. He described you, and they told him you questioned them at the train station. They thought you were an immigration agent and lied to you, too.

"The Monsignor believed them enough to want to speak to the boys himself. The man made a phone call, and about two hours later, a limousine pulled up outside. The two boys came in along with the man you described."

"Luis Augusto," I said.

Gerdie nodded. "The Monsignor asked the boys what happened. Mr. Augusto translated because the boys spoke only a little English. They told the exact story the man and woman told. They knocked into Jackie, and ran because they were scared. Some of their friends and other families had been caught by the immigration service and deported. They didn't want the same to happen to them and their families."

"Did you get the boys' names, addresses, anything like that?"

"We don't care about those things here," said Gerdie. "The Monsignor listened to the boys and looked into their souls. He took them into the church and heard their confessions and absolved them of their sins. Then everyone climbed into the limousine and drove away."

"How old were the boys?"

"They gave their ages as fifteen," said Gerdie. "If you ask me, they looked more about twelve."

I made it back to my pew before the Monsignor wound up his

canned eulogy for the dear departed Jackie Mack. After the mass ended, Damiano arranged the half dozen cars of the funeral procession in front of the church. I fell behind Mel Tucker's Lincoln as the procession wound through Limerick to pass the MacEwan house, joined up with Merchant Street at the north end of Milton village, then climbed the steep incline to the hilltop of St. Mary's Cemetery. We idled while the pallbearers carried the coffin to the gravesite. Then Damiano waved us all to follow. I wanted to hook up with Tucker, but he latched on to Una's left arm while Kate hugged her right. Good thing because the hill was steep and the shaded grass still slick with dew.

Damiano handed out single flowers to each of us while the Monsignor droned the burial liturgy. The Monsignor must have buried two thousand people in his career, but his voice sounded especially mechanical. Maybe it was my imagination, I thought, feeling charitable under the circumstances. But when he ended the prayer abruptly and stood with his eyes closed, I definitely felt he'd rather be elsewhere.

Each of the mourners tossed a flower onto the coffin's burnished metal lid. I'd done this more times than I cared to remember, and the grim finality of this simple act never failed to choke me. Not today. For me, this wasn't the end of Jackie Mack.

Moving down toward the cars, I tried to reach Tucker again. This time, Una grabbed my arm. At that exact moment, her foot slipped from under her, and Kate and I wrestled to keep her upright. Finally balanced, we baby-stepped down the incline while Una showered me with profuse thanks. Meanwhile, Max leaned against the hood of his Volvo, his hands thrust deep into the pockets of his blazer, his head bent but his eyes watching us. Kate noticed, too.

"I'd better talk to him," she said, after we deposited Una in the back seat of the limo.

"Right."

"I hate this stuff," she said.

For a moment, that same feeling from last night coursed between us like a puff of breeze that raises the fine hairs on your skin.

"Be smart, okay?"

"Okay," she said.

Brilliant advice from Mr. All-Thumbs.

From a rocky outcrop above the fourth fairway, Mel Tucker's foursome looked like a lost safari. One golfer tangled with the branches of a bramble bush, trying to fashion a stance so he could flail at the ball lodged against the trunk. Another crawled on all fours, groping through the knee-deep waste area left of the fairway for his ball. A third straddled a drainage ditch and chopped at salad-sized lilypads. Not four holes in the books, and the caddies already dragged ass.

Tucker himself stood alone in the middle of the fairway, his ball resting on the slope of a knoll. He lifted a club from his golf bag and addressed the ball as if he'd forgotten everything I ever taught him about playing from a sidehill-uphill lie. He held the club long instead of choking down on the grip. He aimed straight for the green instead of compensating for an uphill lie's tendency to throw your shot left. And he played the ball in the middle of his stance instead of up toward his front foot. Falling off balance on his downswing, he sliced a veal cutlet of a divot from the turf. The ball wobbled like a wounded duck, nosediving into the drainage ditch only five feet from the other golfer, who shook his fist and cursed at Tucker for not yelling *Fore*.

I kicked off the brake and let the cart roll down the hill. This didn't seem the best time to bother Tucker. But from the looks of this foursome, the most propitious moment might be when all were safely drunk at the bar. I couldn't wait that long.

I caught Tucker just as his caddie fished his golf ball out of the stagnant slime.

"Sorry sight this morning, eh, Kieran?" said Tucker. A dead stub of a cigar bobbed in the corner of his mouth, ashes shaking loose and leaving thin dark trails as they tumbled down his belly. "No one ever did explain to me why that Monsignor fella decided Jackie didn't kill himself after all. You must still be pleading cases like a good ole Philadelphia lawyer."

"I doubt I did anything that mattered."

"Now don't be shy, Kieran. Mrs. MacEwan positively gushed about you. You can take the credit."

I detected an edge in his voice, like he was trying hard to be downhome friendly.

Back up the fairway, the crawling golfer suddenly evolved into *Australopithecus* and yelled to get our attention. He steadied himself, jerked back the club, and flailed a downswing. Grass and mud exploded while the ball nudged along the ground maybe a yard.

"Good," said Tucker. "I'm already two hundred down to three guys who swing like goddam rednecks beating their dogs. Now you're not here to watch this piss poor display of golfing prowess, are you, Kieran?"

"I want to talk to you about Jackie," I said.

"Didn't we just bury him?" Tucker wiped a film of sweat from his face and neck with a handkerchief. Then he rummaged through his golf bag for a can of bug repellant and sprayed his neck, arms, and grayblond mane. "You and I ain't talked this much in years. That what my granny used to say about death bringing the living together?"

Someone shouted, "Heads up!" A shaft flashed in the dark of the trees, and a ball curved lazily into the fairway well short of us. The golfer probing the drainage ditch lost his balance. One leg plunged thigh-deep into the muck. He staggered onto the fairway grass, shaking his muddy pant leg. Tucker's caddie convulsed while Tucker himself frowned, unamused.

"What about Jackie?" he said curtly.

"Did he work for anyone besides you?"

"As a caddie?"

"I mean a real job."

"Kieran," he said, "can you please tell me why in the hell a man with your legal troubles is so damn interested in Jackie this and Jackie that?"

"Jackie's mother depended on him for support, and she's hoping he worked another job with some kind of death benefit."

"She doesn't know what her own son was doing for work?"

"Makes no sense to me, either, Mel."

Another shot whistled, hit a tree limb with a solid *thock,* and bounded backward toward the drainage ditch.

"Okay, what makes her think Jackie had another job?" said Tucker.

"Nothing concrete. But Jackie's sister tells me when their father left, Jackie tried holding several jobs at once, like a young man of the house. His mother always stopped him. So I thought, if he had another job, he might not have told Una."

"What kind of job you thinkin' he had?" said Tucker.

"Anything that didn't interfere with his days. Night shift work somewhere. Hell, maybe he'd be covered by a life insurance policy."

"Far as I know, I was his only employer. And my caddies don't get life insurance."

Tucker wiped the slime from his golf ball and dropped it onto the turf two club lengths behind the ditch. He fingered the six-iron, silently calculating distance and conditions before yanking the seven-iron from his bag. His caddie sighed, dragging the bag away and rolling his eyes. I don't know if Tucker were angry with the match, trying to impress me, or just plain stupid. He was 140 uphill yards from a deep green with a deceptively strong breeze quartering into his face. A career shot might catch the front edge of the green. But his signature flail skied the ball straight up, where the breeze slapped it into a sand trap.

"Goddam," he said. "Maybe I should join G.A."

———————

Another evening of practice down the tubes, but I needed to catch Demo Mike in the narrow window of opportunity between the beach club and the fire house. I staked out the Michaelides home and intercepted Demo bumping his balloon-tired Schwinn down the block.

"Still at large, huh, Kieran?" he said.

"Very funny. Do you have any free time?"

"What for?"

I explained, without going too deeply, that I needed to locate an address through a phone number, but didn't have the area code. If he had the time to hack into . . .

"Hack?" said Demo. "What the hell Stone Age are you from? You don't need to hack that kind of information."

Up in his room, Demo rolled his chair along a bank of computer equipment, throwing a switch here, tapping a keystroke there, while brightly colored windows of utter nonsense exploded on a monitor screen.

"Watch out," he said.

I moved my elbow just as a tiny drawer popped out of a sleek white unit.

"Here." Demo winged me a plastic case. "Lay that in."

I pried a silver compact disc out of the case and placed it on the tray. The tray instantly retracted, and speakers wrapped around the monitor beeped in code.

"That CD lists every phone number in the country," said Demo. "It's an old piece of piracy, but good enough for us."

Since Jackie fell from the westbound platform that morning, I told Demo to skip Connecticut and concentrate on New York City, Long Island, and northern New Jersey. He quickly matched numbers in three of the five area codes, each a private residence. I copied the addresses on a pad and started making calls while Demo expanded his search into upstate New York, southern Jersey, and eastern Pennsylvania.

A woman answered the phone in the Chelsea section of Manhattan.

"Jackie Mack, Ian MacEwan," she slurred. "Nah, I don't know either of them. You wanta come visit, and we'll talk about this over a bone?"

A man in Deer Park, Long Island, cut me off before I finished my spiel.

"I've just come home from work," he said as a baby howled in the background. "My wife's gone out to her job, I'm trying to feed the kids, and you're interrupting me for this?"

A man in Ridgewood, New Jersey, assumed the synthesized voice of a recording as soon as he didn't recognize mine.

"I'm sorry. I do not accept telephone solicitations. Please remove me from your list."

"Kieran," said Demo, "I have something here."

I peered over his shoulder. Highlighted on the screen was something called Bookie's, with an address on Broadway in Saratoga Springs, New York. I punched up the number on Demo's phone.

"Bookie's Bookstore, good evening," said a friendly baritone.

"Excuse me?" I said.

"Bookie's Bookstore, may I help you?" he said, no less friendly. Ah, the pace and charms of the upstate world. Ask downstate store clerks to repeat themselves, and you'll find yourself talking into dead air.

"I'm interested in a Jackie Mack," I said. "Sometimes he goes by the name Ian MacEwan."

"What about him?" said the voice, its friendliness leaching out.

"I want to know why he was carrying your phone number, and if he was headed your way last—"

The phone disconnected. I tried again immediately, but no one picked up. Five minutes later, ten minutes later, same thing.

"A Citgo station near Pittsburgh has the same number," said Demo.

"I found what I'm looking for," I said. "You can shut down now."

Judge Inglisi lived up county, a world away from Milton's tame suburbia. Deer ravaged his tomato patch until he hung panty hose stuffed with human hair from trees along his property line. "Japanese guy collects it from barbershops and sells it door to door," he told me one afternoon, juggling three ripe fat boys with one hand. At dusk, coyotes roamed stealthily through the shadows, ears erect, long tails sweeping the ground behind them. At night, aircraft swooped low and loud, following a trail of runway lights across the reservoir to the county airport.

The Judge greeted me with a sardonic grin, as if he suspected the reason for my visit and planned to amuse himself by acting crochety. He led me to his den, where empty beer cans ringed an armchair and a portly golfer stopped in mid-swing on a six-foot video screen.

"Is that you?" I said.

"Billy Casper, wiseguy. And we're going around at a record pace."

He dug a video game control out of the seat cushion and pressed a button. Casper resumed his swing and cranked the ball skyward. The view shifted to the fairway, the ball bounding past scenery I recognized as one of the cliff holes at Pebble Beach. A readout at the bottom of the screen registered distance and wind direction. The Judge froze the image, fished a beer out of a cooler, and dropped himself into the chair.

"I heard you stuck your face into Jackie Mack's burial problem. Nice work," he said, not meaning a compliment.

"I'm glad I did. Otherwise I wouldn't have found out Jackie torched my shop."

The Judge laughed. He re-animated Billy Casper, who hit a high sweeping hook into the Pacific surf before I wrestled for the control and killed the screen. I quickly told the Judge about Pete giving Jackie a key to the cart garage, the mementoes that disappeared from the shop the day before the fire and reappeared under Jackie's mattress, and the money in Jackie's wallet. The Judge worked himself forward in the chair until his elbows rested on his knees while I ticked through all the people with motives for hiring an arsonist.

"Plausible," the Judge said when I finished. "Especially since Jackie carried the going rate for arsonists."

"But then it gets complicated," I said. "Jackie had an obsession with providing for his mother. Problem was, he couldn't stick with any job, and he had a bad gambling habit. Then something happened. About eighteen months ago he stopped gambling and opened a bank account in trust for Una."

"What a dutiful son," said the Judge.

"Dutiful enough to sock away twenty-five grand."

"Hell, he didn't make that caddying for you."

"Or for Mel Tucker, either," I said. "He had another source of income no one knew about, not even Tucker, who probably knew him best."

"Professional arsonist?" said the Judge.

"The deposits are too regular for that," I said. "I also learned he consulted a lawyer a couple of months ago about a will."

"But he wouldn't need a will if all he left his mother was the joint bank account," said the Judge. "Unless he had other types of assets."

"Or wanted to leave something to someone not covered by intestacy laws."

"Girlfriend?"

"None anyone's mentioned. No one showed up at the wake or funeral."

The Judge lowered himself into a sumo squat, thinking.

"Jackie was headed somewhere when he died," I said. "We had that practice round scheduled, but he suddenly changed plans."

"He was on the run."

"From something, or maybe to something," I said. "No one knows where he was going that morning."

"But you do, right?"

I told the Judge about tracing the phone number in Jackie's wallet.

"A goddam bookstore in Saratoga?" he said.

"I asked about Jackie, and the guy on the other end clammed up immediately, even though I could have been asking about an author."

"Maybe he thought it was a prank. Kids always call bookstores and ask about nonexistent authors. Did it myself as a kid." The Judge squirmed back onto the chair. "You haven't told this to Willie Junior, right?"

"Do I look nuts to you?"

The Judge reached for the phone and speed-dialed his law clerk.

"It's me. Adjourn everything I have on tomorrow's calendar. I don't give a damn. Tell them anything you want." He hung up and turned on the video screen. "You stay here tonight. I want to make an early start in the morning."

"You believe me?" I said.

"Believing you isn't the point. Letting you out of the county while I'm on the hook for your bail bond is."

Judge Inglisi and I are incompatible fliers. He likes rolls, loops, kamikaze dives toward the reservoir, touch-and-goes on vacant stretches of interstates. I dig gentle ascents, trim flight attitudes, shallow approaches toward wide runways. He constantly pushes the envelope of the Cessna he shares with nine other suburban Eddie Rickenbackers. I prefer the middle of the envelope, safely sealed.

"No tricks today," he said as we climbed into a clear sky still streaked with the rosy fingers of dawn.

"Why not?" I said warily.

"Too long a flight."

For once, he delivered. He banked northwest over the reservoir, banked again at the Hudson, and traced the river northward at 5,000 feet. We didn't speak. He squinted against the sun and occasionally acknowledged radio chatter with his version of a Southern drawl. I took in the bends of the narrowing river, the old gray-green heads of the Catskills, the distant hint of the Adirondacks. The hum of the engines relaxed my muscles like a masseuse. I didn't mind the Judge ignoring me. We certainly couldn't talk for two hours without his haranguing me about Deirdre.

He put us down at the Saratoga County Airport. After re-fueling for the return flight, we scared up a ride in a Ford pick-up, circa 1959, rather than wait in line for a taxi. The Judge pulled rank and climbed into the passenger seat. I clung to the sideboard in the back as the truck rattled around hairpin country turns.

"Know anything called Bookie's?" the Judge yelled over the rush of wind.

"Where is it?" screamed the farmer.

"Broadway."

"Never heard of it. But I'll get you to Broadway."

The farmer dropped us at an old red-brick fire house at the top of a wide avenue. We took a moment to orient ourselves, then headed south. With racing season in full swing, the sidewalks were crowded for the early hour. Lots of women in sundresses and men in white loafers. Cars tooled along Broadway, the fancy ones of the successful and the crates of the hopeful and the insane. After one block, the Judge started bitching. Another block and the post office presented me with a brilliant idea. I left the Judge on the sidewalk and asked a postal clerk about Bookie's.

"Across the street and half a block down," she said.

The Judge and I crossed Broadway and spotted a wooden signboard. A pair of shifty eyes stared over the top of an open book. The S in Bookie's was a dollar sign.

"You said Jackie beat his gambling problem?" the Judge huffed as he struggled to keep up with my pace.

"The weight of the evidence points to it."

"Sure is a weird place to visit if he did."

Bookie's was open, but not exactly doing a land office business. A clerk with wiry red hair pulled back into a ponytail from a wide patch of forehead sat on a stool behind the cash register. He had one leg raised, an open book on that knee. A rock singer moaned Dylan-esque on the stereo. The Judge and I faked intense interest in the new fiction shelf.

"I think he's our man," I whispered.

"How do you know?"

"He looks like someone Jackie knew."

"Why? Because he looks like an imbecile?"

I couldn't explain Bear Burkowski's story about Jackie's G.A. sponsor, but I'd have bet the store clerk was the same man. One sure way to tell. I walked up to the register and introduced the Judge and myself as tourists up from New York City way. When the clerk extended his hand for a friendly upstate handshake, I saw the jagged scar between his thumb and forefinger. A name tag decorated with the same shifty eyes as the signboard identified him as Al Sabo.

"Are you gentlemen interested in any special reading material?" he said.

"I'm interested in Jackie Mack," I said.

Sabo's hand retracted immediately. I could see his mind work as if his cranium were transparent, connecting my face with the phone call.

"Who the hell are you guys?" he said.

"Friends of Jackie," I said. "You heard about his death?"

"Yeah, I heard. What's it to you?"

"I'm a golf pro, and Jackie was my tournament caddie. This is *Judge* Inglisi. We're taking an interest in Jackie's death. We think he was coming here when he died."

"What makes you think that?" said Sabo.

"You sponsored Jackie at G.A." I said. "You had a fight with him outside Philly Casino's diner the week before the Super Bowl. That's how you got that scar. Want me to go on?"

The front door jingled. Two well-dressed middle-aged ladies walked in, chirping merrily and greeting Sabo by name. Sabo forced a grin, then returned his attention to us.

"Jackie and I weren't friends," he said. "But we kept in touch."

"About what?"

"G.A. matters."

"Didn't he beat his gambling habit?"

"You don't ever beat it," said Sabo. "And G.A. deals with other types of risky behavior, not just gambling."

"He came up here to test his resolve?" said the Judge.

"I'm here to test my resolve." Sabo raised his head to check on the ladies. "Seeing these summer people is a disincentive for me."

"Oh," said the Judge, pouring a paragraph of irony into a single syllable. He hated words like *disincentive*.

"Did he visit regularly?" I said.

"He liked it here," said Sabo.

"The spring waters," said the Judge.

"Any idea why someone might kill him?" I said.

"I didn't know he was killed," said Sabo "I thought—"

"How did you find out about it? None of his immediate family knows about you, or about Jackie coming here. I don't think it made the local papers."

"Some G.A. people phoned me," said Sabo.

The Judge scowled. He treated every conversation like testimony, and couldn't conceal his impatience with evasions. He thumbed a magazine from a rack and made a big show of reading. One of the ladies looked his way. He grinned, patting some of the scruff he called hair.

"Why would Jackie carry a grand in cash?" I said.

"Not to gamble," said Sabo.

"Maybe somebody killed Jackie to keep him from leaving the fold," piped the Judge from behind his magazine.

Sabo tensed angrily. Even I thought this remark went over the top. I kicked the Judge in the shin.

"How did he stash away twenty-five grand in the last year and a half?" I said.

"No idea," said Sabo, but for the first time he seemed genuinely surprised.

The ladies stepped up to the counter with a few splashy coffee table books. The Judge dragged me out of earshot.

"The guy's a liar, and there's nothing we can do about it," he said. "This is a waste of time."

"Let's wait until they're gone. I think I just got a hook in him."

The ladies paid. Sabo's eyes followed them out of the store, then glazed over as if he were lost in thought. A moment later, he snapped out of his reverie.

"Two or three blocks down Broadway, you'll find Congress Park," he said. "Take the footpath at the public library and follow it around to the Trask Memorial. Sit on the stone bench and wait. You get lucky, you'll know why Jackie was heading here."

"Lucky?" said the Judge.

"Be sure to sit on the bench," said Sabo, unaffected by the sarcasm.

I hustled the Judge onto the sidewalk before he could open his mouth.

"Another unreconstructed hippie from your era," he said. "Sit on the stone bench. Guy's nuts."

"Let's give it a try."

"You believe this shit?"

"What other choice do we have, and, yes, I believe him."

"I'm getting too old for this," said the Judge.

We ambled down Broadway and found the Trask Memorial without any trouble, except for the Judge bitching about the walk. The memorial itself was a bronze winged woman with arms held aloft. Water brimmed in a basin at her feet, then cascaded gently into a rectangular reflecting pool.

"What now?" said the Judge, lowering himself onto the stone bench opposite the pool.

"We wait," I said.

The Judge unlaced his sneakers, peeled off his black socks, and massaged feet as white as marble. I shifted upwind. Three kids on the footpath broke away from their mother and splashed into the pool.

"They allowed to do that?" said the Judge.

A park employee trimming a nearby juniper stopped to watch the festivities.

"Guess so," said the Judge. He waddled to the pool, dipped his feet for five minutes, and came back.

"Damn cold. Is that a spring?"

A tourist map I'd snatched from a rack on Broadway didn't list the Trask Memorial as a spring. Off to our left, across the park's main drive, a Greek-style pavilion covered a pedastaled basin. The waters of Congress Spring poured from the spigot.

"What the hell is it with spring water anyway, other than the yuppies and Madison Avenue getting behind it?" The Judge shook one foot and then the other, two old dogs drying in the sun. "Is it any different from rainwater? Is the stuff sold as spring water even spring water? How the hell can you tell?"

"You take it on faith," I said.

"No more idiotic a notion than Sabo coming through."

We sweltered for an hour. The Judge made three more forays into the reflecting pool while I stayed on the hot stone. Sabo's insistence had the ring of a hypertechnical child's game. If both of us left the bench, we'd lose.

I actually noticed the woman twice. The first time, she walked toward us from the direction of the park's main drive. Our eyes locked at a distance, and she quickly turned off to stand at the edge of a duck pond. A few minutes later, having circled behind us, she strolled across a patch of grass above the memorial. Her black dress looked uncomfortably hot, especially with the swelling in her belly. Then suddenly, after disappearing into the shrubbery, she was beside me on the bench.

"You are Jackie's friend?" she said.

She was rail thin except for the belly. Her skin was bronze, with darker splotches in the hollows beneath her eyes. Her features were girlishly cute, almost pixie-ish. But her brown eyes narrowed warily, as if weighing how much she could trust me.

I introduced myself and the Judge, who dragged himself out of the pool like a walrus in linen.

"I am Mariela," she said, and folded her arms across her tiny chest. "How did you know to come here?"

"A phone number in Jackie's wallet," I said. "We traced it to Sabo and the bookstore."

"Where is that wallet now? Is it in a safe place?"

"Safe from who?" I said.

Mariela turned away, her face pitched haughtily upward.

"It's with his mother," I said. "No one else knows about it. The police think Jackie committed suicide. They paid it no mind."

"Was there money?"

I felt the Judge's eyes on me, trying to catch mine. I could steal his thoughts almost as surely as if he spoke aloud: the money was for Mariela.

"Close to a thousand dollars," I said.

Mariela swallowed hard, her tiny Adam's apple ascending into her throat for a long moment before relaxing back down.

"Jackie and I met a year ago," she said. "I needed someplace safe to live, someplace away from . . . away from down there. His friend Al just moved here. Jackie asked him to take me in until I could find work and a place to stay.

"Jackie visited at least once a month. More in the winter and less in the summer because of his job as a caddie. He came by the Amtrak train. I lived in a professor's house, and we could not spend nights there. Jackie would take a hotel room, and we would stay together. After the baby began to show, the professor and her husband asked that I leave because I was a bad example for their children. Now I live in a rooming house."

The Judge took a sharp breath, registering his usual annoyance at meandering chatter. Mariela fell silent, clasping her hands in her lap.

"Where did Jackie get the kind of money he was carrying that day?" I said.

"He was a caddie."

"I know. He caddied regularly for a man named Mel Tucker, and he caddied for me in tournaments. What else did he do for money?"

"I cannot say."

"Can't or won't," said the Judge.

Mariela met his glare without flinching.

"Mariela, my pro shop was burned to the ground. A fireman died, and I was arrested for arson and murder. Jackie started that fire. I have proof, but I need more."

"If Jackie started that fire, it was not directed at you," she said.

"I know that."

"If Jackie started the fire, it was against his will," she said. "Now I am sorry. That is all I can tell you. I must return to my job."

"Wait a second," said the Judge as Mariela rose from the bench. "Why didn't you go down to pay your respects?"

"What does it matter? My heart is just as sorrowful here."

She walked slowly up the sloping grass and disappeared into the bushes behind the memorial.

"Sorrowful," said the Judge. "Sorrowful about losing her meal ticket. You think the kid's Jackie's?"

"Yep."

The Judge shook his head. "You're as goddam gullible as they come."

"Get your shoes on, and let's get out of here," I said, deciding not to explicate my next brainstorm until we were airborne.

CHAPTER
13

We slumped low in the Judge's Ferrari, peering over the dashboard at the stockade fence that opened toward the kitchen entrance of the MCC clubhouse. Restaurant workers popped out at odd times to fling garbage bags into the dumpster or to hose down stacks of plastic food storage trays. The sun edged past an overhanging maple and baked the blacktop pavement.

"When's he going to show? said the Judge. He wiped a soggy hand-kerchief across his reddened dome.

"Soon," I said. "The checks are usually available about one."

"Screw it," said the Judge. He started the engine, closed the windows, and jacked up the air conditioner full blast. I worried we'd attract attention, but the next worker who tossed garbage didn't notice the Ferrari's purring idle.

My breath was visible before Jose Rojas' heap chugged to a stop beside the dumpster. I winked at the Judge with outward aplomb. Inside, I felt relieved as hell. I'd gambled Jose would pick up his final pay-check rather than trust it to the mails.

Jose spent less than a minute inside the clubhouse, but lingered at the edge of the stockade. He spoke passionately to several workers in succession, ending the last conversation with a disgusted wave before climbing into his car. The Judge slipped the Ferrari into gear, and we were off.

Jose drove toward Milton village, took the Merchant Street cut-off, then hung a dangerous left across traffic onto the New England Thruway. The Judge let him go, waited for a break, then darted onto the entrance ramp. The Thruway is crowded any time of day, thick with semis hauling rigs to Boston. The Judge easily gained on Jose, and set-tled into the middle lane with a semi in between. We lost the semi east of Stamford, and hung back through Norwalk as different cars inter-vened.

Jose exited at Bridgeport. He sped through an industrial section left behind by the Information Age, then zig-zagged through a neigh-borhood with burned-out boarded-up houses and side streets blocked by concrete barriers to discourage drug dealers from cruising for business. The surroundings had improved, though not by much, when Jose pulled over. The Judge tooled past while I noted which of several identical houses Jose entered. We swung around at the end of the street. Several kids stopped a basketball game in a sorry-looking park to compliment the Ferrari.

"You need me inside?" said the Judge.

"Maybe. Why?"

"These kids don't strike me as the Little Rascals. I'll stick with the car."

He dropped me in front of the house and promised rendezvous at five-minute intervals. The front door was unlocked, but swollen stuck with humidity. I shouldered it open and read the names on the mailboxes. Seven were labelled with names other than Rojas. The eighth, for a basement unit, was blank.

I clomped down a set of lopsided stairs, ducked under some heat pipes, and found a door in a wall built of unpainted Sheetrock. A woman answered my knock, opening the door a crack and eyeing me through the links of a security chain.

"Is Jose Rojas here?" I said.

"No."

"Jose Rojas. I am a friend. *Amigo.* Kieran Lenahan. I need to speak to him."

"No Jose here. Go 'way."

"I am *amigo.* Not Immigration. *No federales.* Kieran Lenahan." I enunciated every syllable clearly and opened my wallet to show I owned no federal badge.

"Go 'way," she repeated, not buying my attempt to prove a negative.

"*Amigo,*" I said.

Someone called from inside, and the door closed. Sharp voices traded Spanish, the woman's massacring my name. Silence fell, and the door opened.

Jose looked much different from the night I last saw him at the bar. He'd clipped his two pincer locks, and white hairs surprisingly speckled his four-day stubble. His face seemed drawn, as if he'd lost weight.

"Kieran, hey, man, what do you want?" he said.

"I need to talk to you about the fire, Jose."

Jose stepped out of the door and looked behind me.

"Anyone with you?"

"Just my buddy Judge Inglisi. He's with the car."

"Were you followed?"

"We followed you. No one followed us."

"Okay, come on."

He led me through a cramped apartment. Two young girls stared up wide-eyed from plates set on the kitchen floor until the woman shook a broom at them. Jose closed us into a room barely big enough for a mattress and a suitcase. A bare bulb dangled from a loose socket hanging on a hook.

"Sit, Kieran." Jose kicked shoes and shirts into a corner. "Sorry, I needed someplace fast, and the woman outside took me in to help pay the rent for her and her daughters for this shithole."

I hunkered down beside the suitcase, which lay flat, like a table. A clay figurine stood on the case, surrounded by coins, safety pins, an HO scale toy tractor, two locks of hair bound by thin ribbons, and a photocopy of a green card. The figurine was rudely shaped, like a troll doll with a roundish belly, stubby arms and legs, and an outsized head. Wisps of grass and human hair stuck out of its scalp.

"You followed me from the club?" he said.

"In a red Ferrari."

"Damn, I noticed that car. I need to be more careful." He stepped across the mattress and leaned into the corner.

"What was it with that fire, Jose? You guys knew something that night. You knew it would blow that propane tank you stashed there."

"Hey, I didn't want no propane. But the other guys bought too much electric stuff. CD players and blow dryers. The wires overloaded when we needed space heaters in the winter."

"But you know who set the fire."

"Why would I?"

"Because of your reaction the night I told you about Luis Augusto. Because you quit."

"We are all illegals at the club," said Jose. "Every one of us except for Eduardo. My papers are in for a green card, but I cannot wait in my country because I will starve.

"You cannot imagine what it is like to be an illegal in this country.

We work hard. We cram into places like the monkey house so we can mail money back home to our families. We worry about employers, landlords, INS, IRS. But Eduardo brought us over from the same little town in the Andes. He promised us a safe place to live and work. But soon, I began to see my brother broke his promises. The fire proved to me he is not a man of his word. The others are fools. I tried to tell them not to stay with Eduardo, that Eduardo cannot protect them.

"Kieran, I just want to live and work in my profession. Not mix drinks and smile at golfers. Not hide in a shithole like this."

"What about asking the Latin Cooperative for help?" I said.

"The Latin Cooperative. I would sooner die than join the Latin Cooperative."

"But the Latin Cooperative protects you from those problems, right?" I said.

Jose spat. "I will not talk about the Latin Cooperative. It is bad luck."

"Do you know a woman named Mariela?" I said.

"I know lots of Marielas."

I described the woman in Saratoga. Jose shook his head.

"I believe Jackie Mack started the fire," I said. "What do you think?"

"He slept in the cart garage many nights. We knew he was watching us."

"Why would Jackie be interested in you?"

"Illegals knew about Jackie Mack," he said. "We knew if Jackie had his eye on you, something bad could happen."

"Like what?"

"You could disappear."

"Die?"

"Disappear."

"Could he have started the fire?"

Jose kicked a foot at the grayed, rumpled sheet covering his mattress.

"Did he know about the propane tank?"

"We brought the tank in only the night before the fire. One of the guys already did some of the piping. But nothing was connected yet."

"How did you get it in?"

"Easy. We picked the garage door lock."

"Did Jackie work for the Latin Cooperative?"

"The Latin Cooperative, the INS," said Jose. "When you are an illegal, they are both the same."

Outside, the Ferrari and a police cruiser were parked nose to nose. The Judge and the officer stood alongside, the Judge yapping and the officer laughing hysterically.

"Here's my ex-partner," the Judge said as I crossed the sidewalk.

I shook the officer's hand and folded myself into the Ferrari while the Judge finished whatever the hell he was saying. The Judge crawled in and watched the cruiser reverse down the street.

"Find out what you wanted?" he said.

"Enough."

"Goddam took your time about it. I was running out of stories."

We parted company with the Judge ordering me not to leave the jurisdiction without him. Twenty straight hours with the Judge was enough to try the patience of a Buddhist monk. I drove to MCC with the windows opened wide, breathing huge draughts of summer air and feeling freer than any time since my arrest.

"Where the hell have you been?" Pete said when I walked into the shop. "Schedule has you coming in at twelve and me taking off till two."

"The schedule's tentative these days, Pete."

"That St. Clare guy called again," said Pete. "He said go to his office at four o'clock tomorrow, otherwise he won't show up for the felony hearing on Friday."

Promises, promises. If only it were so easy. Once Willie signed on to represent me, he needed a court order to quit. And not showing up for the hearing, he risked being cited for contempt of court.

"I guess I'm closing up," said Pete.

I nodded. "Take a half hour for something to eat."

Pete broke toward the door, but not quick enough. I asked him to phone Deirdre at the medical center.

"Why? I got nothing to tell her," he said.

"Because if I call, I'll be on hold till the millennium."

Pete unscrewed the baseball cap from his head and punched up the number. "I get as weird as you two, I'm gonna jump off a building."

He wended his way from switchboard to floor to intensive care unit with adolescent surliness. Finally, he snagged Deirdre.

"Nothin's wrong. Kieran wants to talk to you. Hey, this ain't my idea. He said he'd fire me."

Smirking, he dropped the receiver into my hand.

"You threatened to fire him, you bully!" she said.

"Youthful hyperbole." I scowled at Pete.

"Well, you got me, so what do you need now?"

"How old were the two guys you saw running off the platform?"

"Twenties."

"Not teenagers?"

"No," said Deirdre. "Pete's a teenager. These guys were men."

Pete sure would be thrilled to hear that.

"What's it matter?" said Deirdre. "I heard Jackie was buried."

"Do you think he could have been pushed?"

"Do you think he was?" said Deirdre.

"I wasn't there."

"I didn't see anything like that."

"But you could I.D. those guys."

"Yeah, but who's asking?"

"No one, yet," I said.

While Pete was out I called a law school classmate named Mary Graye. Mary had joined a law firm specializing in immigration work at the same time I signed on to practice with Big Jim. The process of obtaining a green card or citizenship was, to be charitable, a form-intensive business. Given the future Judge's prowess at filling out forms, he was lucky his few immigration clients weren't deported to Mars. My first day on the job, he dumped his remaining active immigration files on my desk and threatened me with death if I "took in another client who wasn't a natural-born red-blooded American." I waded through the files, found myself hopelessly lost in an administrative morass, and threw myself on the mercy of Mary Graye to bail me out. She did, Mary being the type who latched on to a subject the way a terrier tussled with a slipper.

A few years back, I'd received an announcement that Mary joined the U.S. Attorney's trial counsel staff at the I.N.S. If anyone could tell me about the Latin Cooperative, it was Mary Graye.

A receptionist confirmed that Ms. Graye was still on staff. In fact, she was now a supervisor in the trial division. Unfortunately, she had left for the day, but was expected back in the office early tomorrow.

Pete returned to duty a half hour late, provisioned for his long journey to closing with two sodas and a pound of French fries from the clubhouse grill.

"I've been thinking," I said, which elicited a screwed up facial expression Pete could have learned only from Judge Inglisi. "Business is lousy now, right?"

"It sucks."

"Let's close down during the PGA, and you caddy for me."

"You're going to play?"

"Why wouldn't I?"

"I don't know. Everyone says you're not. The caddies, the members who still talk to me. Even Aunt Dee says it's just like you to blow the biggest chance of your life."

As if I made a practice of getting arrested before majors. Oh well, at least I was still a topic of dinner table conversation in the O'Meara house, which counted for something.

"I'm playing in the PGA, Pete."

"On Thursday maybe. How you getting out of that hearing Friday to make your tee time?"

"Leave that to me."

"I don't know Winged Foot," said Pete. "Why don't you get one of their caddies?"

"You can carry a bag, and you can walk without tripping over your own feet, right? I want you."

"Well, if I'm going to caddy for you, get your ass out and practice so I'm not embarrassed by you shooting eighty."

"Pete," I said, "shut the hell up."

Randall Fisk hunched over a laptop, his feet propped on two thick phonebooks to raise his knees level with his waist. Halfway down a screen of text, the cursor blinked at the start of a new paragraph. Fisk typed a line and erased it, typed another one and erased it, typed three quick lines and erased them, too. He webbed his fingers and stretched his arms over his head. He pulled a tissue from a box beneath his chair and wiped his forehead and nose. His struggle hit me like a revelation; I never thought of his columns as the products of effort.

I shifted my weight, and the doorjamb to his cubicle squeaked. Spotting me, Fisk clapped the screen shut.

"How long have you been standing there?" he said, spreading his arms to gather any stray electrons leaking around the edges.

"An hour."

"Did you read any of this? It's confidential."

"Randall, after the Doomsday Plan, I'm not interested in your confidential info."

"Didn't you talk to Gerry Corrigan?"

"I did. He told me all about the Doomsday Plan."

"You don't believe him?"

"Believing him isn't the point. No one on the executive committee wanted that fire started. Period."

Fisk's eyes shrank as he slipped into thought. Recomposing that hidden text? I didn't care.

"Thanks for the tip," he said. "Now if you will excuse me."

"Not so fast. I need you to get me into the newspaper morgue."

"What do you think we are? A research library?"

"You owe me, Randall."

"For what? Because the Doomsday Plan didn't pan out?"

"For ruining my sex life."

"How the hell did I do that?"

I told him about the recent days with Georgina and the scene in my apartment after talking to Corrigan. I expected a smug lecture about corroborating sources before levelling charges. But Fisk surprised me.

"Is she that long drink of water?"

I nodded. Fisk's eyes shrank again as the obvious reverie overcame him. Winning a passel of tournaments bought me the right to be held up to his ridicule. But an affair with someone like Georgina Newland gained me new respect from this horny little bastard.

"Wow," he finally said. "You must feel like a jerk."

"Class A."

"That's still not a good reason for me to get you into the morgue," he said. "What are you looking for, anyway?"

"Stuff about the Latin Cooperative."

"You think they started the fire?"

"Do you?"

Fisk reached under the seat for another tissue to blow his nose. "It's the one angle no one's covered."

"Seems to me I'm the only angle anyone's covered."

Fisk drifted off into thought again. Either I tugged on a connection he knew something about or he calculated the price for his half of the bargain. Knowing Fisk, it was probably the latter.

"Just let me finish this," he said. "And don't peek."

I waited at an empty desk outside the cubicle while Fisk pecked away. Twenty minutes later, we rode the elevator to the sub-basement. I envisioned rusty filing cabinets stuffed with moldy, yellowed clippings, and a little old man with a green visor who would notch my request in his brain and dodder up and down the aisles with a wire basket under his arm. Instead, the elevator door opened on a room as clean and as bright as a NASA lab. Several people sat at computer terminals, speaking into headsets, their fingers flying over the keyboards.

Fisk ushered me to a desk where coffee steamed and a sandwich lay uneaten. Presently, a matronly woman returned. She was chief research librarian, and with her pale skin and dark-rimmed eyes probably surfaced about as often as a groundhog. Fisk introduced me as a colleague. She chuckled doubtfully, but sent me to a young woman at the far terminal.

"Don't thank me yet," Fisk muttered as he headed toward the elevator.

I pulled a spare chair beside the table and told the woman I needed information on the Latin Cooperative.

"Narrow it down or we'll be here all night," she said, going on to explain that the computer would pull up all references to the Latin Cooperative ever to appear in any of the chain's newspapers. I needed to narrow the search by adding at least one variable.

I chose all articles that mentioned both the Latin Cooperative and Luis Augusto.

"Hard copy?" she asked.

"Excuse me?"

"Want me to print them out?"

"How long will it take?"

"Twenty minutes, half hour."

I told her to go ahead. She typed in a command, and seconds later the printer at her elbow began spitting pages.

"Sorry," she said. "Machine's pretty slow."

She was Demo's age, plain yet pretty in a way I knew her contemporaries probably didn't appreciate. But I no longer subscribed to the "youth is wasted on the young" philosophy. My recurrent image of growing older was me seated beside some whiz kid at a computer keyboard.

I let the pages build up in the printer tray, then removed the first batch. The earliest article, some six years old, mentioned Luis Augusto's appointment as executive director of the Latin Cooperative. A brief biography described him as an immigrant from La Paz, Bolivia, who had operated a successful landscaping company in Westchester County.

Most of the other articles were short, hardly more than blurbs on the local events page. Longer articles focused on the lawsuit the Cooperative brought against a slumlord, the Cooperative's role in transforming downtown Port Byram into a critically acclaimed center for ethnic Hispanic dining, and Luis Augusto playing Santa Claus for a score of Hispanic children left homeless when a propane tanker exploded in White Plains. The hard copy reproduced captions, but only noted the positions of photos or graphics.

The next batch of articles continued the good press a social services organization generated. But an ominous strain creeped in. A scholarship fund lost its funding. Merchants accused the Cooperative of skimming profits during Port Byram's annual Hispanic Fiesta. The Cooperatives' founder, Ingrid Rodriguez, was arrested on a drug charge.

The printer stopped spitting. I took the entire sheaf to the chief research librarian and asked where I could find the photo morgue.

"There is no photo morgue," she said. "The film library is through that door."

The film library was even brighter and more antiseptic than the research library. A pony-tailed young man thumbed through the articles, made notes on a requisition form, and disappeared into a labyrinth of file cabinets. He returned with relatively few pictures: Luis Augusto on a dais, accepting his appointment as executive director; Luis Augusto outside the Westchester County Courthouse during a break in the slumlord trial; Luis Augusto as Santa Claus, with a cute little girl gaping in wonder at a present, juxtaposed with an aerial shot of the devastation caused by the tanker blast; and file portraits of Ingrid Rodriguez, who stepped down as the Latin Cooperative's president after her arrest, and Luis Augusto, the new president as well as the executive director. I couldn't believe my eyes. Ingrid Rodriguez was Mariela.

CHAPTER
14

Except for the Pentagon, the gray metal bulk of 26 Federal Plaza in lower Manhattan is the largest federal building in the United States. I waited for an hour in bathwater humidity on a line that crossed a stone concourse in the throes of renovation, then snaked into a lobby barely cooled by air conditioning. I cleared the metal detector and asked for directions at the information desk. The security guard seemed genuinely unsurprised that I had an appointment with the chief trial counsel of the I.N.S. Of course, I didn't have an appointment, but I lucked out catching Mary Graye at a free moment.

In law school, Mary wore her thin brown hair extremely long and favored bohemian styles in clothing. Neither had changed, though she looked a bit weathered, as if she spent mealtimes on a tanning bed rather than at a dinner table. We reminisced only briefly, and I needed to remind myself that Mary's curtness came by nature. I could tell that she had become one of those Manhattanites who saw the world like those *New Yorker* covers showing a thick slab of Manhattan in the foreground and cutely drawn landmarks like the Mississippi and the Rockies receding toward the horizon. She knew nothing of my surburban legal tangles.

"The Latin Cooperative?" she said. "What do you want to know about it?"

"Whether it's legitimate."

With all the information I'd learned from other people's computers in the last few days, I expected her to roll back to the terminal on her credenza. Instead, she steepled her hands in front of her face, and took a long exasperated breath.

"Well, I can tell you it started out as a legitimate organization providing genuinely valuable social services to legal Hispanic immigrants who settled in lower Westchester. Now it preys on illegals."

"It's a scam?" I said.

"Not completely. It still provides those services for documented aliens. But it also runs a system for illegals that's close to bonded slavery, basically by furnishing false papers for exorbitant prices, which the illegals pay out of wages earned from jobs the Cooperative finds for them."

"How much could it make on that?"

"You would be surprised at the street prices for documents," said Mary. "A green card can go for anywhere from seven to eight thousand dollars. An employment authorization card for seven fifty to a thousand. And that's just the obvious part of the operation. It could be into all kinds of vice and protection rackets."

"Aren't you supposed to shut them down?"

"We can't. We don't have the money or the personnel. We can't coordinate the actions of our field agents. Our computer system isn't even linked up for different districts to exchange information. That was proposed three years ago. We're still waiting."

"But you know something about the Latin Cooperative," I said.

"That's because I prosecuted its founder."

"Ingrid Rodriguez. She was arrested on drug charges, right?"

"Possession of cocaine with intent to sell."

"But that's a state charge."

"Right," said Mary. "She was prosecuted in state court. She said she was framed by people who wanted to take over the Latin Cooperative and pervert it. She refused all plea negotiations and held out for a trial. But then she changed her mind and pled to simple possession. She wanted a promise that no one would file deportation proceedings, but the D.A.'s office was so angry with her they absolutely refused. I caught the case here and won a deportation order."

"Was there any truth to the story she was framed?" I said.

"Some, but not what she claimed. She and the executive director were involved with each other."

"That would be Luis Augusto."

"We infiltrated the Cooperative during the course of the deportation proceedings," she said. "We found no evidence she had been framed. But we did find evidence they broke up shortly before her arrest, and we did find that the Cooperative was being perverted long before that."

"Is the Cooperative under surveillance now?"

"Even if I knew, I couldn't tell you."

"If I gave you the names of certain people, could you tell me if they are on the I.N.S. payroll?"

"Isn't that asking the same question in a different way?"

"Mary, this is personally very important to me." I told her about the fire and my arrest and my suspicion that Jackie Mack started the fire to burn out the restaurant workers, none of whom joined the Latin Cooperative.

"That's terrible, Kieran," she said with typical Mary Graye curtness. But she rolled her chair back to the credenza and angled the monitor so I couldn't see the screen. "Give me the names. I'll decide if and what I answer."

"Jackie Mack or Ian MacEwan. That's his real name."

Mary typed and waited. "Zilch."

"What about Eduardo Rojas?"

Mary punched in the name and spent some time reading the screen. "Not on our payroll."

"But he's in there, right?"

"Eduardo Rojas Willka," she read. "Born in Cochabamba, Bolivia. Entered the United States in the early seventies on a visitor's visa. Applied for a green card, and returned home to wait for his number to be called. Re-entered legally, and lived as a resident alien until he obtained his citizenship in eighty-one. He and his employer have been cited for employing illegal aliens. Last time, about four years ago."

"What was that last name you said?"

"Willka?" said Mary. "That's an Indian name, probably Aymaran. Most Bolivians of mixed Indian and Spanish blood will append an Indian surname."

"What about Luis Augusto?" I said.

"I don't even need to look for him," Mary said with a laugh.

"What eventually happened to Ingrid Rodriguez?"

"I won the deportation order, and she posted a bond pending her administrative appeal."

"She went free?" I said.

"Happens all the time. State corrections turns felons over to us. We get deportation orders, they post bonds, and they're gone."

"Don't your agents bring them back in?"

"We don't have enough bodies for that," she said. "So we rely on other people to do the job for us."

"Who?"

"Bail bondsmen," said Mary Graye. "They hire bounty hunters."

I thumbed a business card out of a plastic tray. Gerry Geiger, Bail Bondsman, it read, with the open ends of a set of dangling handcuffs forming the two Gs. He pronounced both Gs hard, Mary Graye told me when she directed me three blocks to his office. The building was one of those converted textile plants common in TriBeCa that still retain the large windows and high ceilings of the ground floor showrooms left behind when the industry fled overseas. Soot clouded the small window in Gerry Geiger's third floor reception area. Down below, a truck engine groaned as its rear deck lowered heavy wooden boxes to a gray pavement sunlight never touched. The air inside still stank of tea rose laid down by the woman now in Geiger's inner office. Their voices vaulted through the open transom, hers thin and whiny, his gruff and even.

The woman came out dabbing her eyes and pausing long enough on the threshold for Geiger to call her back. He didn't. He hadn't even left his desk to show her out.

"Another happy customer," he said as I took her place. "What's your story?"

I introduced myself and asked if he had hired a bounty hunter to track down Ingrid Rodriguez. Geiger was balding, tanned, and muscular, the deep seams of his face giving him the weathered look of an old tar who'd heard every damn story in the world at least once.

"Nope," he said, obviously not giving a damn why I wanted to know.

"Didn't you care that she disappeared after her deportation hearing?"

"I took one hundred percent cash collateral from her. Why should I care?"

"Would there be any reason for another bondsman to send a bounty hunter after her?"

"Why, do you know where she is?" He narrowed his eyes for a moment, then broke into a grin. "It's none of my business anymore. As soon as she didn't show up at Immigration, the bond was breached and they issued a deportation warrant. Hell, it wasn't my money."

"Is there any reason for another bondsman to chase her?"

"Not for money," said Geiger. "But with her, there's a good chance someone was on her tail. And not just I.N.S. She acted like she was on the run. Refused to give me her address, telephone number, anything I could use to trace her. Usually that spells trouble and I don't write the bond. But she scraped up the full cash collateral, so I let it go for her."

"But you do use bounty hunters," I said.

"When the situation calls for it," he said. "I feel like the I.N.S. should be grateful to me for bringing these people in, like I'm performing a public service by doing their job for them. But they don't care, and neither do I anymore. I just do what it takes to protect my investments."

"Where do you get a bounty hunter?"

"There's a whole pool of them right out there." Geiger pointed to his window, which opened onto an air shaft. "Only kidding, Lenahan. What I do, and what most bondsmen do, is get guys, and sometimes ladies, you'd be surprised, you think might be tough enough and savvy enough to do the job. You give them a bulletproof vest and a cheap badge. They carry a gun, that's their business. They do a good job, you use them again. They blow it or they get killed, you find another one."

"Ever use one named Jackie Mack or Ian MacEwan?"

"No one by those names," said Geiger. "But then I don't necessarily deal in real names. I pay cash, and I don't think my bounty hunters report their earnings to I.R.S."

I described Jackie physically.

"I definitely didn't use anyone like him. If I'm looking for a Chinese guy, I get a Chinese hunter, not some white guy with a head of hair like a traffic light. Maybe if I needed to hunt down an Englishman or a Swede. But I haven't had that problem in years."

"How many bondsmen are there?" I said.

"Not many left writing these kinds of bonds. The big companies all got out of it years ago. I'd say maybe six or eight like me. Bottom feeders all," he added with a laugh.

"Can you name them?"

"Sure. You want a list, I'll give you one. But don't expect whole lots of information. Most bondsmen won't admit to using bounty hunters."

I phoned Willie Junior from Grand Central Terminal and arranged to meet him at his office in two hours.

"Finally came to your senses, eh, Kieran?" he said. "Finally decided to cooperate with your defense counsel, huh?"

I hung up without confirming or denying either of his brilliantly off the mark assertions. Truth be told, I still thought like a lawyer more than I cared to admit.

Flush with sudden confidence, I wired Georgina a dozen roses from a florist shop in Grand Central's main concourse.

"Do you want a sentiment on the accompanying card?" asked the clerk.

" 'Sorry'," I said. "In big block letters."

Detraining at White Plains, I detoured to the courthouse. I didn't relish returning to the scene of my arraignment, but unfortunately Judge Inglisi worked there. I made it through the lobby without setting off any bells, either in the metal detector or in the court officers' memories. Nineteen floors up I peeked into a courtroom the uninitiated might have mistaken for a sleep lab. Two jurors nodded, a court clerk bobbed and weaved behind a desk, Judge Inglisi propped his chins on a thick fist as his eyes rolled back in his head. All the while, a lawyer examined an accountant-type about a corporate balance sheet that didn't quite balance.

I withdrew from the courtroom without breaking the spell and followed a back corridor to Judge Inglisi's chambers. His law clerk, a thin young man with a severe wedge haircut Pete O'Meara would consider cool, hunched over a motion file as thick as two Manhattan telephone books. Thankful for any interruption, he ran my note in to Judge Inglisi. Five minutes later, the Judge staggered in stifling a yawn. His robe looked as wide as a zoot suit.

"What's the idea of dragging me off the bench?"

"Better than having you fall off."

"Listening to numbers isn't easy." He dropped into his big leather catcher's mitt of a chair and loosened the shoulder pads he paid a tailor to stitch into his robe. "What is it now?"

"I'm meeting Willie Junior in ten minutes. I want you there."

"Hey, I have a job besides keeping you company."

"This is important."

"You found stuff on that Saratoga bimbo?"

"A lot," I said. "And I don't think Willie Junior will like what I have to say."

Willie Junior shared a suite in a building where solo practitioners were stacked like cordwood. A secretary read a magazine in a typing bay while a lawyer pecked at a legal form rolled into a typewriter. Another of Willie's office mates stood transfixed at a window, either daydreaming or contemplating suicide. An elderly gent sat outside one of the offices with an old Macy's shopping bag on his lap.

Willie greeted me and the Judge heartily, closed the door to his private office, and leaned a thick law text against it for good measure. He sauntered back behind his desk, his thumbs hooked under his suspenders, ready to regale me with more insights into my good sense. I cut him off.

"Willie, I'm playing in the PGA tomorrow. Got that? And I'm playing Friday, too, because you are going into court Friday and waiving the felony hearing, okay?"

Willie's face reddened as he twined the suspenders around his thumbs.

"Now, Kieran, I know you object to my unorthodox strategy. Most defense lawyers would have pressed for an indictment, and if the D.A.'s office didn't go for one, would lay back and prepare for trial. But you're not the usual defendant, and I think I can kill this quickly at a felony hearing."

He looked to Judge Inglisi for help, but the Judge raised a hand as if telling him to hear me out.

"Jackie Mack torched the building," I said. "Some time before, he removed a few golf mementoes from my shop he knew meant much to me, and hid them under his mattress. He used kerosene from a space heater I stored under my workbench to start the fire in a closet in the bag room."

Willie rocked on his feet like a man wallowing in breakers until he gained enough purchase to ask how I knew all this.

"Paul Surchuck's report," I said.

"You obtained a copy and didn't inform me?" he said.

"Someone read it and told me."

"Who?"

"One of my many spies."

"The D.A. won't go for this," said Willie. "Jackie's conveniently dead."

"Which may not be a coincidence." I traced the history of the Latin Cooperative from a social services organization founded by Ingrid

Rodriguez to an organized crime machine fronted by the popular, photogenic Luis Augusto. Willie Junior kept twisting his suspenders.

"Augusto wanted Ingrid out," I said. "So he framed her with a drug charge. After her conviction, she was turned over to the I.N.S. for deportation. She posted a bond and skipped. Now sometimes when an alien skips, the bail bondsman hires a bounty hunter to track her down. But this bondsman took one hundred percent cash collateral. He doesn't care if she never shows up."

Willie Junior started to interrupt, but I talked him down.

"Meanwhile, Jackie Mack's been working a job besides being a caddie. Pretty lucrative, too. I can prove this from bank records. According to Ingrid Rodriguez, Jackie met her while she was on the run. I think Jackie was sent to find her and then something happened. Maybe she sweet-talked him, maybe he just liked what he saw. Whatever, he didn't turn her over. Instead, he stashed her upstate, very pregnant, with a new identity and fake papers. So the question is, who wants her found if the bail bondsman doesn't care? The Latin Cooperative."

"How does this get you off the hook for the arson?" said Willie Junior.

"It doesn't yet," I said. "But Ingrid Rodriguez told me the fire wasn't directed at me. I'm pretty convinced it wasn't directed at Boland Brothers carts, either."

"The monkey house?" said Willie Junior.

"None of the restaurant workers are legal, and all resisted joining the Latin Cooperative."

"So Jackie blows it up," said Willie Junior.

"He started a fire intended to scare them without knowing about the propane tank in the adjoining closet."

"And I suppose he felt so guilty he jumped in front of the train," said Willie.

"No, he was pushed," I said, and went on to tell Willie what I learned about Jackie's death while trying to get him buried. A sly smile crossed his face. He was buying this, I thought. My theory still needed work, still had holes wide enough Judge Inglisi could run through with room to spare.

"This is all clear to me now," said Willie.

"It is?" said the Judge.

"Sure, you guys are using me. You never intended me to defend these charges like a real lawyer."

"Willie . . ." I said.

"Willie . . ." said the Judge.

"Willie nothing," said Willie. He snapped his suspenders so hard against his chest it hurt me.

"Kieran," said the Judge, "want to leave me with Willie a second?"

I took a seat outside next to the old gent.

"Bonds," he said proudly, giving the bag a shake. "I need help surrendering them."

I grinned tightly, my ear cocked for a sound I didn't so much hear as imagine: the ominous drone of a Judge Inglisi lecture. Ten full minutes passed before the door opened.

"Willie won't waive the hearing," said the Judge.

"Now what do we do?"

"Friday's a long way off," he said.

I dragged myself home in the late afternoon and found Pete sitting at the top of my apartment stairs.

"I closed up early," he said. "You're not pissed, right?"

"Right."

"We still have some daylight left. Want to run over to Winged Foot and get in some practice?"

"John Daly won at Crooked Stick after driving all night to make his tee time," I said.

"You think you're as good as John Daly?"

"No," I said. "But I'm pretty damn tired."

"You doing anything for supper? Because if not, Mom invited you."

"For good luck?"

"She called it more like a last meal."

We strolled across Limerick, fielding accolades as befitted a knight and his squire on the eve of battle. Front doors slammed, mothers gathered in their children, drivers glared from the windows of slow-moving cars. Great to have the whole neighborhood behind you.

"Screw them," said Pete.

The accolades continued at Castle O'Meara. Deirdre clicked across the front porch on high heels, a skirt that particularly weakened me swishing around her knees.

"She has a date tonight," whispered Pete.

She stopped at the door of her car and looked me up and down as if spraying me with machine gun fire.

"Oh, I see you have a night to yourself," she said.

Typical Deirdre. All I ever needed to get a rise out of her was let it be known I was seeing another woman. It was so easy I always felt as if I were cheating, not on Deirdre but on Deirdre's psyche. In more contemplative moments, uncomfortable questions presented themselves. Was I seeing the other woman for her own sake? Was I trying to get back at Deirdre, or get to Deirdre? After my scene with Georgina, the questions were moot. So I could enjoy the irony of watching the madcap Deirdre tear out of the driveway.

The kitchen smelled spicy. Plum tomatoes gurgled in a saucepan. Bay scallops sprinkled with cayenne pepper soaked in a tray of lemon juice. A large pot of water rose to a boil. Gina O'Meara whacked a head of lettuce against the countertop, then gave me a sisterly peck on the cheek.

"She crazy," she said, an implicit apology for Deirdre. Their attitudes toward me obeyed some unknown law of thermodynamics. If Deirdre had jumped into my arms, Gina would have dumped the boiling water on my head and called me a Casanova.

With dinner not yet ready, Gina shooed Pete and me out the back door. The backyard was a squarish patch of crabgrass cut off from the neighbors and a back alley by a crooked stockade fence. Pete amused himself by banging a few golf balls around with an old pitching wedge. I sat on the steps and dodged the ricochets.

I hadn't touched a club since that evening with Georgina. All logic told me I needed to practice, even if only to whump balls into the carpet I hung over my landlord's clothesline. I usually suffered from an extreme case of nerves the night before a tournament, the kind that stretched every scenario into grotesque taffy renditions of reality. Watching Pete and remembering my own days of playing imaginary backyard tournaments, I focused completely on tomorrow and felt surprisingly calm. Maybe I was John Daly, driving through my own dark night to my personal Crooked Stick. Of course, I didn't expect to win. Playing well enough not to withdraw in embarrassment after one round would be a victory. Making the 36-hole cut, assuming a lightning bolt struck Willie Junior from his high horse, would be miraculous.

I left Pete to his game. Inside, Gina mixed salad dressing in a cruet. Ever temperamental, she opened a beer and chased me into the den until called. I stood at the window, avoiding Tom's recliner and ignoring the family gallery. Four-by-fours and vans lined the street outside Toner's. All the menfolk of Limerick stopping by the pub on a summer evening. Something flickered in the corner of my eye, a candle set on a stacking table arranged like an altar and hidden behind the recliner. A clay figurine—a dead-ringer for the one in Jose Rojas' room—stood beside the candle with a bed of grass clippings, just turning brown, spread around. Tees, a golf ball, and a Winged Foot scorecard lay on the grass.

The golf ball was the exact model Titleist I used in competitive rounds. The scorecard bore my name and hole-by-hole scores in a hand too neat for Pete. The scores added up to an improbable total of 67.

At the dinner table, I asked about the altar and figurine. Gina, ladling out a dish that made my eyes as well as my mouth water, pretended not to hear until Pete prodded her.

"That is an Ek'eko, an Aymaran god of fertility and good luck worshipped by the *cholos* in my country."

"*Cholos?*"

"People of mixed Indian and European blood. My grandmother was one-half Aymaran."

I remembered Mary Graye's mention of Bolivian Indians. "What does an Ek'eko do?"

"It works like a charm bracelet. You build an altar for the Ek'eko and surround it with the objects of your dreams. My grandmother shaped that Ek'eko for me many years ago. I don't use it much."

"I should be honored."

Gina bowed her head, a blush tinging the deep tan of her cheeks.

"Whose idea was the sixty-seven?" I said.

"Mom's," said Pete. "I don't think she realizes what it takes."

"The magic can work," said Gina.

"Hey, Ma, c'mon. This is Winged Foot." Pete turned to me. "I'm just kidding her. It was both our ideas for the score. I took the balls and tees from your golf bag the other day. I'd have taken one of your golf gloves, but you only have one."

I'd tried a lot of tricks to improve my game, but never voodoo. Still, Gina's earnestness touched me, even with Pete poking fun. Much later in the dinner, a thought occurred to me.

"Gina, how do the ethnic Hispanics and the *cholos* get along in Bolivia?"

"Just like this." She lifted the salad dressing cruet. Yellow oil floated atop red vinegar.

Back at home, I capitulated to good sense. I humped the old Oriental carpet out of the garage and moved my landlord's socks and underwear for space on the clothesline. Enough light leaked out of the back windows I didn't need to blind myself with floods. I dropped half a dozen golf balls onto the grass and took a few easy practice cuts with a five-iron. The meal sat heavy on my stomach, and the movement released healthy belches.

Finally loose, I set a ball on a tuft of grass and let fly. The blade caught the ball flush at the equator. The ball sailed under the carpet, crashed through a bush, struck the foundation of the neighbor's garage, and caromed past my chin.

I pocketed the other five balls.

Upstairs, I lay on the bed and studied Jackie's yardage booklet. After a hole or two, I found myself swept away by his skills, his tactical approach to Winged Foot, the confidence of his words. These weren't the ruminations of any caddie. His eighteen meditations sounded like the preachings of a golf guru.

I fell asleep with the booklet open on my chest.

CHAPTER
15

Pete came to collect me at noon the next day. My tee time was at 2:14, so allowing myself an hour for the usual housekeeping matters left me approximately another hour for mental and physical preparation. No need for any more. Whipping up a storm on the range wouldn't compensate for days without practicing. Nor would it prepare me for Pete's get-up: baggy-assed jeans and a Knicks basketball jersey.

"You're not caddying for me dressed like that."

"Hey, it's hot out there," said Pete. "You think we're gonna be on TV or something?"

"That's not the point. This is a major tournament played at an exclusive club."

I tossed him a golf shirt from my closet. Nothing I could do about the pants. I had Pete by a good eight inches, so he'd look just as absurd in a pair of mine.

"Shouldn't you be like catatonic now instead of worrying about my clothes?" he said, shrugging into the shirt.

I should have, but wasn't. I felt calm, too calm, to paraphrase the lines of several thousand grade-B movie actors just before the Indians attacked.

Pulling into the contestants' parking lot at Winged Foot didn't stir up any hostilities. The only hint of a tournament in progress beyond the dense wall of trees was a hush so deep I could hear the whirring of the Goodyear blimp's engines as it hovered overhead.

Winged Foot's name derived from the insignia of the New York Athletic Club, not a coincidence since NYAC members commissioned the noted architect A.W. Tillinghast to create a golf course out of a few hundred acres of woodland in Mamaroneck, New York. "Give us a man-sized course," they instructed him, a line with all the pithy eloquence of Alexander Graham Bell's, "Mr. Watson, come here, I need you." Tillinghast did exactly that, sculpting two championship courses by blasting over 7,000 tons of rock and mowing down almost 8,000 trees.

Major tournaments were no strangers to Winged Foot. Bobby Jones won the third of his four U.S. Open titles there in 1929. Thirty years later, the Open returned, and was won by Judge Inglisi's video alter ego, Billy Casper. Fuzzy Zoeller beat Greg Norman for the Open title in an 18-hole playoff in 1984. But the tournament that defined Winged Foot in the average golf fan's memory, and burned scars into the psyches of several touring professionals, was the 1974 U.S. Open. Hale Irwin, who would eventually win two more Opens, did not win so much as survive the infamous "Massacre at Winged Foot" with a remarkably high score of seven over par 287.

No one expected another massacre this week. For one thing, this was the PGA Championship, and the Professional Golfers Association didn't ask the host club to create the rigorous playing conditions the

United States Golf Association required for a U.S. Open site. The rough would be long, but not as deep as elephant grass. The greens would be fast, but not quite like a skating rink. We'd play approximately the same card Tillinghast designed in 1923.

The PGA Championship was the fourth jewel in the annual Grand Slam crown. Golf's Grand Slam was a near impossible feat. No one has ever won it in a single season, and only four golfers—Gene Sarazen, Ben Hogan, Jack Nicklaus, and Gary Player—have won the Slam over the course of their careers. Of the four tournaments, it commanded the least respect. The Masters had the lush springtime beauty of Augusta National and the ghost of Bobby Jones. The U.S. Open had a century of tradition and the exacting standards of the U.S.G.A. The British Open was played in the cradle of the game, sometimes on links courses older than the United States. The PGA Championship, played on the verge of golf's silly season, had me.

Well, figuratively. The rap against the PGA was its egalitarian nature. It was the championship of the Professional Golfers of America, a body that included club pros like myself, as well as the touring pros familiar to most sports-conscious people. Until 1994, the top 40 finishers in the national Club Professional Championship gained automatic spots in the next year's PGA Championship. But bowing to criticism that 40 nobodies weakened the field, the PGA decreased these spots to 25.

All this talk about which Slam event was best and whether the PGA Championship should remain in the Slam seriously engaged golf scribes and commentators and fans. For me, such ostensibly amusing arguments were reminders that we are a civilization. Roving bands of hunter-gatherers had no time for games; they needed to devote every effort to survival. Okay, lots of day laborers and factory workers don't give a damn about the PGA Championship's role in the Grand Slam.

But just the fact the argument exists, and that guys like Randall Fisk write about it, proves that anarchy hasn't descended yet.

Pete lugged my bag to the caddie yard while I headed to the locker room for a quick change into golf shoes and a drop by the marshals' tent. My two playing partners were club pros I'd met during the national championship in October. One played out of a small private club in Ohio. The other ran a public driving range in Kansas. I hunted them up on the practice range while Pete scrabbled around for a bucket of balls.

"Watson and Grady are three groups ahead of us," said the Ohioan.

"Love and Faldo are three ahead of them," said the Kansan.

I smiled indulgently, not expecting either to be the starstruck type. Luckily, Pete beckoned from a heap of pearly whites. Only a handful of people sat in the bleachers or lined the practice tee ropes. The few players still warming up were the last three groups of the day, club pros all, with starting times too late even for the cable TV feed.

I dusted off about twenty shots and slid my clubs into the bag. The calm I felt driving into the club now blossomed into outright serenity.

"That's all?" said Pete.

"All I need today," I said, my eyes settling on a distant pair of sunglasses topped by a familiar shock of red hair. "Pete?"

"Hey, don't look at me, man. She said she wanted to watch me caddy."

"Oh." My mood perturbed but still intact, I wondered what Deirdre's presence boded for a day that already seemed to bode well.

Mel Tucker intercepted me on the way to the practice green. He wished me luck with a sturdy handshake and a thump on the back. Time shrank quickly now. A microphoned voice announced the 1:58 group on the first tee. Tucker didn't unhand me.

"I got a call from some D.A.'s investigator this morning," he said. "Wants to talk to me about old Jackie."

"His death?"

"That and the fire. Does somebody think Jackie started it?"

"Don't know a thing about it," I said, hoping my honest confusion looked exactly like honest confusion. "Sorry you're getting dragged into this, Mel. They didn't get your name from me."

"Well, don't you worry, Kieran. I'll tell them whatever they ask and then some. Meanwhile, you go out there and win yourself a tournament."

Mel disappeared into a crowd around a concession stand. A D.A.'s investigator called. Maybe lightning had struck Willie Junior, and he talked to Jayne Sokol. I felt elated enough to launch into a back flip. Instead, I contented myself with dropping three balls on the practice green and taking aim at a cup thirty feet away. I preferred stroking long putts just before a round. The longer stroke gave me a better feel for the green than jabbing a bunch of five footers. Two of my snakes plinked into the hole. I was on fire and hadn't even teed off yet. Leave it to the Judge to turn on the garden hose.

"First hole's a real bitch today," he said as the 2:06 group prepared to tee off. "Something like seventy bogeys already."

"No bearing on what I'll do," I said, irked less by the statistic than by the Judge's know-it-all delivery.

"And I suppose if it rains, you won't get wet." He punched my ribs, his standard way of wishing me good luck.

"A D.A.'s investigator contacted Tucker about Jackie," I said. "Do you think Willie—"

"Willie's as thick-headed as his old man. I decided you needed some extra-judicial help, so I had a heart-to-heart with Jayney Sokol."

"You talked to Jayne Sokol? I thought she hated golf and golfers."

"Remember her lawsuit against Willow Run?" said the Judge. "I had the case at the trial level and ruled in her favor. The Appellate Division reversed me, but she's loved me ever since."

We watched the 2:06 group hit. Three club pros from who the hell knew where. Their nerves were palpable. Knuckles a bit too white on the grips, elbows flying a bit too high at the top of the backswing, weight transfer a shade too late on the downward move. The rough swallowed all three shots.

My grand entrance onto the first tee of a major championship awaited. The announcer garbled my name. Pete caught the butt of my golf bag on the edge of the bleachers and disconnected my umbrella. As I bent under the ropes, someone grabbed my arm.

Georgina. Dressed to keep my concentration on the game from the tips of her clunky sneakers to the top of her straw hat.

"Good luck," she said, and planted a whammer of a kiss on my lips.

The first hole is a long par four lined by towering maples and evergreens that press close to the fairway on the left and stand back on a wider swath of rough on the right. I motioned Pete for Jackie's yardage booklet to re-read his "Death down the left side" line. "Don't be fooled by your eyes. No bailout area right," Jackie's notes continued. "Shade on the right side of the sprinkler line." How Jackie expected me to see the sprinkler line, which usually but not necessarily ran down the approximate center of a fairway, was another matter.

The Ohioan lofted a lazy fade into the right rough. The Kansan screamed a duck hook into the left. I teed up. The eyes of my small personal gallery bounced off me like ping-pong balls. I waggled the driver, sighted an imaginary sprinkler line down the center of the fairway, visualized the flight of the ball. An envelope of concentration descended. The outside world fell away, leaving just the ball at my feet and the image in my mind.

I coiled into my swing, paused ever so slightly, and released my body. Spinning out, I caught a white streak darkening as it rose to the apex of its flight, then flashing white again as it crashed to the fairway 260 yards away.

I sprang jauntily off the tee, introducing myself to the group's teen-aged standard bearer and the middle-aged woman who charted every shot for PGA statistics before settling beside Pete's weary shamble and collecting myself for a long day. The ball sat high on a freshly cut swirl of grass, just begging to be hit. I calculated the exact distance to the pin from the daily yardage booklet. Jackie's notes advised a five-iron from this distance, one club less than I'd choose in the dead calm humidity of an August afternoon. "Death above the hole. You can't believe how steep the green is front to back."

"Four or five?" I asked Pete.

"Hey, I thought I was only gonna lug the bag."

What a team, I thought. Notes from a dead man, a surly caddie, and a golfer serene enough to have o.d.'d on beta blockers. The pin was cut in the right front part of the green. If I hit the five-iron and stopped short, I'd face a difficult pitch with little green to work with. Screw Jackie; I went with the four-iron.

Perfect contact. The ball flew straight over the pin, hit the center of the green, and rolled all the way to the back. Only a wiry patch of collar stopped it from rolling down a six-foot embankment.

So much for my brilliance. Instead of pitching uphill, I now chipped down the face of a mountain. I barely clipped the ball with my wedge. The ball plopped onto the green and started to roll, gathering speed as it neared the cup. For a split second, I thought the ball would dive into the hole. But it curled around the rim and, seemingly gathering speed again, nearly reached the huge bunker running along the right side of the green. Another chip and a nerve-wracking four footer saved a bogey. I searched the sky while the Ohioan finished out. Along the southern horizon, a dark cloud puffed into a thunderhead. I promised Jackie not to cross him again.

I ran off four straight pars. I'd like to call them routine, hitting each green in regulation and taking two putts to hole out, but on Winged Foot nothing felt routine. Each shot required enormous concentration, and blind faith in the advice Jackie scribbled in the margins of the yardage booklet. My gallery followed in silence, Deirdre and the Judge together on one side of the fairway, Georgina and Mel Tucker separately on the other.

Randall Fisk waited on the sixth tee. After leering at the females, he wrinkled his nose as he read the black +1 beside my name on the group's scoring standard and the big numbers already rung up by the Ohio and Kansas contingent.

"He's stable," he said to Judge Inglisi, as if speaking of my medical condition.

I birdied the seventh hole to get back to even par, narrowly missed another birdie on the eighth, and saved par by sinking a chip on the ninth. Standing on the tenth tee, I checked the leader board for the first time. Nick Price and Steve Elkington were in at three under par 67. Four more players were a shot back at 68, followed by another six at 69. For a brief moment, I had a vision of myself at the top of the leader board.

No one else suffered from the same hallucination. Weary fans trudged toward the parking lots. A greenskeeper's tractor rumbled through the shadows ribbing the first fairway. The Goodyear blimp sailed toward the county airport. A television crew wrapped the tenth tee camera in blue plastic. Even Judge Inglisi seemed to weigh another nine holes on his feet against an early dinner. Deirdre did exit, and none too gracefully after seeing me take a swig from Georgina's water bottle.

The next four holes quelled any further defections from the ranks. Following Jackie's wisdom, I birdied the tenth, strung out three more pars, then birdied the fourteenth. A computerized scoreboard near the fifteenth tee flashed the leaders. There I was: K. Lenahan −2, a single digit below Price and Elkington. People started popping out of the trees, and by the time I lifted my par putt out of the cup, two hundred people ringed the fifteenth green. A television crew on the sixteenth unwrapped a camera in time to capture what turned out to be my final birdie of the day: a drive just beyond the bend of the dogleg, a perfectly carved three-iron, and a six footer.

We reached the eighteenth in the misty dusk that seems to boil out of the ground in August. I drew a drive to within a few feet of a sprinkler head exactly 190 yards from the center of the green. But standing in the fairway, I had no sense how that 190 yards felt in my golf muscles. The pin, cut left center, blipped in and out of focus. The gathering darkness skewed my depth perception.

I held Jackie's yardage booklet close to my eyes and read his notes. "You're pumped up," he began, as if he knew following his advice for 17 holes guaranteed this heady circumstance. As I factored in the conditions, a tiny flame blazed on the right side of the green. Within about four seconds, the entire gallery lit up.

"What the hell's going on?" said Pete.

"We'll ask your mom's Ek'eko," I said, and smacked a five-iron shot into the ring of fire.

"All I did was light my goddam cigar!" said Judge Inglisi.

Tournament officials surrounded him in a corner of the scorer's tent while I sat at a table to check and re-check my card. The figures were correct; I'd shot a 67. But I couldn't sign the card until the officials decided whether the light show on the eighteenth hole broke any rules. They spoke too low for me to hear, so I followed the discussion by Judge Inglisi's roaring reactions.

"Two hundred people two hundred yards away from him flick their Bics, and you're going to penalize him? You think I organized it?"

Funny thing, the Judge probably was pissed he hadn't organized it. And he definitely was pissed he couldn't browbeat this tight circle of men with his judicial bluster. Eventually, the officials ruled the light incident was a spontaneous event completely outside my control, and that no one had broken any rule by creating an artificial line of play marker during my swing.

Still fuming, the Judge escorted me to the press tent.

"Goddam overgrown yuppies," he said.

"They're trying to be careful," I said.

"Bullshit. If Nick Price had been out there in that kind of dark, they'd have suspended play. But a club pro like you, they don't care if you can't see your hand in front of your face," said the Judge, ever sympathetic when the feeling dovetailed with self-aggrandizement. His internal storm blew itself out before we reached the press tent. "I sent Pete home with your clubs. Don't say anything stupid."

The press tent resembled a ballroom fused with a computer lab. Green velvet drapes and gold bunting hung behind and beside the podium. Four plushly upholstered chairs bellied up to a long oaken table. Down below, green and gold tablecloths covered rows of tables equipped with electrical outlets, modem ports, and telephones. About half the seats were occupied, the rest of the scribes probably too deep into research at the clubhouse bar to give a damn about me.

I took my place on the podium and displayed the expected "aw shucks" attitude as befit a club pro nobody tied for the lead in a major.

"Were you in the zone today?" asked one sportswriter.

"I've been in the zone. This wasn't the zone," I said. The zone was sports slang for a level of performance seemingly touched by an angel, or just plain old supernatural if you prefer to avoid religious overtones.

"Is sixty-seven at Winged Foot your normal game?" asked another.

Randall Fisk slipped into the last row and plugged in his laptop.

"Sixty-seven anywhere isn't my game," I said humbly. "But today I felt imbued."

"Oh Christ," Judge Inglisi groaned from the back of the tent. Laughter coursed through the ranks.

"Can you elaborate?" asked Fisk.

"My tournament caddie was killed last week, but he left behind a yardage booklet with very specific tactical suggestions on how to play the course."

"You followed notes left behind by your dead caddie?" another reporter asked incredulously.

"Well, I did swing the clubs myself."

"How did he die?" someone asked.

That set me off on a whole account of Jackie's death and burial. Laptops clicked furiously, the reporters salivating over the weird turn this post-round interview took. About five minutes into my paean to Jackie Mack, I noticed Judge Inglisi take a call at a phone bank. He spoke for a short time, then began giving me the cut-off signal.

"We've got a problem," he said as we left the tent. A 67 meant *we* had a problem; a 78 and the problem would have been mine alone. "That was Jayne Sokol. She met with Willie, and he still won't waive the hearing. He doesn't even want to adjourn it. My guess is, he's so suspicious he's just going to stick to his pig-headed way of doing things."

"What about talking to Petty?"

"Can't. He and I never got along. Goes back to me nipping him in an election."

Another plan dawned on me. Judge Inglisi and I tracked down the tournament officials in a private dining room.

"Change your starting time?" said the chairman. "These times were set days ago. Changing even one would throw the entire tournament into chaos."

"But I'm one of the leaders."

"As of now," he said. "Did you expect to be again this time tomorrow?"

The Judge dragged me away.

"Goddam overgrown yuppies," I said for the hundredth time as the Ferrari peeled out of the parking lot.

CHAPTER
16

I paced my apartment floor. Part of me felt like a pitcher in the late innings of a no-hitter, hiding down at the end of the dugout so my teammates wouldn't disturb the magic. My answering machine toted the phone calls. Thirty-three, thirty-four, thirty-five. Most came from sportswriters who'd missed me at the press tent and now phoned from bars or restaurants for a comment they could bang into their stories before press time. A few were hangups, no doubt the work of Georgina. None bore the news I wanted most to hear.

I knew the severity of the charges against me, and the gravity of flouting a court appearance while out on bail. Even if Petty didn't send a sheriff to yank me off the golf course, I couldn't trust Willie Junior not to sell me out in my absence.

This sounds like standard golf lunacy, weighing a felony hearing on a murder charge against a round of golf. But remember, I didn't start the fire that killed Mickey Byrne. And tomorrow's round of golf carried all the professional stature I'd been denied.

The phone rang again. Pete this time. I cut off the machine.

"Aunt Dee's on her way, flaming out the ass."

"What about?"

"Miss Newland, who do you think?"

I hung up and pulled a shirt over my head. Nice timing, Deirdre. Might as well turn tonight into a smorgasbord of every problem plaguing my life.

After a minute of pacing, I decided the last thing I needed was a scene with Deirdre inside our old apartment. Talk about blowing a no-hitter. I went out onto the steps to head her off, gradually climbed down, and then wandered onto the driveway. No Deirdre.

A minute passed. Deirdre lived all the way across Limerick, but driving or walking she should have crash landed by now. Especially if she had flames shooting out the ass. I checked in both directions. Not a car on the street or a pedestrian on the sidewalk. No sportswriters laying siege.

I started on the most likely route she would take from the O'Meara house. I knew arguing with Deirdre was not good for my golf head. Death on the left side of the brain, Jackie might have written. But something always excited me at the prospect of seeing Deirdre, some primal connection in the cortex of my being long since layered over by experience.

I found her car on a side road. The front wheels had jumped the curb, with the bumper buried in a bush at the edge of a vacant lot. The door was open, the engine off. The thick chain usually attached to her hospital identification card was gone. A few loose keys lay scattered on the floor mat.

I ran home and dove into my car. Having been abducted in virtually the same way, I knew exactly where to look.

Barreling into Port Byram, I noticed an unusually bright sky and the occasional burst of fireworks. Police cars blocked off the entrance to South Main Street. The Hispanic Fiesta. I wheeled around and turned onto a side street. Parked cars lined every block. The houses and small tenements were dark. No one stared from the tiny porches, no one sat on the stoops, as if the fiesta had sucked everyone in the entire area to Main Street. It was the perfect night to remove the only witness willing to testify to a murder.

I worked my way behind Main and drew even with Liberty Square before parked cars finally choked off the back streets. I ditched the car and ran, glimpsing the fiesta at a distance as I crossed from block to block. Music blared, fireworks exploded, knots of balloons drifted into the night.

The limo was the only car parked in the tiny lot behind the Latin Cooperative's office building. Its engine clicked as it cooled. A tiny stream of water dripping from its air conditioning compressor flowed toward a drain. They hadn't been here long.

I threw open the back door and ran up the stairs, treading as lightly as I could to preserve whatever small advantage the element of surprise gave me. Eduardo Rojas met me at the second landing. Sweat glistened on his brow, and I knew with certainty he'd just run the same flight.

"Let me pass, Eduardo."

He lowered his shoulder into my chest. His wispy body felt surprisingly solid. I bounced backward, caught myself a step down, and sized him up. Solid or not, Eduardo was not as wide as the stairway. I could throw him a fake, zip past, maybe kick him down the stairs behind me.

"I know Deirdre's there. I'm going up."

Eduardo slipped his hand beneath his dark windbreaker. He thought he could surprise me, but I knew he'd pull out his switchblade. I faked left, spun right, leaped past him with a single bound. Too easy, I thought. I glanced back. A pistol with a huge silencer pointed squarely at my head.

I didn't break stride. He could shoot me now or shoot me later, but as long as I kept moving I had a chance. Two quick bounds and I reached the next landing. The stairway angled, bringing me back over his gun. A hand grabbed at my ankle. I kicked free, pulled myself up by the railing. Another bound. Again a hand grabbed my ankle, firmly now. I tried to kick, lost my balance, groped for the railing. My chin struck a riser. My teeth chomped down on my tongue. Blackness clouded my vision.

Eduardo wrenched me up by the hair. The muzzle of the silencer chilled my neck.

"You come with me now, yes?" he said.

He dragged me down the stairs, the gun pressed into my ribs. Blood filled my mouth, ran down my chin, dappled the front of my shirt. Eduardo stopped me at the first landing and reached a handkerchief over my shoulder.

"Clean your mouth," he said.

I expected a limo ride, but once out the back door we headed into an alley that cut toward Main.

"Stop here." Eduardo pocketed the gun but kept its muzzle aimed at me through the vinyl of his windbreaker. "We walk down Main, across Liberty Square to the railroad bridge."

"Where the hell is Deirdre?" I said.

"Move," he said, pushing me. "If I kill you now, no one will notice."

"How does a *cholo* like you become involved with an Hispanic like Augusto?" I said.

"Shut up," said Eduardo.

We waded out into Main. Eduardo could have shot me and no one would have noticed, the noise was so deafening. Music, laughter, singing, screaming. Fireworks popping overhead. Men leaning into gambling booths. Women hawking food. Young couples dancing. Children whisking around everyone's knees. Tall, Anglo, wearing a shirt spotted with blood, I should have stuck out. No one even noticed.

This sea of people spit us out on the other side of Liberty Square. We walked under the railroad bridge, then climbed a set of stairs. The parking lot for the Port Byram train station spread before me, completely filled with cars. In a flash I realized what Eduardo had in mind. I'd see the undercarriage of a train, just like Jackie. I wondered how Randall Fisk and the other sportswriters would handle that scoop.

But Eduardo nudged me away from the platform. We zig-zagged among the cars to the approximate center of the lot. He tugged my arm, and we crouched behind a station wagon.

"That van two, three rows up." He touched a finger to his lips, telling me to keep quiet. "Go ahead."

Cautiously, I peered around the side of the car. A dark van was parked three rows closer to the tracks. I ducked back behind the car.

"So what?" I said.

"She is in that van."

I looked around the side of the car again. A well-timed burst of fireworks exploded low over the train tracks, casting enough light to throw the van driver and a passenger into silhouette.

"What now?" I said. "Who are those guys?"

"Watch and wait," said Eduardo.

I watched, but didn't wait long. The man on the passenger side climbed out and walked around to the back of the van with a length of rope dangling from his hands. He bent down, fiddled with something under the chassis, then fed the rope into the van through a narrow crack between the back doors. He scanned the parking lot, then slid to the front of the van. The driver climbed out, and both men casually walked toward the train platform.

"Eduardo," I said, but he was gone. A switchblade lay open on the pavement beside me.

I scuttled from row to row with my head down and the switchblade clutched in my fist. One row away, I heard the muffled sound of the van's engine, a sinister hum beneath the sounds of the fiesta. The rope was not a rope but a loop of green hose running from the tailpipe into the back door. Twenty feet of open pavement separated me from the van.

The two men stood talking on the platform. One faced my way, the other opposite. They looked to be in their early twenties, with a lean hardness to their bodies. I couldn't get to the next row without one of them spotting me. Circling around would take time, and too much had passed already. The exhaust from the van smelled thick along the pavement. No telling how much oxygen was left inside.

I needed a diversion and luckily got two. An Amtrak express whistled past, whipping up a dusty wind. As the men shielded their faces, a grand finale of fireworks lit the sky. I scrambled across the open space and crawled under the van. The heat must have fused the rubber to the metal tailpipe because the hose was hopelessly stuck. Pulling the other end from the door wouldn't help Deirdre, so I cut the hose with the switchblade and blew several lungfuls of air into the back of the van.

The wind pushed the last of the finale directly over the parking lot. Burnt cinders drifted down as I crawled off to a payphone to call the cops.

They arrived at the Port Byram police station one by one. Judge Inglisi, Willie Junior, Jayne Sokol, her investigator. A detective named Brudney questioned me several times, and tried to fit my story with other pieces of information. A computer check traced the van to a corporation that leased workers to a local cable TV company. The village judge left his bed to sign a search warrant. Deirdre lay in the medical center, unconscious but alive. Her prognosis guarded.

Finished with Port Byram, we all drove to Milton and crammed into DiRienzo's office, drinking coffee and trying to maintain our civility. Change of scenery, change of subject matter.

"We have evidence that exonerates Mr. Lenahan of the crime for which he is charged," said Willie Junior.

"Shut up, Willie," I said. Just like his politician father. He screws me at every turn, then tries to jump on the winning bandwagon.

"Hey, you shut up until you're asked a specific question," said Di-Rienzo.

"What kind of evidence?" said Jayne Sokol.

"Physical evidence showing the opportunity afforded this perpe-trator, as well as testimonial evidence to prove a motive," said Willie Junior.

"Willie," I said.

"Lenahan," said DiRienzo.

Jayne Sokol pressed her hands to her temples as if fighting a throb-bing headache. "Detective, all I care about is someone talking to me in English."

"Let me explain," I said.

"Hold on," said Judge Inglisi. He gathered Willie Junior and me into a corner, but spoke only to Willie. "Look, Kieran has this all figured out. Maybe it better come from him so nothing gets lost in the translation."

Willie snorted, not liking a possible great moment snatched from his jaws.

"You did a good job," I said, punching his shoulder like the old pal I never was.

"Yeah, yeah," he said, and plopped himself into a chair.

I gave Jayne Sokol the same spiel I gave Willie Junior and Judge

Inglisi two days ago. The history of the Latin Cooperative. Jackie Mack's double life. Ingrid Rodriguez pleading guilty to a drug charge, then skipping on the deportation bond. Jackie being sent to find her, probably by the Latin Cooperative. Their love affair, the fire, the mementoes, and Jackie being pushed onto the tracks. If Jayne Sokol had a headache before, she needed brain surgery now.

"Hold it," she said. "This doesn't prove you didn't hire Jackie to burn the shop."

I wanted to ask then why the hell did she send her investigator to sniff out exactly the same theory. But alluding to Judge Inglisi talking to her on the q.t. wouldn't advance my position.

"Except for what just happened," I said. "Those two guys who tried to kill Deirdre are the same guys who pushed Jackie Mack in front of the train."

"Well, I guess it's just too bad for you those guys got away," said DiRienzo. "And even if Port Byram caught them, Deirdre can't make an I.D. until she wakes up. If she wakes up."

"They'll find those guys," I said. "And Deirdre will I.D. them. You'll connect them to the Latin Cooperative, and you'll have a trail heading right to Luis Augusto."

"Augusto wanted the building burned because twelve restaurant workers refused to join the Latin Cooperative?" said Jayne Sokol.

"It's an ethnic Bolivian thing. We can't fully understand it," I said.

She tapped a pencil on DiRienzo's desk. "Let me speak to the detective alone."

Willie, the Judge, and I stepped into the corridor.

"What do you think, Willie?" said the Judge in a clumsy attempt to lift Willie's self-esteem.

"I think I'm quitting," said Willie. "You guys didn't want a lawyer. You wanted a puppet to play games for you. Well, I'm not playing anymore."

"You can't just quit on Kieran," said the Judge. "You need a court order to withdraw as someone's attorney."

"I don't need one to go home and go to bed," said Willie, receding down the corridor without any perceptible movement of his thick-soled shoes. "Nighty-night, guys."

"He doesn't wear sarcasm very well," said the Judge, after Willie slammed the door behind him.

DiRienzo's door opened, and the two of us filed in.

"Where is William?" said Jayne Sokol.

"He went home to rest," said the Judge.

"What we all should do," said Jayne. "Look, I don't understand the entire picture. But enough of what you told me agrees with information my office uncovered."

"Like what?" I said.

"That is for me to disclose to your attorney when the time comes. For now, I'll go into court and A.C.D. the felony hearing."

A.C.D. means to adjourn in contemplation of dismissal. I was sure Willie'd be thrilled. The Judge interrupted my profuse thanks by grabbing a fistful of shirt and practically lifting me off the floor.

CHAPTER
17

The sound of a newspaper slapping onto the landing outside my door woke me too early that same morning. The pages were folded back, with a calling card clipped to the sports section. Compliments of Randall Fisk, it read. His column, titled "A Good Job at Winged Foot," barely reached below the fold. It didn't need to be any longer.

> The national press never heard of Kieran Lenahan. Playing brilliantly through a dusk that gathered endlessly before plunging into darkness, the Milton Country Club pro fashioned a 67 and helped himself to a slice of a three-way tie for the lead after the first round of the PGA. The national press had heard of him now. Having tormented Lenahan in this space for four years, I have no such excuse. *Mea culpa*.

Last week, within a few hours, Lenahan lost his pro shop to a
fire and his tournament caddie, Jackie Mack, to a death the
police only now consider suspicious. A few days later, Lenahan himself was arrested for arson and the murder of a fireman who died fighting the blaze. I wrote a column calling
Lenahan a modern-day Job. Only an editorial board decision
to delete all mention of Lenahan from our PGA coverage prevented that column from running. *Mea culpa.*

Medieval methods of deciding guilt or innocence, like the
joust or the trial by fire, are a millennium out of fashion.
Surely an immoral man is capable of an immortal round of
golf. But one cannot have witnessed Lenahan's performance
yesterday and not have sensed the decency of the man. It is
the hope here that the police solve the mystery of Jackie
Mack's death, and that the justice system absolves Lenahan
of the charges against him. *Mea maxima culpa.*

Normal visiting hours at the medical center ran from noon to eight p.m.
But I charmed my way past the main reception desk and the fifth floor
nurses' station. Most of the staff knew me, and none could keep track of
whether Deirdre and I were on-again or off-again. At least not without
a scorecard.

The police guard outside her room didn't charm so easily.

"Who the hell are you, Mac?" he said, slapping the sports section
to the floor as he lowered the front legs of his chair. He was Port Byram
P.D., and didn't recognize me on sight.

I pointed to my name in the headline of the lead PGA story.

"So what? Two guys tried to kill the lady last night."

"She's my, uh, girlfriend," I said.

The cop cocked his head and gave me a one-eyed squint. I considered citing Randall Fisk's column as a character reference, but decided that might win me a sock to the jaw. The cop opened a flip phone and called headquarters for instructions. I hoped he'd show more initiative if those two punks came back to finish off Deirdre.

"Really?" he said into the phone. "Three? Holy shit. Naw. Quiet here. Got this guy wants to see her. Tells me he's Lenahan, her boyfriend. Yeah, that's the guy all right. Okay."

He closed the flip phone and fogged out.

"What did they say?"

"Them? Oh nothing. You can go in," he said, and resumed protecting Deirdre from behind the cover of the sports section.

Deirdre lay with an oxygen tube clipped to her nose and an IV bag dripping into one arm. A heart monitor pinged, showing 72 beats per minute. Phlegmatic for Deirdre. Wires clipped to the fingertips of her other hand dove off the bed and looped up to a machine with a readout of red numbers bouncing around 90. I'd seen this machine once before when I visited Deirdre during a private duty nursing stint for a little girl with a bad case of asthma. The machine charted the percentage of oxygen in the blood. Ninety percent was a great score on a school test; as a blood-oxy figure, it was a C minus.

I stood beside the bed. I don't think she saw me so much as sensed me blocking the sunlight from the window. She turned her head slightly in my direction, her eyes half open. I raised my hand into her line of sight and, despite myself, signed, "I love you." A faint smile turned the corners of her mouth.

Out in the corridor, I found the guard chair vacant. Several doors down, a different cop joked at the nurses' station. Eight o'clock shift change, I thought. I needed to hurry. My starting time was 9:20.

Winged Foot jumped. The results of the first round focused everyone's attention for the second. Galleries now had leaders to follow. The head of the pack concentrated on positioning themselves for the two week-end rounds. The middle of the pack tried to spring onto the leader board or hang on to make the cut. The bottom-dwellers, basically the 24 other club pros, would play out the string, stow their memories, and head home.

I found myself signing autographs on the path to the practice tee, where my core constituency—Judge Inglisi, Georgina, and Mel Tuck-er—hugged the ropes along with about two hundred front runners.

"Sure can't act like an asshole today," said Pete, who wore a regular golf shirt and jeans barely big enough to fit the Judge.

I warmed up with the same sequence of shots as the day before. The balls climbed into the sky, then knifed to the earth like balata darts tossed at a lush green dart board. The gallery oohed and aahed, all except for the Judge, who always thought a shot could fly a bit longer or a bit straighter, and when that failed, bitched about form. The shots themselves satisfied me. But I sensed a slight instability, as if today's swing was a combination of subtle, cancelling mistakes rather than a smooth pass at the ball. I quit at twenty, less out of superstition than the honest fear I couldn't muster many more.

The Judge must have explained to Georgina and Mel why they shouldn't expect too much from me today because they stopped me coming off the practice green and asked about Deirdre. She looked in pretty bad shape, I said. I hadn't spoken to her doctor, but the only encouraging sign was her being in a private room instead of intensive care.

Georgina kissed me lightly, yet with more feeling than yesterday's whammer. I sensed her relief that whatever danger I faced had passed. Mel Tucker steamed.

"Goddam animals," he said loud enough for several bystanders to turn our way. "First Jackie, then your girl. Can't anybody throw these people out of the country?"

"Bounty hunters," I said, and shouldered past.

I found the first tee far different from the previous afternoon. The sun hit at a lower angle. People crowded the bleachers. The Ohioan and the Kansan bantered with the casual air of men whose fates had been sealed. I paced, grinding my teeth, while the preceding threesome moved down the fairway at an excruciatingly slow pace.

I held the honor based on yesterday's round. The announcer trilled my name with a touch of the brogue. Applause rippled. I teed up, sighted down the fairway. Jackie's advice came to mind as a whisper. I squared myself toward the right portion of the fairway. Then, almost despite myself, I adjusted my line down the left.

The ball screamed off the driver's face. One of the longest, purest drives of my life bounded to the verge of the dogleg. A stunned silence gave way to cheers. The bleachers emptied. People streamed down both sides of the fairway. A minicam crew joined the standard bearer and the statistician as part of the threesome's official entourage.

My drive left me with a ridiculously short approach, much shorter than Jackie anticipated. I debated between a smooth eight-iron and a hard nine before settling on the eight. The pin was cut in the back left part of the green. My shot flew out to the right before its spin bit the air and drew it back toward the pin. The ball landed and stuck ten feet directly below the hole. A few minutes later, I rolled in the putt for birdie. With Price and Elkington still due to tee off, I became the sole leader of the PGA Championship.

I hate starting with a birdie. Sounds weird, but it's true. A birdie lulls you into a false sense of the round. A par keeps your edge. A bogey grabs you by the throat and reminds you this is Golf, you imbecile, and to play well you best bring all your shots, all your sweat, all the experience you've accumulated over a lifetime. Some of my best rounds started with bogeys; some of the worst with birdies.

That birdie was my last of the day. Three straight bogeys, and I was reeling. Another one, sandwiched between two pars Judge Inglisi charitably described as "out the ass," and I was staggering like a punch-drunk boxer. One more to start the back nine, and the gallery jumped ship in hordes. Nothing went right. My swing deserted me. My shots landed in predicaments Jackie Mack never predicted. My putting stroke, so true the day before, deteriorated into slap shots. I was in the midst of what everyone expected of a club pro with the temerity to lead a major. I was in a crash-and-burn.

"Where the hell did everybody go?" said Pete.

We stood on the eighteenth tee. Halfway down the fairway, two marshals snoozed at either end of the crosswalk. Behind the green, a handful of people sunned themselves on the bleachers. The last three of my faithful gathered at the right tee marker. As the Ohioan readied to hit, Mel Tucker slipped into the trees. The Judge edged closer to Georgina. Without Deirdre to engage him, he'd spent most of the morning chatting her up. Her sunglasses concealed her reaction.

A series of cheers, like cannon booming across the landscape, answered Pete's question. Everybody was out there, watching a tournament I felt recede from me. The leader board clicked, registering Price at −6. I was eight shots out, but doubted anyone thought of it in those terms. Kieran Lenahan, the surprise first round leader, had dropped off the planet.

I bogeyed the last hole for a 76 and a two-day total of 143, well within the projected cut line of 146. No controversy followed me to the scorer's tent today. No sportswriters, either. Not even Randall Fisk, who probably believed his half column of saccharine bought him another four years of ignoring me or abusing me with impunity.

Georgina waited outside the tent, her straw hat dangling from its knotted ribbon strap, her long auburn hair flowing thickly over her shoulders. Fatigue clouded my thoughts and dulled my muscles. Deirdre worried me, and lots of unfinished business nagged me. But I still en-

joyed watching men ogling Georgina and knowing that tonight . . . tonight . . .

"See you tomorrow," she said, when I finally emerged from making
my 76 official.

"But I thought—"

"Forget it, Kieran. You're not going to lay a bad round tomorrow
on me. Sunday night, we'll talk."

"Interesting choice of words," the Judge called back to me as he
followed Georgina toward the clubhouse.

The players' lounge was quiet. A few guys loosened their muscles
with gentle calisthenics. Several crowded around a TV to watch the
tournament's cable feed. I changed my golf shoes for sneakers, and sat
staring into my locker. Georgina was right. I should head home, shower,
and sleep through till dawn. An attendant interrupted all this high-
level planning.

"Two guys want to see you outside," he said.

I assumed these were reporters, either overly timid or underly cre-
dentialed since they didn't barge into the locker room. Another wrong
assumption.

"Greetings, Lenahan," said DiRienzo, who reintroduced me to
George Brudney, the Port Byram detective I met last night.

"Afternoon, Kieran," said Brudney, a rangy guy pushing retire-
ment age who acted like he worked at polished edges and smooth deliv-
eries. "Rough day, huh?"

I grunted. I didn't need smooth, and they weren't here to analyze
my round.

"We'd like to know how you ended up at the Port Byram train
station," said Brudney.

"I gave my statement last night."

"Well, he wants to hear it again, Lenahan," said DiRienzo.

Brudney patted a calming hand on DiRienzo's shoulder.

"I thought you had a lead on those guys," I said.

"Tracing the van?" said Brudney. "Nothing's developed yet."

So what was so important? I wondered.

"Humor me, Kieran, okay?" he said.

"Deirdre was on her way to my apartment for a personal squabble," I said. "I went to meet her outside, and when she didn't show up I traced her likely path. I found her car and saw the van rounding the bend. I recognized the van from the day I questioned the people at the Milton train station about Jackie. Things clicked."

"Like what?" said DiRienzo.

I ignored the sarcasm, which DiRienzo wore even worse than Willie Junior. "I knew these were the guys who pushed Jackie, and they would want Deirdre out of the way so she couldn't identify them."

"So you rush to the Port Byram train station," said Brudney, stroking his chin like a grandfather listening to a child's story. "Why not Milton? Why a train station at all?"

"I figured the fiesta gave them good cover. I wasn't thinking carbon monoxide. I was thinking more of the Amtrak express."

"You guessed good, Lenahan," said DiRienzo. "Almost too good."

"Reason this interests us," said Brudney, "is that early this morning we found Luis Augusto and his two bodyguards shot dead in the Latin Cooperative's boardroom."

"And since you're such a great expert on Hispanic-American culture," said DiRienzo, "we want you to come down and explain it all to us."

"Am I under arrest?" I said.

"You want to be? I'll cuff your ass right here," said DiRienzo. "See what all the reporters singing your praises yesterday say about that."

"Easy, Charles." Brudney walked DiRienzo to a water fountain and suggested he douse himself. He returned, slipping a card from his suit jacket and into my hand in one sweeping motion. "I just want to talk. Clear things up. I'm on duty till four. Go home. Collect yourself."

"Yeah, you had a hard day chasing golf balls," said DiRienzo, water dripping from his chin.

"Four o'clock, okay, Kieran?" said Brudney. "I don't want to put in for overtime. But if you don't show, I'll come looking for you."

I met the Judge in the clubhouse bar. Georgina already had departed for some spectating after a quick drink and a sample of the Inglisi wit one on one.

"You caught up a shot since you came off the course," he said.

I squinted at a distant television screen. The leader board showed Price at −5, and a host at −4.

"Any post-round interviews lined up?" he said.

"No."

The Judge dropped me at MCC. I faked unlocking the trailer door, then looped behind the clubhouse to the garbage stockade. The restaurant workers stared silently as I squeezed through the steamy kitchen to the cool of the main dining room. The Milton Lions Club, meeting for their weekly luncheon, listened to a realtor predict an imminent upswing in property values. A few of the Lions watched me pass, then whispered to each other. The switchblade in my pocket suddenly felt like Excalibur.

Eduardo Rojas sat with his feet on his desk and his pant cuffs riding high enough to show he wore no ankle holster.

"Kieran, Kieran, Kieran," he said without inflection.

"I need you to help me, Eduardo."

"For what? I saved your girl. Everything is finished. Now you mind your business." He opened a magazine in front of his face.

I flicked the blade, sliced the magazine in half, and held the knife edge to his nose. Eduardo never blinked.

"You put me in a serious bind, Eduardo. The Port Byram police want to question me about Luis Augusto's murder. I kept you out of it so far, but I won't keep you out of it much longer if you don't help me."

Eduardo dropped the two halves of the magazine and carefully lowered his feet without brushing against the blade. I backed him up with the knife and, without taking my eyes off him, groped through the top drawer of the desk until I found the gun. The silencer was still attached.

"What do you want?" he said. "I am not a member of the Latin Cooperative."

"Then how did you know about Deirdre?"

"I heard a telephone conversation," he said. "Augusto talked with someone about taking care of her. He said he wanted it done quick and clean. He wanted no one getting away this time."

"Prove it."

I prodded him down the fire exit to an old Datsun Z slung lower than the Judge's Ferrari. Rusted coat hangers lashed the rear bumper to the chassis. One fender was primed brown for a silver paint job it might never see. I untucked the front of my shirt and hid the gun underneath, the muzzle aimed at Eduardo's gut.

Downtown Port Byram suffered from a collective hangover. Many of the Hispanic shops were closed. Those with open doors idled in the afternoon heat. Sanitation workers pushed heaps of rubbish with large brooms. Streamers and banners flapped from concession booths lining the perimeter of Liberty Square. Three workers loaded sawhorses onto a flatbed truck.

Eduardo tooled along Main Street, his face its usual impassive mask except for the dark darting eyes that took in everything and missed nothing. He swung around at the north end, a move that gave us a glimpse of the squad car blocking the rear door to the Latin Cooperative's office. Neither of us said a word.

We headed back down Main and through the Square again, seeing more activity than on the last pass. Three children tossed colored milk caps on the sidewalk. A woman dragged a shopping cart stuffed with clothes into a laundromat.

Eduardo pulled to the curb and threw the car into neutral. I twisted in the seat, shielding the outline of the gun from people on the sidewalk.

"We won't find them here," he said. "We must go back to Milton."

I managed a glance at my watch without shooting myself. Two o'clock.

"Make it fast," I said.

Eduardo found a section of Milton I hardly knew existed, a tight grid of streets packed with multi-family houses on an inside bend of the Metro North tracks. A bunch of kids chased a soccer ball down the street. Old women bent over garden plots scraped from tiny front lawns. The hulk of a taxi sat on concrete blocks. A train rushed past, its wake plastering sheets of newspaper against a rusted chain-link fence.

Eduardo eased past the soccer game, hung a right up a steep road, then reversed into an even steeper driveway. Concrete walls rose tightly on each side of the car until we stopped beneath timbers thickly twined with grape vines.

"Wait here," he said, killing the engine.

"I'm coming with you."

"No. You want to find them, you stay here."

I had the gun and the knife, but right now had no choice. Eduardo squeezed around the back of the car and opened a wooden gate in the wall. He returned two minutes later, pushing a young boy in front of him while a woman screamed angrily at his heels. She was the thick woman with the long skirts and derby hat I'd questioned at Milton Station.

Eduardo shoved the boy into the back seat and climbed behind the wheel. The woman leaned through my window, shouting and cursing Eduardo while spraying me with spittle. Eduardo punched the car into gear and shot down the driveway, sending the woman spinning to the pavement.

"Mama," the boy cried as he pounded the rear window.

Eduardo yelled at him in Spanish, then raced us out of the neighborhood before skidding to a stop at the first quiet stretch of road.

"This kid knows," he said to me, then slipped into Spanish. The boy listened, bit his lip, spoke some and then started to cry.

"What did he say?" I asked Eduardo.

"An address."

"For what?"

"An operation."

I turned toward the boy. He was dark, very thin, and young. Twelve, thirteen tops.

"Ask him if he ever spoke to Monsignor Neumann," I said.

Eduardo translated my question.

"*Si,*" the boy said with a whimper.

"About the man who fell in front of the train."

"*El tren, si.*"

"But you never saw it happen, right?"

"No."

Eduardo geared up. The boy stopped crying and leaned forward into the gap between the front bucket seats, pointing, tapping Eduardo's shoulder, directing him in Spanish. Eduardo drove beyond the county airport, where the road curved sharply through fields marked by old stone walls and sudden rises revealed tree-covered hills stretching to the horizon. Eduardo slowed at each house, looking for a name, a number, a mailbox, something the boy told him and he didn't bother to tell me. Finally, he swung onto a dirt drive separating two fields of Queen Anne's lace. He nudged up to the crest of a long incline.

Down below, the drive curved to a modest farmhouse. No cars, no lights inside, no sign of anyone about.

Eduardo rolled us down the hill, and he and I got out of the car. The boy stayed in the back seat, scared. I took the front door, which was locked up tight, while Eduardo moved from window to window along the wide front porch. I stepped down and scanned the second floor windows. One was open. Boost the kid, I supposed.

"Kieran, here." Eduardo wiped dirt from a pane and told me where to look. Through the gauze curtain I could make out computer equipment.

Eduardo went back to the car and pulled the boy out. After some severe talk—obscenities are obvious in any language—the boy ducked under the porch and crawled out a moment later covered with dust and cobwebs. Eduardo brushed a nasty-looking spider from the boy's head. The boy dropped a key into my hand.

We all three went inside, the boy dangling under Eduardo's arm. The Latin Cooperative ran a damn big operation. Several computers and printers, laminating machines, boxes filled with green cards, blank social security cards springing off the floor and curling into a printer.

Prompted by Eduardo, the boy spoke quickly. Amid the Spanish I picked out distinctly English words: *work visa, green card, social security number*.

"He says two men often worked here," said Eduardo. "They create counterfeit documents here. The equipment was stolen from a Department of Motor Vehicles office upstate."

"How does he know this?"

"He and his brothers deliver the documents."

"The two men we are looking for," I said to the boy through Eduardo. "They work here when?"

"*Noches.*"

Nights. I couldn't wait that long. Detective Brudney would shed his smooth grace about five after four.

"Do you know where they live? Where they hang out during the day? A bar? A storefront?"

Eduardo translated. The boy shook his head.

I noticed the photo through a door, standing on a shelf in a tackily decorated den. From a distance, the sky-blue and sun-washed white meant nothing. But as I moved closer, wondering whether this subconscious interest was my way of coping with another dead end, the white portion slowly resolved into two men flanking an upended marlin on a dock.

I bolted from the room, grabbed the boy with one arm, and pushed Eduardo with the other.

"I'm driving!"

I threw the boy into the back seat. Eduardo barely closed the door as I spun a tight circle and shot up the drive. The clock on the dashboard flashed 3:55.

I drove like a bastard, hugging the insides of curves, passing pickups on short straightaways, running red lights at two intersections. I jumped onto the Cross Westchester Expressway, weaved through the traffic, jumped off again at the Port Byram exit. The clock blinked 4:05. Shift change at the medical center; tour change for the Port Byram police.

Traffic slowed. Several car lengths ahead, a county bus chugged up a steep incline. I pulled out, raced through a shopping center parking lot. Eduardo braced himself against the dashboard. The boy clung to the back of Eduardo's seat. Both screamed I was *loco*.

Through the parking lot I bounced into traffic, zoomed past St. Mary's Cemetery, then turned up the big hill toward the medical center. In the exit, around the nurses' residence, past the ER. I jammed to a stop in front of the lobby and burst through the automatic doors.

Visitors lined up at the reception desk, waiting for cards to admit them to the wings. Gina O'Meara stood at the newsstand, gathering magazines. I rushed past everyone, past the security guard, past the elevator bank to the staircase. One part of my mind counted the seconds since my discovery. Another replayed the comments I'd dropped over the last few days, essentially signing Deirdre's death warrant.

Five flights up, my lungs burned, ready to explode. Out on the floor, I quickly oriented myself. The nurses' station this way, the empty chair guarding Deirdre's room that way.

I rushed into the room. Mel Tucker bent over the bed, pressing a pillow with his elbows. I lowered my shoulder, drove it directly into his ribcage. The impact lifted him off his feet. His head banged hard against the thick glass of the window. I tumbled over a chair. Flower pots crashed. An alarm squealed. Tucker stared dopily into space as he melted to the floor, leaving a streak of blood on the glass.

I scrambled to the bed and threw the pillow off Deirdre's face. The heart monitor beeped.

CHAPTER
18

Jose Rojas returned to his job the day after Mel Tucker was arraigned on charges of conspiracy to commit murder, attempted murder, and assault. The feds waited in the wings, ready to bang him for a host of offenses connected with the immigration scams he ran with Luis Augusto.

That first night back for Jose, I kept one eye on the bar and my other eye, mind, and heart on Georgina. Toward the end of the night, Eduardo stopped prowling the tables. He reached across the bar and grasped his brother's hand.

Eduardo and I never talked about the night in the stairwell or the mad dash to the medical center that Friday afternoon. We saw each other many times as the summer ripened into fall and the fall aged into winter. He would seat Georgina and me at the table we reserved every Tuesday and Saturday evening, mutter under his breath, and slink away. He still carried the switchblade. Having carried it myself for a night and a day, I didn't see it so much as sense its tempered blade and ivory handle riding in his jacket high against his heart.

Our longest conversation came one quiet night in late September, before coffee and after Georgina excused herself for the ladies room. Eduardo asked about the tides, which ran heavy through the inlet between Milton Harbor and the Sound this time of year.

"Planning some fishing?" I said.

"Fishing, yes."

That was as close as we came to discussing the gun.

Deirdre completely recovered from her bout with carbon monoxide poisoning. She visited my apartment one night with Georgina in attendance. We all three spoke about the case and Deirdre's health. Quickly out of words, Deirdre said good-bye. I walked her to her car while Georgina, ever discreet, channel surfed from her corner of the living room sofa.

Thick clouds carried a hint of rain, the sharp autumnal showers that knock the first leaves from the trees.

"I guess we're even," said Deirdre. "I saved you, you saved me."

"Agreed," I said. "Let's call that quits, okay?"

We both scraped our feet on the pavement beside her car.

"I have an interview tomorrow," she said. "Third one with the same bank. Think they like me?"

"They love you," I said. "Good luck."

I watched her drive away. She stopped at the end of the road and flashed her lights before turning safely toward home. Yes, we were even. She once saved me from drowning; I saved her from Mel Tucker. These are momentous matters, but our problems always had been the tiny moments and minor crises that build into lives. Would these little things build a life with Georgina? Time would tell.

———

Late in March I met Mariela at St. Mary's Cemetery. A stiff wind whipped among the gravestones. In the distance, sunlight poked through steel-gray clouds scudding above the Sound. Closer below in Milton, the steeples of Church Alley rose above the bare trees.

"The day he first came to me he was covered head to foot with dirt," she said. "He heard about the Cooperative, and he wanted to join. He was a good man then. I still believe it."

"He already knew Tucker," I said.

"Long before, as a boy in La Paz. Tucker stayed at a hotel on the street where Luis begged. He wanted to find tin, and Luis volunteered to be his guide. It shows. Luis had no father. Neither did Jackie. They both fell under his control. The only difference is that Jackie resisted in the end."

"And paid for it."

"Jackie was still a gambler deep down, as Al says," said Mariela. "After Luis and Tucker hijacked the Cooperative, Tucker trained Jackie for jobs Luis' men refused. The monkey house was one. Those men were to die, but Jackie started the fire earlier than planned. He knew they would get out alive."

"Do you plan to come back?" I said.

"I cannot," said Mariela. "The merchants group in charge of the Cooperative now, they will do a good job."

Swaddled in a basket, Ian Rodriguez-MacEwan began to cry. Mariela rocked the basket, and gently set it back at the foot of the Celtic cross marking Jackie's grave. I slipped the wad of bills into her hand.

"From Jackie's mother," I said. "She understands where he was going that day and why."

Mariela nodded, knowing I lied. She lifted baby Ian into her arms and walked down the hill to the road where Al Sabo waited in an old VW minibus.

I almost forgot. I shot 70 - 69 in the last two rounds of the PGA Championship to finish tenth. The prize money made up for my closeout merchandise gamble, re-stocked my pro shop, contributed to Jackie's gravestone, and staked Mariela to the grand Jackie carried the day he died. More importantly, tenth place won me exempt berths in a whole lot of tournaments on the PGA Tour. Tomorrow, Comet Kieran and Georgina leave for Augusta National.

Kensington Books proudly announces
that the paperback edition of
Conor Daly's first Kieran Lenahan mystery

LOCAL KNOWLEDGE

is available this month.

The following is a preview of
LOCAL KNOWLEDGE . . .

LOCAL KNOWLEDGE

The useful knowledge acquired by a golfer based on
the experience he has gained of the best way to play
a particular hole or a particular course.

—from *The Encyclopaedia of Golf*
compiled by Webster Evans
St. Martin's Press, 1974

CHAPTER
1

Miko Onizaka winced as his fifteen footer burned the cup and spun dead on the lip. He stood motionless, the anguish of another defeat setting in. Then he whipped his putter in a furious swing of frustration and stomped toward the ball. The air crackled, the green quaked. The crowd rustled nervously behind me. We all had heard the rumors of blind drunks, violent temper tantrums, fealty to a sponsor who demanded success at any cost. I'd always ascribed these stories to xenophobia. But watching my opponent subtly change from a golf pro to a downsized sumo wrestler with powerfully rounded shoulders and a paunch as soft as iron, I felt a twinge of chauvinism.

Onizaka glared at his ball for a long moment before tapping it in. The crowd held its collective breath as he walked stiffly to the fringe. My caddie plopped my freshly buffed golf ball into my hand.

I cleared my mind, crouched at my coin and aimed the label of my golf ball straight at the cup. Three feet of close-cropped bluegrass separated me from a sudden-death win in the Metropolitan Golf Championship. I glanced around, freezing the scene in a mental diorama. Wykagyl Country Club, New Rochelle, New York. Present day. Onizaka strangling his golf glove, local sportswriters scribbling on notepads, police auxiliary raising hands for silence, golf nuts in all shapes and sizes jockeying for a view. I wanted to remember every detail. This putt meant far more to me than a title and a fat paycheck. The Met winner also earned an automatic berth in the Classic, the local stop on the PGA Tour. I had screwed my one chance at becoming a touring pro. This three-footer was my backdoor to a dream.

I rammed it home.

The gallery exploded in applause. My caddie danced the samba with the flagstick. The sportswriters barked for comments. The police joined hands to prevent a wholesale stampede across the green. I waded through the crush to offer my hand to Onizaka. Shreds of his glove littered the fringe, and I wondered if devotion to good sportsmanship might cost me a working set of knuckles. Luckily, someone grabbed my shoulder.

"Please come with me, Mr. Lenahan."

The county trooper stood a full head above me. Black, articulate, with a ranger hat strapped tightly to his jaw and forearms the size of Popeye's, he radiated a calm detachment in the floodtide of bodies roiling around us. Sometimes the most minor detail reinforces the reality of a situation. I became the Met champ the instant my putt clicked against the bottom of the cup. But the idea of this gladiator steering me safely to a blue and white cruiser parked on a macadam cart path drove my accomplishment home. My stomach fluttered pleasantly. All hail the conqueror.

But when the trooper opened the rear door I sensed something strange. And when he gunned the cruiser clear through the clubhouse parking lot I knew this wasn't a victory procession.

"Where the hell are we going?" I said, my fingers entwined in the cage separating the front and back seats.

"Milton," he said. "You are wanted for questioning."

My chest collapsed against a thumping heart. Minor detail, hell. I was in trouble. Sudden, severe, indefinable trouble. A minute ago I had climbed to the top my own little world. Now I felt like a poor slob who'd been flattened by an air conditioner from twenty stories and stood before St. Peter wondering what the hell happened.

I resisted the normal inclination to jabber my way into deeper hot water. I'd been a golf pro for five years, more than half the length of time I spent as a practicing attorney. A *bete noire* from my previous life was the client who tried to buddy up to his arresting officer. Cops aren't your buddies. They are paid to arrest people, and a good part of the job involves bending what you say into something they want to hear. I wasn't strictly under arrest. *Questioning* was the last word the trooper said before retreating into authoritarian silence. So I settled onto the seat and watched the suddenly unfamiliar scenery whip past while searching my memory for the last crime I may have committed. An ignominious start to my reign as Met champ.

I expected Milton to mean the Milton Police Station, but we skirted the village and turned into the grounds of my employer, the Milton Country Club. The cruiser's suspension bucked down a service road that dipped and curved through wooded hills until it smoothed out at the wide treeless expanse known as the linksland. I pulled myself up to the cage. Two hundred yards beyond the windshield, several Milton squad cars gathered alongside a pond. Their gumball lights flicked bright blue against the hazy July sky.

A siren whooped behind us and an ambulance whisked past, its tires kicking up clouds of grass and sand. The trooper parked behind the squad cars and ordered me out of the back seat. Several cops huddled on a rocky island that supported the twin spans of a wooden footbridge linking the eighth green with the ninth tee.

"Yo, DiRienzo!" the trooper yelled across the water.

DiRienzo straightened up, a hulk in white shirtsleeves towering above the huddled uniforms. His eyes locked onto mine, and he lumbered across the bridge.

"Lenahan," he growled at me, then turned to the trooper. "Thanks, bud. You want to stick around and see how we work?"

A hint of a smirk crossed the trooper's face. "I'll pass," he said. He flicked the brim of his hat in a curt salute and marched to his cruiser.

"What the hell's going on here, Chicky?" I said. DiRienzo's given name was Charles, and he hated the diminutive nickname. I didn't like being hauled away from a tournament, so we were even.

"I'm asking the questions, okay?" DiRienzo's head was about three sizes too small for the rest of him, like a football player minus a helmet. The hairless red arms poking out of his shirtsleeves looked like boiled hot dogs. "You hired Tony La Salle to dive in this pond, right?"

Another Milton patrol car crunched to a stop behind us. A police diver in full scuba gear bounced out. His partner lifted the trunk and began pounding stakes into the hardpan and stringing bright orange tape.

"What happened to Tony?" I said.

"Nothing. Now did you hire him? It's a very specific question."

I noticed Tony now. He knelt on the far side of the island and stared very intently at the water.

"Yeah," I said.

"Want to tell me what the hell a golf pro needs with a frogman?"

"I hire Tony twice a year to dredge golf balls out of the ponds," I said. "Technically, any ball lost in a water hazard becomes property of the club pro."

DiRienzo closed one eye and considered my explanation. I'd

known Chicky since his days as a rookie patrolman pounding along Merchant Street. He wasn't very smart, and compensated by casting suspicion on everyone and everything around him. He owed his detective shield to tenacity and departmental politics rather than any talent for detection.

He thumped my chest with the back of his hand. I followed him across the bridge and instantly saw the object of everyone's interest: several sausage links floating on the dark water about three yards off the island. A dragonfly danced around them, then spun off into the marshes.

A few sausages seemed like a strange reason for the commotion. Maybe I had missed the point. Then the sausages seemed to leap right out of the water at me, and I realized with a sharp jab to the solar plexus the sausages were fingers. Human fingers. Swollen, coated with pond scum, their flesh a garish purple.

I hunkered down beside Tony La Salle, who crouched on a rock with his toes curled into the water. Tony was an ex-Navy frogman who billed himself as an underwater salvage expert when he wasn't shucking clams.

"I was pickin' along when I felt somethin', sorta like a dead fish maybe wedged between two rocks," he said. Dried pond water crusted his hair and mustache. A fresh coat of sunburn raged on his brow. "I pushed and grabbed, and then it popped up like a goddam Jack-in-the-box."

"Any idea who it is?"

"I wasn't using a mask. I was rootin' around in the shallows with my hand. Probably can't see anything in this soup anyhow. I'da had to raise him, and I wasn't gonna do that. I ran down to the call box at the end of the service road. Called the cops from there. DiRienzo ask about me?"

"He wanted to know why I hired a diver. I told him."

"So did I. He didn't believe me."

"Suspicion is his civic duty."

The police diver eased into the water with a nylon net strung between inflatable yellow bladders. His wake rolled lazily across the pond as he submerged. The hand sank out of sight. Draughts of bubbles spiraled in the water.

The diver surfaced and gave a thumbs up. A moment later, two yellow floats popped into view. Slung between them was the body of Sylvester Miles. The left side of his head lay flat against his left shoulder.

Any body in a water hazard is a shock, but Sylvester Miles' grinning death mask shook everyone. He was one of Milton's leading citizens, a man who had parlayed hard work and a war hero's reputation into a chain of clothing stores in Westchester and Fairfield counties. He also was a founder and one-third owner of Milton Country Club. I could say, without sounding maudlin, that he had rescued my golf career from the ash heap.

The diver pushed the float against the island and two cops lifted the body. Water streamed out of collar and cuffs. Heavy objects dangled in the back of Miles' dark windbreaker. The cops laid out the body, and a doctor from the county coroner's office took over. DiRienzo didn't bother us again until the ambulance attendants zipped up the body bag.

"How much of the pond did you cover before you shook hands with Miles?" he said to Tony.

"Three-quarters, maybe a little more."

"Find anything other than golf balls?"

"A few clubs, a rake, a garden hose."

DiRienzo's eyes, already a shade too close together, narrowed into dark slits. "Where are they?"

Tony led us across the bridge to his staging area on the bank of the ninth tee. Three golf clubs leaned against a wire basket brimming with muddy golf balls. Layers of dark brown rust darkened the heads and shafts. The wood handle of the rake ended in splinters dulled by months beneath the water. Algae coated the garden hose, transforming it at first glance into an Amazon snake.

"I'm impounding all this stuff and anything else my men find," said DiRienzo. His tone carried a challenge, but I didn't snap. He could sell the junk for all I cared.

Tony explained where he covered and where he hadn't, and DiRienzo sketched a crude map of the pond in a notepad. Then he focused on me.

"You knew him, right? Miles was a honcho around here."

"Everyone referred to him as the owner, but he's actually one of three." The newness of Miles' death confused my verb tenses.

"Who are the others?"

"William St. Clare and Dr. Frank Gabriel," I said. DiRienzo dutifully scribbled the names. All of Milton knew this triumvirate, but DiRienzo obviously planned to examine the most basic facts.

"Did he play much golf?"

"Not as much as you would think. A round on weekends, maybe another midweek. What he enjoyed best was walking the course in the evenings. His house is right on the golf course." I pointed down the eighth fairway. Behind the tee, the linksland ended at a wooded hill. The gables of a Tudor mansion rose above the treeline. "I ran into him whenever I practiced. Most times he'd be carrying one club and hitting three or four golf balls in front of him. Other times he'd inspect the course. If he noticed anything amiss, he'd tell the greenskeeper."

"Was he out here yesterday evening?"

"I don't know. I played thirty-six holes at Wykagyl and only stopped back here after dark."

"What about you?" DiRienzo said to Tony. "What time you get out here this morning?"

"Seven A.M. I didn't see nothing."

"Do you think someone killed Miles while he was practicing?" I said.

The linksland was forty odd acres of flat terrain dotted by greens, tees, ponds, and tide pools. The only cover was a belt of brush growing along the harbor inlet and a wall of reeds marking the boundary between the club and the Marshlands Nature Conservancy. Not the place where you could commit a crime unnoticed, especially since there always was a foursome or two somewhere on the linksland at any given time of daylight.

DiRienzo ignored the question. He walked back to the island and detailed a rookie to chauffeur me back to Wykagyl. The rookie seemed peeved at being banished from a murder scene, but at least he let me sit in front. And at least I knew where I was going and why.

I gladly avoided Wykagyl's post-Met festivities. I loved the game, loved competition, but hated all the glad-handing and backslapping that followed a tournament. Sylvester Miles' death afforded me the perfect excuse for a quick exit, though the news caused barely a ripple of sobriety as it coursed through the crowd. Besides, the sight of those sausage fingers spoiled my appetite for the hot-cold buffet.

I discreetly pocketed my winner's check and headed toward the parking lot where caddie and clubs leaned against a fence. Concern over my sudden disappearance went only so far as securing payment for three days' not so hard labor.

"You weren't the only one dragged away by the cops," said my caddie. "Onizaka downed a few Scotches in the clubhouse bar, then started ranting about how the tournament was fixed."

"Fixed? I birdied the last three holes to tie him, then the playoff hole to beat him. We didn't even need any rulings from the officials."

"Hey, this is what he was shouting, okay? The barman tried to shut him up, but Onizaka slugged him. Someone called the cops, and they carted him away. Hope they book the bastard. He ain't back yet, see?"

Ten yards down the fence, a set of hi-tech Japanese clubs sparkled in a blue golf bag. Onizaka had built a reputation as a perennial also-ran. He often led in the early stages of our local tournaments, only to self-destruct in the final round. Rumor mongers blamed a Scotch bottle buried deep within the folds of his golf bag. But he'd been stone-cold sober today as his six shot lead dwindled to nothing. I simply blew him away with my late birdie barrage.

I collected my own clubs, and drove back to Milton Country Club. A ton of work awaited me in my shop. Now that I needed a week off for the Classic, I decided to set about doing it.

An unmarked police car hogged my usual space, so I parked near the caddie yard. A group of caddies interrupted debate on the murder barely long enough to congratulate me on winning the Met. My greatest victory upstaged by violence. Christ, what a world.

I heard the shouting even before I opened the pro shop door. DiRienzo demanded access to the bag room and Pete O'Meara, my seventeen year old shop assistant and sociology experiment, refused at the same decibel level. These were confirmed adversaries, DiRienzo having arrested Pete at least a dozen times. Pete locked both hands on the doorjamb and seemed willing to sacrifice his scrawny frame to defend the shop commandment that no one but staff and members may enter the bag room. Great to see a kid thinking independently.

"Shut up!" I yelled.

DiRienzo smoothed the front of his shirt. His suit jacket lay crumpled on the floor, a sure sign I'd just saved Pete from something unfortunate.

"Let me guess, Detective," I said. "You want to see the clubs Sylvester Miles stored in the bag room."

"Yeah. That's exactly what I was trying to explain to this wiseass."

"Pete, you could have let him in."

"But—"

"Pete."

Pete flung himself from the door and plopped onto a stool behind the cash register counter.

"He should have a warrant," he said.

DiRienzo folded his suit jacket over his forearm. "Stop acting like a Legal Aid lawyer, kid. You'll live longer that way."

The bag room was a large storage area behind my repair shop. The members paid me a yearly fee to keep their clubs cleaned and the caddies' fingers out of their golf bags. I explained this to DiRienzo as I led him to Miles' clubs.

"And you leave that wiseass in charge when you're not around? Isn't that like the fox guarding the henhouse?"

"We haven't had one complaint of theft since I hired Pete. That was almost two years ago."

"I know when that was," said DiRienzo. "I was Youth Officer, remember?"

The Youth Officer was Milton's idea of a liaison between the police department and the town's wayward adolescents. The YO theoretically combined a sympathetic ear with the mantle of authority. Talk about foxes and henhouses. DiRienzo as Youth Officer was like the blind leading the insane.

I yanked Miles' golf bag down from the rack. His set was intact, the same fourteen clubs he'd stored since I took over as golf pro two and a half seasons earlier. DiRienzo noted the make of the clubs in his pad. I explained that Miles didn't use these clubs when he practiced. He most likely kept another set at home for his evening jaunts. DiRienzo rifled through the pockets and made more notes about the balls and tees.

"The O'Meara kid minded your shop for you yesterday?"

"As usual."

Back out in the shop, Pete still sat at the register with his elbows on the counter and his hands on his temples. His face was the crescent moon personified. A turned up nose and lots of forehead and chin. DiRienzo placed both hands beside Pete's elbows and lowered himself until his nose was inches from the boy's.

"Did you see Sylvester Miles yesterday?" he said.

"Was I supposed to?" Pete said without flinching.

DiRienzo gripped the countertop, trying to maintain his composure. His knuckles went white.

"Do you keep a record of who plays?"

"Caddymaster does. I don't."

"But you see most people before they go out to play."

"Look, you want to know if anyone played, ask the caddymaster. I didn't see nobody after four in the afternoon. The weather was bad, so nobody played."

"What time did you leave?"

"Seven, quarter after maybe."

"How did you get home?"

Pete stuck out his thumb.

"You didn't cut across the golf course into Harbor Terrace."

"I just told you," said Pete. "I hitched."

"What are you driving at?" I said to DiRienzo.

"Just want to see if maybe he saw Miles on his way home." DiRienzo turned back to Pete. "What'd you do until seven?"

"Things. Cleaned clubs. Changed a few grips. Kieran taught me things."

"He's a big help," I chimed.

DiRienzo looked at me doubtfully.

"I would have left earlier," said Pete. "But Dr. Gabriel needed a golf cart."

"I thought you said nobody played," said DiRienzo.

"He didn't. He said he had to check something out. Kept the cart about a half hour. Otherwise I would have left earlier. He tipped me two bucks, though."

Pete rode home with me, as he often did on evenings I didn't practice until sundown. I expected a deluge of adolescent questions about the murder, but Pete fooled me by asking about the Met. At least someone was interested. I recounted how I birdied the last three holes to tie Miko Onizaka at the end of regulation play, then added a fourth birdie on the first hole of sudden death. Pete wasn't familiar with the Wykagyl lay-out, so I spared him a blow-by-blow and described only the high points. The entire account ended well before we reached home, which then left time for the adolescent questions.

"Do they know like how he got killed?"

"DiRienzo didn't brief me."

"Did he just get dumped in the pond? There were like rocks in his jacket, I heard."

"DiRienzo didn't like say."

"Damn. Sylvester Miles, deader'n hell. Ain't that a bitch?"

Pete and I both lived in Limerick, upscale Milton's only bona fide working class neighborhood. The name derived from the Irish immigrants who settled in this community of converted summer cottages in the early 1900s. The men found jobs with the railroad, and the women worked as domestics in mansions along the Sound. The neighborhood was mixed now, each decade of the century folding in another national-ity: Italians in the '20s, Hungarians in the '50s, Bolivians and Brazilians in the '70s and '80s. Two-family houses sprouted among the cottages like flowers in a weed patch. But the neighborhood kept its name; insti-tutions like Toner's Pub endured. And Limerick's original bloodline still worked on the railroad, which was electric rather than diesel and boasted solid-state cars that passed through town with a whisper. The few remaining domestics worked for successful Limerick boys like Brendan Collins.

Pete hailed from what our therapy-obsessed society vapidly labels a dysfunctional family. His father, Tom O'Meara, was a Metro North electrician who nearly lost a leg in a railyard accident. He settled his claim for peanuts rather than tough out a trial, and spent every penny on transforming his front porch into a private den and buying a second-hand motorboat he moored in the public marina. Mangled and sullen, he collected monthly disability checks, contracted small electrical jobs on the sly, and occasionally used his wife for a punching bag. Gina was a mousy Bolivian immigrant who oozed guilt from every pore. She blamed herself for Tom's accident, blamed herself for his unpredictable blasts of temper, and absorbed his body blows with incantations to *Jesu Christi*. Neither parent paid Pete any mind. Tom couldn't manage his own life, let alone another human being's. And Gina harbored the idiotic notion that if she pleased her perpetually dissatisfied husband, they all three would return to familial bliss. If ever they'd been there.

Small wonder Pete had a police record as long as his proverbial arm before his sixteenth birthday. Vandalism, shoplifting, public intoxication, possession of a joint. Minor offenses in the grand scheme of the criminal justice system, but enough to earn a gangster's reputation in a town like Milton.

I knew Pete's history because I almost became his uncle. I'd lived with his Aunt Deirdre—Tom's younger sister—on and off for five years before the road to marriage permanently forked. Deirdre gave Pete his only sense of direction in an otherwise rudderless existence. She bought him clothes, sheltered him from temptation, and generally tried to instill a sense of values. She even took him into her apartment for six months when Tom and Gina went through a bad stretch and Family Protection Services wanted Pete placed in a foster home.

But even Deirdre was no match for Pete's last run-in with the law

two summers earlier. Youth Officer DiRienzo had convinced the town
judge to sentence Pete to six months at an upstate youth farm for a
relatively minor vandalism incident. Tom O'Meara didn't raise a fuss;
he probably liked the idea of one less mouth to feed. So Deirdre turned
to the Honorable James Inglisi, my former law partner and our mutual
friend.

Judge Inglisi blew into Town Court in typical gruff fashion. He
intimidated the town judge, insulted a social worker, and pissed off Di-
Rienzo, but eventually hammered out a deal. Instead of the youth farm,
Pete accepted two years probation conditioned on finding part-time
employment during the school year and full-time employment during
the summers. I volunteered to hire him as my shop assistant. I'd always
liked Pete. And having grown up in Limerick as a shanty Irish kid myself, I felt an affinity for whatever drove his recklessness.

Pete wasn't exactly the shop assistant from central casting. He had
terminally bad posture and a habit of leaning against any inanimate object within reach. His black hair straggled to his shoulders. He wore
ragged football jerseys and faded jeans. His manners made a grease monkey look sophisticated. But he developed into a damn good shop assistant. He played a decent golf game, showed a talent for club repair, and,
despite DiRienzo's insinuations, was impeccably honest. I couldn't
shake the vague suspicion Pete always teetered on the verge of backslid-
ing. But so far my fears had been unfounded.

I wheeled my car into the O'Meara driveway. Like most Limerick
houses, Pete's was a pastiche of architectural styles: the dormers of a
Cape, the stucco of a Tudor, and the curlicued woodwork of a Victorian. Tom's enclosed porch protruded from one side like a goiter. The
blue light of a TV flickered through the screened windows, throwing
Tom's head into a wavering silhouette.

"There he is," said Pete. "Just my luck he ain't fishing tonight. All
he'll do is sit on that porch and watch war movies on the VCR and

bitch. At least he doesn't hit Mom anymore. I guess he figures I'm big enough to pop him back."

Pete yanked open the door and loped down the driveway to the back of the house. Must be comforting to know you're keeping your father in line.

CHAPTER
2

The next day the club was lively as a dirge. The sun glowed weakly behind persistent clouds. A harsh breeze tossed the red, white, and blue bunting left over from the Fourth of July. Golfers tiptoed past the pro shop and spoke in whispers. Even the caddies refrained from their usual spats. The ambience hardly improved when Randall Fisk popped into the shop just before noon.

Fisk covered the metropolitan golfing scene for a local newspaper chain. Despite his relatively unimportant beat, he fancied himself an investigative journalist and informed his columns with all manner of "serious" topics. One story, devoted to women's restricted starting times at a particular country club, exploded into a tirade on the Equal Rights Amendment. Another, intended as a paean to a toothless septuagenarian caddie, explicated Fisk's bubble-headed theories on redistribution of wealth. Crazier still, Fisk professed never to have played the game. "If I play it, I can't criticize it," he once told me. "Someone must seize the role of watchdog." As if golf were a bureaucracy worthy of a Cabinet post.

My personal introduction to Randall Fisk's journalism was a column about my troubles with the PGA Tour brass. The facts were basically true, but the insinuations bordered on libel.

"Quite an exit you made yesterday," he said. "Or was that an exit at all? Was someone, or some local golfing body perhaps, interested in a urine sample?"

Fisk pulled a wrinkled handkerchief from his pants pocket and dabbed at a single bead of sweat meandering down the curving ridge of his nose. His interviewing technique featured a symphony of twitches, tics, and grunts calculated to annoy his victim into submission. I took a deep breath.

"I was needed here. Someone had an accident."

"That's not what I heard. A blow to the collarbone, another to the occipital lobe of the skull." Fisk shivered. "Stones shoved into pockets and shirt to weigh down the body. These aren't accidents. I understand you identified the body."

"There were several of us. Everyone knew him."

"And this diver." Fisk looked up at the ceiling and seemed to snatch the name physically out of the air. "This Tony La Salle. You hired him."

"To pull golf balls out of the ponds. So I could sell them and donate the proceeds to the caddie scholarship fund." Where was this going, I wondered.

"Such an odd turn of events." He plucked an iron from a display rack and pressed the clubhead to his chin. "You with the well documented, ah, troubles, finally winning yourself a spot on the Tour, however fleeting it may be, only to be whisked away from your triumph by the state police."

"County trooper," I said. "Let's get our law enforcement authorities straight."

Fisk nodded playfully, noting this fact for the record.

"You missed the action yesterday," he said.

"I don't like post-tournament parties."

"I'm referring to your chief rival's tirade."

"I didn't know I had a rival."

"Ah, Kieran, still confusing your public and private selves. You and Miko Onizaka have been knocking heads in these tournaments ever since the Tour banished you to this patch. Therefore, you are rivals."

I wiped my thumb on the glass top of my display counter. Fisk had manufactured this "rivalry" during my first year at Milton Country Club after Onizaka and I battled to a second place tie in the Connecticut Open.

"Why the rivalry?" I had asked him at the time.

"The golfing public needs a focal point for the inexorable Japanese take-over of American golf," he had replied in all his stilted splendor. "I have chosen you and Miko as the standard bearers."

In fact, Onizaka played the stereotypically inscrutable Asian as well as he played golf. We barely traded a word during our several competitive rounds. Strip away the rumors, and I didn't know a damn thing about him other than he worked as a staff pro for a Japanese golf equipment company with a large outlet in southern Connecticut.

"The funny part," said Fisk, "is that your rivalry is bent toward an ironic denouement."

"What the hell do you mean?"

"A little rumor a little birdie told me. Or was it a bogey?" Fisk smirked the kind of smirk I wanted to drive a fist through. "A Japanese concern plans to buy Milton Country Club. And when they do, guess who will be installed as head pro? Miko Onizaka."

"Get the hell out of here!" I winged a set of leather head covers, but Fisk ducked out of the way.

"Ta ta, Mr. Met," he chortled.

The phone rang not long after lunch. A male voice identified himself as Roger Twomby—pronounced Toomby—then fired off a rapid succession of WASP names ending with his own. I recognized the law firm as an estate administration heavyweight, with offices in Manhattan, Palm Beach, and several other communities where the rich went to die.

"We drafted the last will and testament of Sylvester Miles and are counsel to the executor in the probate proceeding. The reason I am calling is that a clause in the will directly involves you."

"I inherited money?"

"Not exactly," said Twomby. "The clause is quite unique. I believe a face to face is necessary. In, perhaps, ten minutes. At the deceased's home."

I left the shop in Pete's hands and drove across the golf course in an electric cart. Sylvester Miles had been my boss, and a damn good one. But we never became friends, never hoisted drinks at the clubhouse bar, never grilled burgers on his backyard patio, never even played a round of golf. I spent the entire ride searching my memory for any hint why he would name me in his will. I found none.

The Miles house stood on a ridge that descended from the posh neighborhood of Harbor Terrace, crossed the seventh hole like the spine of a subterranean monster, and flattened out onto the dun-colored fairways of the linksland. I parked my cart where the stone fence marking the club property line humped over the ridge. The view was impressive, even by Harbor Terrace standards. With one sweep of the eye you could take in the marina, the linksland, the golden reeds of the Marshlands Nature Conservancy, and, at the mouth of the inlet, two rocky islands forming a gateway to the Long Island Sound.

The driveway was crowded. A Milton squad car and an official-looking Plymouth pinned a pair of Mercedes to the garage door. Behind them, a dusty Volvo hissed with recent exertion.

The same rookie who had driven me back to Wykagyl the previous day answered the door. They weren't ready for me, he said, and showed me into a parlor. At the far end of the room, framed by a window bay, Adrienne Miles stretched to tip the spout of a watering can into the hanging pot of a lush spider plant. A sleeveless gold tunic reaching to mid-thigh matched her wiry blonde hair. A black body stocking hugged the rest of her.

Adrienne lowered her watering can, and our eyes locked in that provocative way where you feel you're rushing toward each other on dollies.

"I'm terrible sorry about Sylvester," I said, and the twenty feet of parlor between us telescoped back to normal proportions. She smiled wanly and returned to her plants. After a final long draught into a ficus, she glided past me, eyes averted, and left the room. Musky perfume floated in her wake.

Everyone in town knew Adrienne's story, or thought they did. Fifteen years earlier, Sylvester Miles flew to a fashion convention in Chicago and flew back with a bride. Adrienne was thirty years his junior, so words like *gold digger* and *sugar daddy* rattled behind them like empty cans on string. The club women treated her like a pariah. The older ones saw her as a threat to their husbands; the younger ones criticized her obvious lack of education and breeding. Small wonder she rarely appeared at the club. My only previous contact with her had been idle chatter at the annual Awards Night dinners. She always seemed pleasant, but plainly couldn't wait for those nights to end.

I wandered into the hallway. The rookie stood with his ear cocked against a closed door. Behind it, a male voice thundered unintelligibly.

The door suddenly flew open, and a tall, gangly man collided with the rookie.

"Damn you, too," the man said with a snort. He adjusted a small brown package under his arm and lurched toward the front door with a gait as knock-kneed as a giraffe's.

"We want Mr. Lenahan next," a voice I recognized as Twomby's called from inside the room. "And Mrs. Miles, too."

The room undoubtedly was Sylvester Miles' den. A large mahogany desk angled across one corner. Along the entire back wall, silver cups and pewter plates from Syl's many golf victories twinkled in pools of light. Across a thick burgundy carpet the size of a putting green stood a fully stocked bar. Chicky DiRienzo sat heavily on a barstool, his suit jacket draped across his lap and his omnipresent notebook on his knee. He nodded with a dopey *we meet again* grin on his face.

Roger Twomby stood behind the desk with his hands stuffed into the open mouth of a briefcase. He was a gaunt man with bloodless lips and spindly arms like the forelimbs of a Tyrannosaurus Rex. He lay a single sheet of legal-sized paper on the blotter and offered me a dead fish handshake.

"I presume you know Mr. St. Clare," he said. "He is the executor of Mr. Miles' will."

William St. Clare rose from one of two matching leather recliners. He was a former mayor of Milton, a co-founder of MCC, and Sylvester Miles' closest friend. His body bulged like a brandy snifter. Ambrose Burnside sideburns brushed against earlobes the size of quarters.

"And of course you know Detective DiRienzo," continued Twomby. "He requested to attend these proceedings as an observer, and of course the estate is cooperating, just as the Milton police department is cooperating with us."

"How does a police department cooperate with estate proceedings?" I said.

"Just an expression of good will," said Twomby. "We are all cooperating with each other."

St. Clare opened a closet and trotted out a black and white kangaroo golf bag containing a set of irons. Then he poured himself a drink and lay back in the recliner.

"Please sit, Mr. Lenahan," said Twomby, indicating a wing chair to his right. Adrienne Miles slipped silently into its mate at the opposite end of the desk. Her skin looked smooth as butterscotch, and her hard, strong features promised to age well. She pointedly avoided meeting my eye. Her fingernails held far more interest.

Twomby cleared his throat. "Here is the clause, Mr. Lenahan. Listen carefully. 'I direct my executor to sell at auction my set of *Blitzklub* golf clubs for the highest possible price. In this regard, my executor shall retain the services of Kieran Lenahan, the golf professional at the Milton Country Club, to lend his expertise in obtaining the highest possible auction price for said clubs.' "

"That's it?" I said when it became obvious that the clause had ended.

"The remainder of the clause does not concern you," said Twomby. "Do you understand the direction?"

"I've never heard of a *Blitzklub*, and I've never attended a golf club auction. Otherwise, it's perfectly clear."

"I confess I am mystified as well. I questioned Mr. Miles quite severely when drafting this clause, and he assured me that you would cooperate. Oh well, the clause speaks for itself, and Mr. Miles was extremely adamant.

"Now, although the will has not yet been admitted to probate, we, that is the executor and myself, believe the best interests of the estate dictate an expeditious marshalling of all assets, and since the arranging of an auction requires substantial preparation—"

"You want me to get the ball rolling."

"Exactly, Mr. Lenahan. Now, since the nature of these assets will require—"

"Are these the clubs?"

No one answered, probably because they weren't experts. I reached for the golf bag.

The *Blitzklubs* were the oddest set of irons I'd ever seen. Their design was pure 1990s golf technology: angular heads with the weight distributed in the heels and toes; metal with the dull finish of cast iron and the density of forged steel; a gooseneck hosel slightly offsetting the heads from the shafts. But the decorative features harked back to the Third Reich: *Blitzklub* lettered in Gothic typeface and underscored by a lightning bolt; tiny swastikas encircling the iron numbers; a Maltese cross inlaid on the clubface.

I thumbed each of the irons. The heads bore the nicks and scratches of moderate use. Bits of dirt and grass clung to the grooves. But the sole markings were deep and crisp and highlighted by goldleaf paint.

I pulled the five-iron from the bag. Tiny swastikas ribbed the black leather grip. The shaft was a smooth, shiny gray. An old fiberglass dinosaur, I thought. But when I waggled the club the shaft felt more like graphite than fiberglass.

I stole a glance at Adrienne. She had one palm open and trailed a finger of her other hand along the life line and up the mound of Venus. She seemed less like a grieving widow than a petulant child forced to sit through a boring dinner. She sure didn't give a damn about these clubs.

I emptied the bag and leaned the clubs in size order against the desk.

"The pitching wedge is missing," I said, pointing to the gap between the nine iron and sand wedge. "Can any of you explain that?"

"As I said, Mr. Lenahan," said Twomby. "I questioned Mr. Miles quite severely—"

"You told me. A set of irons with a matched sand wedge should include a matched pitching wedge."

My expert opinion thudded about the room. St. Clare mumbled into his drink. Adrienne played palmist. DiRienzo scratched a pencil across his pad.

"Doesn't matter. I'll do my best to follow the will's directions." I gathered the clubs together. "I assume I may take these with me."

"Of course," said Twomby. "You'll need them in order to arrange the auction, I presume."

"I will."

"Fine," said Twomby. "I can tell you without reading the remainder of the clause that you will receive a commission for your services."

"Who gets the rest of the money?"

"None of your damn business," snapped St. Clare.

I knew that would get a rise out of someone; I didn't expect it to be the ex-Mayor. Everyone bid me good day except for Adrienne. The rookie showed me to the door. As I walked to my cart I noticed the dusty Volvo idling in front of the house. The knock-kneed man stared at me through the window. Then he punched the car into gear and shot off down Harbor Terrace Drive.

Back at the shop, play had dwindled to its late afternoon trickle. I sent Pete home at six and saddled up an electric cart. Despite all the hubbub, I still had a tournament to prepare for.

I loved the golf course in the evening. A hush descended over the landscape. Water hazards smoothed to glass. Shadows ribbed the fairways. And for one magical moment, if you watched very carefully, the grass shifted from green to blue before tumbling into darkness.

The Milton Country Club layout was a unique blend of parkland and linksland. The original holes were built in the 1890s by a man named Tilford, who dreamed of carving a golf course out of a rolling forest of oak and ash. Unfortunately, Tilford routed only twelve holes before running out of room. He offered to buy additional acreage from his neighbor, a man named Caleb Park. But Park resented Tilford's plan for bringing this newfangled game to Milton. He not only refused to sell Tilford one square inch of property, he also forbade his only son Josiah from ever doing the same.

The golf course remained the private playground of the Tilford family until the 1960s, when three leading Milton businessmen—Sylvester Miles, William St. Clare, and Dr. Frank Gabriel—bought the estate and fashioned six more holes out of wasteland obviously ignored by Tilford. Set hard between Milton Harbor and the Marshlands Nature Conservancy, deeded to the town by Caleb Park's son, this terrain so closely resembled a Scottish seaside links that the architect did little more than cultivate greens and tees.

The three owners retained title for themselves rather than spread ownership among the members. It wasn't the normal method of country club management, but the owners realized Milton was a jewel of a golf course. The twelve parkland holes were lush, deceptive, and precisely manicured, and the six linksland holes gave you the feeling of St. Andrews. The club sold annual playing privileges like term life insurance. The members renewed year after year, and the waiting list numbered in the hundreds.

I played the first few holes in decent form, but my swing soon fell out of kilter. By the time I drew even with the Miles house I decided my heart wasn't in golf. A single Mercedes was all that remained of the cars that had jammed the driveway earlier in the day. Despite the thick green lawn, the razor-sharp shrubbery, and the newly painted stucco, the house seemed desolate, as if the death of its owner somehow had extinguished its soul.

I tooled through a flock of Canadian geese scraping for food on the linksland's skimpy fairways. At the pond, the orange tape snapped in the breeze. Tire marks left by police cars tattooed the hardpan. I walked along the tape, not expecting to see anything the cops hadn't noted. Several craters gaped in the pond bank. A swath of divots scarred the fairway where someone had practiced hitting pitch shots across the water to the eighth green. The water was murky as ever.

I crossed the footbridge and parted a screen of reeds behind the green. The tide was out, and a long shelf of mud stretched toward the buoys that guided boaters along the harbor inlet. The previous week's constant sunshine had baked a tiny patch of sand into a flat hardpan broken only by a gash from the keel of a small boat. Below a wash of mussel shells, the sand darkened to mud.

When I was young, the caddies would steal down on hot summer afternoons and skinny dip in the inlet. Not being a swimmer—in fact, being petrified of water—I stood on the sand and watched for the Harbor Patrol speedboat. No one dared swim here now. Silt choked the inlet, and motor oil slimed the water. But I still visited this beach whenever I wanted to think deep thoughts.

Milton Country Club always had seemed as safe and as sheltered as the harbor. For twenty years, no matter how far I ranged, I felt tethered to its fairways. Its parochial concerns of pars and birdies, of matches won and putts missed, of greens fertilized and tees clipped provided a brief respite from the realities outside the stone fence. Now the club had seen a murder.

I wondered about Adrienne. Will readings weren't lively affairs. But she had seemed curiously detached, if not downright uninterested. Or maybe helpless was a better description—a woman suddenly sitting on a fortune and surrounded by jackals ready to tear off hunks of cash with their jaws. Oh well, I had my role. Arrange the auction of those *Blitzklubs*, whatever the hell they were. For a fee. Maybe I was a jackal myself.

A boat engine sputtered, and a familiar looking motorboat festooned with fishing rods drifted past. Tom O'Meara fiddled with the outboard engine. I stepped into the reeds. Tom was the last person I wanted to spot me in a contemplative mood.

People think the job of a club professional is constant amusement. Hell, they see the pro while they're playing a game. *Ergo*, the pro must be having fun, too. In fact, the workday of a club pro is as tedious, and as unglamourous, as a coal miner's. It's just not as dirty or dangerous.

My contract with Milton Country Club requires me to run a pro shop with normal business hours (basically, dawn to dusk), maintain a fleet of electric golf carts (about as durable as five dollar watches), officiate the weekly club tournaments (featuring arguments as childish as kindergarten spats), and teach golf lessons. Unofficially, I am a head-shrinker to golf nuts, a father confessor to unhappy spouses, a registrar of sundry complaints, and, not often enough, the object of female desire.

Playing the game doesn't appear in the job description. That's because the Professional Golfer's Association, the umbrella group to which every club professional must belong, cares more about its members' ability to read a balance sheet than read a putt. We're businessmen in sports togs. But uncage me and I can play a mean game. And with a bit of luck, as happened at the Met Championship, I can show my wares on a grander stage.

Another of my unofficial functions was to attend the wakes of deceased members. Most were quiet affairs. The women sat in the viewing parlor while the men, dressed in muted golf shirts and blue MCC blazers, stood in the foyer swapping golf stories about the departed. The memorial service hastily organized by the local VFW post resembled a testimonial dinner, minus the food.

Miles wasn't just a big man at the club; he was a bona fide war hero, WWII vintage. You wouldn't have guessed it to see him decorating display windows in his flagship store on Merchant Street or lowering himself on rickety knees to line up a putt. But if you knew about his past you'd have seen a hawk in the bent nose, darting eyes, and raked back silver hair. On damp days you'd have noticed a slight hitch in his stride, the result of an ankle wound. And that constant twisted smile? Nerve damage from hand to hand combat, or so the story went. Miles gained such notoriety that the Town Council erected a permanent tribute in the lobby of Town Hall: a helmet, a Springfield grenade rifle, shell casings, and a laminated copy of a *Milton Weekly Chronicle* story about his war exploits.

I shouldered my way through several knots of elderly men clogging the front steps of the funeral home. From all the strange faces and the blue and gold piping, I took them for VFW members from other towns. The air inside reeked of lilies and cheap cologne. A VFW banner hung from the ceiling of the main parlor. Beneath it, an elderly vet stood at a podium draped in black. Between whines of microphone feedback, he railed about how Syl Miles should have been awarded the Congressional Medal of Honor for single-handedly capturing a German mortar nest near Anzio.

Smack in the middle of the audience sat the knock-kneed man who had stormed out of the Miles' house that afternoon. His puffy cheeks and a tousled mass of salt and pepper hair loomed over the bent gray heads of the old vets. Unlike the others, he met each heap of praise with a faint but unmistakable scowl. I certainly never saw him before today, but a strange sense of familiarity, perhaps an intimation of someone I once knew, tugged at my memory.

I backed away from the speeches and joined the usual gaggle of club men congregated in the foyer. No golf stories circulated tonight, just wild speculation about the murder. The police had been unusually stingy with details, and these men, who fancied themselves town elders, were miffed at the lack of info. I listened long enough to fulfill my professional duty, then drifted toward the door. As I passed the main parlor, I noticed the knock-kneed man was gone.

Out on the sidewalk a group of vets surrounded a Milton cop who had ticketed a car with Pennsylvania plates for parking in a prohibited zone directly in front of the funeral home. The owner, a bandy-legged gent wearing a powder blue leisure suit and an olive drab army cap, shook his fist in the cop's face.

"Go after the real criminals," he shouted. "Not innocent people paying their respects to the dead."

Judge Inglisi and I went back twenty years, when his brief fling with golf brought him to Milton Country Club. I was a caddie; he was a portly beginner who showed no sign of ever mastering a full shoulder turn. His caustic exterior never quite fit in with the staid elements of the membership. But his penchant for generous tips made him a darling among the caddies. To us he was Big Jim, and a pisser of a loop.

I was a champion golfer in high school and college, but, being practical-minded, pursued a career in law instead of golf. When I finished law school, Big Jim hired me as his associate. The practice hauled in the usual small town staples: oldsters needing wills, families buying houses, punks grinding through the criminal courts, accident victims dreaming of lottery-sized verdicts. Inglisi & Lenahan lasted seven years without fistcuffs. Then Big Jim fooled enough voters to become county judge, and I headed south for a long delayed golf apprenticeship.

Since my unexpected return to Milton, our friendship trailed off to rare beer-filled evenings. The schedules of a golf pro and a judge meshed very poorly. Still, he was my court of first resort whenever I needed advice or oddball information. He'd bitch and moan and yell at me like a *de facto* stepfather. But he'd always churn out some imaginative ploy or dig up the dope. Though he wouldn't dare admit it, he admired me for casting off a sober profession to pursue a dream. Catch him at a candid moment, and he'd confess he'd rather have been a test pilot.

Most summer evenings, Judge Inglisi drove directly from the court-house to the Westchester County Airport. After terrorizing the skies in a Cessna, he would eat dinner in the quonset hut that masqueraded as a terminal, then wander over to the Air National Guard hangar and trade flying stories with pilots, technicians, whoever might be around. I found the Judge standing beneath the cowling of a turboprop while two mechanics scurried over the wing assembly. Clad in a leather bombar-dier jacket, he looked like a medicine ball with feet. He chattered on, oblivious to the thick smell of jet fuel or the staccato bursts of pneu-matic ratchets. I crooked my arm around his neck in typical greeting. Surprisingly agile despite his weight, he spun out of the hold.

"I'm having a conversation here," he said, pressing tufts of springy white hair behind his ears. A generous nose dove into a walrus mus-tache sprouting from his upper lip. His nostrils flared whenever he was angry, and right now they opened full throttle.

"These guys aren't listening to you."

"Of course they are. I'm a judge."

I dragged him out onto the tarmac.

"You knew Sylvester Miles, right?" I said.

"Bastard conned me into joining that damn club of his all those years ago. Ridiculous, me trying to play golf."

"I meant he was a client before you hired me. I remember seeing the files."

The Judge cocked his head and narrowed his eyes as if listening to the wail of a distant air raid siren. His bushy eyebrows had kept the blackness of his younger days and added intensity to his steel-gray eyes.

"What are you up to?" he said.

"A lawyer named Roger Twomby called me to the Miles house this afternoon. Miles named me in his will to sell a set of golf clubs at auction. But something about the will strikes me as odd. I want to read your draft to get a feel for this one."

"What the hell does an old will that's been revoked twenty times matter?" That siren in his head wailed louder.

"Twomby only read me the clause that named me. He didn't even finish it."

"Maybe the rest isn't any of your damn business."

"He did the same thing to Adrienne, only read her parts of the will."

"Maybe it's none of her goddam business either."

"She's the surviving spouse. And she doesn't seem to have a clue to what's going on. Twomby and St. Clare controlled the whole show. And DiRienzo was there, too. Observing, he said."

The added cast brightened the Judge a bit. "St. Clare must be executor, huh? And the only things DiRienzo observes are what jump up and bite him in the ass. But what the hell do you care?"

"I want to know what I'm getting myself into."

"I'll tell you what you're getting into. Hot water. Now you just won the Met—and by the way, congratulations—and you're about to play in the Classic. Sell the damn clubs and be done with it. Don't get any more involved than you have to. Remember Florida."

"This isn't Florida."

"Neither was Florida when it started. You were doing someone a favor. But the truth is if you minded your own business down there you'd be on the Tour right now, and we wouldn't be having this conversation, or any of the other ones we've had in the past two years."

"I'm not planning anything stupid. Nothing will keep me out of the Classic."

"But you can't contain your curiosity."

I nodded as humbly as I knew how. Some of the steel melted out of his eyes.

"I'd be divulging the secrets of a former client," he said.

"A dead former client. And we were partners, so that rule doesn't apply between us."

I knew I just cleared the last hurdle. The Judge stared back into the hangar, shook his head, and motioned me toward a chain link fence separating the tarmac from a parking lot. The sun hung low over the distant tree line and sprayed pink through the evening sky.

"I didn't do much work for Miles," said the Judge, inserting a thick elbow between the spines of the fence and relaxing his bulk. "He liked to spread his legal work around. He had one lawyer for his business dealings in New York, another in Connecticut. A different one handled his real estate. I was his will man.

"The first one was a typical wealthy bachelor will. Most of the estate went to charity, some to a brother, a few token bequests to trusted employees and former lady friends.

"Then one day Miles contacted me about an incident at a convention in Chicago. He saw a fight in the hotel bar. Older man, younger woman. A real donnybrook. He tried to break it up and ended up clocking the man in the mouth. Loosened four of the guy's teeth. Miles was worried about possible criminal charges. I told him that if he hadn't been arrested immediately, the other guy probably wouldn't swear out a complaint. Especially if the woman wasn't the guy's wife, and the wife didn't know about the woman. Miles was relieved. Then he told me he spent the rest of the convention with her. She was a secretary from Cleveland, and the guy with the dental problem was her boss. They were attending the same convention as Miles."

"Adrienne?" I said.

The Judge nodded. "Miles was nuts about her. Right from my office, he called an airline and reserved three tickets, one going out to Cleveland and two coming back to New York. Flew out there the next day and talked her into marrying him. She jumped at the chance. Hell, she'd been fired before her boss hit the deck."

"Everyone thinks she seduced Miles."

"Hey, everyone thinks lots of things that aren't true. I don't know exactly what happened in Chicago. If anything, it was the other way around.

"The upshot was that Miles wanted his will redrafted from typical bachelor to typical married sap. Everything to the wife, no conditions. No life estate, no trust, nothing. And all to a girl thirty years his junior he met at some damned convention. I told him, as diplomatically as I could, that he should have a prenuptial agreement. May save your life, I told him, kidding around. He didn't laugh. He was so crazy about the broad he wouldn't listen. Wanted no part of a prenup, just wanted that new will. So I drew up the bastard. For the measly fifty bucks I charged in those days, it wasn't worth the argument. I'd land the probate work no matter who the beneficiaries were.

"Things rocked along for a few months. Then Miles came into the office and announced he wanted to cut Adrienne out of the will. I told him you couldn't cut a spouse out of a will in New York. It never would get through probate. So he said okay, let's make things tough for her. So I cut her down to the bone, stuck his brother back in for a song, and left the bulk to charity.

"That started the merry-go-round. Miles came back every month, cutting Adrienne's share, adding to it, writing the brother in, writing him out, changing charities on a whim. Didn't take a genius to figure out they weren't getting along. But he never wanted a prenup, so this was his only choice. I must have done fifteen codicils before I said, Why don't you just divorce her and save us both the heartache. He got pissed off, told me at his age a divorce was worse than a bad marriage. Financially, that is. That was the last I saw of his business."

"What were the codicils like?"

"Aw, Kieran, I don't remember every little detail. They were stupid. Like they might direct Adrienne to buy particular stocks on certain dates and sell them on certain dates regardless of value. Dumb things, because no matter how I wrote the codicils Adrienne always ended up with a fortune. Sometimes it just didn't come as easy as others. From what you told me, old Syl never changed a bit."

CHAPTER
3

Andy Anderson's golf repair shop sat amid the squalor of a half vacant industrial park astride the Metro North Railroad tracks. Despite the early morning hour, Andy already had company. A sports car with baroque fins and numerous spiny antennae butted up against the front door. Double-tinted window glass perfectly matched the deep purple body paint.

I nudged my heap into the adjoining space and squeezed out carefully since the slightest nick probably would activate a modern defense system. As I gathered the loose *Blitzklubs* out of the trunk, the shop door squealed open. I slammed the lid and found Miko Onizaka staring at me.

Black hair bristled above his broad flat forehead, then splayed in a ragged tail over his shirt collar. Wrinkles etched his shirt and pants, the same outfit he wore the last day of the Met. He cocked his head as if measuring me. But despite the hard stare, he reeled just slightly off balance.

I shouldered the *Blitzklubs* and walked toward him, my right hand extended for the bittersweet mix of condolence and congratulations I should have offered immediately after the playoff. The booze smell hit me at five feet. I muttered something vapid about competition. Onizaka sneered, ignoring my outstretched hand, running his dull eyes from head to foot and back again. My fingers twitched, ready to tighten into a fist at the first wrong move. But Onizaka only screwed his mouth into an odd grin, then staggered to the sports car. After grinding gears, he shot away in a cloud of rubber and gravel.

I used foot, hand, and shoulder to loosen the shop's front door. The building was little more than a shack with exposed plumbing, a splintery wood floor, and a potbellied stove. The equipment was just as seedy—scarred workbenches, rusted vises, worn out lathes, carbon crusted etnas, and all manner of screws, nails, wood inserts, and grip plugs arranged in warped cigar boxes. But with Andy's wizardry, this collection of ancient junk took on magical properties.

Andy had come to America to add a dash of international flavor to the professional staff of the renowned Winged Foot Country Club. Never enamored with the country club life, he spent every free hour honing the clubmaking skills he had learned from his father and his grandfather in Scotland. Eventually, he quit his job and set up his own shop. He manufactured one set of clubs per month ("only for the connoisseur") and subcontracted oddball repair jobs from local pros ("most canna even change a grip without buggering up the club").

Andy's knowledge of golf lore was phenomenal. He could regale you for hours about the windswept links of Jacobean Scotland or discuss the evolution of the mashie in language worthy of a physicist. But his real joy came from gadding about the countryside in his minivan and conning valuable golf clubs from unsuspecting antiques dealers.

"Cheerio, Kieran," he said as he steered a rack of newly refinished woods toward a drying room.

Looking at Andy was like looking in a mirror, if I didn't examine the image too closely. We were both reed thin through the hips and squarely wide in the shoulders, as if we wore shirts without removing the hangers. Andy had the hands of a blacksmith and sinews like thick telephone cables coiling down his forearms. Mine were cut from the same die, though an arm-wrestling match would be Andy's without contest. The main physical difference was in our hair. Andy's mop was tawny brown while mine ran to premature gray. Of course, Andy never had practiced law.

The rack caught a seam in the floorboards and nearly toppled.

"Damn!" said Andy, scrambling to save his handiwork from ruin. He steadied the rack and jumped it into the drying room.

"You just missed your rival," he called from inside. "He's had a bit of the barleycorn, I'd say."

"Started right after the Met."

"Aye, and congratulations, laddy. Your fast finish must have had quite an impact on the man."

"I can see that."

"But you didna see this."

Andy's hand reached out brandishing a broken golf club. I recognized the bright blue pistol-shaped grip. Two days ago, it had been Onizaka's mallet-head putter. Today it looked like an elongated barbecue fork.

"He vaporized the bugger," said Andy. "Along with several others. He wants them all repaired right away. And don't you want to know why?"

I didn't answer.

"He thinks he'll play in the Classic," said Andy. "Well, he hopes to, anyway."

"He's expecting me to step aside?"

"You have to understand, Kieran, the man is desperate. Pitiful, too. I arrived here at six this morning and found him sleeping in his car. Talked to me for over an hour, which was bloody torture between his English and the barleycorn. He said his sponsor's pulled his backing and he needed the Met, and the Classic berth, to remain in the U.S. Otherwise, it's back to some triple-decker driving range in Tokyo for him."

"What about his job?"

"Apparently that canna keep him here."

"Forgive me if I'm not touched."

"You donna want to give up the Classic, eh?" Andy said with a laugh.

"No way," I said. "Did he mention anything about my job?"

"At MCC? Are ye not solid there?"

"Far as I know. But I heard it was up for sale to a Japanese company and Onizaka was in line to be club pro."

"He said nothing to me. But he was very clear about the Classic. He wants to play."

I whaled several violent swings with a *Blitzklub*. Fisk, the Judge, the PGA Tour brass, now Onizaka and Andy. I was tired of people picking at the few things I did right in life.

Andy returned, wiping his hands on a greasy rag.

"What do you have there, another replating job—holy shit!"

He snatched the club from my hand and carried it under a light.

"No, yes, no, yes," he debated with himself as he spun the iron to take in every surface and angle. "Bring the rest here, laddy."

He swept clear a section of workbench with his forearm. Then, with a care bordering on reverence, he arranged the entire set with the grips touching the wall and the heels of the clubheads set precisely on line.

"I canna believe this," he said.

"Can't believe what?"

But Andy wasn't listening. He pulled down a thick leather bound volume from a rafter. The binding was broken, the pages loose, and most of the gold lettering on the cover had worn away. But I could see that the title was *Golf Arcana* by H.T. Hillthwaite. Andy carefully opened the pages to the proper spot and stepped back like a painter surveying a canvas.

"Yes," he finally decided. "Where the hell did you get these?"

"Never mind where I got them. What are they?"

"For the golf collector, they are Moby Dick, the Holy Grail, and El Dorado rolled into one. You know nothing about *Blitzklubs?*"

"Never heard of them before yesterday."

"You'll be needing a short history lesson, then," said Andy. "During World War Two, a high-ranking SS officer lost a golf match to a subordinate. Since he couldna believe his lack of talent was the reason, he decided his clubs were to blame and hit upon a plan to develop the perfect set of golf clubs. He knew nothing about clubmaking, so in typical Nazi fashion he confiscated a forge in a small Bavarian village and ordered a clubmaker to design a set of irons worthy of the master race. These are the result."

"Sounds like a fairy tale," I said.

"That's what most people say. The clubmaker manufactured only twelve sets, each with slight variations, before the war ended. No one on this side of the Atlantic has ever seen one. My father once had a customer who claimed to own a set, but those clubs turned out to be forgeries."

"How do you know these aren't?"

Andy handed me the book. There were no photographs, just carefully drawn artist's conceptions. They were Miles' clubs, all right. They had the same heel-toe balance, the same dull metal finish, the same gooseneck in the hosel, the same decorative swastikas and Maltese crosses, and the same lightning bolt underscoring *Blitzklub*.

The text confirmed everything Andy had told me, and added that all twelve sets disappeared when a platoon of Allied soldiers raided the forge shortly after Germany's surrender. The drawings were exact reproductions of the clubmaker's designs found buried in the forge sometime later.

"See these shafts?" said Andy.

"Graphite?"

"Aye," he said, suddenly unable to contain his excitement. "Fancy that, Kieran laddy. Graphite shafts in 1945. These things were the V-2s of the golf world."

He grabbed a camera from the drawer of a paint-splattered desk and snapped several photos of the clubs from different angles.

"They belonged to Sylvester Miles."

Andy kept snapping.

"Did you hear me?"

"That I did," said Andy. "He left them to you in his will, now did he?"

"Not exactly. He directed his executor to engage my services for expert advice in selling the clubs at auction for the highest possible price."

"Did it ever occur to Miles you know nothing about rare golf clubs?"

"That's why I'm here. What can a set like this command at auction?"

"Let me explain how clubs are appraised. These are in near mint condition, but that's less important than you might expect. The critical factor is rareness. Now we know only twelve *Blitzklub* sets exist. That's rare for clubs not owned by somebody famous, like Young Tom Morris' brassie or Bobby Jones' Calamity Jane putter. The main drawback is the missing pitching wedge. But even allowing for that, I'd say the mid-five figure range is reasonable. In the right market."

"For a set of golf clubs?"

"For mythology," said Andy.

"That's crazy."

"Aye, but consider this. A few months ago, an anonymous owner offered a rake iron at auction. The club isna legal now, but was very popular at the turn of the century when you wer'na restricted to fourteen clubs and designers invented all manner for nasty situation shots. The rake iron was built for hitting out of wet lies. Six vertical grooves in the clubface allowed the club to pass easily through the mud or water. Hence the name. Five Japanese collectors locked horns over that one club."

"They're into that, too?"

"Why not? What Japan lacks in an ancient golf heritage it's making up for in collectibles. The bidding lasted for hours. None of the five wanted to be the first to blink. Finally, a man named Hayagawa won out. His bid was ninety thousand."

"Ninety thousand dollars for one club!"

"That was the bid." Andy frowned. "Unfortunately, no one's verified if the sale ever was consummated. Hayagawa isna the type to pay top dollar for something if it can be had any other way. If you know what I mean."

"We'll bar him from the auction."

"Might be pretty sticky. He keeps his ear well to the ground. I'd wager he already knows about these."

"Forget him for now. Where do we sell them?"

"Most of these auctions are held in connection with major golf tournaments," said Andy. "The biggest American auction was at the Memorial in May. The next big one will be at the World Series at Firestone in late August. But the biggest of all will be at the British Open in two weeks time."

"Is any one auction better than another?"

"They're all of a piece," said Andy. "The British one might yield more because speculators flock there."

Two weeks, I mused. Judge Inglisi's lecture from the previous night wound back into my consciousness. Coordinating a trip to the British Open with competing in the Classic was crazy, if not damn near impossible.

"And what would the set be worth if the missing wedge turned up?"

"Low six figures, unless the market suddenly is glutted with *Blitzklubs*. Which reminds me of one other factor. Say Sylvester Miles owned all twelve sets. You could inflate the auction price of any one set because you could guarantee the potential buyer the other sets wouldn't pop up at another auction."

"Inflate the price how much?"

Andy stroked his chin. "A quarter million."

Golf is big business, and any big business spawns economic phenomena that defy all logic. But the idea of intrinsically worthless objects commanding such value struck me as obscene. Why should a length of pipe connecting a leather or rubber sleeve with a trapezoidal hunk of steel cost as much as a house or attending med school? In my world, the *Blitzklubs* would better serve mankind as stakes for tomato plants.

But few people shared my world view, and Andy Anderson wasn't one of them. I had arrived at his shop with the *Blitzklubs* strewn across the back seat like a set of second-hand MacGregors. He refused to let me leave without sheathing the clubheads in bubble plastic, wrapping the grips in packing paper, and swaddling them all in a towel. The back seat wasn't a fitting throne, and the trunk was out of the question. Andy stood them upright on the passenger seat, lashed securely with the seat belt. "Drive carefully," he admonished, as if they were a Ming vase balanced on a dozen Faberge eggs.

I stashed the clubs behind the door of the cubby hole I called my office, then proceeded to sit on the info the rest of the day. Whatever my philosophical stance on the *Blitzklubs*, I was still dealing with estate property and was duty bound to report Andy's appraisal either to the executor or to the attorney. In this instance, however, a more intriguing alternative existed.

Adrienne Miles answered the door wearing a white body stocking and powder blue leg warmers, with a matching sweatshirt knotted loosely around her shoulders. Exertion flushed her cheeks, and two damp strands of blonde hair curlicued past her ears. Aerobics music thrummed in the background.

"May I come in? It's about the golf clubs."

Adrienne bit her lip, then snapped off a neat about-face. We went into a room completely devoid of furniture except for a hard rubber exercise mat, a boom box stereo, and a torchiere lamp. Adrienne shut off the stereo and settled onto the floor, tucking her legs beneath her. I crouched a discreet distance away, as if lining up a putt. The evening sun glared off the shiny surface of the mat.

"What do you know about the clubs?" I said.

"Very little," she said. "Golf doesn't interest me, so I never paid any attention. Syl kept them in his den and used them when he practiced in the evenings. I just assumed they were his practice clubs."

"He never mentioned them to you?"

"No, we—. No, he didn't."

I started to explain the mythology of the twelve *Blitzklub* sets. Bouncing off the eardrums of a nongolfer, it must have sounded hokey as hell. Adrienne spared me the embarrassment by cutting directly to the point.

"How valuable are they?"

"As is, with the missing pitching wedge, the set is worth approximately forty to fifty thousand dollars. With the wedge, the set is worth one hundred thousand, minimum."

Adrienne's eyes focused on infinity for a brief moment. Otherwise, she didn't react. No surprise, no disappointment. Nothing. She untucked her legs and rolled into a split. She may have been on the shady side of forty, but she was as lithe as an Olympic gymnast.

"Did Syl own any of the other eleven sets?" I said.

Adrienne shook her head as if the words jarred her out of deep thought.

"Sorry. I didn't catch that."

I repeated the question.

"I haven't seen any other ones, but I suppose I could rummage around. Why do you ask?"

"No special reason," I said.

The doorbell rang. Adrienne lifted out of her split and loosened the kinks with a heel-toe strut that looked very interesting from floor level. A wall blocked my view of the front door, but Adrienne said, "Hi, Bill," in a voice loud enough for my benefit. They spoke inaudibly for a time. I stood up, half with the idea of moving within earshot. Then Adrienne raised her voice again.

"Someone's here to see us, Billy."

They strolled into the room, St. Clare with his pudgy arm entwined around hers and Adrienne dragging her toes with each step like a blushing schoolgirl infatuated with the nerdy class president. The sight rankled me, though I wasn't quite sure why.

"Evening, Kieran," St. Clare said in a poor stab at bonhomie. He might as well have just told me to scram.

"Mr. Lenahan just stopped by for a moment," said Adrienne. "He has good news about those clubs."

"Oh really?" said St. Clare. "As executor, you should report your findings to me."

Adrienne squeezed his cheeks. "You're such a fogey, Billy. Does it really matter who finds out first?"

St. Clare reddened. He hated being called a fogey more than he hated being ignored as executor.

"I suppose not," he grumbled.

"Well," chirped Adrienne. "The clubs are worth about ten thousand dollars. Double that if the missing club turns up."

I didn't know Adrienne's game, but she had played her hand and I decided to pass.

"Ten thousand, huh?"

"Isn't that wonderful?" said Adrienne.

"Yes," said St. Clare, though he obviously didn't share her enthusiasm. Neither did I, for that matter. I bid them both a good evening and headed for home.

My digs were a two-bedroom garage apartment owned by a young Italian couple with a growing brood. An outdoor stairway shored by unpainted two-by-fours climbed the side of the garage. I snagged a six-pack from the refrigerator and sat on the steps to watch the sky turn dark. I kept replaying Adrienne's cheerful lie to St. Clare. Not that I gave a damn about St. Clare's sensibilities. The man was daft. He had served two undistinguished terms as mayor over thirty years ago, and still swaggered up Merchant Street like an incumbent. He even barked orders at the police during times of public emergency, which in Milton amounted to the occasional power blackout after a thunderstorm. I didn't know if he'd been shadowing DiRienzo's murder investigation. But he sure seemed to take a personal interest in the widow.

The lie was something else. If someone planned to use me, I wanted to know why.

Three beers past nightfall, headlights bored into the driveway and splashed against the garage doors. The light faded. A car engine kicked down, then shut off. Adrienne Miles gradually materialized in the dimness. Vaguely, I wasn't surprised. She fit herself onto a step below me, spine against the shingles and feet pressing a two-by-four. Jeans and a blouse had replaced the body suit, but the effect was the same. I handed her a beer. She popped the top and took a long, healthy draught.

"I owe you an explanation," she said.

"Damn right you do."

"You think I'm terrible for lying to St. Clare."

"What you tell St. Clare is your own damn business. You involve me and it's mine."

"Why didn't you tell him?"

"The clubs are worth whatever they're worth, not whatever you tell St. Clare. He'll learn the truth eventually."

"But you told me their value," she said. "You didn't have to. I know that much about the way an estate works."

"How did you know I hadn't already told St. Clare or Twomby?"

"I knew. You caught me completely off guard. I didn't think you would be so quick with a response about the clubs. And when he showed up I didn't know what to do."

"You didn't miss a beat," I said. "A minute ago you said you owed me an explanation. I'm still waiting."

Adrienne pressed the beer can lightly against her temple.

"I don't want St. Clare to know the real value of those clubs," she said. "Just for a little while."

"Why?"

"I have my reasons."

"Not good enough. The will charged me with a duty, and I take my duties very seriously. Like it or not, you need my help in whatever scheme you have planned."

"It's not a scheme!"

I couldn't see her face very well in the half-light, but her voice sounded genuinely desperate.

"Damn," she said. "When I heard you were named in the will, I thought finally here is someone I can talk to. And when you showed up tonight I thought you really were someone I could trust. But you're just like everyone else in this goddam town."

"Am I supposed to feel flattered or ashamed?"

"Go to hell." She clomped down the stairs and tossed the beer can onto the grass.

I didn't move. The same vague feeling that accompanied her arrival now told me she wouldn't leave. A moment later she was back at the foot of the stairs.

We went into my apartment. She wedged herself in a corner of the sofa, legs crossed and arms folded. A defensive posture, a student of body language might say. Beneath three hundred watts of ceiling spotlights, her skin looked less like butterscotch than too much time in a tanning salon. But she still cut a damn nice, if tightly wound, figure.

I'd cross-examined my share of witnesses. Sometimes it was as tough as cranking a frozen engine. Other times it was as easy as puncturing a tire and listening to the air rush out. I didn't expect Adrienne would be very talkative, so I gave her the old jump-start.

"I know something about Syl and his wills because my old law partner drew up the first dozen or so. You get the money from the *Blitzklubs*, right?"

Adrienne barely reacted at all, which I came to conclude was her way. She just smiled indulgently and trilled a tiny laugh in her throat.

"St. Clare is completely nuts," she said.

"I know all about the Mayor."

"It's far worse than you can imagine. St Clare's relationship with my husband went far beyond friendship. He revered Syl. Maybe it was the war hero thing. Or Syl's self-made business success. Or me. Maybe it was all these things. But with Syl gone, St. Clare's changed. I think a psychologist would call it a personality transference. He's starting to confuse himself with Syl. I wouldn't care so much, but with Syl dead St. Clare's become my husband in his own mind.

"The only thing I know about the will is that I'm entitled to half of what those clubs sell for. The secrecy is St. Clare's way of lording it over me, and that freak Twomby is just as happy not telling me anything. He's heard only Syl's side of the story for years and thinks the worst of me.

"All I want is to get out of this town. I hate it, I always have. Everyone probably thinks I killed Syl for the money just like they think I married him for the money. At least I've managed to convince the police I'm innocent. Detective DiRienzo believes me."

She smiled sweetly to invite my vote of confidence. I didn't oblige.

"Why don't you leave Milton?" I said.

Adrienne rubbed her fingers together in the universal sign for money.

"I don't have any. I don't even know if I have a roof over my head or if Syl left the house to charity, too."

"You can fight the will. There are laws."

"I know all about them. But it would be a fight. Just like a divorce would have been a fight. I don't have any fight left."

"What do you gain by keeping the truth from St. Clare?"

"The element of surprise," she said. "St. Clare has designs on me. He knows I can't afford to leave because I have nowhere to go. The only family I have won't take me in. My only cash is a piddling bank account I'd run through in a month. He actually believes I'll break down and marry him. But he also realizes I'd fly if I could afford it. As long as he thinks the clubs are worth ten or twenty thousand dollars, he won't worry. Half of that won't get me very far, so he'll let the clubs go to auction. But if he knows they're worth fifty to a hundred thousand, he'll hold up the sale forever."

"Of course, all of fifty or a hundred thousand will take you even farther."

"I have no desire to swindle money out of my husband's estate. I want only what is mine, not a penny more or less. When I leave this town, I leave no favors behind."

"Why the hell didn't St. Clare jump for joy when you told him ten grand?"

"He must have been nervous because you were there. After you left, he tried pumping me for what we talked about. I told him nothing. Then he focused on the figures, and I could feel him relax."

I didn't know how to take her. Good liars laced their stories with a ring of truth. Bad ones overcompensated with details. Adrienne had spoken from the heart, or what I fathomed to be her heart.

Don't get involved, the Judge had counseled. I already was involved, and with each passing minute that involvement deepened. I could help Adrienne without compromising my ethics. The auction would take weeks to arrange. By then the Classic would be over, and St. Clare's unrequited ardor may have cooled. Meanwhile, I could say nothing to anyone.

I escorted Adrienne to her car. I didn't tell her my intentions; she didn't ask. But before she pulled away, she lowered her window.

"Syl always thought highly of you. I can understand why."